The
Deep End
of the
Ocean

Jacquelyn Mitchard

VIKING

The
Deep End
of the
Ocean

VIKING
Published by the Penguin Group
Penguin Books USA Inc., 375 Hudson Street, New York, New York 10014, U.S.A.
Penguin Books Ltd, 27 Wrights Lane, London W8 5TZ, England
Penguin Books Australia Ltd, Ringwood, Victoria, Australia
Penguin Books Canada Ltd, 10 Alcorn Avenue, Toronto, Ontario, Canada M4V 3B2
Penguin Books (N.Z.) Ltd, 182-190 Wairau Road, Auckland 10, New Zealand

Penguin Books Ltd, Registered Offices: Harmondsworth, Middlesex, England

First published in 1996 by Viking Penguin, a division of Penguin Books USA Inc.

9   10

PUBLISHER'S NOTE
This is a work of fiction. Names, characters, places, and incidents either are the product of the
author's imagination or are used fictitiously, and any resemblance to actual persons, living or dead,
events, or locales is entirely coincidental.

LIBRARY OF CONGRESS CATALOGING IN PUBLICATION DATA
Mitchard, Jacquelyn.
The deep end of the ocean / Jacquelyn Mitchard.
p.   cm.
ISBN 0–670–86579–6 (alk. paper)
I. Title.
PS3563.I7358D4   1996
813'.54—dc20   95–26234

This book is printed on acid-free paper. ∞

Printed in the United States of America
Set in Centaur
DESIGNED BY BRIAN MULLIGAN

For the two Dans, and for my father and my mother

Acknowledgments

Though there usually turns out to be only one name on the cover, every book's a collaborative effort, and that is monumentally true for this one.

Without the support and encouragement of key angels in my life, it would still be, as it was for two years, four pages on a forgotten disc at the back of a drawer. For getting it out of the drawer, I must first thank the two Janes, my friend Jane Hamilton and my friend and agent, Jane Gelfman, one who said I could do this, the other who said that I had.

I also wish to extend my deepest gratitude and affection to the Ragdale Foundation in Lake Forest, Illinois, where substantial portions of this book were written in 1994 and 1995, especially to Annie Adams and Sylvia Brown. For their expertise, I want to thank police officers Nancy Robinson, Mary Otterson, and Ralph Gehrke; medical specialists Marilyn Chohaney and Tom O'Connor; David Collins of the Matthew Collins Foundation for Missing Children; lawyers Michele LaVigne and Kaye Schultz; and, for special valor, my basketball tutors—Rick, Mike, and T. And for their astonishing faith in me, to Barbara Grossman and Pam Dorman, thank you.

For their endurance and generosity, Hannah Rosenthal and Rick Phelps, Jean Marie and Christian Kammer, Georgia Blanchfield and John Wiley, Steve Schumacher and Victoria Vollrath, Franny Van Nevel and the rest of my Madison circle deserve a medal of honor, as do my friends from afar—

especially my dear Joanne Weintraub, and also Bridget Flanner Forsythe, Deborah Toscano, Anne D. LeClaire and Kobena Eyi Acquah.

Most urgently, let me thank my family for their tolerance in sharing my heart and mind for so long.

To my son Robert, who is my right arm and sometimes my left, and to my sunshine son, Daniel, and my son Martin, the small Hemingway who titled this book, and to the beautiful woman who is my daughter, Jocelyn, and to my daughter of the heart, Christin, bless you for staying the course. When I promised that this was as much for you as for me, I meant it; and I love you beyond reckoning.

Madison, Wisconsin
June 3, 1995

Grief fills up the room of my absent child,
Lies in his bed, walks up and down with me,
Puts on his pretty looks, repeats his words,
Remembers me of all his gracious parts,
Stuffs out his vacant garments with his form.
Then have I reason to be fond of grief.
Fare you well. Had you such a loss as I,
I could give better comfort than you do.

King John, Act III, scene iv,
by William Shakespeare

The
Deep End
of the
Ocean

Prologue

November 1995

Altogether, it was ten years, easily ten, from the hot August morning when Beth put the envelope full of pictures into the drawer until the cold fall afternoon when she took them out and laid them one by one on her desk.

Ten years and change, actually. The summer just past had marked a full year since Beth had learned what happened to her son Ben. And if she counted the whole spiraling spectacle of what came after, it was really closer to eleven. Just weeks before, in October, a front-page story called "Ben: An Epilogue" had appeared in *USA Today*—a belated "one year later" attempt based on a couple of stale quotes from those few people who would still talk to the press. But it hadn't been the story that reminded Beth of the pictures.

She had simply awakened one morning knowing. She would look.

It was raining that day, a chill, insistent November murk. For years, rain had frightened Beth into a concentrated burst of the most habitual quotidian tasks. But, that day, even the rain did not dissuade her. She was, if anything, in a hurry, as if looking at the pictures would put a period at the end of a sentence that had straggled all over the page.

Beth laid the pictures out, only sixteen—a small roll, because Pat had used

that silly little Instamatic then, the one that embarrassed Beth. She laid them facedown, like an old lady laying solitaire in a window seat.

And then she closed her eyes and touched one.

It did not vibrate. There was no voltage. All she felt was Kodak paper, feathery with a skin of dust. Nothing mystical. Beth caught her breath in relief. All those years. The seal had remained tight, like closed paper lips, with the date stamped across it in smeared ink, an astounding prophecy. June third, and the year. June third, a Saturday, because Pat had dropped the roll off at the mall color booth the day she left for the reunion. When he remembered to pick them up, at the end of that erased first summer, Pat had come into the house sobbing and given them to Beth, as if expecting she would enfold him, comfort him by somehow managing to cope with the evidence.

Instead, she had taken the picture folder securely between two flat hands and brought it to her desk. It had seemed important then—she had never been exactly certain why—that she always know where the pictures were, no matter how uncomfortable that sometimes was. For example, there were the times Beth glimpsed the envelope when she opened her desk drawer to reach for her paper clips or her address stamp. She did it quickly, as she once used to gather her speed before rushing past the Goya print of Kronos munching on a child that her grandmother Kerry unaccountably kept on a wall at the turn of the stairway. She felt the same oxygen deficit when she closed the drawer as she did when she put that hideous image behind her.

But she still sometimes saw it, and once or twice she actually brushed the envelope with her fingers. And when they'd been packing for their move to Chicago, Beth had gone purposefully to the drawer as if she actually meant to take those pictures out and look at them.

But she hadn't. It had still been too soon. Too soon to look, too soon to toss.

There were other things left over from Ben that Beth had gradually found the nerve to give away or pack up. On a few rainy days, suffocating days, she had even broken some of those things—a music box, a ceramic picture frame decorated with nursery blocks.

She had never even considered doing that with the pictures. After all, Beth was a photographer; pictures were talismans to her. But she also had a sense that a time might come when she could cherish those photos, particularly the last one on the roll, the porch snapshot. The simple passage of time, or religion, or resignation, might make it her bittersweet delight, a record of Ben the last time she saw him—well, not the last time she saw him, but the last time she saw him as he was, her sunny, uncomplex son, the one who never came to her dreams, though she bade him often, weeping, thinking that at least she need not fear him in her sleep. And so someday, perhaps when she was dying and was sure that frank oblivion was her immediate prospect, when she was sure that she was not going to have to drag herself through more life, she might want to look at those pictures often, perhaps every day.

So she'd need them handy. Otherwise, she'd lose them. That became especially clear when she returned home, weeks after the reunion, and noticed how she had begun to lose everything with remarkable ease, how keys, checks, paper money floated from her hands as if they had their own kinetic lives. Beth would stand in her kitchen unable to remember, as she unpacked a grocery bag or folded laundry, where cereal went and where sheets. She learned to regard it as chronic, like a limp after an accident.

It was only when she looked back at its progress that Beth could see her impairment was a deliberate choice, not a temporary fog that could have burned off when she felt equal to seeing things clearly. The impairment was her training. She taught herself to veer off, mentally, into the tall grass of lost school forms and stuffed peppers, at the first hint that a memory of Ben, or of that day, was about to break the surface.

Beth knew that she could not bear up under those thoughts; and she could not heal without inviting them. And so she had made the choice, it seemed now, to not heal. Instead, she would try to live around the friable edges of a crater, to tread softly and avoid what she had come to think of as the avalanche.

Without success, Beth had tried to explain the avalanche and the necessity of confounding it to her husband, Pat.

She'd tried and sounded like a fool, telling him about people who had a disease—Korsakov's syndrome—that sliced their memory to moments. Such patients, mostly alcoholics, could meet a doctor, a social worker and talk intelligently for long minutes, about the weather, their health, the stories on the front page of a newspaper spread on a desk. But should the doctor or the social worker leave the room, even for a minute, victims of Korsakov's would have no memory of ever having met any such person. Introductions would begin all over again.

That, Beth told her husband, was nearly how she felt—how, in fact, she longed to feel. A virtually functional woman, who would look normal to anyone who couldn't see the key in her back. But Pat, who had watched her become a robot wife and mother, thought her grief irrational. Pat grieved for Ben as a normal person would grieve, as if they'd lost their little boy to child-hood cancer or a wildfire outbreak of some outmoded disease, polio or diph-theria. As time passed, Pat proceeded through grief's "stages," almost in the manner described in Compassionate Circle pamphlets.

Beth couldn't do that. It seemed to her a process as impossible as cutting your straight hair short and willing it to grow out curly.

What she felt about Ben, Beth tried to tell Pat, was as similar to that sort of grief as a biplane is similar to a dragonfly.

Grief, Beth knew. When Beth was eighteen, her mother had died, of a complex series of organ failures and cluster catastrophes that started with a kidney cyst, hurtling toward death with an absurd speed that ended the day she was brought home in an ambulance after breakfast only to leave again in a hearse after dinner. It had been horrible, a train wreck, a blunt invasion of Beth's life.

But it wasn't her fault.

Beth had not teased a pestilent growth out of her mother's kidney. Noth-ing she neglected to give or do or say had drifted off her like contagion and settled on her mother.

Losing her mother had been regular old agony, not a trip to the lip of the avalanche. If she dared to embrace what she really felt about Ben's loss— pulled apart the skeins of stupidity and lack and the truth that everything that matters in life is decided irrevocably in seconds—Beth knew something would happen to her. And it was that, the beyond-grief, the sealing-up of a mind still expected to produce order and plans, which she dreaded.

She'd had little tastes of it, small rock slides that caught her unawares, sending her from room to room, bent over, panic rumbled over longing. Images of him in a closet, or a grave. The churn of her bowels as her brain popped his name. His one-bell Ben name.

And then, unless someone, someone persuasive, Ellen or Candy, was there to redirect her, Beth would begin, feverishly, to rewrite the rest of that day, restring the entrances and exits, and all the elements of plot, revamp the dialogue as if she were an artist who could fill in speech balloons from people's mouths. All the while, above her, ominous rumbles, glacial shifts. Beth would shuffle faster, irresistibly trying to imagine a way to beg back ten minutes, maybe four minutes, long enough to walk back over to the luggage trolley, where Vincent stood, whining and fidgeting, and take Ben back to the hotel registration counter with her. Or perhaps even let the panicky, dropping moments happen, if they had to, for the sake of penance, but then let the tape play in reverse, fast, and see Ben come walking to her, backwards, from the magazine stand or the revolving door, or wherever he had first gone—theories varied. Come walking back and back into her, into her arms, his overround belly pulsing against her hands, his heart beating as it did when he was scared or startled—beating so she could almost feel the outline of it, like Road Runner's in the cartoon, after he outsmarted the coyote— Ben, smelling of red pop and Irish Spring, and if he was hot, a little tang, like the smell of rubber bike handles, because he was too young to truly have hormones. She would feel herself spanking him; she would have spanked him, she would admit to herself, during those rock slides, just once, hard, felt his threadbare favorite denim shorts under her hand. Feel his cupped little rear, so firmly packed it seemed he had water injected just under his skin.

Feel Ben. Ben safe.

It was that palpable sense of presence shoved up against the reality of absence, like hot against cold, that really threatened to buckle the whole mass. Then Beth would have to strain to stop it.

What resulted looked like stoic calm, to editors she worked with, sometimes even to family. And indeed, Beth appreciated that her impairment, like courage, was a state of grace. But only she understood the disadvantages. She knew that for a very long time she had not actually "loved" the children, though she was careful to be mostly kind and sometimes noticing to them. She was certain that Kerry especially, who had never known Beth any other way, didn't feel the difference.

But Vincent did. Especially on those nights when Beth, on the way to school to pick him up, would forget where she was and why. When she'd finally arrive, sweating, Vincent would be standing outside the school, bouncing his basketball in the gathering darkness, looking at her with a scorn so bold that had she been able to feel anything at all about him, she would have been enraged.

On the whole, however, it worked. What, after all, had she given up to protect herself and her remaining children from abuse, or worse? The odd few years of examined life?

A more-than-fair trade.

So, when she turned over the first photograph—even in the full knowledge that the images could no longer hold any dread—she still felt that minute tectonic shift, and the impulse to run from the landslide.

When she fought that impulse down, Beth recognized, all in a wave, what she had really been seeking from the pictures, especially the last one, taken just as they set off for the reunion. The real reason she'd been unwilling to discard them.

She realized what she was looking for, and that it wasn't there.

Not in any of them—not in the picture of Vincent fishing at Terriadne, or of Ben feeding Kerry her bottle. Especially in the porch picture, the worst shot on the roll, intended, really, only to capture Pat's lilacs. She and the children were just a prop for the record of Pat's horticultural triumph. Even so, it had taken forever. Beth recalled her husband scolding Vincent for fidgeting.

But in fact, Beth saw now, it was Ben who had moved.

She wouldn't have recognized him. Beth had not seen her son's three-year-old image for a very long time by then, and in a real sense it was the image of a child she'd never really known. Not her baby Ben. A little-boy Ben she'd only just met.

She stared at the picture, wishing she had her good photographer's loup. There was Jill, Pat's nineteen-year-old cousin, who lived with them then and helped out while she went to school, carrying Beth's cameras and bags. Jill with long hair, looking like a sunny little hippie. There was Kerry, a minuscule infant face above a dress bordered with red and blue and yellow boats. Vincent had still been blond. Beth could not remember her older son, with his brown mat, lush and coarse as bear fur, ever having been blond.

But Ben's face, that was a blur.

Poised to receive that face like sacrament from the drawer bottom, she saw instead . . . not much of anything. She saw details—how very many freckles he'd had on his arms, how long and enormously well-muscled his legs were, even as a preschooler. But his face . . . all you could tell was that his mouth was open. He had been talking. But his features were indistinct. There was no message. Even changed as she now was, on the molecular level—all her old beliefs discarded—she realized that she had still, somehow, expected it.

Beth had been a newspaper photographer and photo editor, working mostly freelance, since college. When she edited, because of the nature of what scholars wrote about, Beth got to see many photos of people who later came to trouble. Soldiers in fresh uniforms with raw shaves. Immigrant families at the metal rails of ships, in layers of clothes, their luggage beside them on the deck. Cowboys. Aviators.

She thought sometimes that in those muddy images she saw a hint, a foreknowledge, of the mishap to come. The clue, she fancied, was the look in people's faces. A vulnerability? A message of departure in the photo grain? To test her theory, she once showed a picture to Pat, an old picture of a sailboat pilot who drowned on a routine pleasure voyage on a good bright day, after a spectacular career. She'd asked Pat, "Can't you see that man is doomed?"

And Pat patiently explained to her that she was crazy, that no one ever had a presentiment of tragedy until after it occurred; those stories of precognition were balm for weak minds, stuff his aunt Angela, widowed from birth, would say if a baby was born breech, or the phone rang twice and stopped. "Could you see in Abraham Lincoln's face as a young lawyer that he was going to be president? That he was going to be murdered?"

"Yes," said Beth, then. "I could."

"Could you see in the newspaper picture of that kid Eric's face, that kid my sister had in her music class, that he was going to be crushed under a semi on the way to graduation?"

"Absolutely," she told him, wondering how Pat could have missed it. But Pat just sighed, and called her "the bleak Irish," the in-home disaster barometer, ready to plummet at a moment's notice.

But Beth had once put stock in such things. Signs and portents, like water going counterclockwise down a sink drain before an earthquake. When she was seventeen, she believed that missing all the red lights between Wolf Road and Mannheim would mean that when she got home her mother would tell her that Nick Palladino had called. She believed, if not in God, then in saints who had at least once been fully human. She had a whole history, a life structure set up on luck, dreams, and hunches.

And it all went down like dominoes in a gust, on the day Ben disappeared. There had been no warning. There never was any, at all.

Part One

Beth

Chapter 1

"I only like the baby," Beth told her husband, as they stacked plastic bags and diaper bags, and duffel bags and camera bags, and Beth's big old Bacfold reflector—all in a pile in the hall.

She was surprised when Pat looked at her with disgust; she knew he didn't want to fight, didn't want to make trouble on the verge of clearing the whole tribe out for a weekend.

It was foolish in the extreme—her plan to take all the children to Chicago, attend her fifteenth high-school reunion and shoot a job—according to Pat.

But once she insisted, Pat, always happiest solitary, was probably looking forward to a bachelor's forty-eight hours, to sleeping late, to shooting pool at Michkie's, next door to the restaurant, after closing. He didn't dare argue, or Beth would be just as likely to turn around and leave Ben or Vincent behind. Still, the look he gave Beth was ugly, and it never failed to surprise her when he was shocked by the things she said to shock him. "Why?" he finally asked her. "You blurt stuff like that out, you don't mean it, and Vincent could hear you."

"I mean it," said Beth. "I really, really mean it." And thought, I don't just torture Pat, I get a kick out of it.

In fact, Vincent did not hear Beth. He was slumped in a corner of the sofa, watching the videotape of *Jaws*, from which Pat had obsessively edited all the bloody footage, his face clenched in what would have been, if he hadn't been seven, and still forgivable, a scowl instead of a pout. He didn't want to go anywhere in the car. He didn't think the idea of going to a hotel and swimming in a big pool with Jill while Mama saw all her old friends sounded like fun. He wanted to stay home and play with Alex Shore; he wanted to go to the restaurant with Daddy. He had told Beth so this morning, eight times.

"You cannot go to the restaurant with Daddy," she finally snapped at him, wondering if she would actually lay hands on him if she heard his wheedling voice just one more time. "Daddy will be working."

"I can sit quiet in the back," Vincent told her stubbornly. "I did it that one time."

It had been the peak experience of Vincent's life thus far—going to spend a Saturday night with Pat at the restaurant he managed for his uncle Augie. He'd been able to go because Beth had the flu, Kerry was just days old, and the last sitter in America was at the prom. The largest thing Beth did with Vincent (she had let him follow her onto a movie set while she shot stills; Paul Newman had shaken his hand), this was nothing to Vincent compared with the fabled night at Cappadora's. His white-haired uncle Augie had carried Vincent around on his shoulders, and Daddy had given Vincent anchovy olives while he sat high on the polished bar.

"Mama was sick then," Beth explained with a patience she did not feel; she hoped, in fact, Vincent could tell how close she was to meltdown. "Mama's well now, and we planned to go all together to Chicago, and you'll see Aunt Ellen, and I need you to help me watch Ben and Kerry."

"I hate Ben and Kerry, and I hate that I have to do everything, and I'm not even going to get dressed." Vincent hurled himself facedown on the sofa, and when Beth tried to raise him, performed his patented dead-weight drag, until she let him drop in the middle of the family-room floor.

Vincent hated his mother. Beth knew it, believed it was because she had waited until he was more than four, old enough to understand the significance of being her one and only love, to have Ben. Vincent liked Ben; he was drawn to Kerry's shell-like smallness; he adored Pat with a ridiculous, loverlike devotion that almost made Beth pity the child. But Beth was sure her older son considered her a food source and an occasional touch for a toy. When she punished him, Vincent looked at Beth in a way that instantly reminded her of what Pat said about house cats: they were miniature predators; if they were big enough, they would eat you. Beth, on the other hand, was drawn to Vincent with an intensity she didn't have to feign. She didn't just want to love him; she wanted to win him. And, Beth thought, he knows that.

Vincent was not forgiving. Ben was. He was delighted to be going out of town with his mother and his brother that morning, as delighted as he would have been to go to the hardware store or sort laundered socks. Ben wasn't just accommodating; he simply expanded, with great good humor and faith, to fill any space you put him in. When Ben was a baby, Beth had actually taken him to a doctor because he smiled and slept with such uninterrupted content. She asked the doctor if Ben could be retarded. The young man, a Russian immigrant, had not mocked her; he had told her, gently, that he supposed the baby could be impaired—anyone could be—but was there a reason for her fears? Did Ben rock, or bang his head against his crib bars— did he seem to be able to hear her, did he look into her eyes?

Beth told the doctor that, no, Ben didn't rock or avoid her eyes. She tried to avoid the doctor's eyes as she told him, "But Ben's so ... so quiet, and so content," sounding like the ninny she was. "He doesn't scream, even when he's got a dirty diaper, even when he's hungry. He's so patient."

"And your older boy?"

"He was more ... present." Vincent had been a thin, wakeful, watchful baby, walking at nine months, talking at ten, telling Beth "Me angry" at a year. The doctor smiled at her. Beth still kept the copy of the bill on which the doctor had scrawled his diagnosis: Good baby. Normal.

Ben had remained undemanding and cheerful. Beth could not imagine how from Pat's cynical idealism, his tense bonhomie, and her melancholy had

sprung this sun child. Beth didn't love him more than she did Vincent but
she had nothing harsh to say to him. Even when Ben was nuts—and he was
nuts frequently, like when he'd come to breakfast with a surgical mask on his
head like a beret and two sanitary pads wrapped around each bicep, loot
from Kerry's birth he'd found stashed under a bathroom sink—Beth could
not find it in her to scold him.

Today, as he waited to get into the car, Ben was lying on the hall floor in
a dust-dappled shaft of sunlight, using his heels to pedal himself around in
a wheel. "I'm underwater," he told her, drunk on the yellow light in his face,
as Beowulf, the family dog, leaped sideways to avoid the human pinwheel.
He had begged Beth that morning to make what he called "mommy bread"
(actually, it was "monkey bread," a sort of cinnamon-scented apology for
nonbaking mothers that Beth concocted from store dough rolled into pretzel
shapes and slathered with whatever sugary spices she could find). But when
she told him she was too busy, he didn't whine. He wandered off, always
busy, absorbed. "Ben's on a mission," Pat said.

Ben's preschool teacher had once, gently, suggested Beth might have Ben
evaluated for hyperactivity. Beth never did. She and Pat thought Ben was simply like one of those dogs you see advertised in the free classifieds: "Needs
room to run."

But even his charm was wearing thin today: Ben had just decided to take
all the medicine and makeup out of Beth's bags and line the bottles up, like
toy soldiers, against the door. Now she stepped on a bottle, cracking it, and
vitamins exploded everywhere.

"God damn it," she hissed. And when Pat arrived, gracefully, to help her,
she had told him the momentary truth: she liked only Kerry, who was un-
formed, dependent in simple ways, and could barely sit up.

"Just get on the road," Pat told her. "They'll settle down. They'll go to
sleep." It was like Pat to think so; the boys hadn't slept in the car since they
were two, and Pat still thought a great pair of Levi's cost $15.95. But Beth
had the idea that she was old enough for tension to show on her face; and
she wanted to be as close to youthfully attractive as it was possible for her
to be tonight. So she and Pat dragged everything out to the Volvo, and

strapped Kerry and Ben into their car seats, and got Vincent and Ben out again to make sure they went pee and had their toothbrushes, when Pat suddenly remembered he wanted to finish the roll of film from their camping trip.

"I'm not getting out of this car," Beth said. "I'll pull it up in front of the door on the grass, if you want. Or I'll yell for one of the neighbors to pose by the lilacs."

"Come on," Pat urged her, with the kind of sexual growl that reminded her of a gentle yen she hardly ever felt for him—at least not in the same way she had ten years before.

But to acknowledge the fact that Pat had tried to move her, she agreed to get out, despite Vincent now frankly on the verge of tears, and Ben singing one line from "House of the Rising Sun" at the top of his voice, over and over.

They stood in the bower the lilacs formed. Pat scolded and then snapped; Beth leaped into the driver's seat. She didn't kiss him. She would see him in two days, anyway. In fact, she would see Pat before the sun went down, Beth later recalled—and she had not kissed him then, either, not then or for months afterward, so that the first time she did, their teeth knocked, like junior-high kids', and she noticed, for the first time, that his tongue tasted of coffee—a thing she had never noticed before, during all the years when his tongue was as familiar in her mouth as her own.

The drive down Route 90 to Chicago was never a pleasure, though she and Pat used to have some fun petting in their old Chevy Malibu, years before, coming home from college for Christmas, to families who were speechless with delight that the two of them were in love. These days, it was simply what it was, a stupid, boring, flat-farms-and-then-suburban-sprawl shot for 150 miles. They made the trip often, because most of both their families lived in the Chicago area. Beth and Pat were considered adventurous for living "up north," in the Madison outpost Pat's uncle had pioneered in 1968.

Pat and Beth had belonged to each other from her junior year at the University of Wisconsin—and even, in a sense, before, as the children of parents who didn't consider it a holiday unless they played poker together. They'd played with each other at picnics, and in friendship emergencies. They went to each other's first communions, to each other's high-school graduation parties.

But they never really saw each other as gendered until the day they ran into one another on the library mall in Madison, three hours before they fell into bed at Pat's attic dump and missed the next two days of classes.

By then, her junior year and Pat's first year of grad school, Beth was frankly frightened. She had had a miscarriage, at six weeks, while sitting in the waiting room of a clinic preparing to have an abortion. Her last boyfriend had used a telescope to spy on her after she broke up with him. She believed that bad men would fly into town to ask her out. The only sex she'd ever had that was "good" had been a front-seat interlude with a friend's fiancé. She was working two jobs—waiting tables in the morning, and at night selling china, with stupefying humiliation, door-to-door to perennially engaged sorority girls. She had no money left for senior year, and she was failing two classes. She felt old. She felt used.

She saw Pat.

He was not handsome, not even when he was young. He had a wide, white smile and straight teeth—"perfect collusion," he called it—but he was short and slight, with unruly curly brown hair and face-saving huge eyes. His shoulders were broad, but his legs were skinny, almost bowed. Pat looked waifish, starving, and was so uncomfortable around people, so eager to please them, that they believed he was the friendliest guy they ever met. Only Beth knew how pure Pat was, how pathologically just. Even when he grew comfortable enough with Beth to know she would stay, and began to enumerate her failures of honesty, tact, and self-discipline, Beth still believed she slept with a sort of knockoff saint.

She was not in awe of her husband—she came to take for granted in Pat everything she admired so lavishly in Ben. But it had been she, not Pat, who had gotten up from that hard bed, more than a dozen years ago, certain they would marry. She knew at last she was safe. The match quickly became family legend: Evie and Bill's only girl, Angelo and Rosie's only son. Beth couldn't help feeling happy for their parents. Pat had gone to college in Madison because his uncle's restaurant was there, and Pat wanted into the business; and so they stayed, marrying in relief after a couple of uncomfortable years of proving they could live together and force their parents to acknowledge it. When she told the judge—another struggle; their parents actually brought a priest to the ceremony in hopes the young people would see reason at the eleventh hour—she promised to honor and cherish Pat, Beth meant it absolutely.

Who would not? Beth thought now, already regretting her cursory farewell, promising herself to phone Pat as soon as she got to the hotel. She knew she was superficially kind and capable of the surface warmth that made even strangers feel included. But Pat, though not happy, was good.

As Beth sat in traffic backed up for three miles around the huge mall at Woodfield, she caught herself wondering if Pat was so tense, so stereotypically the tie-tugging smoker, because he still believed people could be better than they were, that they could measure up if they tried harder. She imagined what Pat would be doing now, alone in the house. He would be trying to impose order on Beth's chaos—checking canisters for the level of staple food supplies, tossing a hundred drawers, putting the screws in bags, carrying the seed packages out to the garage, throwing out the half-empty packs of stale Chiclets. Beth often heard Pat doing this at night, before he came to bed. She had come to associate that rummaging and reorganizing with Italian ancestry, perhaps because her father-in-law, Angelo, did it, too. Too busy all day to attack the details that nagged at them, they puttered, fussily, fretfully, into the small hours. So did her mother-in-law, Rosie, though she was too much aware of disturbing others to rattle about. She folded laundry, reconciled the business accounts, wrote letters to her cousin in Palermo. She was a silent putterer, a busy wraith in a long white robe.

The first Christmas Beth and Pat were married, his parents and Beth's brothers spent two nights in the newlyweds' sordid rented house off Park Street. Beth's brother Ben, called Bick, named Pat's family "the night stalkers." They stayed up late, and then they roamed. "Must be because they're Romans," Bick told her.

Beth had not asked Pat to the dance and dinner that would form the centerpiece of her reunion. He knew plenty of her old Immaculata crowd; he had been two classes ahead of her at the same school. He would have been seamlessly cordial to her friends but it would have been such a strain for him that he might have been sick with a cold for a week afterward. He would have drifted mentally to the stacks of history books he read obsessively, underlining good parts with a yellow marker, like a college kid. He would have been bored, thinking of acres of messy drawer space he itched to attack. He would have found the jokes stiff, the laughter forced, the opportunities for telling old stories and dishing old enemies meaningless and cruel.

Beth, on the other hand, couldn't wait.

She turned the car off, while seven cars back a misfit honked his dismay at the delay. She looked into the rearview mirror. Ben had removed ham from the sandwiches Jill had packed and was wiping down the back window.

"Benbo," she told him sharply, "ham is for eating, not washing." Immediately, disgustingly, Ben popped the smeary ham in his mouth. Beth could have stopped him—but how filthy could it be? Ben picked up and ate floor food every day; he sometimes even put his cereal bowl on the floor so he could imitate the dog. Jill would wash the children. The hotel pool would wash them. Beth was not going to snap.

The traffic inched forward, and she started the car. Vincent was by then poking Ben in the neck, relentlessly, probably painfully, with a yellow rubber Indian chief. She could have stopped him; but wouldn't he then have just done something else? Ben was not crying; and there was a certain high-register urgent tone of crying that Beth had come to regard as her cue for interrupting any atrocity. Today, she would ignore all atrocities except those that broke the skin. She inspected her haircut in the mirror—it was new, and appropriately tousled, and she'd rinsed out the gray with henna. Once the logjam moved, they'd be only half an hour from the hotel, which was near her old high school, in Parkside, Illinois.

"Sing 'Comin' Through the Rye,' Mom," Ben suddenly called to her now, ignoring Vincent's increasingly violent pokes. How could he do it? Beth wondered; how could Vincent poke Ben, who loved him so? (She thought, guiltily, How could I squeeze Vincent's arm? Or yell at him, nose to nose?) And Beth began hum-singing aimlessly, " 'If a body catch a body . . .' "

Ben asked, "Catch a bunny?"

"No, stupid, a buddy! A buddy!" Vincent cried murderously.

Beth closed her eyes and dreamed of tonight—of all the people from the neighborhood she'd see, who would all be wealthier than she, but not so "creative," nor so good-looking, and certainly not possessed of so many lovely children. Good-looking, thought Beth. I *am* good-looking. Not pretty, but objectively speaking, a solid seven on the scale. When Beth thought about her own appearance, the word that came to her mind was "square." She had square shoulders—a cross to her until they became fashionable— and a square chin. (One of her father's favorite dinner-table stories was a re- counting of the first time he'd laid eyes on his only daughter and commented, "That baby has the O'Neill jaw. You could use that jaw to miter corners.") Even Beth's hair, when she let it hang of its own considerable weight, was square, and so, to her continuous despair, were her hips. When she was twelve, her pediatrician had crowed cheerfully to Beth's mother that Beth would "pop 'em out one, two, three with that pelvic structure." And even though until Kerry, Beth did indeed hold the indoor record for easy labors, she still couldn't think of Dr. Antonelli's words without feeling as though she'd been genetically programmed to pull carts like a Clydesdale. Beth's own looks could never hold a candle to Ellen's, though Ellen, her childhood best friend, had spent twenty years telling Beth, "No one ever looks at your butt, Bethie. They never get past the bewitching green eyes."

Ah, Ellen. From Beth's point of view, the whole point of this reunion weekend was Ellen. Ellen was six inches taller than Beth, and thirty pounds heavier, the kind of stacked-up strawberry blonde who still caused men to bump into pillars at the airport.

She was waiting for Beth at the hotel. Ellen, who lived in the same west- side neighborhood where all of them had grown up, a street over from the house Beth's father still owned, had booked a room for the two of them and a room for Jill and all the kids. She'd left her husband, her son, and a thawed tuna casserole up at her northern-suburban mini-mansion and bought a fancy black rayon dress. She'd sent Beth a drawing of it in the mail. The prospect of the weekend had reduced both of them to seventeen: "I think if Nick asks us to sit with them, we should," Ellen wrote on the bottom of the drawing. "His wife won't mind—after all, you fixed them up."

Beth's first love, the most beautiful boy she had ever seen, before or since, the memory of whom could still make her abdomen contract, often ran into Ellen and her brothers, and occasionally worked with Ellen's husband on development contracts. Beth had not seen Nick for ten years; they had met last at the funeral of a mutual friend, a boy who'd gone to Vietnam twice and later committed suicide by driving his car into the path of an oncoming freight train. Under the circumstances, though Beth still longed for Nick, thought of him in a syrupy way that had nothing to do with her real life, they had only touched cheeks near the casket. And Beth had wondered then, as she often did, if she should have married him.

Nick Palladino had long been a tough, no student, the kind of kid who seemed headed for life as a knockout shoe salesman who pumped iron and dated Bunnies from the Playboy Mansion downtown. But ten years later, Beth was a newspaper photographer who could barely afford cigarettes, and Nick owned his own business. Fifteen years later, Beth was a magazine photographer who no longer smoked, and Nick had sold his construction firm for more than it would have cost to buy Beth's whole neighborhood in Madison. He was married to Trisha, his cool, slight homecoming-princess wife, who had lived across the hall from Beth at college. On that floor in Kale Hall, Beth used to write to Ellen, she felt marooned on the planet of the Nordic blondes. And Ellen had written back that no matter what happened, Nick would never love anyone else, that he would forgive Beth anything if she'd go back with him.

In her car, Beth hummed, and remembered Trisha.

Trisha was from Maine, and she had never seen anything like the street feast of Our Lady of Mount Carmel. Pat and Beth took Trisha to the parade, during which supplicants carried the figure of the Madonna, covered with ten- and twenty-dollar bills affixed to her ceramic robes, through the streets. They bought Trisha a paper cup of cold lupini beans and stood with her next to the bandstand, where Beth suddenly sensed Nick before she ever saw him. He'd had on the most beautiful coat, leather the color of honey; and he danced with Beth first, while Pat stood by, radiating tolerance, his ring on Beth's finger. And then he danced with Trisha; he was a good dancer. Beth was sick with envy; they didn't make caramel-haired, light-wristed girls like Trisha on the west side of Chicago. After an hour, there was no turning back. When Trisha married Nick, Beth stood up in the wedding, got drunk, and threw up on her beige organdy dress.

" 'Everybody has somebody—nay, they say, have I …' " Beth sang, swerving across three lanes to head into the home stretch of Interstate 290.

"I love that part," said Ben.

"I hate that part," said Vincent. "Actually, I hate the whole song."

She would not throw up anymore, but Beth wanted to get drunk with Ellen, get drunk and giggle and whisper and rush to the bathroom as if they had important things to conference about in there. She wanted to forget until Sunday that she had had children and a recent Cesarean scar.

Beth had weaned Kerry, though she hated to give her last, least one such short shrift, for the reunion. She'd had her ragged nails shaped and lacquered. Shaved an inch off those square hips with leg lifts.

By the time Beth had eased the wagon under the portico of the Tremont Hotel on School Drive, Ellen was on her, tugging her shoulders, trilling, "You're here! You're here!"

"You will not believe it," Ellen whispered now. "Diane Lundgren is here, and she must go three hundred pounds. I'm serious."

"Who else? Who else?" Beth cried, easing Kerry out of her car seat. But Ellen was by then all over the baby, offering Kerry her necklace of silver filigree balls to chew, sniffing the crown of Kerry's head.

"I'm your godmama, Kerry Rose Cappadora," Ellen cooed, reaching out a hand to each of the boys in turn, pulling them to her with her strong arms and soundly kissing them. The boys, who had grown up believing they were her nephews, didn't struggle; they never failed to regard Ellen, who was as vivid and confident as Beth was dark and unsure of herself, as a sort of natural phenomenon, like rainbows or an eclipse. "Vincent, can you swim? Where's your tooth?" Ellen all but shouted. She kissed Jill—whom she still called "Jilly," Chicago fashion—and shouldered half a dozen of Beth's various satchels and bags. "Let's stow everything, okay? And then Jill can take the babes for a swim or lunch or something, and we'll have a drink."

"It's one o'clock in the afternoon, Ellie!" Beth told her, embarrassed even in front of Jill.

"But we're free!" Ellen reminded her. "We're allowed to be irresponsible.

We're not going to drive. We have no kids." Beth glanced at Vincent, who glowered. He did hate her. Guiltily, she reached down and pulled him against her side.

"I don't even know if I got connecting rooms," Beth told Ellen.

"You did. I stuck it all on my card."

Beth was horrified. "Ellen! You can't do that!" Ellen had money—everybody in construction was loaded, as far as Beth could tell. And though it was Pat's dream to someday own part of the restaurant, and Beth's to someday run an actual photo business with real employees, they were lean now. They had been lean as long as they could remember. Once, when her brother Bick offhandedly told Beth that he and his wife had been in financial trouble, that they'd been "living paycheck to paycheck," Beth felt a stomach thump of panic. Wasn't that what everyone did? Were she and Pat supposed to have a reserve, a cushion, already? In their early thirties? Did other people?

The economic gap between Ellen and Beth usually didn't matter. Ellen sent Beth crazy things in the mail—sheets from Bloomingdale's, pounds of chocolate, five hundred dollars once, when Beth had gone crazy on the phone and cried because she couldn't buy the boys new clothes for Easter. Beth sent Ellen gallery-quality prints of her best photos; they were framed, expensively, all over Ellen's house. Ellen paid at restaurants when they ate together; she sent Kerry savings bonds as if the country were at war.

But there were times Beth balked.

"You can't pay for me," she told her friend now.

"It's, what, it's seventy bucks or something," said Ellen. "Who cares?"

"I care," Beth replied, tempted, trying to seem more genuinely proud than she actually was. "I think I can write this off, anyhow, because I have a job on Sunday. I'm shooting the antelope statues at the zoo for a brochure." Ellen's attitude reversed instantly. She was part-owner of her husband's business, after all; a write-off was a write-off.

"You're going to have to go up there in that mess and rearrange it, then," Ellen told her. They straggled into the lobby. It was jammed; virtually all the out-of-towners who'd come back for the reunion were registered there. Beth almost gave up. Dozens of people she recognized milled past her; it was like watching a movie peopled with stars from a previous era—all familiar faces, all altered, with names she couldn't summon to her tongue. Did she really want to spend fascinating moments negotiating a credit-card transaction with a twenty-two-year-old in mall bangs, who, Beth already realized, would mess the whole transaction up anyhow?

"Elizabeth—the fair Elizabeth Kerry!" The tallest man in the lobby lifted Beth off her feet. Wayne Thunder was both the first American Indian and the first homosexual Beth had ever known. "I'm gay because of you," he told her once. "Because you didn't regard me as a sex object." Wayne was a management trainer for the phone company; he was madly successful, lived in Old Town, came to spend every Thanksgiving at Beth's house.

"You have brought some children...." Wayne intoned. "Who are these children?" Ben and Vincent jumped up and down. They were crazy about Wayne, who brought them boxes of illegal fireworks; Beth and Pat had been asked to leave the neighborhood association after Wayne set a neighbor's hedge on fire. Holding Ben in one arm, Wayne told Ellen and Beth conspiratorially, "I saw Cecil Lockhart. She looks just like Gloria Swanson now. She has white hair—on purpose." The antique flicker of annoyance Beth still felt at the mention of Cecil Lockhart's name took her by surprise. She realized that she had been hoping that Cecil—the swanlike, gray-eyed girl who grew up next door to Ellen, the chief and constant rival to Beth for Ellen's best-friendship—would skip this occasion. Cecil (whose real name was Cecilia) was, Beth judged, the only of the Immaculata graduates from her year to have made more of herself as a creative soul than Beth had. And it rankled.

Cecil was an actress. She had taught acting at the Guthrie in Minneapolis and at the Goodman in Chicago—she was very much married. Cecil was, Ellen told Beth now, still a size six, with a belt. Ellen knew; she'd seen Cecil last year at an arts ball. Cecil had had the distinction of being the first of them ever to have sexual intercourse—at fifteen. She'd liked it. She couldn't imagine, she told Beth once, in junior year, ever going a month without doing it.

Beth noticed abruptly that the cheerleaders had arrived. They were grouped at the desk, eight of them, still a unit, as if they had moved smoothly through adult life in pyramid formation. Their husbands, all large-necked and calm, stood behind them. When they saw Beth and Ellen, they surged.

"Bethie!" called Jane Augustino, Becky Noble, Barbara Kelliher. They draped their arms around Beth, whom they remembered chiefly as the short sidekick to Ellen, their Amazonian colleague, who'd inherited nothing from her Sicilian father but a name. Ellen, a revolutionary who read *Manchild in the Promised Land*, had never really embraced the soul of cheerleading; she had done it, she confided to Beth, for its surefire potential as guy bait. Even fifteen years ago, Beth couldn't have done a round-off for money. But now, she gladly embraced all the women who had formed the top tier of high-school popularity, noting carefully Barbara's chunky thighs and Becky's resolute blondness, accepting their compliments on Kerry's sunny, one-tooth smile. Then, when she spun around to grab the luggage trolley, she stumbled into Nick Palladino's chest.

"Where did you get all these kids?" he asked. Beth's stomach bubbled.

"Just made 'em with things we already had around the house," she said. She and Nick hugged; Trisha hugged her. Nick and Trisha were wearing white cotton suits that would have looked ridiculous on anyone else. On them, the suits looked like a spread in *Town and Country*.

Beth dragged Jill to her side. "Nick, this is Jill, Pat's cousin." Ellen was hugging Nick, who turned to Vincent and shook hands.

"I came this close to being your daddy," he told Vincent softly, not quite enough out of Trisha's hearing to please Beth. Beth smiled madly and concentrated on working her way to the front of the check-in line.

"My daddy is Patrick Cappadora," Vincent told Nick with homicidal intensity.

"Jill," Beth said, "push this cart thing over by the elevator and then take the keys and park the car, okay?" She handed the baby to Ellen and lifted Vincent onto the luggage trolley. "Vincent, I want you to hold Ben's hand. Real tight. You can look around and you can stand on this funny cart. But hold his hand while Mama pays the lady. And then you can go swimming." Vincent gripped Ben's hand limply.

"I love you, Vincent," said Ben, straining to get closer to the toys in the newsstand.

Vincent smirked.

"He loves you," Beth said. "Can't you be nice?"

"I love you, Ben," said Vincent wearily. "I'm hot, Mom. My neck is killing."

And then—and Beth would never be able to banish it, no matter what other random, dangerously precious scenes she was able to sweep from her mind—Vincent had one of those flashes of egregious tenderness that he had only with Ben or Kerry, never with Beth. And never, even, with Pat, because Vincent's love for Pat didn't flicker between attachment and irritation, it was utter.

Vincent reached out and clasped Ben around his belly and pretended to get one of his fingers stuck beneath Ben's arm. "Tickle, tickle, you old fuzzhead Ben," he said, and Ben writhed in ecstasy.

Well, good, thought Beth.

She said, "This will only take one minute, now. See? Jill is getting the bags. You just stand here." Nick had drifted away. She could see Ellen, a sherbet-colored crown above the other women's heads, surrounded by men, making Kerry's hand wave bye-bye, up and down. Beth pushed through the backs in front of her. The counter girl was on the phone, talking to someone at the airport, explaining nastily that no, there was no shuttle of any kind, and no, she had no idea what taxi companies operated in the area, and in any case she was very busy. Bored, she finally turned to Beth, who could barely see Vincent, bobbing up and down on the luggage trolley, and said, "Yesssss?" Beth was caught unawares; she'd been scanning the doors for a glimpse of Jill; how long did it take to park a car? She plopped her purse on the counter, nearly spilling it into the girl's lap.

It probably took five minutes. Even though the girl was slower than weight loss, even though Beth gave her a gas card by mistake first, and the girl ran it without realizing it wasn't a Visa. Absolutely not ten minutes, Beth would tell the police later, even though Beth ran into a cousin of Pat's, and her old lab partner, Jimmy Daugherty, now a cop in Parkside. Ten minutes at the outside, no more.

At last, clutching a sheaf of carbons, her wallet, and Kerry's pacifier, Beth made her way back to the elevator. Vincent was standing slumped against the wall, slowly pushing the trolley back and forth with his feet.

"Where's Ben?" she asked.

Vincent shrugged expressively. "He wouldn't let me hold him. He wanted Aunt Ellen. My neck is killing, Mom. I got a heat rash."

Absently, Beth checked his neck. It was ringed with small red blotches. "Wait," she said. She scanned the lobby for Ellen; there she was, easy to see. Beth whistled. Ellen plowed toward her, Kerry in her arms.

"Do you have Ben?" Beth asked, and she would recall later that it was not with panic. Not the way she had felt, instantly, at state fair when Ben was two and wandered away, and the crowd closed around him. She didn't feel that bottom-out sensation that preceded frenzy. Ben was in the room. The room was filled with people, all good people, grownups who knew Beth, who would ask a little kid where his mama was. "Ellen, Ben took off. We have to find him before we can do anything."

Ellen rolled her eyes and headed for the newsstand. There were toys on spinning racks there—kid bait. Beth went outside and scanned the sunny street in both directions, then came back in, circled the elevator, and darted into the deserted coffee shop. Had the lone waitress seen a little boy in a red baseball cap? No. Beth squatted down on her knees and looked through the crowd Ben-height. But all the legs ended in heels or oxfords. She ran back to the elevator. "Vincent, think hard, which way did Ben go?"

"I don't know."

"Didn't you watch?"

"I couldn't see him."

It was then that Beth's breathing came in gasps, and her hands tingled, the way they did when she'd narrowly avoided smacking another car, or almost turned her ankle. Ben! she thought. Listen to me with your mind. Ellen came slowly through the crowd, pulling Beth to her with a look.

"He wasn't over there."

"Ellenie . . ."

"We should get the manager."

"I don't know; maybe if we just wait . . ."

"No, we should get the manager."

The counter girl said the manager was at lunch, and if they wanted, they could fill out a form describing what they lost.

"What we lost is a kid!" Ellen screamed at her.

The girl said, "Whatever. The manager should be back at—"

Ellen charged across the room and leapt onto the luggage trolley. She was five feet ten, and even before she yelled "STOP!" a score of her old class-mates had turned to look at her. But when she did yell, talk ceased in the lobby as if a light switch had been flicked. A phone was ringing. A bellman, outside, called, "Chuck!"

"We need to all look for Beth Kerry's little boy," Ellen said. "He's three, his name is Ben, and he was here a minute ago. He's got to be in the room. So divide up. Look all around where you are. And if you find him, pick him up and stand still."

And they all did that. They set down their bags where they were, and the whole room burst forth like a choir: "Ben? Ben?" in a shower of different timbres of voice, Beth's the loudest. Jimmy Daugherty cut the room into halves by walking through, and assigned people quadrants. Nick took off at a lope down the first-floor corridor. Twenty minutes later, a few small groups of newcomers were greeting one another again, but most of the faces nearest Beth watched her for direction, in their eyes a kind of embarrassed pity.

Ben was gone.

Chapter 2

It was Jimmy who said they might as well call the police—not that the kiddo wasn't somewhere right nearby, anyhow, but it could move things along quicker, you know? Jimmy knew everybody at Parkside; in fact, if not for the reunion, he'd be working today. "It'd be my shift, Bethie, and these are good guys. We'll get the troops over here." The station house was less than a mile away.

"Bethie, you'll feel better," he said. "He's probably asleep in a linen closet."

The manager, a chubby, fancy man, was back from lunch now. Waving his hands, with large gestures intended to play across the room, he had berated the counter slut and brought Ellen coffee—believing she was the child's mother—and checked the doors to the swimming pool to make sure they were locked, and summoned security, which turned out to be two hefty older men in ill-fitting purple livery.

Beth sat on the luggage trolley skinning her hair back from her face with her hands. In her mind's athletic eye, she was trotting the length of the corridors, shoving open every door that was ajar, calling Ben in a clear, Doris

Day voice, welcoming him. In fact, her legs were gelatinous, she could not stand. Vincent was curled behind her, holding Ben's blanket, asleep. Jill had taken Kerry upstairs and put her down on a bed.

It was five minutes to two. Beth had been in the hotel less than one hour.

After the first, fruitless search, the lobby had drained of alums. Beth watched people slink away, talking low, not quite sure what they dared do. Were they to continue greeting each other as if nothing had happened? Join in the search? Go out to lunch? Go home? Two guys were in the bar, drinking, watching a football game on the high, slant-mounted TV; but they hadn't been here when Ben went missing. Beth didn't blame them, though she would have had she recognized them. Husbands, she thought. Not my friends.

When Jimmy came back from the desk phone, he said, "It was just what I thought. They'll send a bunch of guys over here, no problem, and they'll floor-by-floor it, and they'll find him in no time."

Ellen asked him, "What if Ben went outside?"

Jimmy looked pained. "I . . . uh . . . some guys will be looking outside, too. But Bethie, there have been no . . . accidents reported." Accidents? Beth shoved a deck of her brain over to accommodate new alarm. He could have been run down by a car, picked up by a felon, knocked into a ditch, flattened by a train. . . . Beth seized herself, forcibly. She tended to embrace panic as a matter of course; Kerrys did that—no hangnail was too small for a short fulmination.

But Ben had been missing now for one full hour. Ben had never, unless Beth was on a job or out for dinner twice a year with Pat or giving birth, been out of Beth's sight for one full hour, in the three years of his life.

So this was serious. Too serious for panic. Beth needed to call upon the self that, in her newspaper days, calmly started printing photos of a fire at midnight and finished by one a.m., in time for the first press run. The self that once found a way to pull and snap Vincent's dislocated arm back into place, while his limb dangled like a plunger on a rubber band. Who stanched bleeding foreheads, who made children who ate muscle relaxants throw them up. That self struggled in her grasp and broke free. She smoothed her face. It welled with oil, as if she hadn't washed for days.

The clock, meanwhile, lurched ahead. In the moment that she spent on her face, another eight minutes passed.

Ben had been missing for one hour and eight minutes.

"Bethie," Jimmy was saying, deliberately casual. "This is Calvin Taylor. He's my partner. Everybody's coming. Slow day at the old station house. Cal, this is Beth Cappadora. It's her boy."

Beth looked up; she felt small, like a pond resident. It felt good to look up, good to be down where she could do nothing, ruin nothing, take charge of nothing. She wondered if Taylor could see her at all. Calvin Taylor was slender and spectacled, spoke with a Jamaican lilt. "Don't worry, mother," he said genially. "We haven't lost a child yet."

He squatted down next to Beth and asked her a series of soft questions about Ben—his size, his age, his clothing, where he was standing when she last saw him. Beth murmured in reply. When Wayne came over, Calvin Taylor shook his hand and asked about the results of the first-floor search. And then he said, again genially, "Well, Mr. Thunder, sounds like nothing left for us to do but open a few doors." Wayne all but beamed with pride; the police had commended him! Beth almost laughed aloud.

Jimmy and Taylor told the manager, who was lurking, to get a passkey; they would have to open two hundred rooms.

"Ah, there are guests, though . . ." the manager said nervously.

"We'll knock," said Taylor.

The lobby filled with handsome young men—almost all short, Irish, Italian, a couple of black guys, one tall Germanic blond. A woman with long brown hair in a bun, looking awkward in a uniform clearly not styled to fit the contours of her body. She came over and sat down beside Beth on the trolley. "Scared, huh?" she said. "Don't worry. We'll find him. I mean, I've been a cop for five years, and I've looked for a dozen kids, and we always find them." She stopped and looked at Beth, who was pulling her own hair now, rhythmically. "We find them, and they're okay. Not hurt."

Beth did not know what to do with Vincent; she supposed she should comfort him. She looked at him, as he twitched in his sleep.

"Would you like something to eat?" the manager asked Ellen. He was florid now, and smelled thickly of cigarette smoke.

"I'm not his mother," Ellen told him. The manager, now sighing audibly, turned to Beth.

"Would you like something to eat?"

Beth considered. She did not see how it would be possible to eat.

"I'd like a vodka and tonic," she said. The manager's mouth made an O in surprise, but he bustled off, literally snapping his fingers to the bartender.

"Paperwork," said the brown-haired police officer with the artful bun. "I have to ask you a couple of things, Mrs. Cappadora. I mean, even if we find him in five minutes, there has to be a report, of course. And we need the most detailed description we can get to send out to other departments—if we need to do that, which we probably won't."

Beth knew she was supposed to find this soothing, this routine-ness, this scoffing at the absurdity of it all. It was meant to assure her that any minute a tousled Ben, with a fistful of baseball cards given him by a friendly police-man, would be carried out the elevator doors like a silver cup. Everyone would be smiling, everyone would be chiding Ben, "You gave your mama a scare, partner. . . ."

". . . three?" asked the police officer.

"Yes," said Beth. "What?"

"He's three, your son?"

"Just turned."

"Date of birth?"

"April first."

"April Fool's Day."

"Yep."

"And he has, what . . . brown hair?"

"He has red hair. He has dark red hair. Auburn. And a red baseball cap. He's wearing an orange shirt with red fish on it. And purple shorts. And red high-top gym shoes. Those are new. Parrots." Beth bit her lip; she knew how that sounded—as though she didn't care enough to match colors in her kids' outfits. But who noticed what a kid wore to ride in a car? She slid her eyes over to the brown-haired officer. *She* would. The officer was probably a caring mother.

And why, she asked herself suddenly, don't they tell one another what Ben looks like? Is there a therapy or a strategy in the repetition?

"And Mrs. Cappadora, where did you say you lived?"

Beth hunkered down and talked. She concentrated on precision and detail. She pretended she was Pat. She told the officer about Ben's language skills and his fears (windstorms, all bodies of water, blood) and his habit of hiding in small places (once, horrifyingly, but just for a moment, the dryer). In detail, she described Ben's birthmark, the mark in the shape of a nearly perfect carat—an ashy-colored inverted V that sat just above his left hip. The birthmark had been something Beth considered having removed, she told the officer, but the dermatologist said it was nothing, just an excess of pigment, and so she left it alone. Sensing the officer's restlessness, Beth next talked about Vincent—who had awakened and gone off with Ellen to get a sandwich. He was a difficult kid, but he loved Ben and was protective of him.

"Kerry's named after me," said Beth. "I mean, not Beth, but that's my last name, Kerry. Before I got married. We were going to name Ben that, Kerry ... at least I wanted to, but Pat—that's my husband—he said, 'Why not just name him Fairy?' So we named the girl that instead. Ben's named after my brother. . . ." She babbled; the lobby was filling up again, with police officers Beth hadn't seen before.

As Beth watched, two of them set up a folding table in a small room off the lobby that probably was used to hold coats with a number of cellular phones and a compact radio that squawked and crackled.

"What are they doing?" Beth asked.

"They're setting up a command center," a young female officer whose name tag read G. Clemons, told her.

"What for?"

"Well, to stay in touch with the station, and to take any calls that might come in from the state police or other departments."

"Other departments?"

"Yes. Or tips from people. Or any kind of calls. I mean, if we knew for sure that anybody else had been involved in this, it'd probably be a larger operation already. But the kind of tips we're going to be getting might—"

"Tips? But how would anyone know where to call?" Beth asked, and then what G. Clemons had alluded to jabbed her. One person might.

"Just a minute, Mrs. Cappadora." Tucking stray ends into the careful roll at the back of her head, Officer Clemons spoke briefly with Detective Taylor. He took the sheet of paper she'd been using, made a few jottings on it himself, and took off for the phone.

"We're putting out an ISPEN, Mrs. Cappadora. That's 'Illinois State Police Emergency Network.' Alphabet soup, huh?" The bun bobbed in concern. Beth thought, she's still trying not to scare me. "That frequency is monitored by all departments statewide. For example, this is District Three, near Chicago, but we pick up way into the western and northern suburbs. . . ."

"You have a lot of police officers for such a little city."

"Oh, these aren't all Parkside police, Mrs. Cappadora," said Officer Clemons. "They're from Chester and Barkley and Rosewell, too."

Beth stared at her. "So you're worried."

"We have to take the disappearance of a child this small, after this length of time, very, very seriously, Mrs. Cappadora."

It was three p.m. Ben had been missing for two hours.

There were two cops at each of the exits Beth could see, and the slice of the circle drive that lay inside her vision was filling with blue-and-white cars, like a puzzle with pieces sliding into place. Jimmy Daugherty crossed in front of the revolving door. Beth excused herself and wobbled, thickly, to his side. She asked Jimmy for a Marlboro. He lit it.

"Bethie," he said. "Pat will be here soon, right?"

Beth was startled. "I didn't call him."

Jimmy ground out his own cigarette with a vicious twist of thumb and forefinger. "You didn't call Pat?"

"I thought we'd find him right away, and Pat had to work." She sounded like the kind of light-witted ninny who would soon begin to complain that she was missing her favorite soap. She tried again: "No one told me to call Pat!" That was worse. In the valley of the gathering shadow, who doesn't call your nearest? The child's father?

"Let's call now," Jimmy told her gently.

Beth thought, well, I'm not going to.

"And your folks? They're all still here, huh?"

Not them, either, thought Beth. No chance.

Pat would not have left a three-year-old to wander off alone. He would have made quick, fail-safe preparations—waved Ellen over, or waited to leave Vincent and Ben with Jill. He would have given the three minutes that safety demanded, not waded off blunderingly the way Beth did, trying to cut corners, shave time, consolidate motions. He would not do what Beth did when she set a hot glass dish on a corner of the counter at home and tried to make one phone call and then let the dish fall. He was full of foresight.

All their parents knew that.

Beth said no, she would not bother their parents now.

"I guess that's probably best, actually," said Jimmy. "Because you could have a family situation here, where the grandparents wanted the child—I mean, Bethie, I'm probably not exercising the kind of judgment I usually do because I know you and Pat and the Cappadoras. But who knows? Actually, my supervisor said the first thing I talked to her that we have to get somebody over to their house and talk to them."

"To Rosie and Angelo Cappadora's?"

"Right. Pat's folks. I know them, but we don't need to broadcast that we're coming."

"You mean you think that Rosie and Angelo could have Ben?"

"Anything's possible. A family feud—"

"Oh, that's so nuts, Jimmy. Rosie and Angelo worship Ben."

"That's just what I mean."

"And there's nothing with Pat and me or anything. They don't even know I'm in Chicago. Neither does my dad."

"People do strange things, Bethie."

Cop wisdom. Full-moon talk. This was all happening too quickly. All these people were too concerned all of a sudden. Couldn't Jimmy see how time-wasting and absurd it would be to send a police car to Rosie and Angelo's manicured ranch house to ask them if they'd stolen their grandson whom they didn't even know was in town? Didn't Jimmy grasp that she didn't want to see her dad or Pat's parents? To have them see her? She had always seemed unusual to Angelo, unusual to her father, perhaps even to Rosie, who liked everyone. But now, with this, if the parents came, there would be no escaping.

Jimmy led her to the telephone, wrote down Beth's home number in Madison, and dialed it for her. But when the phone began to burr, she felt as if she would have diarrhea, right there, and handed the receiver to Jimmy. Ellen came back and took her to the bathroom, and because Beth's legs would not bend, actually helped her sit down. Then Beth went into the bar and ordered another vodka and tonic; she didn't even attempt to pay. She had no idea where her purse was, or her shoes. Or Jill. Nick Palladino had come down and brought Vincent a small football on a rubberized string. Vincent was batting it up and down. Wayne and Nick and a couple of the cheerleaders' husbands stood around the bar. Beth watched their jaws work up and down.

". . . to help," said Nick.

"Huh?" asked Beth.

"She's torn up. She wants to go home," said Nick. "But I'll come back."

Trisha wants to go home to the children, Beth thought. To their two little girls, make sure they are safe, hold them and smell them. She said, "No, you don't have to. Unless you want to go to the party."

"Oh, Beth, I don't think they'll have the party," said Nick. "At least, not unless they find Ben, you know?"

So grave. So grave so fast. Grave enough, this perhaps-not-temporary loss of her child, to cancel a year-planned event for two hundred couples? If it's so grave as that, Beth thought, logically I should cry. She tried to let her eyes fill. But they would only lock, pasted open, staring at Nick's suit buttons, which had little, silver whales on them.

"I'd do anything for you, Beth," Nick told her.

"Oh, okay," Beth answered. Was that an appropriate reply? She searched Nick's face. His beautiful eyes looked puzzled. I should have married Nick, Beth thought, no matter how unintellectual he is. Then I wouldn't have had Ben to lose. That would be better. Her glass was empty.

Jimmy Daugherty came back and said he'd phoned Pat—Pat wasn't home.

"You have to call the restaurant."

"You guys have a restaurant?"

"His uncle's. Cappadora's. 741-3333."

Jimmy wrote it down. On the way to the phone, he added, "Don't worry, Bethie. Look around you. The Marines are here! And bliss is coming."

He sounded sure. She sipped her drink, prudently.

Ellen had ordered a pizza. Vincent wanted pizza, and the hotel didn't serve it. Discipio's was only a mile or so away, said Ellen. Jill, she told Beth, was lying down ... upset. Ellen had given Kerry to Barbara Kelliher. "And don't worry, Beth, she's right in her room, number 221, and Becky's with her. Kerry's safe, Beth."

Beth decided against telling Ellen that it didn't matter; she didn't really care whether Kerry was safe, unless Ben was found. She said, "Oh, good."

Wayne, the police, and the purple security men were rounding up everyone in the hotel who was connected with the reunion; they'd assemble in the ballroom, for what Beth pictured as a sort of ghastly dress rehearsal of the evening's planned assembly. The police would make small groups and then search the hotel rooms left vacant once again, in case they'd missed something. Everyone not connected with the reunion had been shuttled to the Parkside Arms, three blocks away, because the ordinary customers, only half a dozen couples, had been unnerved by the droves of uniforms in the lobby and the cordons outside.

The manager was furious and kept asking when the investigation would be complete. "Hasn't started yet, buddy," Jimmy told him.

"I thought this place didn't have a shuttle," Beth remarked to Ellen.

Ellen stared at her, glared at her. "What?"

"Never mind." Beth's glass was empty. She held it up and Ellen took it to the bar.

It was five p.m. Ben had been missing four hours.

Beth could feel her stomach boiling; she was actively nauseated; she probably needed to stop drinking. But there was the process of getting smaller, which had started when she first met the sergeant. That was wise to continue, Beth knew for sure. She accepted another drink from Nick. The brown-haired bun officer was back.

"Now, Mrs. Cappadora ..." she began.

"Beth," said Beth. It was such a long name, hers and Pat's; if she kept using it, this would take all night. Night. No, not yet. Outside the window, it was still bright afternoon, the sun spilling wavelike over the round shadow caves made by the hotel awnings.

"Well, you can call me Grace then," said the bun.

"Grace Clemons," said Beth.

"Right!" said the officer, as if Beth were very, very bright for her age. "One thing that sometimes happens is, parents sometimes have fingerprints taken of their children—"

"Fingerprints?" Beth shouted. The lobby went still for a long instant; then a phone rang and the burble of voices quietly resumed. And then Beth remembered: "I did, actually. We had this school program—Identa-Kid, through Dane County. We did both boys."

Beth thought Grace Clemons might literally jump up and down. "That's so wonderful, Mrs. Cappadora! Now we have a good tool, a real helper, for finding Ben."

Am I thick, Beth thought, or is she talking to me in layers? If they were to find Ben, why, they would bring Ben to his mother, and he would wrap his legs around me like a cub on a trunk. Who would need fingerprints? Fingerprints were for criminals—and victims.

Beth felt as if she heard a far-off engine sputter and then catch. That was it. So far, so fast. Children taken to hospitals, found in weeds, children whose hands were not damaged, but their faces ...

"Now, this Identa-Kid program, Mrs. Cappadora, would that be through your local police department?"

"Uh, no—Dane County, I said."

"County sheriff?"

"Yes."

"And that's which county?"

"*Dane* County." Didn't I just say this? Beth wondered.

Grace Clemons summoned one of the cops manning the phones and told him to get in touch with Dane County stat and get a fingerprint fax. You don't understand, Beth wanted to explain. I had Ben's fingerprints taken so that he would not ever be stolen or lost. It was preventive medicine, kept in the cabinet like Ipecac, to ward off poison by the fact of its presence; it was not ever intended to be used.

The brown-haired bun was talking again. Clemons. Yes. Grace. "Tell me what happened when you first came into the hotel. Now, your friend Elaine—"

"Ellen."

"Ellen was with you?"

"She met me in the parking lot."

"In the parking lot?" said Grace Clemons. "How did she know you were in the parking lot?"

"Well, she was looking for me. She would come out and look, and go back in. And then we got here."

"And besides Ellen, who was the first person you talked to?"

"Well, my boyfriend ... I mean, my ex ... I mean, my boyfriend from high school, Nick. And Wayne. My friend Wayne. He's Pat's friend, too. And the cheerleaders." Grace Clemons looked disappointed. Beth wondered what she'd done wrong. Her glass was empty. She held it up. Ellen materialized from somewhere and took it.

Beth said, "I have to get up for a minute."

Jimmy Daugherty had somehow found time to take off his suit and put on an ordinary summer-weight jacket and shirt. Jimmy was still as lean as the swimmer he'd been senior year, with crisp brown curls and a Marine-recruitment-poster jaw. Beth thought absurdly of Superman, ducking into the cloak room. He had told Beth he was a detective in plainclothes, and these were certainly plain. He'd even showed her his gold shield, as if to reassure her that they were both grownups now and not going to fight about who had to pith the frog in lab.

Now Jimmy approached Beth with a tall, willowy woman, ash-blond, with the kind of languid, manicured hands Beth associated with the Shorewood mothers for whom she sometimes shot photos of garden festivals. She wore a short plaid skirt and a long cotton sweater. He's going to introduce me to his wife, thought Beth. Is this possible? And then she remembered, Jimmy was married to the little Ricarelli girl, Anita—a child bride who had given him four boys before her thirtieth birthday.

"Beth, this is my boss," Jimmy told her. "This is Detective Supervisor Bliss."

"I'm not really his boss—who could boss Jimmy? I just head up the detectives," said the woman, smiling.

"You're a police chief?" she asked stupidly.

"No, just of detectives. . . . Well, my name is Candy Bliss."

Beth laughed, snorted; she couldn't help it, but was instantly mortified.

The woman's green eyes lighted with a kind of conspiratorial joy. "I know—it sounds like a stripper, huh? My sister's name is Belle, can you beat that? Belle Bliss? I'm the stripper; she's the gun moll. The stuff parents can do to you, huh?"

She stopped, and pressed one slender finger against a deep line just between her arched brows. "I can't believe I said that. Mrs. Cappadora, I want you to know, we are going to find your little boy. Can we sit down?" Jimmy drifted away.

"Jimmy doesn't have to work; he took a night off," Beth said helplessly. She did not want Candy Bliss to think her a greedy person.

"Oh, I think he wants to," said Candy Bliss. She gave Beth her dazzling smile, then turned to Grace Clemons, and Beth saw the smile vanish, as if Bliss had run a washcloth over her face.

She said, "Description?"

Grace Clemons said, "Already out, and they're doing the leads now."

"What leads?" Beth asked. "Who saw him?"

"Not those kinds of leads, Mrs. Cappadora. It's a computer network," Candy Bliss explained. "Law Enforcement Agency Data Systems. If anyone were to be able to run this child by obtaining his name or date of birth—"

"He has no idea what his date of birth is."

"Well, his name, then—it would come back on the computer as a hit. We'd have a location for him."

"A location?"

"A hospital, if he got hurt—a lone child if he was picked up by a unit."

She turned her attention back to the other woman. "Detective Clemons, I can take over here now. I'm going to want you to do press if this keeps up for very much longer, so start preparing a statement." She shot a look at Beth. "Ben answers to his name?"

"Yes."

"So I guess, maybe, okay, use the name, and heavy on the description. Just . . . let me have a look at it before you go with it."

Switch. Turn. Radiant smile again. "Now," she said, "here's the deal."

Odds strongly favored finding Ben within the next hour or so. "Children disappear all the time. Even in a little town like this. We have kids wander off from the carnival, from the playground, the library. From day care— there's major hell to pay when that happens. They walk down the block, turn the wrong way, and get lost. The thing is, someone always finds them. And what we're seeing now, I think, is just that gap in time between someone finding Ben and bringing him to a police station, or calling the police while they have Ben at their house. . . ."

"So you're saying you think he's no longer in the hotel, period," Beth began.

"It's been a little too long for that now. And this search has been pretty thorough."

The next step, said Candy Bliss, would be to create target maps of the immediately surrounding area; then search systematically—go door to door along the short block of stores that ran parallel to the cemetery, cut over to the high school to check the sports equipment sheds, the fields, the bleachers, any place that might attract a kid's attention.

"There are a lot of fathers and grandfathers here who are pretty upset," said the detective. "We're getting a fair number of volunteers dropping in who are off-shift tonight. By the way, that's why it took me so long to get here. I wasn't working tonight. I apologize. It was my nephew's birthday, way up in Algonquin."

"Oh, I'm sorry." Beth nodded.

"You mean, to take me away from it? Oh come on, that's fine. He got what he wanted out of me anyway. Little Tykes wagon."

"Ben has that, too. Santa Claus. How old is your little nephew?"

"Well, actually, he's three today. He's three."

Beth reached for her glass and drained her drink.

The pizza arrived then.

It was five-thirty. Ben had been missing four hours and thirty minutes.

The pizza delivery kid in his red-and-yellow smock barely made it through the revolving glass door when Pat flew in as if out of a hailstorm and jostled the kid to one knee. It was 150 miles from the restaurant to Parkside, maybe more. Pat would later tell Beth he didn't really know how fast he drove; but she calculated it had to be close to a hundred miles an hour. No one stopped him; he paid no tolls. He left the door of the freezer open at Cappadora's and the lip of the cash register hanging out, the tray stuffed with money. Augie wasn't there, only a seventeen-year-old waitress and the busboy, Rico.

"Where is he?" asked Pat of the manager, who happened to be the first person in his line of vision.

"The little boy?" said the manager. "You'll have to talk to the police about that matter."

"Paddy," said Jimmy Daugherty with the kind of easy, instant intimacy Beth craved from fellow Irish. "We haven't found him yet. It shouldn't take long, though."

"What?" Pat cried. "What? Where's Ben? Where's Beth?"

Hastily, Beth stuck her half-filled glass behind her and scrambled to her feet. Pat rushed at her, grabbed her, held the back of her skull in his free hand as if she were a child. "Bethie," he told her, speaking slowly, as if she were hearing-impaired, "tell me how this happened. Tell me where Ben is."

Beth made a small motion; should she shrug, try to speak? Explain?

Pat let her go, not entirely gently, and said, "Okay. Okay. Can I smoke in here?" Four people offered him a light. "Okay, okay," Pat said again. "Now, where is there in the hotel nobody has searched? The basement?"

"Just food storage down there," said the manager. "And it's locked. All the doors leading to storage are locked from the outside."

"Ben would love food storage. He grew up in a restaurant. Freezers and cabinets." He gestured to the manager. "You take me there."

"I don't see why," said the manager.

"We were going to anyway," said Calvin Taylor, appearing. As they walked off, Vincent appeared screaming, "Daddy!"

Pat waved for Vincent to stay back, stay with his mother.

"Your husband," said Candy Bliss. "That's okay. He needs to do something. We all do. And what we'll do is just go through that first half-hour once more. Is that okay, Beth?"

This was liturgy, then. Christ have mercy upon us. Lord have mercy upon us. Mercy upon us as many ways and by as many names as possible, over and over. Beth's part was to answer.

Had she seen Ben wander off? Had Vincent? Did Ben have a history of attention deficit or other neurological disorders? Did Ben have seizures? Was he drawn to shiny objects?

Seizures? Shiny objects?

"Huh?" Beth asked her. "Of course he liked shiny objects. All kids like shiny objects." She explained to Candy Bliss that she had seen nothing, nothing but one glimpse from the check-in desk of Vincent's head bobbing up and down.

"Well, then let's ask Mister Vincent," said Candy Bliss. She got up and settled herself on the luggage trolley, where Vincent cringed. "You wanta help the cops, Vincent? We got a lost brother here." Vincent stared around her, at Beth. Beth nodded faintly. "First, I want you to point for me in which direction Ben walked away."

Vincent sat back down on the luggage trolley and coiled back against the wall beside the elevator, hiding his eyes with uncharacteristic reluctance, until Beth walked over and settled him on her lap. Then he buried his face against Beth's midriff and violently shook his head. Beth eased him up and brushed the sweaty hair off his forehead.

"You can help find Ben. Old fuzzhead Ben needs you," she told him. Vincent squeezed his eyes closed; like her, Beth thought, he wanted to shrink to a dot.

"He's shrinking," she told Candy Bliss, who blinked once, quickly, and then looked away.

"Come on, buddy," the detective urged Vincent. "Show me where your brother went."

Vincent stuck out one limp and skinny arm and pointed toward the center of the room.

If Ben had toddled—Beth caught herself using the word, making Ben tinier, more babylike than he really was—off in that direction, he would have come gradually closer and closer to Beth.

He had been trying to come to Beth.

"Did you poke him?" Beth asked Vincent, suddenly, ferociously.

"No, I didn't touch him one single time!"

"Was he frightened? Did he want me?"

"No—Ellen. He wanted me to get Aunt Ellen. He said he was peeing his pants."

Beth loosed her arms from around Vincent; he flopped forward. She clawed her face again—Ben helpless, Ben embarrassed and looking for a trusted grownup, any of his "safe grownups," to help him use the bathroom. Had he seen her? Had he called? Had he tried to find a washroom on his own? Beth stood up, reeled, sat down heavily on the luggage trolley.

"I can think of better places to fall than that thing," Bliss said. "Why don't we get you on a couch?"

Lie down, Beth thought. It was the suggestion you made all the time in disasters, to people waiting to hear about the survivors of downed aircraft, to the stranded, to those in hospital emergency rooms awaiting the results of doomed surgeries. Have coffee. Lie down. Try to eat something. She had said it herself, to Pat's cousin (Jill's mother, Rachelle) last year, when Jill, then a freshman, had been hit by a car on her bike and had a leg broken in three places. Rachelle had listened; she lay down and slept.

Beth supposed she should lie down; her throat kept filling with nastiness and her stomach roiled. But if she lay down, she wanted to explain to Candy Bliss, who was holding out her hand, it would be deserting Ben. Did Detective Bliss think Ben was lying down? If Beth ate, would he eat? She should not do anything Ben couldn't do or was being prevented from doing. Was he crying? Or wedged in a dangerous and airless place? If she lay down, if she rested, wouldn't Ben feel her relaxing, think she had decided to suspend her scramble toward him, the concentrated thrust of everything in her that she held out to him like a life preserver? Would he relax then, turn in sorrow toward a bad fate, because his mama had let him down?

Surely this woman would understand how urgently Beth needed to remain upright.

She smiled brightly at Candy Bliss and said, "He's not dead."

"No, of course not, Beth."

"If he were dead, I could tell. A mother can tell."

"That's what they say."

"It's true, though. They talk to you with their minds, your kids. You wake up before they wake up—not because you hear them cry; you hear them getting ready to cry." Beth had never thought about the sinister extension of that link before—that if Ben were now being tortured or suffocating, she would feel a searing pain in her, perhaps in her belly, her throat. She was, instantly, entirely sure of this; there would be a physical alert, a signal at the cellular level. She strained up on the end of her spine, to raise her aerial, her sensors. She felt nothing, smelled and heard nothing, not even a whisper of breathed air past her ear.

And then Pat came up out of the basement of the hotel, yelling, "Where's your phone? I have to call my father and mother, and my cousin, my sisters!"

No, Beth thought, not them all. And yet, perhaps, if they came—and then went—she could follow her feelers, delicate feelers deranged by all this light and sound, into the night, clear. She could rise up from this pond bottom, from where she watched Pat, and let Ben pull her to him. Pull his mother to him with the gravitational force of their bond.

It was seven p.m.

She watched as Vincent soundlessly, furiously threw himself on Pat—and Pat had sufficient presence of will to show love for Vincent even now, to bury his face in Vincent's neck. "Don't worry, Vincenzo," he said. "Papa will find Ben."

Mama, Beth thought. Mama will find Ben. Maybe.

She leaned forward, delicately and slowly, over the edge of the luggage trolley, and vomited on the tile floor in front of the elevator.

Chapter 3

Italians were good at this sort of thing. In a jam, Irish would tremble and supplicate theatrically; but Italians knew what mattered in this world: that everyone needed food and shelter, that an army ran on its stomach, that children had to be bathed and put to bed. Except at funerals, when they indulged hysteria at a time when it availed them least, Italians did what needed doing.

Beth's mother-in-law, Rosie, came in the revolving door carrying the car keys. She'd driven. Angelo would have wanted to, but he was older than she by ten years, a little loose behind the wheel at the best of times. Rosie, who was boss, didn't trust him in a crisis.

Rosie was little, light-boned, not at all the stereotypic black-shawled Sicilian mama—she had a pageboy, and wore a silver-moon pin on her plum-colored jacket. She looked chic, thought Beth, and collected, as she patted Beth's cheek and murmured *"Carissima"* and exchanged a look with Pat (no words necessary). Then, without asking for a progress report—Rosie assumed she would get that if there were progress—she took the elevator upstairs to fetch Jill and Kerry. Jill's mother, Rachelle, Rosie's niece, was at the

house. Jill would be happier with her mother. Ellen offered to ask her husband, Dan, to come for Vincent, so he could play with her son, David; but Rosie silenced her with a smile. "Vincenzo will go to the house, Ellenie dear," she said. "It's better."

Ellen, who had known Rosie all her life, would not have thought of arguing.

For Beth, there was an almost festive interval when Rosie arrived. She knew she smelled of puke and booze; but Rosie, who normally frosted her eyes to behavior she called *"stupida,"* had not noticed, or had chosen to overlook. Angelo barreled in with a tray of cream horns for the police and set them down on the table where the phone bank burred steadily. The officers smiled faintly, exchanging looks. Beth thought, They don't understand: you give something, you get something. They'll remember the cream horns and make one more call.

Angelo grabbed Beth and searched her face, kissed Pat on the mouth. "My God in heaven," he said. He ripped the paper covering from the cream horns. One was out of place; Angelo, by long habit, turned it and set it in line with the others.

Rosie and Angelo were first-generation, but far more pragmatic than earthy. They were caterers; it was not possible for a Mob wedding to take place on the west side without Rosie and Angelo's braciole and cream horns, their ice swans (tinted) and Champagne fountain. And not just Mob—Rosie and Angelo did weddings for ordinary Catholics who weren't even Italian, and for Protestants and Jews. They marinated chicken breasts in mustard and red vinegar; they sprinkled nasturtiums in the salad bowls before anyone else did it; they made a miniature of the towering wedding cake for the bride and groom to freeze and to thaw at the birth of the first child. They knew how to do things.

They had never had a child mortally ill or a grandchild lost. They had been married forty years, and for all Beth knew, their life's severest tragedy had been the death of her own mother, their dearest friend. Even so, Beth could see they would do the right thing. They would help find Ben and they would forgive her.

By contrast, Beth's father, Bill, was red-faced and dazed when he arrived.

Not because of the crisis; he'd been golfing, with the firefighters—he'd been a chief, through most of Beth's childhood, though he was retired now ten years. Beth had not even told Bill she'd be in town—she had the job to shoot, after all, and the reunion dinner and brunch would consume all the time up to that. "What are you doing, sweetheart?" he asked Beth, straightening his sweater and leaning down to take Beth's hands. "What is this about Ben? Is he in the hospital?"

Rosie had left a message at the nineteenth hole, and a kid had run out in a cart to bring Bill in.

"Bill, Ben's missing. . . ." Pat told him.

"Missing? But Ben's only two. Where?"

"He's three, Bill. Here. They think he's somewhere in the hotel. . . ."

"Is he three? That's right. Did somebody call the police?"

Pat sighed.

"Well, sure," Bill went on. "I see all the blues. Did somebody call Stanley?" Stanley was the chief of police in Chester, the west-side suburb where Bill had served as fire chief for twenty-three years.

"It's Parkside, Bill," Pat told him. "They got this jurisdiction. But there's Chester police here, and Barkley, too. Even Rosewell."

"Well, but Stanley could help out." Bill could never be anything less than pugnaciously certain that a guy he knew could put matters straight. These cops, they looked young, he told Pat.

"Where were you, Patrick, when the baby walked away? Where was Beth?"

Ellen explained the whole thing to him then, while Beth got up and wandered into the bar. She could see the bartender scan her denim shirt, which was still damp and stained where Ellen had sponged away the vomit. But the bartender, a Hispanic guy with an elaborate mustache, gave her the vodka and tonic she asked for.

"Rosie!" Bill bawled when Rosie came back down into the hall, carrying the sleeping Kerry, leading Jill, who was holding Vincent's hand and carrying his football and overnight bag. "What's going on, sweetie? What's all this?"

"Give Grandpa a kiss, Vincenzo," Rosie told Vincent, and Vincent, who was ordinarily shy at first around Bill, turned up his face to be kissed. Bill picked Vincent up and embraced Angelo.

"Ange, what's this? Where's the baby?"

Beth slammed the drink. She didn't feel a flicker of tipsiness, or even nausea—the liquor descended tenderly, like hot chocolate. She began to grow small again. Her father was not rising to the moment; it was his habit to act as if the world perplexed him. Beth was sure it did not; it was only Bill's way of getting someone else to manage. When her mother was dying, Bill stood in the hospital hall, his face collapsed in a frown, while doctors explained that Mrs. Kerry needed dialysis, and even that, perhaps, would not clear the—

"Wait," Bill had told them. "This cyst, if you remove this cyst, why then . . . ?"

There was an almost comic quality to the combination of unlucky breaks and Bill's bewilderment at each of them. Did we say two weeks? she imagined the doctors telling her father. We meant two days. Every palliative surgery, every new regimen of antibiotics intended to drive off the deepening infection revealed another complication, another mass of necrotic tissue, another absence of function. The doctors continued to probe and prop and confer. Bill continued to ask them when Evie would be cured, not how much time was left. Beth and her brothers, Paul and Bick, floundered, pitying Bill for his vacuity, hating him for it, wanting him to take charge of them as he did a squad at an industrial fire, wanting to take charge themselves and shake him, tell him, "Dad, she's dying."

But the train of Evelyn's illness kept careening downhill; and still, Bill was perplexed when Evelyn died. "She doesn't look like she could be filled with poison," he told Beth at the funeral parlor. "Does she? Does this figure?"

He looked at Beth this same way now. As if she would clear matters up for him.

"We got an unidentified. Elmwood Hospital," one of the stocky younger officers called. Everyone stopped. Candy Bliss was across the lobby like a sprinter, taking the phone. "Yes, a boy. . . . No, I don't think so." She scanned the room for Beth. "Can Ben speak Spanish?" Beth shook her head and the detective asked her, an instant later, as if inspired by a random thought, "How about Italian?"

"Just swear words," said Pat. No one laughed. Pat said then, "He speaks English. *Sesame Street* English."

"We'll call you back," Candy Bliss said.

The child was older, she told Beth. He'd been hit by a car riding a bike; he was in stable condition. Had to be four or five at least. And Elmwood was ten miles away, easy. But he did have auburn hair. Beth looked up at her. Candy Bliss pressed a forefinger between her eyes. "Jimmy!" she called. "You saw Ben, right? Take a run over there and look at this little boy, okay? What's the harm?"

Jimmy was already grabbing for his coat.

"Who are all those people calling?" Beth asked.

"Mostly other departments, calling back to tell us what they've been hearing, that's all," said Candy Bliss. "Later, when ... well, if we have to inform the press, we'll get a whole ton of calls from everyone, including Elvis, saying he's seen Ben."

"Cranks."

"Aliens. The Easter bunny. And genuinely lonely people who watch reality TV shows."

"And what if one of them has?"

"That's why we listen to the Easter bunny."

Past them proceeded an almost mournful parade of half-familiar faces, refugees from the reunion. A few people were staying, Ellen had told her, mostly those who were going to stay over a few days anyhow. And they wanted to help. But the majority of the people were going home, or out in large groups for dinner.

"Can we still stay here?" Beth asked. She wanted to be good, the model complainant, the kind of patient the dentist liked best because she kept her mouth open so wide.

"Of course, absolutely." She smiled at Pat. Now he had to hear the recounting, find out about the odds. "Anyhow, it's a beautiful night out there; he wouldn't even really be uncomfortable."

Beth gaped at the clock.

It was 9:15. Ben had been missing for eight hours. A work day. A day of school. An amount of time that would not be accidental. She jumped up, sweating. "It's so late!"

"That's what I mean, Mrs. Cappadora. In a sense, that's an advantage. Now it's quiet out there, and we can really start getting a sense of what's going on in the town. The canine unit is on the way, and we're getting helicopter support from Chicago. We have a neighborhood patrol, too—"

"Helicopters?" Beth asked.

"Equipped with infrared sensors, Beth. When things quiet down, they can scan open areas. They pick up objects that are giving off heat. A person, lying down maybe."

"Or a person dead."

"Or a body, yes. But that's not what we're looking for here. We want to be able to pick up a sign of Ben even if he is trying to hide from being seen, for example, in some bushes. See?" She excused herself for a moment and whispered to one of the cops on the phone, almost too low for Beth to hear, "Are they *breeding* the goddamn dogs or what?"

"Where's Rosie?" Beth asked Pat, gripping his hand, which was icy and wet. "Where's Rosie?"

Rosie was about to leave, to take the children home. But she came to Beth, humming so softly it sounded like a purr, and pushed Beth's tangled hair behind her ears as if Beth were a little girl. In Jill's arms, Kerry was absorbed in her bottle, but Rosie took Vincent firmly by the hand and told him, "Kiss Mama. You'll see Mama soon. We'll go to sleep at Nana's."

His eyes were wired with overtiredness, and something else, a confusion she had never seen before in her linear-minded eldest. Vincent leaned over. Beth hugged him perfunctorily; but for an instant, surprising her, he clung. Then Vincent took Rosie's hand and walked a few steps without looking back. All at once he stopped.

"Mom?" he called.

Beth heard him, but had no energy for an answer.

"Mom?" Vincent called again, conversationally. "Did Ben get back yet?"

Rosie said firmly, "Not quite yet. Very soon." But Vincent was looking straight at Beth's eyes, his comically too-bushy brows drawn down in absorbed attention.

"Mom," he said, "I asked you a thing. Did Ben get back yet?"

Beth said, "Sweetheart. No."

Vincent said, "Oh."

Beth covered her face, scoured it with her fingers. She looked down at her nails. The creamy-coral guaranteed-two-week manicure was smudged and split.

Angelo and Bill didn't leave. They stayed in the lobby, sprawled in armchairs, though the manager officiously encouraged everyone, over and over, to "relocate" to an upper-floor lounge. People walked into the Tremont lobby, looked at the command center, and took a quick powder. Ellen and Nick Palladino were in the bar; Wayne had mustered a volunteer force of fifteen schoolmates to take their own cars and cruise the cemetery, the parking lot of the school, Hester Park. Beth had overheard a cop tell another that it was like bumper cars out there, but that no one had the heart to stop them.

Supporting Beth under one arm, Pat brought her to a more comfortable chair by the piano. Candy Bliss followed. She wanted a picture of Ben for distribution to the media. It was getting late now, and she didn't want to miss morning paper deadlines.

Did Beth have a picture? She had dozens—she'd brought a score of them for purposes of bragging, for the reunion.

But she had no idea, she told Captain Bliss, where her purse was.

Pat found it under the luggage trolley. It was wet, the contents halfscattered. He held out a picture of Ben in his baseball shirt, grinning with his Velcroed catch mitt held close to one cheek.

Beth would wonder later, What had she been imagining? Had she believed, as very small children do, that because Ben was out of her vicinity, was invisible to her, he had in fact been suspended in a pocket of the universe? That he sat on a bubble, safe but estranged, waiting for his mother to notice him again, so he could resume being real? Had Beth believed that because she, his own mother, could not see him, Ben had stopped existing as a complete being who could feel terror and bewilderment?

Ben was a real child in the urban night.

"Ben!" Beth screamed. And again, as the fragile crust of her muddled restraint cracked and then broke entirely, "Ben! Ben! Ben! Ben!" It got easier.

"Ben!" Beth screamed. "Ben!" When Pat put his hand over her arm to try to ease her down, she leaned over and seized it in her teeth, biting hard, drawing blood. The room took on the aspect of a hospital emergency room, a sudden bustle. Pat and Jimmy tried to strong-arm Beth; but she tossed them off as they scrabbled to grab different parts of her. She was an eel, a thing coated with resistant gel. The manager ran for the purple security guards, who watched in pity as Beth thrashed, blocking her path to the door every time she got to her feet. She was strong, famously strong. She noticed everything: Pat's bleeding hand; the fearful, furtive glances; the looking away of the de- parting couples who had to pass through the lobby. She saw Nick with his shiny charcoal-brown head of curls in his hands; she thought he might be crying. His back was heaving up and down. Beth stopped stock-still for a deep breath, and then she screamed again, "Ben! Ben! Ben!"

Candy Bliss told the manager tersely, "Call a doctor."

"I don't know a doctor," said the formal, chubby manager.

"Well, don't you have an emergency physician on call to the hotel?"

"We've never had ... What does she want?"

"You simple—" said Candy Bliss, letting out stored breath in a huff. "Shit. Call 911."

Beth was wearying; her arm muscles burned. But she only had to look at the bright banquet of children's photos—primary-colored, gleaming—on the coffee table and she would feel the scream percolate up again, as impos- sible to resist or contain as an orgasm. "Ben! Ben! Ben!"

The manager brought Candy Bliss a portable phone. "The mother is hav- ing trouble.... Yes, exhausted.... Yes, you can hear her.... Well, no, not a transport.... Send someone out."

"Christ God, Beth, please stop!" her father told her firmly.

"Ben!" she screamed at his heavy, veined face. He looked like a hound, sad-eyed and pouching. A bluff, once-handsome man, features blurred by years of gin gimlets. "Beeeeennnnn!" Tears formed in Bill's eyes. Pat was repelled—shivering, he backed away from the couch where Beth struggled.

Beth looked at the clock. It was blurred. Could it be eleven? She screamed, "Beeeennnn!"

A paramedic, very cute, slipped a blood-pressure cuff around Beth's arm.

And the doctor who arrived, minutes later, in a jogging suit, squirted golden liquid out of a syringe; the drops flicked down. "We need to get you some rest, here," he told her, swabbing parts of her arms and hands with alcohol, whatever patches of skin he could reach as she flailed. "Listen," he said to the room at large, "we need—"

Nick charged across the room then and half-lay on top of Beth; he smelled wonderful, spicy. His chest was harder than Pat's, bigger. He held her left arm against her body while the paramedic extended the right. The shot was painful, stinging, aching as it seeped in. "Bethie," said Nick. "I know, I know."

"What the fuck?" Beth said, laughing. "You don't know. *I* don't even know."

The medicine was spreading her legs, stilling her chest, compressing her jaw; she felt a line of saliva gather at the corner of her mouth. It was anesthetic. "You can operate now," she told the doctor; he didn't know it was her small joke.

And then black wings brushed her face. And fell.

When Beth awoke, she was tucked hard into a huge bed. Tucked so hard she was nearly straitjacketed.

Ben.

Every available light in the room was on. Directly beside her, in a second king-sized bed, Pat was asleep on top of the bedspread. "Pat?" she whispered. He was oblivious, snoring.

Beth had to pee. She got up, danced sideways for a step, then made her way into the lush, cream-tiled bathroom. She peed, steady, calm, purged, as if the medicine had deadened a section of brain stem. She wanted to brush her teeth. I am doing the things people do, Beth thought, still wanting to eliminate my body's wastes, clean myself, quench my thirst. Unbidden, Beth thought how even when her mother died, she and Ellen were stunned, not that life went on, but how quickly life went on, and how unchanged it was. People could not wait to eat or to get a newspaper. The young priest had told Beth this eating, this talking, these were affirmations of life. He was the humanist kind; he thought he could trick people into Catholicism by pretending the program had been revamped. Beth knew very well, back then, that she did not want to affirm her life and health. She knew that even more securely now. She simply wanted to be shed of bodily urgencies. She forced open a window crosshatched with wire, and craned her neck up and out. There was an alley down there, narrow, and a wall, the other wing of the hotel, that went up farther than Beth could see. A cat was down there, stirring among the dumpsters. Beth tapped the glass; the cat looked up. She saw its gold eyes snap and its maniacal grin. She did not feel Ben, neither his death or his reaching. She slammed the window closed. Pat gargled a snore. You dumb boy, she thought, looking at him. I don't like you.

Opening the closets, cracking the drawers, she found no luggage. Nothing of hers. She could not find a clock. Pat winced in his sleep.

Beth looked out into the corridor. It was absolutely hushed, dim-lighted. She could not find her shoes. Faintly, from outside, she could hear the whump of beating helicopter blades.

Down in the elevator, in the lobby—it was lighter, but still. At the desk, a young blond woman slumbered on her cupped hand. When Beth approached, she sat up and stifled a little shriek.

"Where are the police?" Beth asked her.

"Oh," said the clerk, instantly sympathetic. "They left."

"They left?"

"Well, that is, they didn't *leave*—there are a lot of them outside. But they took the phones and stuff down and went back to the station." She brightened up. "Channel Five was here. And Seven—Eyewitness News. They set up stuff right here in the lobby for the ten o'clock news. But the lady police chief wouldn't let them wake you up."

Beth nodded.

"I need my things."

"Ah, toothpaste? A toothbrush? I can get you one."

"No, my own things. My bag."

"I think it's locked up." The young clerk pawed through a ring of keys, found Beth's duffel, handed it over to her. Beth dragged it to a washroom off the lobby. She removed her reeking shirt and pulled on a T-shirt over her jeans. She found a cotton sweater, bright with red and gold beads. For the luncheon on Sunday. Red shiny flats. She put all of it on. Bodily urgencies.

She washed her face and brushed her teeth. As she shoved the toilet articles back into the bag, she saw Ben's clothes tumbled among her own underwear, and Kerry's tiny tights, her footie pajamas. Ben's rubber sandals. His Blackhawks jersey. She was such a bad, haphazard packer. Beth zipped her duffel and lay down on it, her forehead on the tile floor.

Then she rose, lugged the duffel back out to the counter.

"I have to go out," she told the clerk.

"Do you want me to call someone? Your friend—" she glanced at a clipboard in front of her—"Ms. DeNunzio?"

"I just have to go out."

"It's the middle of the night. No stores are open."

Ben had been missing more than twelve hours. This girl thought Beth wanted to go shopping. The girl asked, "Do you want a coffee?"

Beth said, "No thank you," and walked out into the night, which was balmy, Floridian, cleansed.

A half-dozen squads ranged around the circle drive in a loose ring, including a van Beth assumed from the array of electronic plumage on top housed a portable communications center. Cables snaked from the van across the sidewalk, under and through the doors of the Tremont. The fabled Eyewitness News truck was still there as well, its white-eyed lights giving the whole dark stretch of pavement an Oscar-night feel; and a group of what Beth assumed to be print journalists were talking with one of the young detectives. *They* were talking, but he was just smiling and shaking his head. She watched the photogs, their arms draped with the heavy groceries of their profession, lining up to shoot the squad cars under the arch that said "Tremont Hotel." Boring stock shot, Beth thought; that should be me taking it. Or I should be in it, to make the shot better. She crossed behind the van, and not a single person seemed to notice her passing.

Out on the quiet street, street lamps—the hazy, muted halogen kind her father put so much stock in—threw the only illumination.

Ben. A moonless night.

Looking across the street, Beth could see the blue roof lights of Immaculata. There was no traffic to dodge. Beth crossed the street, growing stronger on gulps of air. She peered into the door of C Building. Inside, all was darkness. Think of C Building, she told herself—that's something that won't hurt if you think about it. In C Building, the juniors and seniors would congregate before school. A sophomore could come in if she was dating a junior guy; but these miscegenetic relationships were barely tolerated. Beth could see the door to the student council office—the door for which Beth, as an officer, had her own key. She and Nick would draw the curtains after third lunch, lock the door, and lie on the meeting table, sweating and probing. All through the afternoon's trigonometry and English III, Beth's stomach would ache and contract. She had believed then that everyone who looked at her knew, could see Nick's handprints on her as if they had been impressed with luminous paint.

She walked through the courtyard, past the statue, past the marquee that read "See 'Dracula!' at Olde Tyme Dramatics" and "Welcome Home Immaculata Class of '70!" Out past the field house, the tennis courts, out to the field.

Just before the gate to the bleachers, she crossed the red wooden bridge that spanned a tributary of Salt Creek. For a generation, village engineers had tried to dam the little stream; in spring, its swollen overrun made the football field a slippery marsh. Nothing worked. The creek always re-established its course. The bridge was so defaced with carvings the paint was virtually nonexistent. It looked red only from a distance. Teenagers from years that followed Beth's own youth, teenagers more skilled at tagging with a spray-paint can, had scrawled ominous messages: "Men of the 2-and-2, Arise!" "Spick Power Rules!" There were also the usual romantic epitaphs: "Justin Smashed My Heart," "Christine Blows Ryan."

Beth once would have swung herself down, briefly, to see whether the heavily etched marks that proclaimed "Steven and Ellen 4-Ever More" were still there. "4-Ever" had not even spanned junior year; Ellen later said Steven Barrett's band-major lips made her flesh creep, though it had taken her six months to decide that it wasn't her fault. But Beth knew the carving remained, a chestnut. Tonight, instead of looking, Beth stood over the stream, no more than half a foot deep, intent on seeing a clue.

But she knew she needn't look for Ben here.

Ben would not willingly go near water. "It is impossible," the YMCA instructor once wrote to Beth, "to evaluate Benjamin's progress at swimming because he refuses to get into the water." When they swam, even in a bright, shallow pool, Ben attached himself to Beth's waist like a python. He would relax his legs and kick near the steps, with tentative joy. But if Beth walked out farther, even if the water was only up to her ribcage, he would brace himself around her, seem to want to meld into her. A solid, sloppy swimmer who loved water, Beth could not imagine the origins of this fear—had she ever terrified the children with drowning tales? Held them under for a panicky instant, intended for a tease? Never, not ever. There had been that one time when Ben fell off the pier at Lake Delavan. But hadn't her brother snatched Ben out of the water instantly, almost before his face got wet? With Beth screaming like a Comanche the whole time at Vic to be more careful . . . Vincent swam with quicksilver efficiency, had since he was four. Even baby Kerry now struggled to get out of Pat's arms and paddle.

When they visited Pat's aunt in Florida, Vincent ran into the waves; Pat had to chase him and explain the undertow. Ben would not even walk on the damp sand. "There is too much water," he told Beth, solemnly.

"Ben," she had coaxed him then, "come in, just a little. Mama will hold you."

Ben, stolid in his neon-pink trunks, pointed. "Is that the deep end?" His terror was like a scent on him. He didn't even trust Beth to get too close to him, as if she would overwhelm him and rush him into the water. Beth thought, back then, *he's hostage to us*—to people so large we could compel him to do almost anything. She could not remember ever being so small, vulnerable, so dependent on goodwill.

"There's no deep end of the ocean, Ben," she told him gently. "That's the shore. And it goes on and on, all along here, for miles. You have to go out and out a long way before it gets deep. That's way out there, where the boats go."

"So this is the three feet?" Ben persisted.

"Not even that, Ben. It's not even as deep as a pool, along the edge here. Look, it isn't even up to Vincent's knees."

"I don't want to go in the deep end of the ocean," Ben told her. "Sharks are there. Do I have to go?"

"No, no, Benbo," Beth had said, scooping him up, unsure whether she should just stomp out there and dip him, get it over with. She didn't want her boy to grow up timid, shy of this, of that. "Don't be afraid. I would be with you. Mama would never let the ocean snatch you away. I would hold you tightest and tightest, wouldn't I?"

"You know what?" Ben told her then, buying time. "You can go to the deep end. You can go there. You just start walking, until it goes over your head and then you keep on walking on the bottom. But then if you want to go back, that's too hard because the water just rubs all the, all the . . ."

"What, Ben?"

"All the feet marks away. You can't ever turn around and go back. You can't find it." And Beth, chilled, sat with him, all that long afternoon, high on the brow of the beach, scooping sand.

Bracing herself on her hands, Beth climbed to the top deck of the bleachers. They were slippery with dew, tacky with chipped paint. She held her arms and shivered. Wind from the cloudy sky seemed to reach down for her. Hunt. Prod. Beth lay on the bleachers, stretching herself out to fullest length, and emptied herself of tears, until the shoulders of her sweater were soaked, and her forehead pulsed against the wood.

When she looked up, not at a sound, but at something else, a disturbance of the air, Candy Bliss was standing at the foot of the bleachers. She held a plastic zip bag, small enough for a sandwich. In it was Ben's high-topped shoe, so clean and new the red parrot still glowed in the dark.

Chapter 4

Finding the tennis shoe changed everything.

It was the shoe that made Ben kidnapped. It proved for Candy Bliss that Ben had not wandered away on his own.

The knowledge that her child was in a stranger's hands should have accelerated her panic, but in fact it seemed to slow Beth down.

The shoe, Candy explained, had been found on a low shelf in the newsstand, low enough that Ben could have put it there himself. But it was tied neatly in a tight bow, in a way that most three-year-olds could never have done alone; and he could not have taken it off without untying it, either. "It's not conclusive, Mrs. Cappadora," said Candy Bliss. "But it's enough to start on. And, of course, that's how we felt anyway."

"That someone abducted Ben?"

Candy nodded. "It just ... that whole lobby full of people. You know, hiding in plain sight...." She shook her head. "Beth, now, you're sure Ben couldn't tie?"

"God no. He could barely cut pancakes with a fork. He was three." She snagged her lip with her teeth. "He's three."

"Well, I'm never sure. I mean, I'm close to my nephew, but you have to live in the same house to really commit all those developmental stages to memory. And this is my first . . ."

"Your first?"

"My first case involving a child so young. Of this kind."

"I see. Other kinds?" Beth asked.

"Well, in Tampa I used to work juvenile. Back when I started, that's what a female officer in the South did. And later . . ."

"Later?"

"Well, homicide."

"I see. You don't have children of your own?" Beth asked, amazing herself at her even-measured voice, because she knew that if she looked behind her, she could see herself galloping back and forth across the verge of the parking lot, under the moon, keening and shuddering.

"I don't," said Candy. "I . . . kind of wish I did."

"Maybe soon," Beth said, thinking, For Christ's sake, what are we talking about?

"Uh, well, I think not. I'm thirty-six. Maybe. Anyhow, he can't tie, and you can see how this bow looks." Beth stared at her son's tiny shoe as if it were a chip of meteor, an extraterrestrial phenomenon.

The service door swung wide as they approached, a young officer anticipating them from a cue Beth couldn't discern. She walked blinking into the sharp light reflecting off the stainless-steel expanses of sinks and stoves and straight into the muzzle of two huge and straining dogs.

"McGinty!" cried Candy, as if she'd just found her long-lost brother. But the barrel-chested, red-haired uniform cop was looking at Beth.

"Mrs. Cappadora," he said softly. "This is Holmes and this is Watson." The bloodhounds sat down, respectfully enough, at a silent gesture from McGinty's right hand. "We call them the bionic noses. We scented them off your little boy's shoe . . . and they got as far as the parking lot. We scented them again, and they went straight to the same place, to a spot in the parking lot a little west of the front entrance. We assume the car was there. . . ."

"The car that belonged to whoever it was who took Ben," said Candy.

"I know what he meant," Beth snapped. "I'm not stupid. I was a newspaper photographer for years." Candy nodded, tight-lipped. Pat showed up then, his face blurred with sleep, his hand still seeping under the bandage from Beth's bite, and Candy sat down with both of them. After the state troopers assigned to the case arrived, they would expand their survey of mapped coverage areas for ground and air searches. There would be computer searches, with the help of the list provided by the reunion planners, and the first individuals they would concentrate on interviewing would be those with criminal histories.

"Criminal histories?" Pat asked. "Kids from Immaculata?"

"Not kids anymore," said Candy. "And yeah, in any group that big there's a fair chance we're going to turn up some people, maybe spouses, with histories involving—" They both looked at Beth, and Candy continued, "Abuse. Or assault. Or something."

"With children?" Beth asked.

"Maybe."

"Like?"

"Like, for example, your friend Wayne. Beth, there was a statutory offense, involving a juvenile. In the seventies."

"Wayne is as close to my children as their blood uncles. Wayne would never hurt Ben. This is because he's gay. . . ."

"Which is what I thought, Beth, and it turned out that the kid was sixteen and he was nineteen, and it was probably just a romance that got some parents all juiced . . . see? Most of these things turn out to be nothing, but we check them all. . . ."

Ellen wandered into the kitchen, zeroed in on Beth, and enfolded her. In sweats and a ponytail, Ellen looked reduced, frail and young. She held Beth against her as Candy explained that it would be wise to get the parents' lie detector tests out of the way. They could visit the technician today or wait until Monday.

"You think Beth arranged for Ben to be stolen?" Ellen asked.

"No, but most kidnappings are domestic in origin. They're custody-related, or they turn out to be problems with relatives or former caregivers," Candy Bliss explained.

There were lists and interviews and the first Crimestopper poster of Ben's face to approve; Beth—luckily, she thought—looked away at the last minute, so she never saw Ben's trusting eyes look back at her from the black-and-white photocopy. Ellen helped Beth take a bath, drawing Beth's jeans down over her hips, handing her into the tub as she would have helped a brittle-boned grandmother. While Beth lay in the water and Pat paced, smoking, in the bedroom, the phone rang almost incessantly. Ellen would answer, crisply, "She's asleep," or "No, they've lived in Madison more than ten years." Dressed in Ellen's clean clothes, so long on her she looked like Nellie Forbush in her sailor suit in *South Pacific*, Beth sat in front of the mirror and dried her own hair. Some time in the late afternoon, Officer Taylor asked her what she remembered about her classmate Sean Meehan. His second child had died four years before, a crib death that never felt quite right. When Beth began to dry-heave in the sink, the doctor, whose name Beth never knew, showed up again and gave her sample packets of tranquilizers. But when she couldn't keep those down, either, he gave her another shot; and she slept, hearing everything, even her brother Bick's voice—she tried to wake up to talk to Bick, but couldn't fight her way through the slumberous layers. At one point, Pat sat her up and they watched a grainy, early-morning news video of teams of neighborhood volunteers and Immaculata classmates walking the forest preserve and the golf course shoulder to shoulder. When Ben's baseball-cap picture flashed on the screen and a young woman said, "A community is mobilized to find little Ben," Beth screamed and Pat turned the set off.

A bellman from the Tremont staff brought up a tray of cheese cubes and fruit, with a card tucked in it that reminded them they ate compliments of the Tremont, part of the nationwide chain of Hospitality Hotels. Ellen forced Beth to eat grapes and a single cube of cheese. Coffee materialized. Beth drank four cups.

It was still light when Candy came up into Beth's room and asked her if she was ready to talk to the press.

Beth said, "Of course not."

Candy winced. "Well, you don't have to. But I want you to if you can. You don't have to talk to a bunch of reporters, just one. I have one picked out. She's okay. And you *could* talk to everybody. You could talk to Channel Five,

Seven, Two, Nine ... the *Tribune*, the local paper, the *Sun-Times.* They're all here."

"I don't want to talk to anybody. Let Pat talk. He's a good talker."

"But Beth, you're the mother. People respond to mothers. They see your emotion."

"You want me to cry in front of these people."

"No, I don't want you to perform," Candy said.

The sedative's still-warm brandy in her blood made Beth bold. "I'm not the crying-in-front-of-other-people type," she said.

"You are so," Ellen put in.

"If I was," said Beth, "I'm not anymore. This is my kid, *my* kid. . . ." Beth felt the nausea crest and recede. "You don't understand."

"No," said Candy. "I don't. But I understand how far-reaching these reports can be, and how many people watch, and how we can get their eyes working for us."

"Look," Ellen told Beth. "You are going to do this. You are going to do this because it's one thing you can do to help find Ben. Now, sit up and get ready."

"I look like a sack of shit."

"That's okay," said Candy, and Beth thought, remembering her newspaper days, yes, of course, this is a tableau: the grieving mother she had herself photographed five or ten times, eyes dreadful with sleep deprivation, cheekbones like rocky ridges. "But you don't want to look frightening," Candy went on, "or they'll think ..."

"They'll think what?"

"That you're nuts and you did it," said Ellen as she went to get her makeup bag. Candy watched as she smoothed Beth's hair back and secured it with a gold clip.

"Put on a little eye shadow, Beth," Ellen said. Beth stared at the pot of greens and blues and beiges.

"Let me do that," Candy suddenly said briskly. "I'm very good at makeup." And, Beth would later reflect, more times than she could ever imagine why, Candy really *was* good at it: the discreet taupe orbs she sketched under Beth's brows made her look wan but not wild; the minimal amount of cover-up she applied did not hide the pouches that flanked Beth's nose, but muted them.

"Now, what I'm going to do," Candy explained, brushing gently, "is bring Sarah Chan up here with her crew. And we'll do her first, because she's on deadline, and they troubled to send an anchor, and Channel Two is the top-watched news. And then if you want to do anybody else, you can—they're all going to have reports anyhow. There will be a lot of lights, Beth." Beth thought briefly of a gynecological exam, of her doctor telling her the patient litany, "Now, I'm going to insert the speculum. . . ." She interrupted Candy.

"I know about lights, I'm a photographer."

"Okay. And all you'll have to do is answer her questions. They're taping, so if you need to go back over something, if you're nervous—"

"I'm not *nervous*," Beth said, more violently than she meant; she didn't need to compel Candy to despise her, too. "Can I see the press release?" she asked then, trying to sound helpful, even sane. Someone went to get a copy and Beth scanned it; it was not lyric prose: "No witnesses as yet to the disappearance . . . several promising leads . . . a full-scale investigation."

"You don't mention the shoe," Beth said.

"And we're not," Candy told her. "That's our hole card. Only one person, probably one, knows why that shoe was there. We'll never get anything physical off the canvas, like—"

"Like fingerprints?"

"Right. But that's what we'll use for the confessors."

"Confessors."

"The people who say they took Ben, when they call."

"People will call?"

"Oh, they have, Beth. They already have. There are chronics out there who just want the attention, and maybe some people who are genuinely guilty of something and so tormented they have to confess to something else. They all come out of the woodwork, Beth."

And Beth locked on an image of a darkened room, a moon-pale face with a phone receiver clutched tight next to it, speaking quietly, whispering, perhaps afraid someone in the next room would hear . . . and then Sarah Chan, slim as a pleat and fragrant in her blue suit, knocked at the door and the room filled with a bristle of cables and light poles. Pat sat down next to Beth on the sofa.

"Touch her," said Candy. And Pat placed his arm along the back of the sofa, resting it just shy of Beth's shoulders.

"Mrs. Cappadora," said Sarah Chan, "I want you to know that all of us want to do everything we can to help find your little boy. You know how these things are. They really draw people together. A whole city will be praying for Brian—"

"Ben."

"For Ben. I'm very sorry about that. I just got here and I haven't really brought myself entirely up to speed."

Beth couldn't say anything.

"Mrs. Cappadora?" Sarah Chan prodded.

"I understand," Beth gulped, finally.

She suddenly recalled a moment from her newspaper days—shooting a family whose only son, a teenager, had died hours before in one of those hideous northern Wisconsin county-trunk car wrecks. All at once the boy's old grandmother said loudly, "Oh, well, we used to do the same thing. My husband and his buddies would have a big tin bucket of beer on the floor in the back of the car, and they'd drive up and down raising hell. Oh, my yes, we did. They all do it." Beth was dumbstruck, her fingers fumbling with her old Hasselblad (the editor wanted mournful portraits, not news shots). Was she supposed to agree: kids will be kids, kids will be incinerated in old Chevys?

Sarah Chan's breezy reference to "how these things are" stunned Beth in exactly the same way, she realized, but now she was on the other end of the lens.

"Mrs. Cappadora, are you ready?" asked Sarah Chan.

"Let Pat talk," Beth pleaded.

"We agreed," Ellen told her firmly. "I'll be right here."

And so the tech attached a necklace mike to Beth's shirt and did a sound check.

"Mrs. Cappadora, before we begin," said Sarah Chan, "I know I shouldn't be asking you this, but if you could manage not to talk to other media, I think this might have a great deal more impact."

"Get over yourself, Sarah," said Candy in a warning tone. And the videographer, a young woman in tight jeans and a huge Harvard sweatshirt, trained the lens on Sarah Chan.

"We're here in the room of the Tremont Hotel in Parkside where the Cappadora family waits and wonders and grieves," she said. "Less than twenty-four hours ago . . ."

"Sarah," Candy said. "Do the stand-up later. Let's get this over with."

Abruptly, Sarah Chan sat down next to Beth and Pat on the sofa. "Now, remember, we'll be taping, so if you feel as though you haven't said exactly what you want to say, we can always stop and start over," she told Beth soothingly.

And then she changed, became glowing, her face that of a veritable madonna of empathy. "Beth and Pat, this is the town where you grew up. Could you ever have imagined that something like this could happen in Parkside, in a lobby filled with all your friends from high school?"

"What kind of question is that?" Pat asked, and Chan made a tiny cutting gesture to the photog. "I mean, of course not. This is a small town. Beth and I grew up with these people. We know these streets like the back of our hand."

"But the possibility still exists that someone you know actually took your little boy," Sarah Chan said sorrowfully, gesturing for the tape to roll again.

"It exists, but I don't believe it's possible," said Pat in what Beth considered his best Scout voice. "Whatever has happened to Ben didn't have anything to do with Immaculata."

"Mrs. Cappadora . . . Beth," Sarah Chan asked then, "your feelings now must be unimaginable. . . ."

Beth said, "Yes."

"I mean, the combination of fear and wondering how long it will take, the grief. . . ." Beth stared at the line of thin pancake that bisected Sarah Chan's face neatly at the neck, like a mask, and said nothing. The reporter tried again: "We really have no idea how you must be feeling tonight, the second night—"

"You really have no idea," Beth agreed.

"So," said Sarah Chan patiently, "is there anything you would like to ask our viewers, the people of Chicagoland, who care deeply about your loss?"

Beth sat silently.

"Beth?" Sarah Chan urged her.

"Yes," Beth said. "I want to say something to the person who took my son Ben from this hotel lobby." Please have mercy on me, Beth thought. Please have an ounce of human heart and bring me my baby, she thought. I beg you to spare him, she thought, and said, "It's that . . . it's that I don't expect you to bring Ben back." Sarah Chan gasped audibly, and even the photographer jumped. Beth felt Pat cringe from her, as if he'd been stung.

But Candy Bliss held up her hand, as if to hold back traffic, and Beth looked straight and long into her eyes. As long as she watched Candy's unblinking blue eyes, she knew with an utter certainty that she could continue. And so she did.

"I don't expect you to bring Ben back, because you are a sick, heartless bastard."

"Mrs. Cappadora," Sarah Chan breathed. "Beth . . ."

"I don't expect you to bring Ben back because if you could do this thing, you either don't understand the nature of the hell we are going through, or you don't care."

She cleared her throat. "So, I am not going to appeal to you. But anyone else . . . anyone who sees Ben's face, and who has a heart, you know that whoever is with Ben is not me or Pat. It's not his mom or dad. So if you could, what I want you to do is, grab Ben. If you have to hurt the person, that's okay. I will reward you; my family will reward you; my friends will reward you. We will give you everything we have." Beth paused. "That's all," she said.

Sarah Chan looked up at Candy. "We can't use this," she said in dismay.

Evenly, Candy asked, "Why not?"

"Because it . . . because it's not . . . I mean, pardon me, Mr. and Mrs. Cappadora, but if somebody really does have the little boy and they hear this, it's going to just infuriate . . . No one expects her to say—"

"You're afraid that people are going to dislike Beth because she's angry at the guy who took her baby? Because she doesn't want to beg a kidnapper? You think she's not sympathetic enough?"

"It's not that ..." said Sarah Chan.

Candy pressed one finger against her forehead. "These are your choices, Sarah. Either you use that or you get nothing else. And I will go downstairs and get Walter Sheer or Nancy Higgins or whoever else I see in the lobby, and Beth can say the same thing again, and they will use it, and they will have this exclusive and you will not."

"Detective, I don't see why ..."

Candy stood behind Beth and placed her hands over Beth's head. They felt to Beth like a cap of benediction. "Because she told the truth, is why," said Candy Bliss.

Chapter 5

On Monday afternoon, over Beth's objections, Pat insisted they leave the Tremont. Though she could not begin to tell him why, she knew that the close heat and the cooking smells, the family-funeral atmosphere of Italian coming and going that would permeate her in-laws' house could strangle her. If that was possible, it would be more unbearable than the hotel, which was, while terrifying, at least muffled and anonymous. You didn't bump up against someone you owed something to every five seconds.

But Pat was resolute; this was stupid. She had not seen Vincent or Kerry in nearly two days. Pat wanted to be with his parents and his sisters. "And I have to tell you, Bethie, I think you'll get more of a grip if we go home to my mother's. You'll . . . come around a little," he said. "Every minute we sit here, we're just looking at where it happened."

And so they walked to the car, the manager following them out onto the sidewalk and across the parking lot, explaining more than once that, of course, there would be no charge for their stay, and that the management of the Tremont, and indeed all Hospitality Hotels everywhere (everywhere in the galaxy, thought Beth), was deeply sorry for their ordeal, as if their rest

had been disturbed by a noisy air conditioner. Reporters followed the manager, some actually calling out questions: Had there been any word from the kidnappers? Did the FBI have any serious suspects? Beth had never understood before how people besieged by press people managed to ignore their insistence, especially under conditions of enormous stress.

She knew now. You did not hear them. They were not even annoying, like black flies. Angelo had said that the phone rang all day at his house, reporters trying, as they explained, to expand on the "family perspective." A police officer stationed at the Cappadoras' usually simply took the telephone, explained politely that no one in the house could comment on an ongoing investigation, and hung up. When Angelo and Rosie's Golden Hat catering trucks left their store on Wolf Road, news vans sometimes trailed after the drivers. Even as Beth got into the car, a young writer from *People* magazine was putting a business card into her hand and literally closing Beth's fingers over it, telling her that *People* had a reputation for caring, exactitude, and results. "Talking to us will get the word out in every airport and drugstore in America," she warned Beth. "So call me." Beth nodded, closing the door and locking it, rolling up the window. She crushed the card and pushed it into the ashtray.

And yet, she thought, press, police, or family—after all, what did it matter? People could move their mouths at her if they wished. She was not, anymore, real. She was a faux woman, a toupee human. She was already putting into place her cloak of invisibility, tucking the edges of dark cloth around her mind to screen out information and light. She could go to her in-laws' house, or Madison, or Amarillo, or Uranus. She would find neither stimulus nor peace.

Pat had accused her, softly, of being "spaced out." His own face was rough with an eruption of hives; he stank of smoke; his hair was oily. When he lay down to sleep, he cried out. Beth offered him her drugs to shut him up, but Pat said he needed to be alert, to help the police any way he could. Beth thought otherwise. The only way she could help the police or anyone was by standing far enough from herself to deflect idiocy, the strong urge to slobber and gibber and scratch.

As they stepped into the living room from Angelo and Rosie's front porch, Vincent threw himself on Pat, and Beth held him briefly, stroking his hair. Jill presented Kerry to Beth to cuddle and feed; but when Pat saw that Beth did not notice when the bottle became disengaged from the baby's mouth, he took her and fed her himself, until she fell asleep. Pat's sister Monica made pot after pot of coffee and could not pass the piano without playing a few bars of something. His sister, Teresa, simply asked everyone who came through the door, "What are we going to do?" until Pat, sharply, told her to stop. Beth sat in a huge wing chair just inside the door, and everyone who passed her, coming into the house, seemed about to genuflect. The Comos came, and Wayne Thunder, twice, and a dozen of Angelo's business friends, who brought fruit in baskets and pans of lasagne, though Wayne said that bringing lasagne to Rosie's was even more egregious than coals to Newcastle.

Neither Beth nor her brothers had been able to eat lasagne since their mother's death, when it had seemed for months that the lasagne in the freezer was like the loaves and fishes—that it would never be gone, was breeding on its own. They had given lasagne to the mailman, to strangers collecting for environmental organizations, to the families of school friends.

But Rosie now accepted each new offspring with effusive grace. "We haven't had any time to cook—how kind," she would say in wonder, when in fact Rosie had done nothing but cook since Saturday morning, obsessively, serving full meals to whoever was in the house, and, even now, in the hot center of a June afternoon, had turned up the air conditioning so that she could bake pork chops with peas and tomatoes in the oven without causing anyone to stroke.

Just before dinner, when Rosie was elaborately setting the table in the formal dining room with its mirrored wall, Beth heard Angelo in the kitchen talking with another man, an unfamiliar voice. Something tripped an alarm in her, and she got up and walked around the end of the hall, until she stood just inside the door of the bathroom next to the east kitchen wall.

He saw her anyway.

"Charley," said Beth.

"Bethie honey," said the man, who wore an immaculate white shirt, red tie, and blue pinstripe with an almost undetectable thread of crimson.

"Bethie honey, I swear to God. I swear to God. What is this world?" He held her against him, and in spite of herself Beth felt that unmistakable surrender to the embrace of an Italian man her father's age, the feeling that you had managed to crawl onto shore and been cut on the sharp stones, but everything would be all right as soon as you got some dry clothes on.

She didn't know his real name. Yes, Beth suddenly thought, she did know it. Ruffalo. His daughter was named Janet. Charley Ruffalo. But she had never called him anything except Charley Two, though of course not to his face, because he said everything twice. In some obscure, village-linked way, he was related to Angelo—they called each other "cousin"—and Charley ran what Pat lovingly called the most profitable single-truck delivery company in the Northern Hemisphere. "Bethie," he said now. "I've been doing my best. I've been doing my best. I've talked with some guys. And Bethie, Angie, I swear to God, I swear to God, there's nothing. There's nothing out there."

He meant, Beth knew—and Angelo knew she knew—that Ben had not been taken by professional criminals.

"Thank you, Charley," she said, and heard Angelo take a breath, sharply. They spoke in Italian. Charley kissed Beth, his cheek soft as a leather glove soaked in Aramis.

"Eat," said Rosie, with not even a trace of her usual vigor. Everyone sat down. Vincent ate heartily, and so did the current Parkside cop in residence, a black kid named Cooper, but none of the other adults, so far as Beth could observe, did anything but cut up their chops. Teresa's husband, Joey, finally threw down his napkin and stormed away from the table, Teresa bustling after him, casting back an apologetic look at her mother. In the middle of the nondinner, Bick showed up to tell Beth that their older brother, Paul, who'd just returned from a business trip, was on his way. "I didn't know what to tell him, Bethie," Bick said. "Is there any news that isn't on the news?"

From the rim of her eye, Beth saw the young cop stiffen. But she said in her mind, This is my brother, fool, a lawyer, not a gossip columnist, and said aloud, "They found his shoe. They found Ben's shoe in the newsstand."

Bick held her again. "So they think someone has him?"

"They think someone has him."

"So did the local cops call the FBI?"

And so Pat explained the complexities of kidnapping law, as best he understood it—Beth was certain he didn't fully understand it—about how it was either a federal crime or it wasn't, depending on whether the kidnapper crossed state lines or air space above state borders or Lake Michigan or an ocean, and that it was a state crime if the kidnapper took the abducted child from one end of California to the other, even by air, and that every state's law on the matter differed slightly. And in the middle of it all, Beth's head began to throb and she went upstairs in search of her drug bottle and fell on Rosie's bed, while in her dreams voices came and went like tide, Candy's and Angelo's and Bick's and, finally, one voice that said, "Mama?"

Beth screamed. She sat up in bed and screamed again. And then Vincent, who stood next to the bed in his T-shirt and underpants, screamed also and burst into tears. Rosie came running down the hall with Monica at her heels and scooped up Vincent, muttering, "*Dormi, dormi*, Vincenzo, sweetheart."

"What the fuck, Beth?" Pat grabbed her arm ungently.

"I thought—I thought it was Ben." He let her go then and cradled the back of her skull in his hand. Ben was their come-into-bed child. Though he fought the process of going to his room, once asleep, Vincent had slept, sprawled, independent and entirely confident, from babyhood. But Ben rarely passed a night without slipping into his parents' room, vaulting his crib bars like a gymnast until Beth took them down in defeat, crawling and then walking into his parents' room, sometimes leaving the sheet between Beth and Pat soaking cold in the morning. "I walk-sleeped," he would explain to them in recent months, since his language had become fluent. It was Ben, also, who called Beth "Mama," not "Mom" or "Ma," as Vincent did. In her sedative blanket, Beth had not recognized Vincent's voice.

Staggering, she got up and made her way down the hall to the guest room. It was the first time in all the years she had known Rosie—basically all the years she could remember—that her mother-in-law had looked at Beth with true scorn. Cradling Vincent, who was falling out of sobs into a hiccuping sleep, she motioned Beth away. Beth walked out onto the terrace off the guest room. Joey and Teresa were staying in there, though evidently they were not yet asleep. There were cars parked all up and down the block, reporters sitting on blankets sipping coffee and Coke from paper cups as if they were at a music festival. They did not see her. There was a Parkside squad parked at the corner of the block, an orange sawhorse set up as a desultory roadblock—as Beth watched, a Channel Nine van drove right around it. Behind her, Joey opened the bedroom door.

"Joey, have you got a butt?" Beth asked.

"Bethie, I didn't know you smoked anymore," Joey, the gentlest of men, told her softly.

"I don't," she told him.

They sat side by side on the terrace and watched the reporters mill, some doing stand-ups for the early broadcasts, their backs to the lighted, entirely presentable shuttered front of Rosie and Angelo's white stone ranch.

"We'll find him, Bethie," Joey said fiercely.

"Oh, Joe," said Beth, putting her arms around him, overcome with tenderness for this kid brother-in-law, tenderness she could not seem to smooth over her own, real little boy, at last asleep again down the hall. And why not?

"Bethie, I would give my right arm, my leg, to find Ben."

"I know, honey," she said.

Teresa came out in her nightgown. "I'm pregnant," she said abruptly.

"Jesus fucking Christ on a pony, Tree," her husband hissed, getting up.

"Joey, it's okay. Congratulations, Tree," Beth told her. "*Buona fortuna.* How much?"

"Two months," said Teresa.

"Does Pat know?"

"No. Should I tell him? Rosie knows. She said I shouldn't tell you. I'm sorry I told you. My mouth just opened. I'm crazy in the head, Bethie. We're all crazy."

"I know," said Beth. "Got another butt, Joey?"

After Joey and Teresa lay down on top of the quilt, Beth sat watching the sky drain of darkness. She repeated in her mind the periodic table. Oxygen. Nitrogen. Carbon. Silicon. Sodium. Chlorine. Neon. Strontium. Argon. She knew there were some they hadn't had when she was in high school. Technetium? Californium? Or was she just making that up? The cigarette burned her fingertips. She lay down on the painted wooden floor. Kerry was crying. Someone would feed her.

At eight, Candy came to take Beth and Pat to a lab in Elmbrook for their lie detector tests. Later, Pat told Beth the young technician had made the same speech to both of them: "Relax," he said. "Physically, this will be the least painful thing that ever happens to you. I always tell people to relax, but of course they can't relax, it's a polygraph—who can relax? But it doesn't even really matter if you can't relax, because I'll be able to read your baseline whatever state you're in. And I imagine your state right now is pretty rough. Now, I'm going to start with the question that's the hardest. What's your name?" Both Beth and Pat learned afterward that their answers indicated deception when they were asked if they were responsible for Ben's disappearance.

"That's no biggie," Candy told Beth. "We can always run it again if we have to."

When they got back to Rosie and Angelo's, Ellen was there to drive Beth to the volunteer center in the basement of Immaculata's church hall. Beth asked, "What volunteer center?"

"You know," Ellen said. "Leafleting and searches. This lady came yesterday morning from Crimestoppers and taught us how to set it up. These first seventy-two hours are critical."

There had been three hundred and twenty Immaculata graduates. And there must have been, Pat later said, a hundred and fifty people connected with the school alone in the church hall basement, leaving out the handful of Rosie's neighbors, Bill's lady friend, and the scattering of friends who grew up with Beth's and Pat's sisters and brothers. Nick's wife, Trisha, was there, and all the cheerleaders, and Jimmy Daugherty's wife, and twenty other mothers, classmates, and classmates' wives. There was the principal of Immaculata, the only remaining nun on the whole teaching staff, and four other faculty, including Beth's ancient English teacher, Miss Sullivan, ten years retired. Wayne, whose management training job with AT&T was so intense he estimated he took three days off a year (all Sundays), was there, having canceled all his appointments indefinitely for only the second time in his working life. (The first time, he took a four-week cruise to Australia on a boat with nine hundred other gay men. "We were in the middle of the ocean and I couldn't get a date," he despairingly told Beth later. "I might as well work.") Wayne was in charge of the media, he told Beth. He would screen all requests for interviews and photos and pass on those he thought might advance the search. Even Cecil Lockhart had signed up to come, but then couldn't at the last minute because her mother had taken ill. "But she sends her love, Beth," said Ellen. "And I really believe she meant it. She's going to come and work when her mom gets better. You know, she has a little boy not much older than Ben, from her second marriage—or her third, or her fifth. I didn't even know that, but she sounded so sick over it. Everyone does, Bethie. Everyone."

Just after Beth and Pat arrived, Laurie Elwell walked in, carrying a stack of three-ring binders. She looked as though she had been in bed with flu and shouldn't have gotten up. Since college, Laurie had been Beth's best friend in Madison; she sometimes thought her only friend. She was no more like Beth than the moon is like a hubcap—even as a college freshman, she was cool and self-assured in a way Beth was relatively sure she herself would never be, even as an adult. Laurie was one of those girls who already seemed to know everyone in the financial aid office; presidents of sororities left messages for *her*, not the other way around. Laurie seemed to have been born with an open trunk to the essential information of the universe, and, as the binders proved, she intended to keep it all on file.

Beth and Ellen fought and hung up on one another at least once a year; but Beth's relation to Laurie was as free of the dark underpinnings of child-hood and common origin as a summer afternoon. They had met at the time people reinvent themselves, talked each other through the panicky boredom, the manifest prides and fears of parenthood and long marriages.

When Beth saw Laurie and the others, she thought, only for an instant, Now is the time of the reunion. Now I will be able to act.

Beth had said that Laurie could win the Nobel Prize for Organization; and she was in laureate form. The long tables usually used to hold the food at parish teas and wedding breakfasts were covered with phones and stacks of leaflets, posters on red and yellow and blue paper. Pat picked one up, and Beth read the bold-print headline, HAVE YOU SEEN BEN TODAY?, over a thankfully unfamiliar picture of Ben that Ellen had taken last summer in her yard and a phone number Wayne had commandeered for its unforgettability: the numbers spelled out FIND BEN. From one of her notebooks Laurie removed and unfolded a detailed map of the west-side neighborhoods in three panels that, stapled together and tacked up, covered the better portion of one of the walls.

"We'll have a red team, a blue team, and a yellow team," she told Beth and Pat, opening another binder to computer-printed lists she had compiled over the telephone with Wayne and Ellen. "The captains of each team will be responsible for assigning blocks for the team members to leaflet. And then each team will have volunteers here who'll coordinate calls we get from each of the areas."

"When are you going to start leafleting?"

Laurie looked surprised. "Why, now," she said.

"How long can you stay?" Beth asked.

"Well, forever," Laurie told her.

Candy spoke briefly to the assembled volunteers, telling them that every piece of information they gathered was potentially the one nugget of information that could lead them to Ben. "You can't overestimate the importance of your being here, both to Beth and Pat and to us," she said. "You are going to be our eyes and ears in this area for the next few days, and however long or brief the time you can give is valuable time." She told about the shoulder-to-shoulder searches planned for open areas later in the afternoon, and how even those who had to work during the day could join the police in those efforts in the light hours of the early evening. She warned volunteers against attempting to interview residents or to conduct searches on their own. "We have to be one body, with the head of that body right here," she said, turning to Pat. "Pat, do you have anything to add?"

Pat's eyes misted. "Just that we thank you. We thank you. Ben thanks you."

It was Anita Daugherty who stood up and began to applaud, and then everyone else stood and joined in. The peculiarity of the gesture stunned Beth, who turned away and fled for the stairs to the first floor; she supposed it meant encouragement, solidarity. But it sounded like a pep rally, and with volunteers laden with leaflets about to surge up the stairs behind her, she felt like a sick animal in search of a refuge to lie in.

The Chapel of Our Lady opened directly to the right of the altar. There,

Beth had taken her flowers to lay in front of the Virgin as a first communi-
cant in her white miniature of a bridal dress. There, she had always believed,
she would come as a bride. Now, she wished only that the little sky-blue
room with its faded gilt stars on the ceiling had a door to close behind her.
Beth knelt and folded her hands. "Hail Mary, full of grace . . ." she said
softly. But they were words. They came from nowhere but the back of her
throat. In all her life, Beth had felt only twice that she had actually prayed—
that is, established a connection between herself and some other consciousness: once in her mother's hospital room shortly after Evie had died; once
the day the bleeding stopped, when she'd believed she was miscarrying the
pregnancy that turned out to be Ben. For most of the rest of her life, though
she knew her Confiteor, her Rosary, her creeds (in Latin at least) as well as
she knew the spelling of her name, she had felt outside herself when she said
them, even when the linguistic power of the words themselves made her
throat close with emotion. "Holy Mary," she whispered again, thinking, If I
cannot believe now, if I cannot ask for help now, even given the strong doubt
that I would ever be heard except by atmosphere, that I would ever receive
anything but the borrowed peace of meditation, if I cannot uncurl my closed
hand even a little, I am not deserving of Ben. I have to pray for Ben, she
thought. "Holy Mary," she said, the words clicking, dry against the dry roof
of her mouth, sounds. "I can't," Beth said.

She smelled Candy before she saw her, smelled the distinct lemony bite
that underlay her cologne, like a telegram of cleanliness. The row of blue-
velvet-padded kneelers extended a full five feet along a gold rail in front of
the white marble folds of the Virgin's gown. A few feet from Beth, Candy
knelt, one hand over her eyes.

"Are you Catholic?" Beth asked.

"No," said Candy. "I was just waiting for you."

"There's nothing to wait for," Beth sighed. "I'm done. I never got started.
I can't pray."

"My mother always said there's no right way to do it."

"I don't believe."

"In anything?"

"I mean, I don't believe in God."

"Atheist?" asked Candy.

Beth snorted. "No. That takes too much courage."

"Maybe it's faith that really takes the courage. The belief in things unseen."

"Sounds like you were raised Catholic," Beth said.

"Well, I was raised Jewish," Candy told her, standing up. "And there are plenty of comparisons. Guilt. Misogyny. You name it." She reached out her hand and touched the Virgin's marble fingertips. "But some other stuff, too. Like you move the house to take care of someone. You sacrifice everything for a child—and of course you remind the child of that for as long as you live." Candy looked up at the serene face of the Madonna. "She was a Jewish mother, Beth, you know? And if anyone would help you now, maybe it would be a Jewish mother."

"I guess that should be easy to accept right now. They say there are no atheists in foxholes, right?"

"Beth," said Candy, not pausing, "maybe you don't have to believe everything. Maybe you don't have to know how to pray. Maybe you have all you can do right now just to hold on. Maybe holding on is enough."

Beth looked up at the statue of the Virgin. "Hold on, huh?" she whispered. "To what? To *her*?"

"If you want. Maybe."

"And what if there's nothing there?"

"Then ... you can hold on to me."

Chapter 6

Even Laurie really couldn't stay forever.

"I'll come back every weekend until Ben's found," she told Beth, her hand cupping Beth's chin, her eyes fastened unwaveringly on Beth's eyes with Laurie's special earnestness. They both knew she could not come back every weekend—would not—and yet nothing about that reality negated the loving hope that underlay the promise. "There's still a lot more that we can do. Everybody says so. The woman from Crimestoppers says. This week, we'll do the bulk mailings to all the states where every graduate lives now, and they'll be distributed by volunteers there. I'll do a bunch of them from home. By Sunday, we'll have the highway billboard the Firefighters' Association is buying—Bethie, a hundred thousand people are going to see that every day. Jimmy's wife is going to work on that connection with the National Center for Missing and Abused Children. And then there's that TV special coming up, the one called *Missing*—Sarah Chan says we have a very good chance of getting on that, especially now that Ben's been . . ." She stopped.

"Gone so long," Beth finished for her. "Gone so long that the fact of him being gone so long is the story now."

"Oh, God," Laurie said.

It was the end of something. No one would say it, but they felt the decline, saw it in the faces of the Parkside officers, fewer each day, in the eyes of the volunteers, down after two weeks to a core group of twenty or so. The scent of Barbara Kelliher's Chanel No. 5 had become a kind of leitmotif in Beth's days; it preceded Barbara into the basement room at Immaculata, and behind it would come Barbara's unfailingly strained smile, and the single-minded devotion with which she attached her stack of marked maps and phone messages that had come in the night before. It had occurred to Beth that for a few of the volunteers, the search for Ben was a real labor of love—but not love for her. They hoped, by finding him, to keep lightning from striking their own houses. It was the best, most defensible kind of guilt, the kind that made bystanders jump into freezing water to save collies or derelicts—and thereby save themselves. Beth loved the center, its smell of newly opened reams of medium-weight bond and stale coffee, with a near-romantic fervor. It, and Candy's obsessively cluttered office on the second floor of the Parkside Police Station, were the only places Beth felt sheared, however briefly, of Ben's loss; of the weight she sometimes felt would compress her into a flake of skin.

It was at the center, just after saying goodbye to Laurie, that Beth found out about the tip. A sighting that, unlike others, sounded real. A woman from Minnesota, who refused to leave her name, had called to describe a little boy she had spotted in a shopping center in Minneapolis, walking beside a gray-haired woman in a huge hat and sunglasses. The little boy, she was certain, was Ben. He had been eating a hot dog. It was the hot dog that somehow certified the tip for Barbara. "I think you should go talk to Candy and see if she's going to follow it up," suggested Barbara. "I could drive you."

"I can drive," Beth told her. "Thank you."

She didn't, in fact, have to drive. The car piloted itself into the Parkside Police Station parking lot; she simply had to hang on to the steering wheel. But without quite recognizing why, once she got there she drove out again, the few blocks to Golden Hat Gourmet, where she went into one of the cold cases and got a few cannoli.

Joey, who was working the lunch takeout, wrapped them up for her.

"Hungry, Bethie?" he asked hopefully, glancing at Beth's loose jeans, cinched tight with one of Pat's belts. Her hipbones now poked at the pockets like bunches of keys.

"Yep," she told him, stretching her mouth in what she believed still looked like a smile. "Got a cannoli craving, like Tree."

He hugged her, slipped her a Camel, and Beth left, settling the white box with its bowed string beside her in the passenger seat.

No one in the locked offices at Parkside questioned Beth's presence anymore; they simply buzzed her in wordlessly. Though there was an elevator, Beth always took the stairs, and today when she opened the steel door that would lead directly around a corner into Candy's open office, she heard Candy say, "... to have somebody go up there and check things out."

"You have to pardon me, Candace," an unfamiliar male voice replied, "but there's no way he's going to free up a team to drive to fucking Minneapolis to talk to some coupon shopper who thought she saw a kid. I mean, Minneapolis? There wasn't one person at that reunion from Minneapolis. There are sixty full-time cops on this department, not six hundred."

"How far the hell away is Minneapolis? People drive all the time, McGuire," Candy said, her voice stiffening. "It's a mobile society."

Beth made herself still to listen.

"Candace, I know how you feel about this, but this kid is dead. This kid is dead, and from his point of view that's probably a good thing, and—"

"Don't say I know it, because I *don't* know it." Beth heard the familiar sound of Candy tapping her eraser on her blotter. "Anyway, this is interstate. I'm going to call Bender."

"And he's going to say, 'Good afternoon, Detective, call me some time in the next century or when hell freezes over.'"

"It's a legitimate alleged sighting across a state line."

"It's just another—" The plainclothes cop, whom Beth had never seen before, turned and noticed her. "Uh, hi, Mrs. Cappadora."

Beth smiled.

"Beth, come in," Candy told her fiercely. "See you later, McGuire." The detective left. "You heard, didn't you." It wasn't a question.

"I heard the part about some guy named Bender."

"No, you heard the whole thing. But what you need to know is that this is going to be my excuse to call the FBI, and that's who Bender is—Robert Bender, he's the agent who heads up the bureau in Chicago."

"The FBI," said Beth. "Why?"

"Well, not because we couldn't do the work ourselves," said Candy Bliss. "Though we do have this delicate resource problem. We do have this problem of brass who get fretful if we don't solve a case and get an airtight confession by lunch." She coughed. "But this is supposedly the reason why the FBI exists, to support local jurisdictions involved with federal offenses."

She got up and paced. "My own personal perspective on FBI agents is that as criminal investigators, they're great accountants. The actual reason they exist is to hoard computer data banks and show up briefly when it's time to make an arrest. Particularly if there are cameras. But I don't want you to share this sick perspective. So why am I telling you? I'm thinking out loud. Tired." She pressed her forefinger on the minute lines between her eyes. "Fucking suits. But hell, maybe Bender's having a good day. I think I'll call him. He tried to pat my rear once. Maybe there's a sentimental attachment."

Beth sat down, without being asked, and watched as Candy dialed the telephone.

"Bob!" Candy's voice was so genuinely jovial Beth couldn't believe her previous rancor had been equally authentic. "Yeah.... Oh, sure, well preserved, that's me." She paused. "No, actually, three guesses and I'll give you a bump on the first two.... Bob, yes, you are a genius. The thing is, we have a sighting in Minnesota." Pause, during which Candy took the receiver from her ear and placed it against her forehead. "No, Bob, it feels just right.... How did you hear that? ... Well, of course, we'll check it out first, but she could've walked in off the street, too, Bob. Shit, there's nothing that prevents old ladies from walking into hotel lobbies.... Okay.... Okay. I'll call you back."

Candy buzzed her secretary and asked her to send Taylor to go over the Tremont guest lists again for unaccompanied senior citizens, women or men, and chat with the manager and the staff. As she talked, an anxious-looking intern brought in the mail. Candy began to slip through it absently, finally coming to an oversized bubble-lined book mailer stuffed nearly to bursting. Hanging up the telephone, she grinned at Beth.

"Another one," she said.

"You mean, stuff from a confessor?" They'd sent hand-drawn maps leading to nonexistent addresses and abandoned buildings where they said Ben was being held. They'd sent articles of brand-new clothing they said were Ben's. They'd sent photos of husbands they believed were responsible for the kidnapping, and—eeriest to Beth—long, rambling audio tapes in which they described how happy Ben was now that he was finally living in a Christian home. She suspected there were other tapes, sinister ones, that Candy never shared.

Candy had told her early on that there were only three reasons someone would take a child: to get at that child's parent, economically or personally; to want a child and be crazy enough to think it was okay to take someone else's; or, in the very slimmest slice of a single percentage, to savage that child. Of the three, Candy told Beth, you hope for the crazy wanna-be parent, because that person will care for the child tenderly.

So the package could contain anything: a bloody T-shirt, a pair of already threadbare purple shorts, slashed and stiff with—

But Candy said, "No, I mean stuff from Rebecca, my former buddy in the academy, who is now a stockbroker." Using her thumbnail, Candy stripped open the mailer and shook out an astonishing pile of fuchsia and aqua garments—a tunic, elastic-waisted pants, a scarf, and a belt. "See, my buddy Rebecca gains and loses about thirty pounds every six months or so. It's a very expensive habit, because as soon as she starts getting fat, she starts mailing all her thin clothes to me." Candy shook her head. "The thing is, even when she looks good, Becks looks like the fortune-teller at a street fair. And so I end up taking these clothes to Saint Vincent De Paul—fortunately, Becks lives in California, so she never knows. And they probably cost hundreds of bucks."

Beth smiled. "Sounds like a muffled cry for help to me."

Candy held up the mailer. "Actually, it's a padded cry for help."

And Beth, to her horror, laughed, instantly covering her eyes and feeling that she was about to choke. Candy was on her feet and around the desk in seconds.

"Beth, Beth, listen," she said. "You laughed. You only laughed. If you laugh, it doesn't mean that's a point against our side. If you laugh, or read a book to Vincent, or eat something you like, it's not going to count for or against us on the big scoreboard of luck." Beth began to cry. "You have to believe me," Candy went on. "It feels like if you watch a movie, or listen to a song or do anything that makes you feel anything more than like absolute shit, that little moment of happiness is the thing that's going to be punished by losing Ben forever. But Beth, that's just not it. You're not going to kill your son because you laughed."

Humiliated even as she did it, Beth reached out and took Candy's hand, holding it against her cheek. Abruptly, Candy snatched it away, and Beth jumped up, nearly knocking over the chair.

"I didn't mean anything ..." Beth said.

"I know, I know," Candy said. "I'm a jerk. There was absolutely nothing wrong with what you just did. I'm just an oversensitive jerk."

"You can't get involved," Beth said uncertainly.

"No," said Candy. "I mean, yes, to an extent. You can't get so involved you lose sight of things that could help people. But what that was about was ... I'm a woman, I'm a detective supervisor, I'm Jewish. And I'm gay, did you know that? Every possible kind of weirdness. So, I feel like the eyes of Texas are upon me, all the livelong day. I feel like every time I hug Katie Wright from Crimestoppers, somebody thinks I'm making a pass at her. . . ."

"I wasn't trying—"

"I know you weren't. Jesus, I'm a jerk." Candy sat down. "But you know what? These bad clothes have given me a good idea. There's somebody I want us to go see, okay, Beth? You game?"

"Who?"

"There's this lady—the guys call her Crazy Mary; her name is actually Loretta Quail. Bad enough. Anyhow, what Loretta does is she helps people find stuff. Lost dogs. Lost money." She looked hard at Beth. "And sometimes, lost people." Once, Candy said, a young mother from Parkside drove off a bridge into a creek in the middle of a snowstorm. Her car went in head down and sank; the seat belt apparently malfunctioned. "She drowned in five feet of water, Beth. But the thing was, we didn't know. We didn't know what the hell had happened. This woman was going out for a bag of diapers. And she just never came back. The husband was a weasly little guy—we thought, you know, this woman's in the backyard under the play structure. They hadn't been having too good a time. But no, he was home the whole time with the baby—this lady was just gone. And so was her car. And none of her friends had seen her. She never got to the store. Just, you know, into the fourth dimension."

And so, Candy said, somebody mentioned Loretta. "You have to know, Beth, I'm a very kind of this-world person. So I thought, Well ... you hear departments have pet psychics, but you never think ... Anyhow, old Loretta sniffed this young mother's ski jacket just like those dogs Holmes and Watson, and said she was in her car under a mountain of snow, looking up. And Beth, that's just where she was. We found her the following March when the creek thawed, still in her seat belt, looking up at the roof of her car. The mountain of snow was what the village plowed off the street into the creek."

"So you think she might help find Ben."

"I think I'm going to offer this as an option to you, which I want you to keep under your hat. Except you can tell Pat, of course."

"I don't want to tell Pat."

"I think you should."

"Well, I don't want to tell Pat. When can we see her?"

"I'll call her now," said Candy; but the telephone rang, and Candy made a despairing motion that sent Beth out the door. As she watched through the glass, she got the impression Candy was arguing; her hands gave her away—she cradled the phone between her cheek and shoulder to gesture as if the caller could actually see her. She hung up and immediately made another short call.

Finally, looking spent, she came out and smiled. "Bender. He's decided as how he might mosey on over. Later," she said thinly. Beth, suddenly remembering the cannoli, handed over the box. Opening it, Candy said, "You keep doing this and I'm going to need Rebecca to mail me the *other* size." Grabbing a chunk off one end of the cannoli, she said, "Let's go see Loretta. She's home."

• • •

Loretta Quail's house was in what Beth's dad liked to call a "changed neighborhood"—in other words, in Bill's opinion, a block that had long since lost the battle. Black middle schoolers, including one girl that Beth noticed to her shock was hugely pregnant, were playing pavement hockey in the street. Loretta's house looked like a threadbare fairyland in the midst of boarded windows and defeated lawns. From one end of the long hedge to the other, garishly painted ceramic elves disported themselves in various pursuits, from carving pumpkins to playing cards on a toadstool. When Loretta herself opened the door, a gust of trapped interior air, smelling of onions and spray starch, fastened itself to Beth's face like a wet washcloth. The inside of the house was as precious as the outside—every available surface was covered with china cats, carved wooden cats, stuffed cats, and not an insignificant number of the breathing variety. Beth counted six cats as Loretta took Candy's hand and led them inside, bustling back from her kitchen with a tray of mugs and a covered pot of tea. It must have been eighty degrees in the room, and Beth could see stray hairs clinging to the mug even at a distance; but she followed Candy's lead and bravely accepted herb tea and took one of the muffins that Loretta, to Beth's dismay, said she'd made herself.

"So, Loretta, you know we're here about Beth's son," Candy began.

"Oh, yes, of course," said Loretta. "And I knew you would come. But I thought it would be Friday. I had a dream last night that it was going to be Friday. I saw Beth in it." Dear God, thought Beth, madly glancing around the room at the hell of cats, she's nuts. Why do nuts women always have cats? Why not dogs, dogs who are just as excited to see you after you drive up to the corner to get milk as they were when they first met you, instead of cats, who, as Pat always said, regarded people as warm-blooded furniture? To keep her eyes to herself, Beth stared down at Loretta's ample thigh in its armor of polyester, a blue that did not exist in nature. Why did nuts women aged about sixty-five who kept cats also wear stretch pants? With flowered blouses that looked chosen carefully for their potential to make the wearer look like ten miles of bad road under a tablecloth? Because something like these clothes had looked good on them when they were young? Because everything else looked worse? As she let her glance slide upward to Loretta's tightly furled perm, like a head full of late-spring buds, she heard the woman ask

Candy, "So, do you want me to do a trance? Or just give you some impressions?"

Beth thought, How about a side of slaw with that? She felt wildly, hideously embarrassed. Not ever in her life—not once, even the single time she'd dropped acid as a college senior—had Beth ever had an experience she considered truly extrasensory. Hunches, feelings, semiprayers overlaid with coincidences—those, yes; her family of origin ran on those things, as if superstition were gasoline. But though the inside of her brain was lined with her grandmother Kerry's tales of dead aunts whose spirits jetted to Chicago without benefit of airplanes to warn that Katie or Mary from Louisiana had died in the flu epidemic, Beth herself had never smelled Evie's cologne, or felt her mother's spirit brush past her, even though several intelligent friends who had lost parents had assured Beth that these things would happen to her.

So when Loretta began explaining the origin of her gift, how smells had begun "throwing" her into trances when she was six, Beth had to struggle with muscles jumping in her face. It was impolite, but on reflection Beth realized that Loretta was probably used to clients who behaved oddly. She didn't seem bothered when Beth put her hand over her eyes as if the light were too bright. Sounding as though she were reciting from a script, she explained to Beth that the first time it happened was after she'd survived an attack of measles, and that in the trances "it was always the same thing—I'd see things in the funniest places. Things I couldn't explain. They weren't mine. A wallet under the wheel of a wagon. A man in a bus station, trying to hide his face behind a bandanna. A ring in the vent of a clothes dryer. And after a couple of years of these things going on about twice a month, I started to tell my mama, and my mama started to tell her friends, and it turned out that every single one of these things was lost. The people, too. And when I remembered every single one of the pictures—I used to call them 'my pictures'—I'd seen, well, God in heaven, people found all kinds of things."

"Are you ever wrong?" asked Candy.

"I've never been wrong," said Loretta.

"Never?"

"There have been times when people haven't found the things they were missing. I can't always say, 'This jewelry, or this document, is in a file cabinet in the basement of a house on Addison Street.' I can't give everybody an address. There have been times when I haven't been able to trance, usually because the people who had lost the things didn't really want to find them. You know, like a teenage girl might be a prostitute. That happens a lot. But every time I do see something, I really see it. It's where I see it. I know that. Most of your psychics average about fifty percent; and the ones in the magazines and the newspapers, I don't think even twenty percent of the things they say will come to pass ever does. They're just good public relations people is all. Most of them will tell you this is a gift from God, even while they've got their hands out for the gimme. Well, I believe in the Lord, but I don't think this is a gift from God; I think it's a wiring problem in my head. I've helped out more than five hundred people. But I've got this idea I shouldn't trade on it. I've never taken a nickel for it and I never will. I've never talked to the press and I never will." She glanced ironically around her tiny living room. "If I had, I'd be living at One Michigan Boulevard instead of here. I've found some . . . pretty valuable things."

She held out her hand for Ben's shoe, which Candy slid from its sealed plastic evidence bag, put her nose inside the heel of the shoe, and inhaled deeply. She grinned at Beth. "New shoes," she said. "But you can definitely tell he's in there. Yes indeed."

Loretta took another bite from her muffin, turning the shoe one way and then another in her large hand. Then, all at once, she dropped the muffin. Beth yipped. The big woman lolled back in her chair; her mouth dropped open and a line of saliva slid slowly down the crease between her lip and the edge of her jaw. Beth stared at Candy, who held up her hand warningly. Just as abruptly, Loretta sat up and dusted the crumbs from her legs.

"Well," she said. "This is a funny one. I saw the little boy, but I only saw him for a second. Saw *him*, that is. The rest of the time, I saw what he was thinking. That's only happened to me about twice before in my life."

"What was he thinking?" Candy whispered, slowly, hunching forward in her chair.

"Well, he wasn't so much thinking . . . it was, he was dreaming. Yes, that's absolutely it. Dreaming. Asleep. He was in a polished wooden box. He was lying on some soft lacy material. The box had a big lid that was shut over him, curved. . . ."

"He was dreaming he was in this box?" Candy urged her.

"In this . . . kind of box. Longer than he's tall. . . ."

There was nothing else it could be, nothing. Beth didn't want to scream. She tried to hold her mouth closed with both her cupped hands, but she opened her mouth anyway and screamed, "I knew it!" Her knuckles against her front teeth began to bleed.

"Beth, wait! Hear her out!" Candy tried to keep Beth on her chair, but Beth was up, trying to shake Candy off. All the cats in the room stood up, hissing.

Mildly, Loretta turned to Candy, shaking her head. "Sometimes, this is what happens when you tell them. They don't want to hear. Do you want me to stop?"

Chapter 7

"I don't know why cognac," said Candy, shoving the snifter at Beth as she sat down at the table in the first chain fern restaurant they came across. Candy had squealed into the parking lot as if the motor were on fire. "Maybe because in the movies, they always give you a shot of brandy if you have a shock. Works for me."

Candy sat down across from Beth at the sticky four-top. "I want to eat something. You want to eat something?" The more time she spent with Candy, the clearer it became to Beth that Candy ate enormous amounts of food, always, and never looked anything but concave; perhaps, Beth thought idly now, she was bulimic. As Beth shook her head, dismissing food, experimentally sipping the cognac, Candy told a waitress, "I'll have a . . . smoked chicken pizza, with double cheese and . . . shrimp too." Leaning over, she told Beth, "If my mother were dead, she'd be rolling in her grave."

"Why?" Beth asked.

"Because the cheese and the meat and the shrimp—this is probably the most trayf thing you could eat." She grinned at Beth's bewildered look. "You know, not kosher. My mother had a kosher kitchen. But I got to be eighteen,

you know, I grew up in Florida, for God's sake. And I thought, If you're not going to eat lobster, why live? Anyway, that's just the smallest part of why the Jewishness never caught on—religiously, that is."

"It never seemed like much of a religion for women," Beth ventured.

"Not like Catholicism, huh?"

"No, I didn't mean that. It's just as bad. But I don't really do Catholicism. I told you that."

"But at least you don't have to immerse yourself in scummy water once a month so you'll be clean enough to sleep with your sacred husband."

"Did you ever do that?"

"I told you, Beth. I don't have a husband, right?"

"Sure, right."

"But of course, if I did, I wouldn't. That's the real dark side of religious belief. You might as well handle snakes or something. Drink some more of your brandy."

Beth drank. She could picture the beaker of her stomach being coated, the outline of it glowing red, maybe purple.

"Do you feel better now?" Candy asked. "Because I want to tell you something."

"You can tell me."

"I don't think what Loretta meant was what you thought she meant."

"It was obvious."

"No, she never said that. After you were out in the car, she repeated to me that if she didn't *say* the child was dead, she didn't *mean* the child was dead. She would have said that."

"You heard her. You heard what she said about the curved wooden box."

"Well, Loretta can't account for what she sees in trance, Beth. She says that all the time; people have to tell *her* what stuff means. That box could have been anything. A symbol of some kind. I mean, this woman has a little light in the piazza. We can't know for sure what she meant, but when I go back and talk to her—I'm not taking you—I'm going to ask her for more to go on. More impressions. I just don't want you to give up because of what some loony said. I mean, Loretta is a very nice loony, but really, Beth, we have no proof that anything at all has happened to Ben."

Candy ordered Beth another drink and went on. "I shouldn't have brought you there."

Beth said, "I wanted to." Candy eating her pizza was like a fire ant, tiny, delicate, and absolutely voracious. She whacked the pizza into six neat slices and nibbled each methodically to the crust. "Don't you eat your crust?" Beth asked, embarrassed by her motherly tone.

"My mother told me it would make my hair curly," said Candy. "So, of course, I wanted my hair just exactly the opposite way."

"You look like Gloria Steinem," Beth said, wondering if she was getting drunk.

"So says everyone," Candy replied, polishing off the pizza, ordering herself a vodka and tonic. She looked up sharply. "I'm not on duty, Beth. I just want you to know. I wouldn't have a drink if I was on duty. I mean, I'm not on duty any more than I'm ever not on duty. I come in on almost all my days off."

"Why?"

"Very tedious personal life."

"Come on."

"No, I really do have not much of a life. It's not uncommon for female cops."

"Why?"

"Well, this life, this work, it's hard enough for a guy who has a wife and the wife runs the house and stuff to have a normal life. But for a woman, who doesn't have a wife at home, it's almost impossible. You can just do so many things. I mean, if I join the book club, I'm going to make it to one meeting a year, and at that meeting my beeper's going to go off."

"Don't you go on vacation?"

"Once a year, up north in Wisconsin, with my sister's family. And a few days in spring to see my mother in Florida when she's there."

"And don't you have a ... partner?"

"Not now." Candy brushed her forehead.

Beth didn't know what to say next. Was she being too personal? What the hell, Beth thought.

"Is there a lot of—" Beth paused, gulped, and went on—"a lot of prejudice against you on the department?"

"Not as much as in my own family," said Candy, smiling broadly, her even teeth so perfect Beth wondered, Can they be real? "No, not anymore. You can't be overt about that stuff much anymore. But when I was a kid, and I started, you had to be really sure nobody ever knew. I mean *nobody.*"

"Not even your . . . chief guy?"

"Especially not brass. Because you couldn't get hired on a department if you were what they called then a 'deviate.' They would do these background checks on you, talk to your family . . . they still do this stuff if you're going to be . . ."

"What?" Beth asked, speaking carefully now, aware that she would slur if she didn't enunciate. "A spy?"

"No, even if you're going to be in the FBI, I think. Certainly, politicians and judges and stuff."

Candy then described her rookie-cop self, a twenty-five-year-old self, as resembling, for want of a better comparison, James Dean. Beth, increasingly sleepy, tried to imagine dainty, long-legged Candy in leather biker boots tucked into jeans, with her long, soft, straight hair ear-length and slicked back from her forehead. "It's hard to picture," she said.

"For me, too." Candy laughed. "I always liked pretty clothes. I was on homecoming court, high school and college. You ask my mother, she'll say that my desperado period was my first attempt to kill her." Candy combed her hair with four fingers. "But I think it was, I'd figured out I was gay and I thought there was one way you had to look. That you had to look like a man." It was in a gay bar, she said, that someone had passed Candy, who was then working as a research assistant for a lawyer, a want ad for Tampa city "police matrons," and dared her to apply. "That's what we were then. We couldn't go to the academy. We couldn't work with anything but juveniles. That was the standard." She applied, and got the job largely because of the glowing recommendations of her neighbor, a nearsighted old woman who had her confused with the sweet-faced teacher at a Christian preschool who lived across the hall. "She's a wonderful girl," Candy recalled the neighbor telling the officer who came to check out applicant Bliss. "Very quiet and religious."

And who could doubt a sweet little old lady? "They regretted it, though," sighed Candy. "Because after a couple of years, I started noticing guys I'd trained advancing through ranks, getting paid twice what I was, and I sued, and I won . . . I won my gun."

"You didn't have guns?"

"The chief used to say, 'I don't want my female officers to be killers.' Jesus." Candy shook her head. "Now they pick the daintiest little cutie-pie things they can find to go undercover with the drug wolves. They play better."

"Are those cutie pies gay, too?"

Candy motioned for another drink, and as she did, her eyes narrowed and locked on a space just over Beth's shoulder. But she tried to go on as if she weren't staring. Did Beth dare turn her head, follow Candy's eyes? "Uh, no," Candy said. "Not all. There are plenty of female officers who are straight now, not that there are plenty of female officers, I mean . . . Beth, will you excuse me a moment?"

Beth did turn then. She didn't recognize the officer, who wore a state trooper's ample felt hat and kept his arms folded in front of him the entire time he talked to Candy, towering over her, looking down at her as if she were a child. Only his head moved, gesturing repeatedly to the right, as if he were pointing outside the window to his sleek black-and-silver squad. Candy looked back at the table, and Beth thought instantly, She's sober. She's sober, and that means this has to do with something big, awful, with me. She felt the crotch of her jeans dampen minutely as her bladder, never strong since Kerry, began to let go—got up and rushed for the washroom, where she cursorily threw up the brandy, scrubbed her tongue and her face with soap and paper towels, and combed her hair.

When she came out, Candy was standing in the foyer with Beth's purse over one shoulder and her own over the other. The table had been cleared; the state trooper was standing outside, next to his car. Crossing the room, Beth thought, would not be possible. Would the other diners notice if she got down on all fours and began to crawl? She was sure she could make it then, with the stability of four limbs and the nearness of firm ground. She took one step, wavered, and Candy came striding over to her and took hold with a vise-clamp grip under Beth's armpit. They walked out into the parking lot, dazzled with the late-afternoon sun.

"Beth," said Candy, "you're right. I know you're scared, but this isn't necessarily anything either. We have to know, that's all. We have to know."

"What?" Beth gasped. "What?"

"We . . . that is . . . they have found a body," Candy said. "It is a child, and it is a boy. But that's all we know, Beth. That's absolutely all we know."

"Where?"

"Well, the body was found by birdwatchers in Saint Michael's Reservoir—that's near Barrington, you know? North of here, maybe an hour. It's been there some time, maybe much too long for it to be Ben. But we have to know."

"I meant, where is he? Where is he now?"

"Beth, I am going to drive you to your in-laws' house, and then we will decide who will go to the county with me to do an identification. It does not have to be you. It does not have to be Pat. It does have to be someone who could make a reasonably certain identification of Ben if Ben had died. Someone who knows Ben very well."

"I'll go."

"No, I think—" Candy opened the door of her car and absently ducked the back of Beth's neck with the heel of her palm, as if Beth were handcuffed and liable to hit her head on the side of the car—"I think we'll just get to Angelo's and then we'll decide on this. No one is going anywhere. I mean, we have time." Candy slipped the buckle of Beth's seat belt into the notch and locked it.

"Is he dead?" God, thought Beth, how she is looking at me! "No, I mean, I know he's dead, but *how* did he die? Was he murdered? Did he drown?"

"There hasn't been any time to determine what the cause of death was, Beth," said Candy. "The body was only found a couple of hours ago, and the state guys did the match from our bulletin, and the child will be taken by ambulance to the county about the same time as . . ."

They pulled into Angelo's driveway, which was thronged with photographers and print reporters, who for once seemed to have outflanked the TV people; it was, after all, a long time until the ten o'clock news. But a Channel Two truck screeched into the driveway before Candy could even open her door, blocking her. She was out and crouched like a prizefighter before Beth could move. The reporter's feet hit the pavement at the same moment.

"Move your car," Candy said quietly.

"Chief," pleaded the reporter, a blond man in his early thirties, "is it true? Did they find Ben Cappadora's body?"

"Move your fucking car," said Candy, not raising her voice. "You are obstructing a police vehicle."

"Just wait one minute—"

"Taylor," called Candy, and Calvin Taylor came loping down from Angelo and Rosie's porch. "Can you please arrest this man for obstruction while I get Beth in to her family?" Taylor made as if to reach into his back pocket, and the young reporter turned and fled, the truck backing out of the drive directly into the path of another of its species. Candy rushed Beth up the front stoop, while reporters called, softly, as if from a great distance, "Have you seen the body, Beth? Is it Ben? Are you okay, Beth?"

A reporter on the porch stepped in front of Candy as she shoved open the door. "I'm from the *New York Times*," he said with well-bred earnestness.

"Good career move," said Candy, closing the door behind her.

Beth was reminded of a child's picture book, in which a ring of wide-mouthed frog brothers and sisters gathered each night around the edge of the bog to hear their mother tell a story. Angelo and Rosie, old-people fashion, had their three sofas arranged end-to-end against three walls—no fancy conversation nooks and parlor tables at odd angles for them. And on all three sofas were arranged the silent cast of main characters, at least those who could be assembled so quickly: Ellen, Pat, Monica, Joey and Tree, Pat's parents, Barbara Kelliher. Pat got up immediately and enfolded Beth in a hard hug; she could smell his sweat—a wild, high animal odor unlike anything she'd ever smelled on her husband's body. No one else moved. The two phone lines in the house, the police line and the family's, rang incessantly, though Beth could hear officers, more than a few, talking in the kitchen. As Pat held her, Beth's father and her brother Bick burst through the back door; Beth heard her father say, "Jesus bleeding Christ, these vampires, these vampires! Where's Bethie?" She ran from Pat's arms into her brother's; Bick was big, and she could lean on him without feeling she was going to have to bear the weight.

"Is it true, Bethie?" he asked. "Is it Ben?"

"I don't know, I don't know," she said into his sport coat lapel, finally, blessedly, able to cry.

"Folks, listen now," Candy said. "We would ordinarily try to do some fingerprint analysis here first. But in this situation, this body has been exposed to . . . wildlife elements, and there is damage to the extremities. So Ben's fingerprint record is not going to do us much good. What we can do is wait for the forensic dentist . . . this shouldn't take more than a couple of hours to get—"

"No," said Bick hoarsely. "We want to know if it's Ben."

Candy pressed her finger to the spot between her eyes. "Of course you do, of course you do—okay, okay." She motioned to several officers who stood just inside the back door. "McGuire, Elliott, I'm going to drive Beth and Pat. Taylor and those three from state will stay here with the rest of the family; you two drive whoever else wants to come, or we can get the other guy— what's his name?—Buckman—to drive somebody. Okay?"

"I am not going," said Angelo suddenly, the first to speak. He's old, thought Beth, dumbfounded, as if seeing her father-in-law again after many years. He's an old man.

"I think I should stay here with Rosie and Angelo," Bill offered slowly, as his son cast him a glance of pure spite.

"It's okay," Beth told Bick. "Don't worry. So long as you go."

"I'll identify the body," Bick said, holding Beth harder.

"Mr. Kerry," Candy asked him gently, "are you sure, first of all, sure you want to go through this, and secondly, sure that you know the child well enough . . . ?"

"Ben is my nephew. He's named after me. I've known Ben since the day he was born."

"But have you seen him often enough recently . . . ?"

"God damn it to hell!" Bick shouted, startling Beth. "I see my nephew all the time!"

"I'll do it," Pat whispered.

"Paddy, no," Beth told him. "No. You can't."

"He's my baby."

"No, you can't and I can't."

"Okay, let's go," Candy instructed, and the officers formed a phalanx of broad shoulders around them, shoulders in blue cotton and corduroy, military in their resolve. Candy opened the door. Ellen held one of Beth's hands, Pat the other. The cars were lined up nose-to-tail in the driveway. "No news, no news," Candy called briskly to the now-teeming crowd on the lawn; Angelo's June roses were a mire of mud and trampled blooms. "Let the family pass by now."

As the officers threw open the doors, Beth drew back. "I don't want to ride with Pat," she said suddenly. Pat stared at her. "I mean, I don't care if he rides, too, but I want my brother." What, she thought, what's wrong with your goofy face, Pat? "I have to tell him something," she finished, gesturing stupidly, fingers to mouth. Pat turned away. Then there was the airtight swish of the instantly locking squad-car doors. The reporters ran for their cars and vans, but they didn't dare go as fast as Candy did when she slapped on her portable Mars light and hit the expressway, a hundred miles an hour, talking quietly to the officer beside her the whole time as if they were driving five miles an hour in a parade.

Beth had stood outside a great many morgue doors, some at hospitals, some at prisons, some at disaster sites, photographing stretchers with their cased black-plastic burdens. But she'd never been inside one. It looked like a school corridor, with frosted glass windows in blond doors. Candy led the marching V of officers surrounding them to an elevator. "This is what Cook County defines as a waiting room," she said, pointing to a shaky collection of green leather sofas and chairs, some gouting stuffing. "I'm going to take Bick upstairs. What he is going to see is a view of the child's face and pertinent ... well, through glass. If he has any questions, we'll come back for Ellen. Or someone."

This, thought Beth, was not like the hospital. There were no heroic medical gymnastics taking place out of sight in noisy, isolated, sterile rooms overhead, no frantic last measures to preserve a life, just so everyone could believe that every stop had been pulled out, every last hope, however futile, exercised. She remembered the atmosphere of bustle outside her mother's door in intensive care; legions of nurses and caissons of equipment rumbled in and out at the speed of light. Here, people Beth assumed were doctors, perhaps even medical examiners, strolled, perusing clipboards; technicians carrying trays of tubing moved briskly but not frantically. Pat leaned against the wall, under a sign that pictured a burning cigarette enclosed in a red-slashed circle, and smoked; Beth noticed the floor was, in fact, littered with butts.

"It's all over here," she said, not realizing until Ellen looked at her that she'd actually spoken.

"We don't know that, Beth. There is every reason to believe Ben is still alive," Ellen replied firmly, in her very best Ellen voice, the voice that said there was a better than fifty-fifty chance that Nick would come back to her in senior year after he'd fallen in love with the Swedish girl at drama camp. And he had. The voice that had told her, when Kerry didn't move inside Beth for a full week, that babies near full term sometimes hardly moved at all, that it was perfectly normal. And it was.

"No there isn't," Beth said pettishly, wanting to tell Ellen all about the psychic, wanting to tell Pat—had that been just a few hours ago? Had no-body told Pat about Loretta? Where had Pat been anyway? Beth realized with a shock that she hadn't seen Vincent or Kerry at all—who had her children? Who cared? "No," she told Ellen again. "There's not every reason to believe that." She breathed in slowly. "Anyway, it's probably better if he isn't—"

"Oh Christ, Bethie, be quiet now—you're talking out of your mind," said Joey, and Pat lit another cigarette.

The elevator doors sighed open. It was Candy. Everyone strained forward. She held up both elegant hands. "They're getting the procedure ready now. Bick's fine. I just wanted you to know that this is going to take a little while. Hang on. I'm going to come down here with him as soon as I possibly can. Okay, Beth? Okay, Pat?"

Everyone slumped back against the green leather seats. There was to be a wait, then. Beth felt like a hostess, like she should be offering everyone something to drink. No one spoke—a minute by the huge clock on the wall. What would a regular woman say? Beth asked herself. A regular woman would ask about her children. "Ellenie," she began carefully, "who's taking care of—?"

She did not get to finish, because Bick came lurching out of the stairwell, his arm over his eyes, the click of Candy's heels close behind him, and then she, too, out the door. Wait, Beth thought—we were supposed to get a wait. "Wait!" she said aloud, as Bick fell down on the sofa next to her, hunched over, tears pouring.

"Bethie, Bethie, it's not Ben," he said.

"Uh . . . wait," Beth said again, trying to lift one of her arms, her impossibly waterlogged and heavy arms.

"Are you sure?" Pat was on his knees in front of Bick, searching his face.

"He's way too small, and his hair, it's red hair, but it's like strawberry blond. He's really a baby, Bethie—oh, he's somebody's baby, Bethie. His little face was like he was asleep—he wasn't even wrecked, not his face—oh, Bethie, it's not Ben."

"Oh, thank you, God," Pat breathed. "It's not him, it's not him! It's not Ben." Pat stopped, looking hard at Beth. "Beth, aren't you glad?"

Beth said, "Glad?"

Chapter 8

The house was what she had been dreading, thought Beth, the house after all. When Pat turned off the engine and got out of the car, he did not seem to notice that Beth didn't get up, even when Kerry, vigorously using one of her lexicon of four words, began wailing, "Out, out, out!"

To Pat's back, Beth said, "It wasn't you. It was the house."

Pat ignored her; he rarely responded to what Beth said anymore. And that was just as well—half of what Beth said made no sense even to her, at least out of context.

"You were hurt because I stayed in Chicago all summer. You kept saying I should come home, and I kept saying I couldn't," Beth tried again. "But now I know why, honey. It wasn't because I thought I would really find Ben. And it wasn't that I didn't want to be with you. It was really that I didn't want to go into my house. See?"

Pat had already gone inside. She was alone in the garage, literally talking to the dashboard as the automatic light winked out overhead and the door slid shut behind her, severing the reach of the pale afternoon sun. Pat had taken the baby out of her car seat and gone inside. I'm cold, Beth thought

suddenly. She resisted the urge to hug herself warm and sat in the dark car with her arms neatly aligned along her sides. *I'm cold, because it's a cold day in August.* You got them in Wisconsin, even in the baked-hard center of a string of droughty days, a single day of surprise chill that wagged a warning finger under your nose of the season to come.

Fall. A brand-new page. The time that for most of her life felt to Beth like the real beginning of the year, perhaps because the resumption of school seemed to signal a toughening of expectations. That summer, as one hot vivid day slid through a sweaty night into another, Beth had stopped wondering where she was when she awoke, heart racing, alone in Rosie's guest room. It was as if she had never had a home or a job or a family. She had been born to the routine—out of Rosie's icy house into the breathtaking blast of the driveway, the murmur of the reporters (whose names she knew by now, who maintained a kind of beach-party atmosphere on the lawn even though no one, not one of the family, not one of the volunteers, ever gave them an interview), into the Find Ben center, the round of paper-folding and stamping people gave her to do, until, after an hour or so, she felt fretful. Out into the heat again, bum a Camel from Joey at the catering company, past a handful of reporters in the lobby of the Parkside station, up past the Cappadora command center in the second-floor conference room (everyone waved), up the short flight, turn, into Candy's office.

Candy. Why, Beth wondered then and later, did Candy let her sit there for hours, watching her talk on the phone, listening to her conversations with other officers, her instructions, her interviews, even, occasionally, her rebukes of subordinates, her tense interchanges with the chief or the president of the village board? Probably, Candy had understood from the first that Beth was unable to really take in and record substance, to digest or collate the intricate overlapping webs of the investigation and its politics. Candy let Beth sit in her office, Beth felt, rather like you might indulge an old dog with the kind of worshipful eyes that made you forget how capable he was of fouling the carpet. Only there, under the protection of Candy's delicate efficiency, did she feel elementally linked to Ben, or even elementally alive.

The rest of the time, there were roles, all with certain motions to perform:

brave, obedient daughter-in-law; grieving mother; plucky friend; loyal wife. She could do them, however awkwardly. But the motions were themselves exhausting in their ultimate uselessness. Like brute and repetitive muscle exercise, they ate time and kept Beth in shape for . . . for what? For the resumption of a life, an altered life, post-Ben, which Beth couldn't really imagine, but which she figured might sometime be expected of her. What she did know was that some sort of reckoning, some sort of relinquishment, would precede stepping up onto the verge of that life. And though she didn't know when the step would have to be taken, she did not want to take it without Candy beside her. If she did, oh, it would be worse than dying, worse then remembering the day Ben had called her "my beauteous grape"—the day she had come to believe that Ben was not just good and lovely but stuffed with poetry—worse than the photocopied stories she sometimes got hold of in the center before anyone thought to stop her, stories about sexually tortured babies kept alive for months, photographed in their agonies. Beth was afraid that she might kill people, or masturbate outside, or drive Angelo's Lincoln Town Car through a crowded preschool playground. So she did all the good-girl things, and hoarded her real consciousness for Candy's office, for the few moments of the hour or many hours she spent there each day when she could drop all her masks.

For Candy, there was evidently no such thing as too bluntly. She did not look away when Beth said she hoped Ben was dead, not because she could ever stop missing him but because then at least she could know that he had stopped missing her. When she said Vincent and Kerry would be better off without her, Candy didn't disagree; she simply reminded Beth that she had to play the hand she was dealt. Two weeks after the body of the baby who was not Ben was found, Beth read in the *Tribune* that the odds of finding a child decreased geometrically after the first week. And Candy had simply told her that this was true, but to ignore it, because that the first thing a cop learned was that there were lies, damned lies, and statistics.

Candy further pointed out that the child who'd been found in the reservoir, finally identified as two-year-old Chad Sweet of Glen Ellyn, missing for four months, had not been kidnapped. He'd drowned accidentally when his seventeen-year-old father took him fishing without a life preserver. The terrified kid had been afraid to tell anyone but his equally terrified eighteen-year-old girlfriend, the baby's mother. So, while Candy did try to give Beth a hopeful spin on the facts where possible, she did not tell Beth to keep making novenas for a miracle, as Tree did. She did not keep bugging her to let just one big, national magazine do an eight-page spread, the way Laurie did ("Why not spread the goddamn net wider, so that the just-one-person who needs to see Ben's face will? Why not, Beth?").

Most of all, Candy did not tell Beth to go home. Everyone else—Rosie, Ellen, even Bick and Paul, whose love Beth counted as primal—had made this a litany. Candy had waited for Beth to feel ready to talk about going home.

That happened one evening when Beth was hanging around Candy's office late, and Candy had seemed to notice Beth afresh as she stood up around seven to turn out her office light.

"Do you want to go get some dinner?" Candy asked.

They took hot dogs from Mickey's and drove all the way down to the Lincoln Park lagoons, out to the grassy edge of the ponds, while a dozen or so black boys, each sleeker and more beautiful than the one before, threw handfuls of illegal fireworks across the water at one another. The air around them throbbed with old Motown tunes from the open windows of their cars. Beth hesitated when the boys looked their way, at what must have seemed two old and impossibly crazy white women picking their way through the hot night.

"Don't worry," Candy said. "I have a gun." At Beth's look, she laughed. "For Christ's sake, Beth. They're only kids throwing firecrackers. Not that I don't mean it. If they start to kill each other or us, I'll shoot them." They sat down on the dry grass.

Beth said, then, "Everyone thinks I should go home."

"What do *you* think?" Candy asked, halfway through her own bag of fries and already eyeballing Beth's. Beth nudged it toward her.

"I think they have a point. I don't want to, though."

"Do you think if you leave, we won't find Ben?"

"Maybe. I don't think you'll find Ben anyhow, not really. I just don't...."
Beth leaned back and lay on the grass—how impossibly winsome and sweet,

a starry summer night, the kind of night that once invited something, a clean two-mile run, lovemaking, rocking a baby on the porch. "I don't think I can go back and start up life as if none of this ever happened."

"Do you think anyone expects you to do that?"

"I don't mean just Ben missing. I mean, as if there was never any Ben."

"Do you think anyone—?"

"No. No, nobody expects me to go on like that. Except maybe *I* expect me to do that. Because I think it's the only way I can go on at all."

"I know that when people lose a child or anyone significant in their lives, they often find it helpful to get some counseling."

"Detective Supervisor Bliss, you sound so professional."

"Come on. There are groups, Beth, grief groups. They do really good work—I mean *really* good work."

"If I go to one of those things, that means it's all over."

"No, it doesn't. It means that a part of it is beginning. The part where you try to take stock of what you can do and how you can do it. You have to survive, Beth."

"That's it. That's just it. I don't want to survive Ben. I don't want to try to outrun him—it—this. I don't want to survive it and I don't want to face it."

"So you stay here and live in the corner of my office. Which I don't mind. But I'm going to have to start hanging my coat on you eventually."

"I should go home."

"Beth, you do whatever you need to do. But however lousy a mother you feel like right now, you are the only mother Kerry and Vincent have."

"What a bargain."

"I think they could do a whole lot worse."

"Oh, I don't."

"I do. And if you go home, Beth, it doesn't mean that . . ." Beth looked up from the ground into Candy's dove-colored eyes, which were always all-iris, eyes that looked made for a camera. "It's not a trade, Beth. I've told you this. If you give everything else up, it doesn't mean you get Ben. If that was the way it worked, I'd tell you to do it."

"I know."

"You have these two great kids, Bethie. I would give my right arm to have a kid like Kerry."

"People do it. People ... like you do it all the time."

"No, not people like me. Gay women, yes. But not people like me. I mean, I could. But Beth, you don't become a cop because you're a rebel. I'm a deeply conventional person, Beth. I know that sounds crazy, given my ... well, just leave it at that. I always thought I'd have a husband and kids. I just couldn't ever see the husband."

"But you could ..."

"No. Sometimes I think ..." Candy paused to stuff her mouth with a fist-ful of fries. "There's this guy. We're old buddies. He was my law professor—I went to a year of law school, during my Watergate period. He had a crush on me, a bad crush, and I had to tell him I didn't do men, that is, not anymore. Which is to say, I have, in my life, though I can't imagine why I'm telling you that. Jesus. Anyhow, Chris and I, we hang out. We get Chinese, maybe once a month. Watch Spencer Tracy movies. He's probably, Chris is probably forty-seven or something now. And he's this perennial bachelor. Dates young women. Coeds. I have sweaters older. And then, of course, me. We go to the ballet and stuff. To his big firm gala things. I tell him, Chris, I'm your beard—you know what that means, Beth?" Beth nodded; she didn't. "I'm like his surrogate wife for places he can't take the young chickies."

Candy lay back on her elbows, Beth wincing over the contact of the grass with the fine beige linen. "A few Christmases ago, I had this party—I told you I'm a bad Jew—and he brought this girl. Beth, I don't think she could drive yet. And I told him, 'Chris, you're going to be hanging around the middle school soon. This is getting fairly despicable.' And he looked at me so sadly. I thought, I had this flash, he's gay, or he's something, and he's not out to himself. Not at all. But what he said was, 'I'm tired, Candy. I want a son. I would marry you, Candy. You name the day.' "

Candy went on, "And since that Christmas, I've thought about it. I've thought, why not? We have a lot of laughs. He's still looking at the teenagers, but they aren't looking back that much anymore. With what I make, if I had

a kid, I'd have to chain it to the bed while I'm at work; and my work is crazy.
But if I had enough money to cover it all ... Chris is richer than God. I
mean, why not? He'd have his kid ... I'd have a kid."

"But you'd be betraying ... who you are."

Candy smiled slowly. "Don't we all do that, Beth? Shit, can you please
point out why I am telling you all this?"

The teenagers were drifting back to their cars. The air smelled of cordite
from the last wisps of firework smoke.

"I don't mind," Beth said, thinking, That was lame. "I'm glad you did."

"I guess I am because this is horrible, what's happening to you, Beth. It's
the worst, the absolute shits. But it doesn't mean you should throw away everything else with both hands."

She doesn't see, thought Beth sadly. Not even Candy. She doesn't see that
if I can't be Ben's mother, I not only don't want to be anyone's mother, I don't
want to be anyone. Even being dead would be an effort. I want to be a lay
sister, scrubbing the same patch of stone cement floor every day, scrubbing,
scrubbing.

"And one more thing," Candy said, wadding up the paper wrappings. "If
you go home, it doesn't mean I'll forget you or stop working to find Ben. I'll
work every day, Bethie. As long as it takes. And if you want to call me every
day and make sure I'm working, you can. And I'll call you, too. All the time.
I promise."

So three weeks later, Pat came with the baby on Saturday night. And Beth
told him she would be going home on Sunday. Pat's face reflected comic-
book disbelief, dropped jaw and all. There was a hushed sort of festivity in
the house afterward; she could hear Joey and Tree hanging around to sit up
late in the kitchen with Angelo—even the reporters seemed restless. As if it
were part of the choreography, Beth let Pat make love to her for the first time
since the reunion; he'd brought her diaphragm to her, unasked, several weeks
before, in mute appeal. She had taken the box in her hand and laughed, right
into his crumpling face. But then he had done the most touching thing, a

thing Beth realized objectively she had not sufficient grace to do. He had turned back to her and asked, "Why don't you want to? I mean, it isn't really the actual sex I want. It's you. It's your love."

"I love you, Pat," she had said. "It's just that making love would be something so ... ordinary, so ..."

"Normal?"

"I guess."

"Do we have to never do anything normal again, Bethie? Is that what we have to do for Ben?"

"I don't know if I ever can. Do anything the way I would have done it ... before."

"I don't know if I ever can either, Beth. I know that I'm lonely, though. I feel like I didn't just lose my kid but my wife, too. Like I'm a widower, and I don't want to be."

I do, Beth thought, but she said, "Let me take a little time."

And when it finally happened, it wasn't so bad. Beth had not even been able to imagine that her body would open for Pat; but it turned out to be an accommodating body, after all; and though she felt as though her insides were covered with skin, as though Pat's shudderings and urgings were calisthenic rather than romantic, the tenderness she experienced for him, though at a distance at least equal to the width of the room, when he finally rolled over beside her, cupping one of her breasts gratefully in his hand as he fell asleep, made it a good thing to have done. Pat whistled in the morning as they packed the car.

Just before they left, when Angelo and Rosie and the girls were lined up on the curb, Ellen's Saab screeched to a halt behind them. She had David in his Sunday-school clothes on the seat beside her. Beth jumped out of the front seat to hug her.

"I thought you were going to leave without saying goodbye," Ellen told her, instantly beginning to cry.

"I called you."

"I was on the way."

"It's the right thing."

"I'll be back next weekend."

"And I'm going to keep everything going. . . ."

"I know, Ellenie. You're the top, you're the best."

They hugged, but Beth felt the slackening, the dip. The principals were leaving; who could expect the supporting actors to go on with the show alone?

"It's all my fault," Ellen said suddenly.

"What?"

"I put your room on my card, so you had to go up to the desk and take so long getting it straightened out. . . ."

"Ellenie," Beth said, trying to be gentle. "I would have had to go up to the desk anyway. . . ."

And yet, how many times had she thought exactly the same thing?

"I even talked you into coming, remember? You said you were still too fat from Kerry. I made you come."

"You didn't."

"I made you come. I signed you up without even asking you, Beth, remember?"

"It doesn't matter, Ellen. It just happened. It just happened."

Pat got out of the car and put his arm around Ellen's shoulders. "We all feel like it's our fault, El. If I didn't let Beth take the kids . . ."

Let, Beth thought—*let?* You *made* me take the kids.

"I'm a bad friend," said Ellen, sobbing now. "I went out with Nick when you were in Michigan the summer of junior year. . . ."

"Did you sleep with him?" Beth asked.

"No." Ellen was genuinely shocked, shocked so that her tears stopped midstream.

"Well, that's okay then," Beth said. Why were they talking about this? "You could have told me that seventy-five years ago, Ellenie."

"Why would it matter if I slept with him?"

"Because I never did."

"None of it matters," Pat put in. "We could trace this all the way back to the Korean War." He turned to Beth. "We have to go, honey. Vincent's with the Shores. We have to go by and get him. . . ."

Both of the women turned to Pat, and, as if drilled by their combined glance, he quietly folded himself back into the car.

Ellen asked, "Where does he get off?"

"He's worn out, too, Ellenie. He just wants to get home."

"Do you?"

"Sure," she said.

Pat talked about as far as Rockford, mostly the fact that two of the new waitresses seemed to consider the cash register at Cappadora's their personal savings account. After a while, he stopped talking and sang with the radio. The baby fell asleep. Beth fell asleep, only to waken, sweating, at some minuscule shift in pressure, as if the landing gear had slid out of the bowels of the plane.

They were turning the corner onto their street. They were pulling into the driveway. The garage.

Beth had no idea how long she sat in the cave of the garage, alone.

What roused her again was her surprise at the cold, the snaky lick of cold under the summer canopy. Get up, thought Beth, and then, No, sit here a bit more. Postpone the beginning of the post-Ben period just a little more. She heard a rustle in the dark from the corner of the garage, where the snowblower was stored, and her heart did thump then. A rat. A fat, bold raccoon, waiting to bite. She threw open the car door and nearly knocked Vincent over.

"Baby!" Beth cried. "I didn't see you! Did Dad call you to come home?"

Vincent buried his face against her belly, nearly knocking Beth back into the seat. And suddenly, easily, she was holding him, too, pulling him up onto her lap.

"Mama," said Vincent, wriggling in sensuous joy. Beth froze.

She held Vincent back from her and looked at him. She had not seen him since the Fourth of July, more than a month ago, and if she were honest, not really seen him all summer. He was a leggity thing now, his last summer's shorts crowding his crotch like a bad bikini. "Mom?" Vincent asked her, wonderingly, switching back to his own word. She kissed him on both cheeks, asked him how T-ball was going, did he hit a home run? And then she set him down and picked up her purse and went into the house, Vincent skipping around and around her like a puppy.

She started to think about Bob Unger, a reporter she knew years ago at *The Capital Times*. She'd gone to Three Mile Island with him, during the meltdown crisis at the nuclear power plant. At night, after everyone filed, it was party city, war stories and card games on top of fourteen-hour work days. One night, Beth and Bob started necking in his car. She had been a tiny bit pregnant with Vincent. No one knew; they wouldn't have sent her to a place where even smart people thought it was possible to end up glowing in the dark for life. But because she was pregnant, her hormones had started to race, arousal catching her unawares. She and Pat had been having sex twice a day; and at that moment, with hunky, prematurely gray science-guy Bob, she wanted to get down to it right there on the seat. But then Unger had slipped his hand under her sweater, and Beth suddenly sat up, smiled, punched him on the shoulder, and said, "I think we're both worn out, buddy."

She'd all but run for her room, a tumult of physical pulses at war with the big feeling—relief. Adrenaline prickles ran down both arms.

She felt that way now. Why? What had she avoided?

Vincent jumped into the house ahead of her, and Beth stopped on the threshold, steeling herself. Laurie had been here, boxing up the most obvious toys, storing some of Ben's clothes. And yet, Beth knew the house would try to take her under to the deep cold places. She would have to kick aside the bathroom stool he still used to pee. A sock would turn up, or his cowboy hat—there, right there, right now, she saw his duck umbrella against the magazine rack in the living room. Had no one else seen it? Moved it? All summer? Vincent stood in the hall, looking back at her, his thick brows drawn down, and she almost grabbed for him again, actually began to extend her arms, and he began to come forward.

But then she folded her arms back against her own body. She forced herself to smile.

What? What was it? Why couldn't she reach for her wild child and pour into him all the baby-clear affection she had felt for Ben? It wasn't Vincent's fault that Ben had never gotten old enough to sully the purity of that baby love. It would be easy, one of the right motions.

But if she did that, what would Ben have been? A sort of delayed miscarriage? No, thought Beth. No. There was no one to punish, no possibility of atonement. Only survival, through a silent celibacy of the heart. Any solace at all would be a signal to the universe that a mother could get along with one child more or less.

Oh, Ben, thought Beth, letting the door of her own house close behind her with a thud. I almost cheated on you.

Chapter 9

"Eighty percent of us divorce," said Penny, shifting her considerable bulk to perch more comfortably on the edge of the folding chair. To be fair about it, it was a sort of pygmy chair: Beth noticed that even slight Laurie filled her seat to capacity. And Pat looked like a giant slouched on his.

Fingering the laminated button she wore that pictured her murdered four-year-old, Casey, Penny went on, "That's thirty percent more than the general population. If half of American couples divorce over the ordinary stresses of life, people who lose children the way we have lost children endure just that much more stress. And it gets you down below the surface of the water in the marriage, where the undertow is."

That's why this meeting of Compassionate Circle, Penny re-emphasized ("for the benefit of those of you joining us for the first time"), would focus on the effects of the loss on family relationships. The meeting last year on this subject, she added, flashing an astounding from-nowhere chorus girl's smile—as if the leaden door of a safe had opened in her sad, fat face—had been among the best the group had ever held.

In her own chair, the seat of honor to Penny's right, inhaling Penny's hypnotic almondy scent, Beth fantasized, and not for the first time, about the possibilities of insanity. Were she crazy, truly crazy, Penny's earnest voice would be no more than background buzz. Laurie would not have been able to drag her and Pat here. The genuinely crazy had a certain aloofness, a dignity, a madnesse-oblige. People left them alone. Did catatonics in hospitals, she wondered, really see the people they pretended to ignore, or notice the drool soaking their clothes? And did they simply refuse, from perversity, to indulge in a sentient reaction? Was true madness simply a will so ultra-strong it overcame ordinary human response? Or were such people really wandering so deep inside, on a broken landscape, so intent on minding their own footing, that the world outside receded?

That's what I want, Beth thought. To be really checked out. Few ants short of a picnic. Few bricks shy of a load. Few pickles short of a jar. One oar out of the water.

But even as she longed for it, she knew she couldn't manage it. Insanity simply managed to elude her. In a short half-hour at Compassionate Circle, two of the thirteen participants had already used the word "breakdown" to describe their immediate circumstances following the loss of their child.

Beth didn't doubt them; she simply wanted to know, How did you do it? The best she could summon was a sort of perpetual sluggishness, in which she noticed almost everything she didn't do but almost nothing she actually did.

At first, it was just bed. Beth behaved as if she had one of the long, sheet-sweating diseases of childhood. She had her huge, delightfully full bottle of little blue footballs left over from the doctor in Chicago, and two of them sent her into a dreamless torpor for six hours at a time. When Pat came home from the restaurant before the night rush, she made sure to get up and hold the baby on her lap and look at Vincent. Then she handed the baby back to Jill and went back to bed. The children had seen her. They knew she was alive.

Soon she began to notice that she smelled. Her underwear was crusty; her oily head felt as though it were crawling with lice. So she showered, put on clean underwear and a T-shirt, and got back into bed, virtuous. If she went on like this indefinitely, would the children be able to say they had never had a mother? Of course not. They would be able to say they had a mother and she was home all the time. A stay-at-home mom, which Beth had never been. Surely Pat would never expect her to work again.

Still, she was only thirty-three. She didn't drink very often. She didn't smoke anymore, or hardly ever. Her blood pressure hovered at about a hundred and ten over seventy. Her weight was within ordinary limits. She wouldn't be running or taking aerobics classes anymore; but she had done those things for years, and thus was in relatively toned-up shape except through the hips. Her mother had died young, but that was more in the nature of an accident than the outcome of hereditary prophecy. Her grandparents had lived to great ages.

All that Kerry longevity meant that—barring unforeseen event or medical calamity, or suicide, and Beth knew she could never do it, even "accidentally" with the blue pills—she would live her threescore and ten. She was damned if she could see what she would do with it. People would reasonably expect her to get out of bed. The thought of getting up and playing with Vincent and Kerry, or going to a supermarket or planting a bulb or frying an egg—these were outside the realm of the performable. In Chicago, she had done human things—she had driven, she had spoken—so as not to let down Candy, Ellen, Barbara Kelliher, and the band of volunteers. She could go back—consult private detectives, work harder on the solution. But she could not imagine seeing those west-side streets, ever again. Just picturing the tulip-covered yellow "I" at the corner of the high-school driveway made her reach for her pillow and bury her head.

But a few weeks after she'd come home, Laurie brought dinner and several boxes of Ben's Missing poster to Beth's house. Beth could hear Laurie calling in the downstairs hall. She squeezed her eyes shut tight.

"I know you're awake, Beth," Laurie said, upstairs now. "I can see your eyeballs moving." Laurie sat down on the bed. "Why aren't you up?"

"I was up," Beth answered. "I just had to lie down for a minute."

"Jill says you haven't gotten out of bed in a week," Laurie replied. To this, Beth said nothing. "I know you don't feel like getting up, but you have to. Your muscles will atrophy. You'll get sores."

Beth said, "I don't care. I want my muscles to atrophy."

Laurie ran four miles four times a week, even in snow. Once, she had fallen on wet ice in front of a neighbor's house and walked up onto the woman's porch, holding the skin of her elbow together over shards of exposed bone. She'd told the woman to call 911 and sat down on the porch to wait for the ambulance. "Beth, it isn't just the inactivity. It's foolish. You don't even know what happened to him yet. If you won't talk to the TV people and you won't make phone calls, at least you can mail off some of these things to people who have called from all over the country offering to post them. It's the least you can do for Ben. I'm sorry, honey, but you're just about worthless the way you are right now."

"I don't care."

Laurie clicked her tongue once. "Beth," she said. "I've never said anything like this to you. But get the hell up, now, or I'm going to stop being your friend and then you'll be in far worse shape than you already are."

Beth swung her feet over the edge of the bed and put them on the floor.

And then, Beth did get up most mornings. The signal often was a phone call, from Candy or Laurie or Rosie. There was another body to identify; Bick had done the duty. The boy, in Gary, Indiana, was at least seven. Another call: Did she know that there was now a billboard of Ben's face on I-90, right near the huge shopping center? Yes, Beth would reply, yes to everything, sure. And then she'd get up and brush her teeth. She might spend the whole day curled in a corner of the couch, furtively watching the street, but she did get up. Twice she went out to get the mail. The only truly ferocious moment was the early Sunday when she got up in the murky dawn light, peeked into the boys' room, and saw Ben curled up in his bed.

Pat came running when she screamed; Beth had peed her own legs.

"It's Vincent," he had explained, holding her up as she trembled. "It's just Vincent. He sleeps in Ben's bed now. He has since the night I brought him home. At first, I used to move him, but now I don't. I think . . . I think it makes him feel better, Beth. He sleeps with Ben's . . . with Ben's rabbit, Igor, too." Pat had carried her back to the bed, brought a warm wet towel and washed her, and then, somehow stimulated by the sight of her uncovered legs and hips, made love to her. Beth thought, as he gravely strained and plunged, he would get more response from screwing a basket of laundry. The children slept on. Pat's breathing was the only sound in the continuous universe.

In the middle of September, Laurie brought them to Compassionate Circle, a group she'd discovered in her PR-chick days, when Laurie had done trifolds and newsletters for almost every socially worthy organization in Madison, which was a hotbed of support programs. But the lost children of Compassionate Circle parents hadn't died of cystic fibrosis. Some of them weren't dead at all. Laurie said the catalogue of bizarre stories was truly stunning. Of them all, the group's president, Penny Odin, had the most macabre story. Her ex had picked their four-year-old son up on his birthday, phoned her an hour later, put the child on the phone, and, as he talked to his mother, shot him in the back of the head.

"Why would anybody with that kind of pain want to hear about me?" asked Beth.

"I thought maybe you might want to hear about them," Laurie suggested softly. "They say it helps to know you aren't the only one."

But, Beth thought, I am. A line from a poem snaked back to her: "there was no other." Mine was the only one. What did the myths and miseries and coping strategies of other busted sufferers have to do with her? She agreed to go to one meeting, only if Pat would come, too. Compassionate Circle met, as everything seemed to, in a church basement. Beth had come to think of church basements as a kind of underground railway to emotional succor—trailing all over America, where people in transformation, grieving, marrying, giving birth and dying, were gathering around scarred tables in rooms with walls covered by children's crayoned pictures of the Annunciation.

"The part of the name of our organization, Compassionate Circle, that has always meant the most to me is the word 'compass,'" Penny was saying now. "A compass is a circle, and it contains the four directions, north, south, east, and west, all in one circle. For many of us, there are also are four emotions—joy and sorrow, knowing and mystery. For some of us, that mystery is literal. We don't know where our children are, living or dead. Even for those of us, like me, who know what happened to the child we lost, there is mystery. I believe Casey is one of the brightest singers in God's choir. But I don't know it for sure, because I haven't passed over to that plane yet. Still, every gray hair I get is a joy to me; it brings me closer to my little boy, and to our reunion." She smiled that saucy smile again—a hundred pounds ago, Beth thought, Penny must have been a looker. "Join hands now," Penny urged.

Beth wouldn't, until Laurie jerked her closed fist up from her lap.

"We meet in a circle, in the hope that healing goes around and around, as we used to sing in church when we were children," said Penny. "That's what we're here to find out, if we can have wholeness in our lives, in spite of our wounds. I think we can." She picked up a stack of pamphlets and began passing them out. "These are some of the most common problems that oc-cur in families that lose a child. Sexual dysfunction. Acting out on the part of siblings who feel ignored or betrayed or scared. Different goals—one par-ent who wants to get back to business as usual and one who gets stuck.... We've all told each other our names and the reasons we're here. Now, who would like to talk about some of the matters this pamphlet suggests?"

Jean was the mother of a pregnant teenager pushed off a cliff by her older married lover. Jean almost levitated from her seat with eagerness. "When Sherry died, the turning point for me was her funeral. I went and looked at Sherry in her open coffin, and though the undertaker had done his very best, you could see from the way her muscles were all tensed up in her neck that she had been in unbelievable pain when she passed...."

Beth looked spears at Laurie. Was she supposed to sit here and listen to this? Laurie replied with her own shushing look, and Beth slumped in her chair, trying to lose herself in the whorls of the pattern on the pamphlet cover, a compass surrounded with rays, like the sun. "And my husband's whole goal in life," Jean went on, "was to get the man who killed her con-victed. He was furious that there was no death penalty in Wisconsin, be-cause, actually, this man killed two people, my baby and her baby. He was on the phone with the police and the lawyers all day, and I just didn't want any part of it. I mean, it wasn't going to bring Sherry back, was it? He wanted to file for compensation for us—money we would have gotten if Sherry had grown up, money for our suffering. The guy who killed her had a lot of money; he had a really good job on the line at the auto plant. I didn't even care that much about that. So, I would try to go along with him, but he could tell I wasn't really interested in it, and he started saying it was because I never cared about Sherry as much as he did."

Jean and her husband were separated now, two years after her daughter's death. Jean was learning to line-dance and, for the first time in her life, was going to college, studying to be a nurse. Her husband lived in a small apartment by the lake, his only furniture a foldout bed and filing cabinets crammed with all the documents and newspaper reports on Sherry's death. It was, said Jean, a virtual shrine to Sherry—with candles that burned night and day under pictures of her all over the house. "He's going to burn himself up one day."

"Maybe he knows that," another man, Henry, put in. "I was pretty self-destructive after my wife snatched my son. In bars all the time. Picking up one woman after another. Just trying to find some softness or love. Waking up in the morning with a head the size of New Jersey...." Appreciative laughter rippled around the table.

A very young woman, who had not let go of her husband's hand for the entire duration of the meeting—which Beth noticed, with dismay, was now almost ninety minutes—spoke up then. "You know," she said, "I'm wondering if there's something wrong with us, because we really haven't experienced any of those problems. Jenny's death just brought us closer, closer to each other and closer to God." Jenny, the couple's two-year-old, had been crushed under the wheels of her caregiver's car as the woman (who was, unbeknownst to her employers, drunk) backed out of the driveway one night after work. "We've found that whenever one of us needs a shoulder to cry on, the other one is always there. We look at Jenny's pictures, and though of course we're sad, and we'll always be sad, we try to remember the joy she brought us, and we find that very healing. We were lucky to have had her."

Laurie wrote on the corner of her pamphlet, shoving it noiselessly across to Beth: "They probably didn't want kids to begin with." Beth covered her face with one hand.

"So, we're finding that this experience," the young mother went on, "difficult as it is, has actually been a time of growing ... so that when we have another child, and we're sure we will—"

"Why are you here, then?" Henry asked bitterly. "If you're doing so great, how come you want to come and be with people who aren't doing so great?"

"Henry," Penny reminded him gently. "You know the covenants of the Circle. We don't begrudge and we don't grudge. Everyone has a right to work through a loss in their own way...."

"But they don't seem like they need any help," Henry said.

"But we do," said the woman. "We need to know that we're not alone."

"Of course you do," said Penny, turning suddenly to Beth. "Now, our newest guests, Pat and Beth, are just starting along the road some of us have been on for a long time. All of you have read about Ben Cappadora, Beth's little boy. We have every reason to believe that your son will be found, Beth, but your family must be experiencing some of these reactions of mourning. Do you feel like talking about it?"

"No," said Beth, and then, surprising herself, she asked, "How did you get how you are?"

Penny looked puzzled. "How did I ... ?"

"How you are. So accepting. So kind. Were you always like that? I mean, before?"

Penny nearly laughed. "I sure wasn't. The first few months after Casey was shot by my ex-husband, the only thing I allowed myself to feel was rage. Rage at my own stupidity for trusting my ex-husband with my son, because I knew he was strung out about half the time. Rage at the man himself, for doing what he did. I quit going to church, and I devoted myself to eating everything in the house that wasn't nailed down...." She gestured to her bright red tunic. "You can see the results of that. If you would have told me that I'd ever feel any different, I'd have said you were a fool, you just never understood what I'd been through...."

"So how?" Beth asked again, feeling a rush of admiration, a wish to graft some piece of Penny's peace under the skin of her own heart.

"Well, what I did, Beth, was ... I finally forced myself to ... do things like look at the pictures of Casey after he died," Penny said, with the first trace of hesitancy Beth had heard in her voice all night. "Casey was shot at point-blank range in the back of the head. And I forced myself to think, What did he feel? What did he know? And the answer was, he knew nothing. He was talking to me, and then he was gone, just gone. When I looked at it from Casey's point of view, I had to think that he died, but he died happy and painlessly and quickly, and that the person it hurt most wasn't him. It was me. And my . . . and my ex-husband. Because Wisconsin isn't a death-penalty state, he has to live with this forever, even now that he's sober."

"And you feel sorry for him? Does he get some kind of pass because he's crazy?" Beth asked.

"I guess, no, I don't feel sorry for him," Penny said. "I do feel, though, that his regret and grief are a kind of justice."

Beth looked up. Pat was on his feet. He hadn't said a word beyond his name all night, but he now said, "I'm so sorry. I can't stand anymore."

"I understand. Do come back," said Penny. "Anytime. Any time you want. Or call me."

"I will," Beth said.

Outside, the last of the light was draining from a perfectly transparent fall sky. Beth breathed in, heavily, the smells of the church's patch of wild roses, the bus exhaust from the metro on its way up Park Street.

Laurie asked Pat, "Are you okay?"

He said, "I just felt as though I couldn't . . . I never imagined there was so much suffering in the world."

Oh, Pat, Beth thought, there just never was in yours.

But that night, she couldn't forget Penny Odin's foolish, saintly face. Did Penny sleep? Beth got up and walked into the boys' room and stood over Vincent as he lay curled on Ben's bed. Each of the boys had a shelf over the head of his bed for books and toys; each one had a designated side to the closet, neatly labeled with stick-up letters spelling out their names.

Laurie had done her work sensitively and well. Only a few discreet things hung well back in Ben's side of the closet. His toys were mostly gone (also boxed and stored in the crawl space, Beth knew, out of sight but not forgotten). There had been an easing of Ben's imprint, a consolidation, but not a clean sweep. Thank you, my dear Laurie, Beth thought, kneeling down at Vincent's side. Thank you for letting me be able to come in here.

Vincent had always slept hard. She had never seen him wake easily; he was like a cold-cocked prizefighter—he woke disoriented, bleary, looking plucked as a newly hatched chick. But now he rolled in his sleep, twitching, sweating like a racer. Maybe he's sick, she thought. He'd asked her a lot of odd questions since she came home.

"How many bad guys are there in Madison?" he had asked. Vincent wasn't the kind of child to be fobbed off with something easy.

She'd said, to get it over with, "There are thirty."

"Are you sure?"

"Yes."

"Who said?"

"Detective Bliss. She counted."

"How many are there in Los Angeles?" he'd asked then.

Beth had sighed. "There are two hundred," she'd told him.

What he was really asking was, Am I next? Beth knew that. What could she tell him? What could she feel, in front of his asking eyes, except accused and resentful? Hadn't she let the bough break?

A memory, a safe one, flitted past her face like moth wings. Just before Ben was born, Vincent had stared at her belly and said, "You'll like the baby. But it won't be the same. You won't like the baby as much as you like me." And Beth had feared the same thing.

Indeed, Ben had managed to perfect for himself the role of second child, undemanding and delighted, the one she knew she would never need to worry about, never need to worry about . . . and she hadn't.

She hadn't worried at all.

Now she should be worrying. About Vincent. But it was all gone, that mother radar, along with her belief in it. She could do nothing for Vincent. Leaning low, she whispered, "I love you." Studies had shown that even in deep sleep, people could hear, could even learn languages that came to them on paths of the subconscious. Perhaps it would work, and he would wake up feeling loved, even if he wasn't sure who loved him. Or whether she was still around.

Vincent

Chapter 10

December 1985

Vincent had thought it over and he decided he would ask Santa for Ben. What he really wanted was a Lionel train or a radio-controlled boat, but the way he figured it was, if he asked Santa for Ben, he might get the boat and the train, too, because asking for Ben was an unselfish wish. Santa would be impressed, and everyone would be happy. His mother. Grandpa Angelo. Everybody.

Vincent would probably be happy, too, because, to tell the truth, after six months, he was getting sick of not having Ben around. Kerry was cute, but you couldn't really play with her yet. Plus she was a little smelly and boring. And his mother was still acting like she was sick, sitting around all the time, except once in a while yelling at him if he got too loud. It wasn't like she never yelled at him before Ben got lost; but in between yelling, she used to do stuff with him and be funny. Now when he tried to make her laugh by singing Elvis or something, she didn't even notice. He had the feeling that getting Ben back for Christmas would be about the only thing that would make her goof around. The way things were now was annoying.

Back in Chicago, he hadn't minded because he could do anything he wanted. He never had to go back to school for the last week before summer break, and he still got passed into second, and got almost all Es, even though he was pretty sure he was only going to get an S in math because he goofed with Andrew P. the whole time. His teacher even wrote him a note and sent him some Geoffrey dollars. There was a lot more hugging and petting him than Vincent strictly liked, some of it from old people whose breath smelled like the wooden sticks the doctor used to hold your tongue down. But the police gave him all kinds of stuff—baseball cards, a play badge that was real metal and wouldn't break if you left it on your shirt when it went into the washing machine, and so much gum he had to make a special place in a drawer to store it all. The lady with the blond hair who was a police officer even though she was really pretty gave him a piece of the stuff bulletproof vests were made out of. Grandma Rosie sewed it inside his Batman shirt for him. (He later put on that shirt and his dad's fishing hat for Halloween, until Alex's mother picked him up to go trick-or-treating. She took him back to her house to put some face paint on him, all the while saying to Alex's dad, "Enough's enough—really, enough's enough"—like face paint was that expensive.)

But at first, he liked that everybody who came over gave him something. Grandpa Bill's friends gave him dollars, paper and silver ones. He saved up eleven dollars the first week. And when he whined and wouldn't eat, they just took the plate away and gave him anything—cookies, or even the kind of cereal his mother wouldn't let him have, the kind with little marshmallow people in it. Uncle Bick even went out at night to get it at the store, just because Vincent wanted it . . . which actually almost gave Vincent the creeps.

It made him wonder if they were all telling him the truth, and whether Ben was really killed instead of alive but not here. And letting him have anything he wanted actually made him miss his mom even more, and he already missed his mom a lot. She was never around when they were in Chicago. Sometimes she called up and said, "Hi, Vincent." His dad was around more often, but had this new, really hard way of hugging him that was also creepy.

All in all, though, Chicago was better. Grandpa Angelo used to put him in their big cannonball bed at night to sleep—not just the first night, *every* night. And even when he couldn't sleep, people were talking out in the living room. Police and grownups.

Now, at home, when he couldn't sleep, he just sort of sat there. His mother never made any noise at night. Kerry never made any noise. Unless it was Monday, his dad was always gone at the restaurant at bedtime. Vincent hated just sitting. He understood now why adults knew how to read fast. A long time ago, he and Ben used to figure out quiet ways of getting out of bed and playing with their cars until they started hitting and laughing and somebody caught them. But Vincent was afraid to do it on his own. It just seemed really dangerous to disobey, even though he was pretty sure his mom wouldn't even notice.

Getting to sleep had always been Vincent's best thing. His mother used to say, "You're the best sleeper of all." All you did was shut your eyes and float, like you were in a big, warm tub. But since the thing happened in the lobby, Vincent couldn't just fall asleep anymore. For one thing, he had the room to himself now; and though he liked being able to spread his stuff out on both beds, it felt weird having nobody to talk to at night. For another thing, he was all of a sudden almost afraid of the dark. It wasn't just one of those things kids feel. He had a good reason to be scared. After all, the kidnapper would probably come and get him, too. It made sense. That kind of bad guy, the kind they told you about at school, who would come up and ask you for directions and grab your arm right in front of your own house, and give you drugs and touch you inappropriately, would definitely want the other brother, too. And if the bad guy asked, Ben would say where Vincent was. Ben knew the number of their house.

Vincent got so nervous, he told Uncle Joey about it, and Uncle Joey said no bad guys better dare ever come near Grandpa's house or he would take them out.

"Do you know what that means, buddy, 'take them out'?" Uncle Joey said in a rough voice. And Vincent had nodded his head, though he didn't; but Uncle Joey was a bodybuilder, so he figured it meant he would punch the bad guys.

But people always said stuff like that to kids, didn't they?

They said you would always be safe, and they would keep you safe, but then you could fall on the playground toys and break your collarbone with them standing right there. You could get kidnapped in front of a million people. And the bad guy probably didn't even need to give Ben drugs or candy. He probably just told him what to do, because kids like Ben did what grownups told them. Even Vincent, who usually didn't, even he sometimes did what certain adults told him to, like when his mom told him to eat eggs, even though eggs made him want to barf.

Once, before they came home, he dreamed that who took Ben was a witch, like in "Hansel and Gretel." Grandma Rosie said there were no such things as witches. Vincent didn't really believe her. It was just another sort of lie adults told kids to make them not be scared. If there were no witches, how come there used to be in the olden times? When all those stories were written? Where did they all go to? Didn't they have babies who grew up to be witches?

There was also the third thing. The smell thing.

It was the only thing he really remembered about the day Ben got lost, that smell. And he couldn't really smell it; he could just remember it. Like all the different powders and perfumes in Mom's makeup bag, all mixed, and then this stinky cooking smell. Uncle Augie would say in a restaurant that wasn't owned by somebody they knew, "Bottle gravy." Like at Thanksgiving, when his mother had opened up a jar of turkey gravy because they forgot to bring gravy from the restaurant—it was just like that smell. It made Vincent so sick he couldn't eat anything, and his dad said quit trying to always be the center of attention, and his mom said shut up about it, and she didn't eat either. She took him upstairs and lay down on the bed with him, which was actually pretty nice. He had no trouble going to sleep that time, and they slept all day.

Most of the time, though, his mother didn't put him to bed or wake him up. She put the baby in bed and said, "Night-night, Kerry," and then she would just stand there in the hall, for so long, with her hand on the knob of baby Kerry's door.

Vincent would get his pajamas on and come back out there. Then he would brush his teeth and come back out there. After a while, he would go and get in bed. He didn't know if it was his bedtime, because he couldn't tell time on the upstairs clocks, only the one on the VCR that had actual numbers. A few times, he didn't get up in time for school, either, but when he told his teacher that his mother forgot to wake him up, they said it was okay, they wouldn't mark him tardy. After a while, a couple of times, he didn't go even when he knew it was time, when he could see other kids going to school on the street. He just watched TV until his mother came down with the baby.

She just said, "Did you eat?" She didn't ask him, "Aren't you supposed to be in school?" Once she asked, "Is it Sunday?" That time, he got up and left. They were halfway through journals when he got there, but his teacher didn't say anything except ask him if he had any breakfast. Vincent said no, and the teacher's face got all hard, like she was going to cry. She gave him part of a doughnut. After that, he just said he ate.

After school, he mostly went to Alex's. He had heard Alex's mother say, on the phone, "Yes, of course, Vincent's here, too. I'm filing the adoption papers next week." And he had to ask his dad if Alex's parents were really going to adopt him. His dad told him, "Of course not," and said, "Maybe you should come home some days after school."

But Vincent didn't like to get home too early. Not until Jill got done with classes. The baby would be asleep. And his mom would be sitting in funny places. Once down in the basement in her darkroom, on the floor in the dark, but not doing anything. Once in his bedroom, next to the bed that used to be Ben's but was now his. Once right in the kitchen, on the floor. That was the scariest time. She had a cup of coffee next to her that had scummy stuff on top and a bug stuck in the scummy stuff, and he'd had to yell, "Mom, ick! Don't drink that!" because when she saw him, she picked it up and started to drink it. And she'd tried to laugh then, a sort of scary heh-heh laugh. And she just put the cup back down on the floor and sat there.

But even if he went to Alex's right after school, he couldn't eat over every night. He had to come home when Alex's dad got back from work, which was about five o'clock. There were times, of course, when he didn't go to Alex's at all.

To get to Alex's house, he had to pass his own house on the other side of the street. And there were some afternoons that he could see that somebody's car was in the driveway, like Laurie, who would probably have one of her kids with her, and the kid and Vincent would go play in the treehouse or have jumping contests off the swings.

And even if one of the kids wasn't with her, when Laurie was there it was like his mom woke up. It was like they turned on her remote control or something. She answered things when they said them, and if they had to sit around and mail and stamp packages of Ben's Wanted poster, Mom would do that right along with Laurie. If Laurie brought a salad for her, his mom would eat it. She would make coffee. She would seem to see Vincent, too, when Laurie or a neighbor was there. She would say, "Would you get me the stapler, big buddy?" in a voice that sounded almost like her old voice, except if you had actually heard her old voice you knew that this one was a toy version, a lot faster and smaller.

Those nights, things would be really great, because by the time Laurie left, Jill would be there, and she would warm up whatever Laurie brought for dinner—not that he didn't love the food from Cappadora's, but you liked to have American food once in a while, too, like fried chicken. That would be a whole day, from the end of school until bed, when he didn't have to be alone with his mom, if it was one of the nights when Jill didn't have a night class, which she did three times a week. But if she didn't, she would read to him and run a bath for him and even stay in his room until he fell asleep.

Once, he woke up in the middle of the night and Jill was still right there, sleeping on the bed that used to be his with her clothes still on and no covers. Vincent got up and put the comforter over her, trying to fit it up around her shoulders without waking her up. But she woke up anyway, and hugged him. He felt awful then; he was afraid she'd leave. But she just turned over and went back to sleep. Vincent liked that so much he told Jill she could sleep there any time she wanted, instead of the guest room she lived in. But when he said that, Jill started to cry, so he didn't tell her it again. His bed was not as comfortable as Ben's, it was true. His mattress was older, because Ben had peed his to death and he got a new one, and Vincent's had a major saggy place in the middle. He didn't really blame Jill.

Vincent knew Jill was going to go home to her real home, with her mother, his auntie Rachelle, for Christmas anyhow. She'd be gone a whole month. Dad said Stacey, the cashier from Cappadora's, was going to baby-sit him and Kerry some nights "until Mom feels better." Stacey wasn't really mean or anything, but all she ever did was watch TV. And she wasn't going to come every night. Even when she did come, she wasn't going to be there at ten o'clock at night, after his mom and the baby were asleep and his dad wasn't home yet.

That was the part Vincent dreaded, being up when his mom was asleep.

By the time vacation started, a week before Christmas, Vincent had his routine pretty well figured out. He could look forward to Monday nights being pretty good, because Dad was home; Tuesday and Wednesday nights would be pretty bad; Thursdays okay because by that time of the week, one of Mom's friends usually was starting to call to see if she was okay; Friday would be okay. Saturday okay about half the time because he could usually talk his dad into taking him to the restaurant and letting him fall asleep on the couch in Uncle Augie's office.

Sundays were the worst. Dad had to open, and so he left right after lunch. He always looked really upset when he left. He kept saying, "Beth? You're all right now, aren't you?"

And his mother would say, "Sure. I'm fine." Then she would watch out the window when his dad left, like she could still see his car pulling down the driveway backwards an hour after he left. A few times, Vincent asked her if he could go out to play. She said, "Okay." But Vincent didn't; he didn't feel too good about going out to play, even if there was new snow, until Kerry was down for her nap. If she threw all her toys out of the playpen, his mom wouldn't put them back. Vincent did, even though it drove him nuts that Kerry would just throw them out again.

On Sundays, the phone would ring all day. Sometimes, his mom would pick it up. Sometimes, she wouldn't. A couple of times, after she picked it up, he heard her yelling swear words—like "You sick buster!"—and then she called his dad and he had to come home from the restaurant so his mom could go to bed. His dad was pretty upset when that happened, and once he even called the police in Madison.

So Vincent answered the phone most of the time now.

Often the person who called would be Detective Bliss, who said to call her "Candy." Or the lady from Compassionate Circle. Or Uncle Bick. Uncle Bick always made him actually get his mother, even if Vincent said she was asleep, and he could also make her talk, even if in just one words.

Two times, though, it was a man Vincent didn't know. Except he knew it was the same man. He sounded like he was calling from a room with all the sounds sealed out of it, a room that didn't even have normal noises in the back, like TV or cars going by. He asked, "Are you the brother of the little boy?"

Vincent told him, "Yes."

And the man asked, "Do you know why he was stolen?"

Vincent said, "No."

The man said then, real whispery, "Do you know how our Lord Jesus Christ punishes sinners? That he who disturbeth his own house shall reap the whirlwind?"

It wasn't what he said that scared Vincent, but how angry he sounded. Mad at Vincent. Like Vincent was the one who stole Ben. Vincent tried to tell him, "My mommy's asleep," even though that embarrassed him a little, because he usually didn't say "mommy" anymore; but the guy just kept right on, hissing, "Do you know about Benjamin in the Bible, son? Vanished into slavery in Egypt? Do you know what sick people do to little boys like your brother?"

The one time, Vincent called his mother, and something in his voice made her shake her head and sit up—she had been watching a bass-fishing show that he was pretty sure she wasn't really interested in. "What?" she said. "What?" He just held the phone out and shook it. And his mother took it and when she heard the man, she really yelled, "Don't you ever call my house again, you—" *f* word, *a* word, *p* word.

The next time the man called, Vincent just said, "I believe in God," and hung up. The man called back and left sixteen messages. "Pick up the phone, if you want to know what really happened to Benjamin," he kept saying. Sixteen times. Vincent counted. Then he never called back again. Vincent figured it was the kidnapper. But when his dad heard the tape he said it wasn't; it was just a sick buster who had nothing better to do with his sick life than scare women and children. He gave the tape to the police in Madison. They came over to the house in a squad car to get it.

Vincent started to think he could tell whether it was a good call or a bad call by the ring. If it was Aunt Tree or somebody, Vincent thought it could hear a kind of friendly bounce in the ring. If it was police or strangers or guys wanting to sell his parents some graves or houses or something, it would have sort of a distant sound, as if it didn't really know where it was ringing. So he tried to only pick up when he heard the bounce, and by Christmas vacation he had determined that he was right about twenty times out of twenty-five; he kept count by making a little tiny ink mark on the bottom of the kitchen table where they put the raw, crummy wood that didn't have the gray covering on top. It was entirely possible that he had ESP.

Usually it was Grandma Rosie who called.

Grandma would say, "Is your mama there, Vincenzo?"

And Vincent would say, "Yes. She's sleeping." Even if she wasn't. Because if he gave his mom the phone, she would just hold it and listen to Grandma Rosie, hardly saying anything, and he would hear Grandma Rosie's little phone voice getting louder and louder on the other end. Which made him want to jump out of his skin, because he couldn't really tell his mom to say something.

When Vincent told Grandma that his mom was sleeping, though, that was another problem. She would say, "Hmmmmmm." He could hear her tapping on the table with her little silver pen, the one she used to write orders at the Golden Hat. Then she would say, "Where is the baby?"

And he would say, "Sleeping, too." Even if *she* wasn't. He could tell that was what Grandma Rosie wanted Kerry to be doing, because people always thought babies were better off sleeping. Then Grandma Rosie would ask if he was watching television. She would ask him to spell a couple of words— usually, two easy, like "ran" or "fat," and one hard, like "nose" or "high," which could fool you. She would say, "I was thinking my car might come up to Madison this weekend. But Grandpa said no, too many people getting married this weekend. Everybody's getting married on the west side, 'Cenzo." She said that almost every time. Except just the past week, she was saying,

"Soon we will be there for Christmas," and asking if Vincent had been a good boy, and what Saint Nicholas would bring for him.

That was when he told her he was asking for Ben.

He could tell right away Grandma Rosie didn't like the idea. She said, "Oh, Vincenzo. *Carissimo.*" Like he had said he got suspended for fighting or something. Vincent had actually expected her to be proud of him, and have her voice get all purry, the way it did when he sent her the recital tape the first year he took Suzuki violin. But, he figured, probably she was just tired. He asked to talk to Grandpa Angelo. Grandpa would probably like the idea better; he was really missing Ben. Grandpa said it made his heart feel like a bone in his throat or something—Vincent couldn't exactly remember the way he described it. But Grandpa hadn't been home. And Grandma Rosie got off the phone really quick.

Vincent thought he'd have to tell Dad, and see if Dad would help him with the letter to Santa. He didn't want to tell his mom.

Christmas Eve was going to be on a Monday, and on the Friday night before, Uncle Paul called to tell Vincent's mom they'd be up that night. Then, Vincent started getting really excited. Uncle Paul's twins, especially Moira, were really nuts and rough, for girls; he always had a good time with them. "Can the twins sleep in my room?" he asked Uncle Paul. "I have an extra bed now that Ben's gone."

There was a long pause, in which Vincent could hear somebody's car phone or radio click in and out on the line. "Uh, okay," said Uncle Paul. "Let me talk to your mom."

Grandpa Angelo and Grandma Rosie arrived Saturday morning. Vincent's dad had to make three trips to the car to bring in all the presents. Vincent began to read the gift tags on the packages out loud: "To Kerry, from Santa." "To Beth, F.U.F.I.L." (that sounded like a swear, but Grandpa Angelo did it all the time; it meant "From you father-in-law," and it was funny because Grandpa had an Italian accent). Then there were a whole stack of boxes that said, "To Ben from Grandma and Grandpa." "To Ben from Santa."

Vincent followed Grandpa Angelo out into the kitchen. "Grandpa," he said. "You made a mistake. These are for Ben, and you know, Ben is kidnapped right now...."

Grandpa's eyes got all red in the white part. "I know, 'Cenzo," he said, squatting down. "But Grandma and me, we think if we keep on believing that our Benbo will come back to us, the Lord will answer our prayers. And so we buy him gifts, so we don't forget our Ben, and so he will have them when he comes home."

"I'm going to show my mom."

"Okay," said Grandpa Angelo. "In a little while." He looked around. "Where's the Christmas tree?"

Vincent felt bad. He knew that he could have told his dad that nobody had remembered to put up a Christmas tree; but he was afraid his dad would cry if he did. So Vincent ran upstairs without answering Grandpa and got his mom. She usually didn't come down until around lunchtime, but she came right down today, and she had on normal clothes instead of her red Badger sweat pants with the holes in them, the ones she slept in and wore all day. She had on black pants and a white shirt tucked in. Vincent was proud of her. She kissed everybody.

"Mom," Vincent said, tugging on her arm, "I want to show you something special."

But he didn't get to show her Ben's presents right then, because Aunt Tree and Uncle Joey drove up. Aunt Tree told everybody she didn't know whether she should come or not, because she was starting to have breaks and hicks. Vincent assumed this had something to do with Aunt Tree's baby, still in her tummy, and he was right.

"Ahhhhh," Grandma Rosie said. "Maybe a Christmas baby!"

"They have hospitals right here in Madison, Tree-o," Dad said.

"Little early yet," said Grandpa Angelo.

"Just a few days," Grandma said. "Easier, anyhow, if it's a little early. Her first one." Aunt Monica wasn't coming, because she was spending Christmas with a boyfriend. Even though she had long nails and could play the piano, Aunt Monica didn't have a husband yet; she always told Vincent he was the only man she could count on.

Aunt Tree couldn't run upstairs, and she hadn't wrapped all her presents yet, so she made Vincent her "lieutenant," telling him to get her the tape and the ribbon shredder. And then, just when he was about to show his mom the

gifts for Ben, suddenly Dad's buddy Rob came with a tree—an already decorated tree!

Vincent smelled it, and it wasn't fake. Rob said Delilo's Florists had given
it to Dad for free. The tree made everything look better. Everybody took a
long time putting the presents under it. Vincent went to get his Playskool tape
recorder, to hide under the tree behind some of the packages. He planned to
turn it on right before he went to bed, in case he couldn't stay awake long
enough, so that he could tape Santa. He figured that if he could be the first
kid in America to actually prove there was a real Santa, he could get on TV.
He'd told Jill about this idea, and she told him it was excellent. Tonight would
be a test. If he could hear what the grownups said on his tape after he was in
bed, at least until it clicked off, then he knew he'd catch Santa for sure.

Rob stayed for a glass of wine, and Aunt Sheilah had already taken the
twins up to bed by the time Vincent finally got the chance to tell his mother
about the gifts for Ben. She was sitting on the couch, holding a cup of coffee
but not drinking it, and he walked up to her quietly and said, "Look, Mom.
All those presents are for Ben. Grandpa and Grandma brought them. Wasn't
that nice?"

Grandma Rosie was sitting across from Mom, embroidering on a picture
she was making for Aunt Tree's baby, and Mom didn't even look at Vincent.
She just walked over to the tree and held up one of the packages and said,
real flat, "Rosie."

Even to Vincent, Grandma looked up as if she was guilty, like she'd been
caught passing notes in school with the word "piss" written on them.
"Bethie?" she asked softly. "What, dear?"

"What are these?"

"Presents for Ben."

"You brought presents for Ben."

"Yes."

"Rosie, why did you bring presents for Ben?"

"Because," Grandma Rosie said, in her talking-to-a-kid voice, "I believe
that Ben will be found. And I want him to know that his family didn't forget
him, when he is found."

"Do you have the impression that we have forgotten Ben?"

"No, my dear."

"But we didn't get Ben any presents."

"I understand that."

"In fact," said Mom, "to tell you the truth, I didn't even want to have this whole . . . go through this whole big holiday act. I didn't want to do anything except sleep through it. And when you do this, when you act like he's just out of town on a business trip and he'll be back anytime, Rosie, do you know what that does to me?" Her voice was getting loud, and Vincent heard the chairs scrape as his dad and Rob got up in the kitchen and came out to see what was the matter.

"Beth," Grandma Rosie was saying, "no one meant to upset you."

"But you *knew* it would upset me."

"Bethie," said Vincent's dad, "please. You know what they said in the Circle. Everyone needs a ritual."

"But I don't, Pat!" Vincent's mother was crying now. "And I'm his mother! I don't want to do a bunch of stupid things to pretend that my baby is alive and on his way home, when that's the cruelest lie in the world! I don't want to rub my face in all this shit!"

"Beth honey!" Aunt Tree said then. "Take it easy. Ma didn't mean anything."

"Take it easy? Take it easy?" his mother cried. "How can I take it easy when nobody except me seems to want to accept that this is over—it's *over?* And we're just all going to go on acting the way we always have, eating and sleeping and baptizing babies. . . ."

"What's my baby got to do with this?" Aunt Tree asked, grabbing her tummy; she was mad. "Listen, Beth. You've got to snap out of it at some point. No one can talk to you. I can't. Pat can't. If you don't have any hope at all that Ben will come back—"

"Come back? He's not even four yet! What's he going to do? Get an Amtrak schedule?"

"What I mean, Beth, is that if the rest of Ben's family wants to keep up hope, that's our business. It's not an insult to you. And furthermore, Beth, what do you care? How does it affect you? You're an . . . island, Beth. You don't care even care about my baby. . . ."

"No. I don't."

"Well, you should. Life goes on."

"If I never hear anyone say 'Life goes on' again, it'll be too soon, Teresa." That was a first. Vincent had forgotten Aunt Tree's real name.

"And you don't care about my mother or my father, and the fact that they're as knocked out by this as you are. And that they don't know what to make of how you're behaving. Now, I have to admit, I would be curled up on the floor. I couldn't go on like you do. But you have withdrawn from the whole family. And that's okay, but if you do that, you can't control—"

"Tree," Vincent's dad warned, very tired. "Tree, wait—"

"No, Pat. You're all too scared to say this, but I'm not! We try to call, she won't talk to us. We write, she won't answer us. We can't talk about anything in our lives that doesn't have to do with Beth's grief. She's like Deirdre, Mother of Sorrows—nothing in the world can ever be as bad as what she's going through, so she's just opted out of life completely."

"That's right. That's my choice."

"But it isn't *ours*, Beth. You don't own every choice about Ben. He was ours, too. And we haven't decided to give up. We still go over at night and mail bunches of leaflets to people in New York and Kansas and Oklahoma. We still talk to the police. We still want to believe that there's hope, and you can't stop us, and I don't know why you want to, because you aren't going to find him by sitting on your duff all day and—"

That was when Vincent decided he had to tell his mom that there was a very good chance things were going to be fine by Christmas morning, that Ben would be back.

"Mom," he said, "I have to tell you what I did." He wondered if, actually, this was going to be sort of a lie, because he hadn't actually written a Santa letter. He had simply tried praying to Santa, because Grandma Rosie insisted he was a saint and you could pray to saints any time you wanted; they were up there waiting for it. So he took a deep breath and said, "Wait a minute, Mom. I asked Santa to bring Ben home. I think he'll do it."

It was like freeze tag.

Nobody in the room moved. Nobody spoke.

Then his mom got up and carefully put down her cup and dug her hands up under the roots of her hair and stumbled out of the room toward the stairs. Vincent looked at his dad. Once, on Mother's Day a couple of months after Kerry was born, he and his dad had brought his mother a whole basket full of wild roses, and she had put her face right down into them and cried and cried, and when Vincent asked why, his father told him, "She's happy, Vincent. I know it sounds funny, but sometimes adults get so happy that they cry."

Was that it?

Grandma Rosie was leaning her head on Aunt Tree's shoulder. Grandpa Angelo got up, jingling his car keys, and said he was going to take a ride over to the restaurant and see Augie. Vincent's dad picked him up and said, "I think it's time for bed, slugger. Just a few days until Christmas. Gotta get your rest." Vincent struggled to get down. Why was everyone mad at him? Did they think it was mean to ask Santa for your own brother? But even though for once he was glad to go to bed, he wanted to switch on his tape first. "I just want to look at that one big present, Dad," he lied.

When they were up in his room, and his father had bounced him on Ben's bed and laid him down and sung a couple of verses of "Davy Crockett," Vincent asked, "Remember that one time when all I did was bop Ben on the head very softly and he bit me?"

"Yeah. I put Ben in our room to separate you."

"When it was actually Ben's fault."

"Well, you did bop him."

"Very softly. And he bit me very, very hard."

"He liked to bite. But he stopped that after he got bigger."

"Yeah," said Vincent. "I just wanted you to know, Dad, I forgive him for that."

"Good," said his dad. "I'm glad. Now, go to sleep. The twins are already out. They're good little girls, not sneaky little monkeys who run around all night. Don't you dare wake them up." He kissed Vincent and said, "I love you."

"Where's Mom?" Vincent asked then.

"She's in her room."

"Is she sick?"

"A little, yeah. A little bit. Even grownups have fights sometimes, Vincent. You know that. It'll all be better in the morning."

But in the morning, it only got worse, because instead of talking loud at each other, everyone was so polite. At least the tape had worked pretty well. He heard his dad say to his aunt, ". . . the amount of stress. And she doesn't answer it because she thinks half the time it's going to be the police saying they've found another kid or some nut trying to tell her we killed him."

"But even given all that, Paddy, she needs professional help. She really needs professional help."

"Maybe," said his dad. "Yeah."

Then they started to talk about Monica being stuck up and all kinds of stuff Vincent didn't even care about.

But professional help. That, thought Vincent, was a great idea. He hoped his dad really meant it. If his mom had a professional helper, someone who did helping for a job, right in the house all the time, she would have to wash and change her clothes every day, because the helper would make her. She would have to change Kerry more often, so that Kerry didn't soak through the front of her little sleepers every day before Jill got home. Vincent couldn't change diapers, because Kerry was too wiggly; he'd tried, and she just rolled over and over until she was away from him. His mom had to do it. If the helper could get his mom moving, so she did more things without taking forever, she would have more time, because as far as Vincent could tell, she wasn't doing her picture work anymore at all. They could maybe take walks. Maybe make a mobile; she used to like to make mobiles out of wire hangers and cut-out stars. He might be too big for that now, but he didn't care. He'd do it if his mom wanted to. And after a while of doing normal things again, she would start to realize that even if Ben was gone right now, she still had even more kids than she'd lost. She had double the number of kids she'd lost.

And he was pretty sure he and Kerry together made up for one Ben. Maybe even one and a half.

Chapter 11

Not long after the *People* magazine landed on the stands, seven months to the day after Ben was taken, Candy passed through Madison, unannounced, on the way to a forensics conference in Michigan. Beth later believed she had made a special detour; it was like Candy to anticipate how Beth would feel when she saw the cover, which was a full-page bleed of the second Missing poster, with no headline other than "1-800-FIND BEN" and a little kicker that said, "Before Their Very Eyes: The Strange Disappearance of Ben Cappadora." No teases on movie stars' pregnancies or stories about diet doctors. Just Ben.

Laurie had brought it to the house the day it came out.

Beth wouldn't talk to her, even after Pat pleaded through the locked bedroom door. Finally, Laurie told Pat to go away. "Bethie, listen," she said. "You're going to hate me for this, and I know it. But it's been a long time now, Beth. The police are getting nowhere." Beth could hear Laurie lightly rubbing the door, as if she were patting Beth on the back. Laurie went on, "You see that magazine at every doctor's office in America, Bethie. And when that reporter called me, well, I decided that I was going to talk to her even though I knew what you'd think. It was the right thing to do, Bethie. I love you. I love Ben. And I've just always thought this paranoia about the media was . . . unreasonable. So, even if you never speak to me again, I'm glad I did it. And you should know, Barbara talked to them, too. And so did Wayne. And so did your sister-in-law Teresa. And if you hate them, too, I'm sorry for you. Beth, when you're ready, I'll be waiting to talk to you." Beth could hear Laurie's silent presence outside the door, like a drawn breath. "Okay, Beth. 'Bye now."

The magazine was on the floor outside Beth's bedroom door when she opened it an hour later. She sat down, right there, in the opening between the lintels, and flipped to page sixty, thinking, absurdly, They always make you wait for the cover story, no matter what it is, they make you wade through sixteen things about the ninth-grade genius who figured out how to make a computer out of a clock radio, or the model who had two babies in eighteen months and starved herself back to perfect flatitude in six weeks.

She thought she could read the first paragraph. That, she would allow herself, though she could feel the cold and crush shimmering above her even as she folded back the facing page, the one covered with photographs she barely glanced at but couldn't help recognize. She'd taken most of them her-self, after all—a Christmas photo of her three kids that had been the center-piece of a card: newborn Kerry, Vincent, and Ben in Santa hats, all of them with their tongues sticking out. A picture on Laurie's picnic table of Ben and Laurie's son in clown makeup. Laurie had that one framed in her living room.

On the first page, it was just the first Wanted poster. Beth could look at that—she'd seen it so often that it had finally become meaningless. She no longer wanted to claw her wrists when she looked at the cockeyed tilt of Ben's baseball cap, the crease in his nose when he smiled. And down below, a glam-orous shot of Candy talking to reporters outside the Parkside station, look-ing up, clearly irritated by the photographer, but still every-hair-perfect despite the grim set of her jaw.

Okay, thought Beth. You can read one line. Two. "When Beth Cappadora took her children to the fifteenth reunion of her high-school class in Chi-cago, she expected a time of togetherness with old friends, not the beginning of a nightmare that would tear apart a family, old friendships, and the very fiber of a community. . . ." Beth slapped the covers together.

She knew what the rest would entail—a couple thousand words of breezy, bathetic prose wrapped around pictures that would make even women waiting for mammograms count their blessings as they read. Enough. It was done. It was there and existed and she knew it and that was it. Since she need never leave the house again, she thought gratefully, she was not going to have to see supermarket eyes averted in recognition and shame. She was not going to have to see the tight, pained half-smiles of teachers. Pat would, though. He would probably revel in the sympathy; he seemed, she reflected, to like sympathy in direct inverse proportion to the loathing Beth felt for the same glances, notes, and little hand-hugs. He'd even said, one night, how heartwarming it was, how startling a confirmation of the basic good in human beings, the letters and the offers of support that caused the mail carrier literally to heft armfuls of stuff up onto their porch; it would never have fit in any mailbox. Laurie, Beth believed, took the letters home. She could see Laurie eye the growing piles nervously every time she came over, and then, a few days later, Beth would notice the piles were slim again. She could not imagine, nor did she try, what manner of pity and grotesquerie those letters contained.

On her bad days, after Kerry fell asleep on her bottle, Beth took baths. She sat in the water until it was scummy and cold, looking at her spindly arms and legs, white as carp, floating under the surface. By the time she came out, it was four or after, Jill was often home if it wasn't a late class day, and she'd gone to get Vincent at the Shores'. Beth could start waiting for dark. Deep dark came early now, and as soon as it was deep dark, a person could go to bed. Bed, for Beth, was a nearly erotic sensation. The falling away of the day was her most precious moment of existence. The nights when Jill had class were nearly intolerable. She had to sit on the couch while Vincent read his chapter books or went over his spelling lists, knowing she should get up and tell him that children did not do homework effectively in front of television, but unable to do it. After a while, he would get up, gingerly kiss her, and go to bed.

And then Beth would have the last fifteen minutes, the fifteen minutes to get through that she usually spent watching Paul Crane, across the street, doing endless chip shots on his frost-nipped lawn under the lights from his garage. After fifteen minutes—it was a reasonable interval—she could run for the stairs. Vincent would be in bed. She would even look in on him, blurring her eyes to avoid seeing the bed he lay in, and say, "'Night, honey." He never answered. He fell asleep quickly. That was good.

On good days, Beth sometimes went downstairs into her office and threw things away. She filled bags with out-take shots, old negatives and contracts, her clips, her anthologies, phone numbers she would never need again. She liked the feeling of stripping away her former life, liked the release from any obligation except living until night. One afternoon, Pat had discovered her throwing away her Rolodex and stopped her. Beth let him—she could always throw it away some other day, when he was at the restaurant.

She thought, briefly, of actually dismantling her darkroom, but she knew that she would never be able to dispose of huge stable objects such as sinks and trays without Pat's noticing. At night, she would mentally scan her own room, thinking of what things she could throw away the next day. Shoes, perhaps. She had far too many.

When Candy showed up on the porch that afternoon, Beth had had a good morning. She had showered and fed Kerry her cereal on her own. She let Candy come in, returned her hug, and felt puzzled by the way Candy held her at arm's length and looked her over, top to bottom.

"Beth, what you are wearing is very strange," Candy said.

Beth asked if Candy wanted coffee. Candy said, "Sure." And Beth went into the kitchen to measure out the coffee in spoons. Laurie always said it tasted better if you measured it.

"Did you hear me, what I said before?" Candy asked, when they were sitting at the kitchen table, Candy holding a drowsy Kerry in one arm.

"Yes," Beth said. She tried to remember.

"You are wearing something that looks funny." Beth was, in fact, wearing ordinary wool pants. They were pants from the seventies, which she had discovered not long ago during a closet raid. She had no idea how much weight she'd lost, but on impulse she had tried on these pre-childbearing pants, with their wide legs and eccentric wraparound belts, and found that they nearly fit. There had been perhaps three pairs, which Beth now wore regularly, with either one of her sweatshirts or one of Pat's shirts.

"I've lost a lot of weight," she told Candy. "And these are just fine for working around the house."

"What about for *working* working?" Candy asked then.

"I'm ... uh ... retired," Beth said. "I can't imagine ... you know. I took pictures of news things and people and weddings and stuff, Candy. I couldn't do that now. I don't think I could take pictures of ... food, even."

"But you might want to—you know, sometime," Candy said. "Don't you think? I mean, didn't you always work?"

Beth nodded.

"Oh," Candy said. "That's what I thought." She went on to tell Beth that the seminar she was attending was being held at the big new conference center west of town. "The Embassy's cheaper, though, so I'll get a room there." But Beth told her no, of course not, she must stay here, it would be fine. Candy smiled. "I'd like that." What the conference was about, she went on, was the psychological profiling of felons. "It's the big new thing," Candy explained. "You get to find out that almost every criminal is between twenty and forty, medium height, white or black, drank milk as a child, had a little trouble with alcohol in college, and had a mother who always bugged him to practice the piano."

"I think I dated that guy," Beth said.

"I think my brother was that guy," Candy agreed. "It's my belief that this is all bullshit, actually. I don't really think there are any more bad guys percentage-wise than there ever were. What I think is that there are simply more people, you know? There are more people, and less room for them, and less money."

She was not mentioning Ben, Beth noticed. That would be because there was nothing new to say. Beth had learned not to ask. Candy would tell her anything, no matter how seemingly minute or insignificant. But attention was shifting away from the case. Beth knew that.

"Did you see the story in *People* last week?" she asked Candy then.

"I was hoping you didn't," Candy told her. "But actually, Bethie, much as

I despise most of the sharks, I really think this isn't such a bad idea. It's like free leafleting. Every kid goes to a doctor's office sooner or later. It could be our key, you know? One of those reality TV shows would probably be a good idea, too." She paused, swirling the coffee gone cold in her cup. "You or Pat would probably have to chat, though."

Beth said, smiling, "No."

"No for you or no for Pat?"

"I'm not his mother. I don't care what he does."

"Oh, so that's how it is, huh?"

"I mean, I don't care who he talks to. He doesn't seem to do it much, anymore, though."

"Maybe he can sense you don't like it."

"Maybe."

"Beth—" Candy said then, and waved to Jill as she came in the door from school, handing her the baby, who woke up and kicked in delight, saying "Joo! Joo!" and gurgling. "Do you have any money?"

"Do you need some money?"

"No, I meant, do you have any money in the house? I thought we could go shopping."

Beth started to laugh. She thought she might laugh hard enough that the coffee would come up in brown strings, so she tried to keep it under some semblance of control. Everything, it seemed, made her stomach revolt in recent months. "Candy," she finally gasped. "I don't go shopping. What would I go shopping for?"

"Some clothes, maybe."

"I don't want any clothes."

"Would you do it for me?"

"No."

"That's not very hospitable. Maybe *I* want some clothes."

"You live in Chicago. They have much better clothes there than they have in Madison. Anyway, you always wear the same thing. And they have beige blazers anyplace."

"Beth, that's not true. I have a quite varied wardrobe at home. Leather studded with nails, mostly. Some gold lamé. What I want, I want to go shopping. Jilly," she called, "where's a good mall?"

Jill, changing the baby, called back, "West Towne. The Limited and stuff."

"Sounds good." Candy got up. At that moment Vincent opened the door. To Beth's astonishment, he flew into Candy's arms, holding her, wrapping his legs around her as she picked him up—easily, Beth noticed, fragile as Candy looked.

"Did you bring Ben?" he asked.

"Sport, not yet." Candy looked about to cry. "I'm sorry. I'm going to keep on looking till I find him, though. I promise. So, Vincent, school okay? Playing basketball?"

Vincent slid his eyes over toward his mother. "I'm not playing this winter."

"Oh, well, time enough for that. Listen, Vincent, I have a big problem."

"What?"

"I'm taking your mommy to the store, and I have to have someone to guard my badge while I'm gone." She took out the leather case that held her gold shield. "This is a detective's badge. It's very valuable." She winked at Beth. "It's real gold, for one thing. And it has powers. Do you have any idea of anybody who could guard this thing, I mean guard it with his life, while I'm gone?"

Vincent lowered his voice. "I think I could do it."

"I don't know." Candy pretended to back off a step. "I don't know, Vincent. You're a smart kid and all, but you're only what—eight? This is the kind of responsibility I wouldn't normally let even a kid, like, twelve do for me. It would have to be a very trustworthy kid."

"I am," said Vincent. "Ask Jill. I make my own bed."

"Well, Jill, what do you think?"

"I think the captain is up to the assignment," Jill said. "But you can't take it to Alex's or anything, big buddy."

"Can I ask him over and show it to him?"

Candy pondered, tapping her teeth. "Can this . . . Alex be trusted?"

"He's my best friend," Vincent confided.

"Well, then, yes. It's unorthodox procedure. But this once, okay." She turned to Beth. "If you haven't got any money, have you got some bank cards or something?"

"Yes, she does," Jill sang out. "They're in the envelope taped to the fridge. They won't recognize her signature, though. They only know mine. I'm Beth Cappadora now."

"Not today," Candy told her, palming the card. "Do you want to put on something . . . ? Well, it doesn't matter. Come on, Beth. Let's go."

The light off the snow was pitiless on Beth's eyes. Her ancient pea coat felt bulky—she hadn't been farther than the mailbox very often since fall. Even the motion of Candy's car was like a fresh sensation, something only vaguely familiar. "It's cold," she told Candy.

"It's January, Beth," Candy said. "It's traditionally cold in January."

"It's just that I haven't been . . . getting out much."

"So I see."

At the sight of the teeming mall—didn't people know Christmas was over? What did they find to buy, endlessly buy, forever?—Beth nearly begged for mercy. And people who read *People* might recognize her face. (Had her face been in the story? It had definitely been in some stories.) People would remember. They'd stare.

"I don't know, Candy," she said, trying to sound just a little bored, restless. "It's so crowded in these joints."

"We'll only go to one store. I just don't know what one store. So bear with me."

They ended up at a place called Cotton to Cotton. "I like cotton," Candy said. "It never wrinkles, and if you put a lot of it on, you're as warm as if you were wearing wool. Layers, Bethie. That's the ticket."

And Beth was stunned; Candy was as good at clothes as she'd been at makeup that horrible night. After studying Beth's face in the relentless fluorescent overheads for a few long moments, Candy said, "Purple. Teal. Gray. Real blue. Maybe a little red." And she'd gone off for armloads of skirts and tunics and vests and belts, sweaters and jackets, which she'd draped over Beth as she stood, mute as a mannequin, in the middle of one of the aisles.

After forty minutes, Candy had filled four shopping bags, and Beth had surrendered her card. On the way home, she told Beth, "Now, the deal is, you can wear any one of those things with any other one of those things. So if one is dirty, just pull out another one and put it on. They all go together, even the belts. And you can wear black shoes with every single thing. Flats or heels. You do have black shoes, don't you?"

"Yes," said Beth.

"So you don't have to think about it. You just pull out whatever is there and you put it on. See? And when we get home, I'm going to hang them all in your closet for you, in one place, and then we're going to take all the disco pants and . . . make a bonfire or something. Okay?"

"Okay," Beth said.

The clothes still had the tags on them two months later when Laurie, who had called a dozen times, increasingly sorrowful, showed up one night as Pat was just about to head back to the restaurant. Beth, upstairs sitting on her bed, heard her ask Pat, "She still won't talk to me, will she?"

"I think she would," Pat replied. Beth could tell by the muffling of Pat's voice that he was giving Laurie a hug. "I think she's over it. I mean, Barbara Kelliher has called her a zillion times telling her how great the response was to the story, how she's had to have new posters made five times. I think she understands."

"I think she hates my guts," Laurie said. But Beth could hear her tripping up the stairs; even on this errand into Rochester's mad wife's room, Laurie was bouncy.

"Hi," she said.

"Hi," said Beth.

"What're you doing?"

"Curing cancer," Beth said. "I just put away my test tubes."

"Oh, well, good," Laurie said, sitting down on the bed. "Can you please just forgive me? Just get it over with? We are never going to agree on this, Bethie, but we've been friends for a thousand years, and you know, you have to admit that you know, I would never, ever do anything knowingly to harm you."

"I know that," Beth said.

"Good, because I have something I want you to do for me."

The nerve, Beth thought. But she asked, "What?"

"I want you to take a picture."

"I don't do it anymore."

"Just this once. There's a lot of dough in it. A lot."

"How much?" Pat asked, walking in.

Beth said, "I don't do it anymore."

"They'll come here."

"I don't do it."

"Just let me tell you." It was a wedding announcement picture, but the bride—the daughter of a client of Laurie's husband, Rick—couldn't go to a studio for the shot.

"Why? What's wrong with her?"

"Nothing. Except she's ... very pregnant."

"Big deal."

"Well, Beth, her family are immigrants from China. To some people it still *is* a big deal. She's very modest."

"Not when it counted," Beth said, starting to feel like some evil old spider crouched in her den, which wasn't how she'd intended to appear at all.

Laurie sighed. "Anyhow, this girl's mom and dad are modest, and very rich. So I said I knew someone who could take the picture in a very private setting, and make it look ... like she isn't. A real magician. You," Laurie said.

"You could do it, Bethie," Pat put in. "You wouldn't have to go out."

"Take a picture of a pregnant woman? Me?" she sneered. Oh, Pat, if money had lips, we'd never have kissed, Beth thought. "You've got to be nuts."

"Please, Bethie, this once," Laurie pleaded. "Let me get over my guilt by doing you a good turn. If you hate it, just never do it again."

"This is not a good turn. This is a setup," Beth said. "Anyhow, I can't, because I threw out all my paper and stuff."

"I'll get you paper. I'll get you supplies," Pat offered eagerly.

Beth sighed, longingly thinking of her pills and the lure of her down comforter.

"When?" she asked.

•   •   •

It was an astounding thing, what happened. When they came, the boy chip-
per, the girl sullen, both their mothers glowering, Beth set them up as briskly
as she would have arranged fruit on a plate. And when she began to shoot,
she realized that this was exactly how she saw them. She remembered what
a high-school art teacher had told her, one of those tiny, utterly basic things
that transform a pattern of thought: that when most people see a cup on a
table, they think of it as sitting flat, so they draw it sitting flat. In fact, she
had told Beth, the bottom of the cup really looks curved, and that was the
correct way for it to be rendered. "It's the difference between seeing with
your brain and seeing with your real eye," the teacher had explained.

And, for the first time in her professional life, Beth saw the couple as a
series of angles and curves, planes and shadows, not as people with emotions
and histories, people who had writhed in love and spat in disgust. She saw
them not with her brain—her brain, she reasoned later, was gone—but with
her photographer's eye alone. She lit them as she would have lit statues, as,
in fact, she had lit statues and architectural pictures.

The portraits that resulted were stunning. The very, very wealthy father
gave her a thousand dollars. Laurie turned up more subjects willing to come
to Beth's lair. And by late spring, Beth grew willing to go out to them—to
shoot pictures of people-as-things that both the subjects, and, later, publish-
ers praised for their sensitivity and humanity. Even, after a while, children.
They were just smaller apples and oranges in baskets.

The first time she had to travel to an assignment, she pulled out a skirt
of deep lavender and a red tunic, tied it with a black sash, and slipped on a
pair of black shoes. She looked skinny, still, eccentric, and . . . not bad. By the
time summer came, Beth, looking back on several months of increasing business, realized she had found a key, thanks to Candy's wiles and Laurie's
stubbornness—a way to fill hours and appear productive, without the need
to feel or even think very much, not even about whether her belt matched her
shoes. She sent Jill back to Cotton to Cotton for more hues and shapes when
the first ones succumbed to washing. It worked.

Beth had found what passed for a life.

Vincent

Chapter 12

His mother said even she didn't know what the square box built into the wall on the staircase was supposed to be. She told Vincent once that back when she and Dad were kids, people liked to put telephones in little nooks all over their houses. "This house was probably built in the sixties. Maybe that's what it was," she said.

"Why would anybody want a phone in the middle of the stairs?" he had asked, eagerly. But by then his mother was looking past him, the way she did that made Vincent turn his head to try to see the person she had spotted somewhere just behind him. But there was never anybody there.

Grandma Rosie told Vincent she thought the people who originally owned Vincent's house were good Catholics. "They would have a figure of Our Lady in there, or Saint Anthony," she had said last Christmas Eve, when she passed Vincent crouched in the square den of a hole on her way up to bed. "It is not for little boys who are trying to stay awake all night so Santa will pass by this house and leave no presents." She took his hand and led him to bed.

Baby Kerry, who could talk now, called the box her "baby house." She took her dolls and her phony waffles and the syrup bottle that looked like it was really pouring in there, and he would pretend to be the customer while she pretended to sell him waffles. Or you could sit there, all tucked up, like Vincent imagined mice would feel in their holes, and see right down into a corner of the kitchen—the corner that had the sink and the Mister Coffee. And if the dishwasher wasn't on, you could hear everything anybody said down there.

That was how Vincent got to hear about how his mom was trying to kill his dad.

First, his dad put his hand on his mother's top, around one of her boobies, which he did a lot, and which Vincent thought usually meant his dad was trying to be nice—the way Grandpa Bill did when he messed up your hair. Vincent didn't like anyone to mess up his hair—he liked his hair just so, nice and flat and soft—but he knew that with Grandpa Bill, this hair-messing deal was like hugging. So he put up with it. That's what the boobie thing was, too. But his mom didn't like it any better than Vincent liked getting his hair ruffled. She pushed his father's hand away. Then his father kissed her. She smiled then, and looked down, down into the sink, as if she were trying to find a contact lens.

"Bethie," said Vincent's father. "Honey, we have to talk."

"I have to print," his mother said. "I have four phone calls to make. I have to get Vincent ready for school."

"He isn't even up yet."

Ha-ha, Daddy, thought Vincent.

"Well, he should be."

Vincent's dad sighed. It was a big sigh, meant to get his mom to turn around and say, "Okay, what do you want?" But she didn't; she just kept on messing with the sink, and finally his father tried again:

"Dad wants an answer, Beth. He wants me to think about this seriously, and make a decision within the year."

"So make a decision within the year, Pat," said his mother.

"After all, Beth, this is what all this goddamn work I've put in was for. . . ."

"Pat, I've heard all this—"

"This is what all the years I've spent at Cappadora's, and before that, filling cartons of potato salad at my dad's—"

"Pat, we've been over and over this." Watch it, Dad, Vincent thought. That's the voice you don't want to hear, the voice that came right before Mom's fingers went like a lobster claw around your upper arm. Dad was pretty smart. He got up and put his arms around Mom again; he kissed her. She let him.

"Kiss, kiss, kiss," his dad said softly, almost as nice as if he was talking to one of the kids. "Don't we ever just fuck anymore?"

Vincent had heard his dad use the *f* word before, but not in such a nice voice. He leaned forward; they weren't looking up, so they weren't going to see him anyway.

"Pat," said his mother. "I have to get the baby up...." Kerry was not a baby anymore, she was going to be two, but everybody still called her that.

"We have time," said his dad.

"Okay. You go upstairs and get my diaphragm and fill it up with gunk, and then ... let's see, we'll have about eight minutes before I have to get some food in Vincent before he gets on the bus ... want to do it right here? I can make toast at the same time?"

"That's a lousy thing to say, Beth. It isn't like I'm on top of you every second. We have sex about as often as we pay the water bill."

"Talk about lousy things to say ..."

"And anyway, I don't see why you need the gunk and the diaphragm every damn time."

"Because I don't want to get pregnant every damn time."

"Beth, that's another thing...."

Vincent's mom got quiet. His dad didn't get the message, though; he kept right on talking: "It's been well over a year, Bethie. We both know that Ben—"

"What's that got to do with it?"

"Jesus, Beth. Don't you give a damn about the way I hurt?" Vincent's dad started to go out into the hall; Vincent shrank back against the sides of the box. "I mean, Bethie, I was the guy who had three kids. Everybody thought

I was nuts, you know? *Three* kids? But one of the worst things is, for me, that the house was so full of their noise before. I would want to run up the walk at lunch—"

Vincent's mom flashed across the lower hall so fast he barely saw her. She opened the front door. It was a thing she did a lot, just opening the front door and letting the air in, even if it was really cold. Just standing there, blowing out her breath.

"Pat, I don't want another child," she said.

"You said you would think this over."

"I *have* thought it over. And every time I think of having another child in me, and that maybe it would be a boy . . ." Her voice got funny, like she had a bread ball stuck. "Pat, it isn't going to change anything. Don't you see that? Just so you can be the guy who has three kids again."

"Not just that. I'm not a fool."

"No, I mean, it would just be numbers. It would be a compensatory child. Like a replacement part. Like getting a new gravy boat so you don't spoil the set."

"You're a bitch," said Vincent's dad.

"I have no doubt," said his mom, "that I'm a bitch. But the fact is, I'm not going to have a baby and I'm not going to move to Chicago so you can start a restaurant with your dad. If you want a new baby and a restaurant in Chicago, you need a new wife."

"Is it so wrong for me to want us to be a family again? Have a normal life again?"

"Pat. There is no such thing as having a normal life again."

Vincent heard the door bang shut, and he had the feeling his mom hadn't done it.

"There would be, if you even tried. . . ."

"Pat," said his mom, and it was her being-nice voice, the voice she used to try to get him not to open the door when she had pictures in the bath and the red light was on. "Do you know what it's like for me?"

Vincent's dad said nothing.

"Do you?"

Nothing.

"It's like I'm always under this giant shelf of snow or rock, and if I move, if I change my position even a little, the snow is going to start to slide, and it's going to come down on me and bury me...."

"Oh, Beth ..."

"No, it really is. I don't dare to think about him for a full minute. I don't dare to think about the reunion for a full minute. If I thought of having to live where I'd drive by the Tremont every day of my life ..."

"We wouldn't have to."

"Pat, I hear you and Tree talking. You and Monica. We'd all be together again. In the old neighborhood. The kids under the table while the adults play poker. Just like the old days. Don't you think I know that Tree hates me for keeping you up here? Away from your parents, who want you so bad, so much more now that they're grieving? Don't you think I know that my own father thinks I should come home, where Bick can help me, because I'm such a mess?"

"Everybody hates you, Beth, right? Nobody understands how—"

"But if I move, Pat, if I move one inch, that avalanche is going to come down on me and you'll have to raise these kids by yourself—"

"Which I already practically do."

"Okay, okay. I accept that. Pat's always been the good one. Pat's the rock. He's the one who's held that poor crazy woman and those little kids ... like the *People* story, Pat. Didn't you love it? 'His hands sturdily on the backs of his wife and his remaining son.' You're such a hero, Pat."

"And you're such a martyr, Beth."

"I have to get Vincent up." Vincent got up onto his knees, ready to take off for Ben's bed and dive in if she moved. "But Pat, you know, you can't force me to do anything. You can't. You can't threaten me like when we were in college, because I don't give a damn if you leave, or ... or ... or if you screw every pizza waitress in Madison."

"What?"

"I mean, you don't have any power over me, Pat. The worst already happened."

"I love how you say 'it happened.' Like it was a tornado or something." There was such a stillness in the hall that Vincent could hear Kerry's mouth open in her sleep, with a tiny pop. Pretty soon she would come waddling down the hall, and that would be good, he was hungry, and they were going to fight ... The sunlight spun the dust over and up, over and up. Vincent put out his hand to let it rest on his palm. They weren't done. He could wish all he wanted, but they weren't done, and he might not get breakfast at all.

"What do you mean by that?"

"Nothing," said Vincent's dad. It was his dad's lie voice, the voice he used when he said "I'm not tired," so Vincent knew something else was coming. "I mean nothing."

"You do. You mean it didn't just happen."

"It just happened. Forget it, Beth."

"No, you've been keeping it inside, and you want me to know that you blame me. Don't you think I already know that you blame me, because *you* would never have let Ben get lost, would you, Pat? You'd never have been such a bad, shitty parent, who only cared about herself—"

"I never once said that, Beth."

"Said it? You didn't have to say it. It was evident, Pat. That line around your mouth, Pat. You hate my guts, and you blame me for losing your son."

Vincent saw his dad blast out of the living room like he was going to grab his mother and knock her down.

"Okay, Beth! Do I blame you? Sure as shit I blame you! Candy blames you, and Bender does, too. So does Ellen. Don't you think everyone thinks that if you just had a minute to take care of your kids, none of this would ever have happened? Just because they don't tell you? Does a wall have to fall on you? Yeah, you were lucky all your life until now, Beth. You could do everything half-assed and get away with it, because I was there to clean up after you!"

"You piece of shit," said Vincent's mother. "You self-righteous—"

"I'm not self-righteous, Beth. I'm right! I'm just right! Kids don't just vanish like smoke, Beth. They don't 'get lost.' People lose them."

"I hate you, Pat," said Vincent's mother.

Vincent jumped up and ran down the hall into Kerry's room. His head was hot like he had a fever. He raced over to the baby's crib and let down the bar and, reaching up, clamped his whole hand over her little nose and mouth.

He didn't want to kill her ... he loved Kerry. She was struggling now, trying to get his hand away, trying to breathe, her big gray eyes scared, bubbling tears ... Vincent didn't know if he could let go yet, but finally Kerry twisted her head just right and opened her getting-blue lips and began to scream, not a baby-wet cry (Vincent knew the sniffly-wheezy quality of that; he'd heard it a million times, first with Ben) but a horror-movie scream, like a big girl's ... and Vincent's mom was up the stairs like she had wings, knocking him to one side as she pulled Kerry out of the crib (Kerry's lips were starting to get pink again), screaming, "What did you do to her? Vincent, answer me! What did you do to Kerry?"

His dad was right behind his mom, and he grabbed Kerry out of her arms, and they held her between them, his dad saying, "Beth, she's okay— remember, the doctor always says if they're crying, then they're okay.... It looks like she lost her breath for a minute...."

Then, his mom was crying, holding Kerry in her arms, and his dad tried to pull his mom against him, but she shoved him away, harder even than she'd shoved Vincent. His dad grabbed Vincent's arm and pulled him off the floor. "Get your sweatshirt on," he said. "We're going for a ride."

"He has school!" his mom screamed.

"Not today!" his dad yelled back.

"Where are you taking him?"

"Somewhere safe, Beth! Safe from you! You're going to kill me off sooner or later, but not him!" And Vincent was practically lifted off his feet as his father skimmed him, with his sweatshirt only one arm on, down the stairs and out into the garage.

"Daddy," Vincent said, "wait a minute. I got to get my vitamin."

"I'll wait in the car," his dad said, fumbling for a cigarette in his shirt pocket.

Vincent ran back into the house—good, she was still up in Kerry's room; he could hear her humming and crying, the floorboards squeaking as she walked Kerry back and forth. Working quickly, Vincent went first into his dad's office, where he set the alarm for 11:00 p.m. Then into their bedroom (he had to pass Kerry's door for it, but the door was shut, so that was okay), where he changed the alarm setting from 6:30 to 4:30 in the morning. And then, he couldn't think, yes . . . okay, the stove timer. He could barely reach it. He set that for 5:00 a.m. Maybe that wasn't all the alarms in the house, but that was all he could think of so fast. She would notice, for sure. He could stand right next to her face while she slept, he could even put out his finger and touch her eyelid, and she wouldn't ever wake up. He'd called her a dozen times, when he had his running-away dreams, but she'd never wake up, though sometimes his dad did, if he called more than once. She would notice this, and he wouldn't care even if they did come back tonight, which he had a feeling they weren't going to, because his dad had grabbed his little bag with his toothbrush and shaver in it. He wouldn't care if the alarms woke him up, too. Or even Kerry, though this wasn't her fault.

Vincent snatched an orange Flintstones out of the bottle on the sink and jumped into the front seat of the car. "Belt," said his dad, staring ahead, and Vincent snapped it on and sat back. They went down the belt line, past the turnoff on Park Street for Cappadora's, past the road that led to Rob Maltese's, his dad's best friend's, house. Past the car wash. To the Janesville exit, the sign that his father once said meant, "We're going to see Grandma!"

"Are we going to Chicago?" Vincent asked.

"Don't you want to go see Grandma Rosie?"

"It's a school day, Daddy. It's not Sunday or Friday even."

"Sometimes, we could go see Grandma Rosie even in the middle of the week, like in summer."

"But why?"

"Just to see her. Don't you ever want to see your mama? I just want to see my mama," his father said, in a little-bitty voice that scared Vincent much more than the *f* word or any of the yelling in the hall. Pat lit a cigarette and rolled down the window. "Don't tell Mommy I smoked in the car," he said, like he always said.

"I won't."

"Okay, pal."

Vincent leaned against the arm rest; his father was singing with the Rolling Stones on the radio, using the heels of his palms like drums; Vincent thought he might fall asleep, if he wasn't afraid of the running-away dream, the dream which wasn't so scary in itself as the way his dream self kept wanting to look behind him. He knew that if he looked behind him, it would be the worst thing, worse than the flabby white monster with the big red mouth he saw by accident one time when he got up and his dad had *Shock Theater* on in the middle of the night.

It would be worse than that, Vincent thought; he wanted to tell his dad that, but his eyes were blurry.

"Wake up," said a voice, a voice that always sounded like it had a cough in it, or stones under it. Grandpa Angelo. "Wake up, *dormi*-head." That was the Italian word for "sleepy," part of the song Grandpa Angelo sang when Ben was little. Vincent was sweaty and shivery, but he put his arms up and Grandpa Angelo lifted him out through the window of the car and held him against the rough wool of his blue suit. Grandpa Angelo wore blue suits all the time, even on Saturday morning in the house, even when he went to get a fireplace log or spray the tomatoes. Grandma Rosie said wearing the blue suit all day made Grandpa look like an immigrant, but he told her, "Rose, a businessman has a big car and a clean suit. Not just at business—all day long." Except playing cards. When Grandpa Angelo used to play cards with his friends—Ross, Mario, and Stuey—he wore his stripey cotton T-shirt with straps over the shoulders. You could see the tufts of white hair stick up from Grandpa's shoulders over the straps, like feathers. If he saw Vincent, he would pull him down on his lap and rub his cigar cheek against Vincent's, and put red wine from his good glass on his finger and let Vincent lick it off. He would ask Vincent, "Now, Maestro, do I ask this most illustrious dealer for one card, or two?" And even back then Vincent was not so little he couldn't tell when the red or black numbers had a gap in them—and he would shake his head no, because Grandpa told him the time to draw to an inside straight was never, ever, never; it was madness and doom. Sometimes, when the weather was hot and the locusts were caroling loud, Vincent would even fall asleep under Grandpa Angelo's white iron patio chair, the chorus of locusts and the slap of the cards and the sound of Italian swears and the hot, almost too sweet smell of cigars all wound around and around him until they seemed like one thing. And he would wake up shivery and sweaty, the sky changed from sunny to sunsetty, or from fresh to shiny overhead, just like it was now.

"My little love," said Grandpa Angelo. "My best boy." He carried Vincent up onto the front stoop, under the cool shade of the big green awnings. Vincent was deeply fond of the awnings, the only ones on the block, and of the shiny green, absolutely square hedges that looked like plastic but smelled like vinegar.

"I love you, Grandpa," Vincent told him, nuzzling. And he did, too. He also loved his grandpa Bill, but his grandpa Bill always seemed to be a little nervous around Vincent. Like he would ask him, "Hey, Vince, you married yet?" Like a nine-year-old kid would be married and not even tell his own grandfather. Grandpa Angelo just gave you penne and red sauce, or white sauce if your tummy was upset, and wine from a spoon and Hershey's kisses from his pockets, and let you pick the grapes and tomatoes and only laughed if you dropped one—and not a phony, grown-up, really-mad-behind-it laugh, either. He really didn't care what a kid did as long as a kid said his pleases and thank-yous and didn't be a *diavolo*—Vincent didn't know exactly what that meant but knew it was a bad guy.

They were passing the kitchen, going outside to the backyard, when Vincent heard his dad say, ". . . what else to do, Ma. I can't take anymore."

"Patrick, *tesoro mio*," said Grandma Rosie, who was getting his dad coffee. "She's not herself. You must give her time."

"I have no more time, Ma!" Vincent realized, to his terror, that his dad was crying. "I want to have a life, Ma, not this . . . prison on Post Road that Beth never goes out of—I mean, not willingly, just up and down to her darkroom. . . . Ma, I want out of this!"

Grandma Rosie swiveled her head around, fast, and then said in a big voice, meant for Vincent's dad, too, "Vincenzo, *carissimo*! Grandma will come and see you in a minute."

Grandpa Angelo carried Vincent outside, set him down in one of the white iron chairs, and brought him a glass of orange juice. "In a little while, we'll have pasta, eh? But first, we give your daddy some time with Grandma."

"Daddy's crying," said Vincent.

"He's so sad, 'Cenzo," said Grandpa Angelo, sitting himself down heavily in the chair opposite. He started flicking through the tapes on his bench, next to his big tape player. "We must have some music now, eh?"

"Why?"

"Good for the soul!" said Grandpa.

"No—Daddy. Why's he sad?"

"He's sad because of your brother, dear one. He's missing Ben."

"And he hates my mommy. She said."

"No, Vincenzo, your daddy loves your mommy. He loves her since he was a little boy like you. She's his best buddy."

"I think Rob is his best buddy."

"Well, she's his best buddy and his true love. It's just ... here!" said Grandpa, finding a tape. "It's just she's so sad and he's so sad, they forget their love."

"Mom forgot my school conference three times. The principal had to call. And then Dad went."

"Well, you see then. This is so hard a time for us. For me, too. I think of my Ben and it crushes my heart." He patted his leg and Vincent came to sit on his lap. "Do you ever get sad, 'Cenzo?"

"Sometimes."

"When?"

"Today was once. They were fighting and they ... they scared Kerry. She yelled."

"I used to get sad when I was a little boy," said Grandpa. "I would get sad so many times because I missed my papa. I've showed you pictures of my papa, Vincent. He was such a big man ... so big and loud ... and he sang the Neapolitan love songs, with the voice of a Titian angel, my father. You know, that is why you are named Vincenzo, after him. And Paul, after your mama's brother Paulie."

"And what about my daddy?"

"What about him?"

"Is he named after somebody?"

"Yes," said Grandpa Angelo. "And this is another story about sadness. When your papa was born, I was on the road, selling cooking things. This was before we had our business, long before. I was far away, and I couldn't get home; and Grandma Rosie was just a young girl, having her first baby. The nurse who cared for her was from another country, like us—she was from Ireland. And when Grandma Rosie was frightened and sad, and crying out for me, this nurse—I think she was called Bridget, they're all called Bridget—prayed for Saint Patrick to ease her and bring forth a good baby. And Saint Patrick did do this. So, though this is an Irish name, this is the name Grandma Rosie gave your daddy."

"Where was he?"

"Who? Your daddy?"

"No, *your* daddy, when you were missing him?"

"He died, Vincent. He died in the first of the World War. He was a cook—all us Cappadoras, we cook, eh? But the bad guys attacked the camp, and your great-grandpa was shot, and he died right there, right where he was. He was buried there, too, not at home. I never saw his grave." Grandpa Angelo looked hard out at the grape arbor near the backyard fence. "And my mama, she had to clean houses, we were so tired and so poor. We missed my papa, and we were forbidden to say his name, because it would break my mama's heart. And that's when I discovered the opera. There was a teacher at the school in our village, and he had the record player, and he would play the operas and tell us to close our eyes and imagine what the places they were singing about looked like. The words sounded funny to me then, Vincenzo, because they were all so *sad*! So sad I thought they were silly; I was only a young boy, not even as old as you yet. In *La Bohème*, he was singing, 'Your tiny hand is frozen,' and I thought, How silly. And yet—and yet, the music was so magnificent! . . . The only true opera is Italian, Vincenzo. You know this. Like the only true food. We have to be nice to all the other people, and say, 'Oh yes, oh yes, this Mexican food is very good,' but we know better, eh?"

"Yup," said Vincent. "We know better."

"And so, when I was a grown man, and I, too, was a soldier, I was very afraid that I would die. This is in the second of the World Wars. I am an American soldier now, an American citizen, fighting against the evil of my own nationals, and the Japs—mostly for me the Japs, on the islands in the Pacific Ocean." Vincent leaned harder against his grandpa's chest, trying to picture his round, brown, white-haired grandpa thin and young like his dad, and scared, like his dad. "I was so afraid, I'd get this record player, which I bought, and I'd play the music. *La Traviata*. Not the Germans, not their pig music. The real opera. And it would make me happier and not so scared."

"How could it make you happier when it was so sad?"

"That's what I'm going to show you," said Grandpa Angelo, and he turned on the tape. There was a lady singing; she was singing pretty loud, but you could still tell she was about to start crying. The words were all jumbled up, like the singing on the tapes in Cappadora's.

"What's she saying, Grandpa? What's she talking in? Italian?"

"Yes, Italiano, Vincent. Just listen."

But Vincent proudly repeated the only words he knew in Italian besides *bambino* and some swears: "Non parlo Italiano."

"I know, but listen. I will tell you what she says. The singer is Mirella Freni, a great star. She's older now, but she was very young when this recording was made. She's talking to her little boy and she's saying, 'Tu, tu piccolo iddio'—my little god. She loves her little boy and he's going away, and she's having a broken heart."

"Why's he running away?"

"He's not running away, Vincenzo," said Grandpa. Vincent could smell the gravy cooking in the house and he was meanly hungry, but he didn't want to be rude to Grandpa. Even though Grandpa was right about the opera, it did sound a little silly, to call a kid "God."

"Why's she calling him 'God'?"

"Because she loves him so much he's like a . . . like a saint to her. That's how parents love their children. That's how we love your papa. And how your papa loves you and Kerry and Ben. And your mama, too."

"So where's he going?"

"Who?" said Grandpa, who looked as if he was going to get up and jump around in his joy over the singing lady.

"The little boy."

"His papa is taking him to America. See, the mama, she's Japanese. Her name is Madama Butterfly. That's the name of the story. By Puccini. The papa, he's a bad guy. He fooled the mama and made her think she was his wife, but he got another wife. Very *malo, malo.* Bad. And now she's giving her baby to him."

"Why, if he's so bad?"

"I don't know, Vincenzo. Because she's poor, I guess. And because she's so sad that the papa doesn't love her that she wants to die. And if she loses her little boy, then she will want to die even more."

"My mommy didn't die," said Vincent, a throwing-up feeling creeping up. He held Grandpa Angelo tighter.

"No, no, of course not. If your mommy died, where would she be when Ben comes home? In heaven with the angels?" He kissed Vincent, his chin rough, smelling of his cologne, the heavy, fruity scent of his drawers and closets. "We pray for Ben to come home. And this mama, she's a Jap, you know, Vincent. The Japs are a crazy people. *Pazzi.* They think that if somebody does something bad to you, or if you screw up, you got to die over it. That's a crazy thing, Vincent. Regular people, like Italians and even Irish, like Grandpa Bill, they get up and kick somebody in the gool if he does bad to them. They get up and they have tenoots. . . ."

"What's tenoots?"

"Nothing," said Grandpa. "They have *coraggio,* they have bravery. They try to fix something."

"Eat!" called Grandma Rosie from the back door.

"*Momento!*" Grandpa yelled back. "Now, listen to this part, Vincent. This is also sad, though it's supposed to be happy. This is why opera is so great. There's a whole story. If you like, I will copy this tape for you, so you can play it at home. In this part—this is the most famous song in the whole thing, it's called 'Un bel di.' "

"What's that?"

Grandpa spelled it out for him; it wasn't spelled like it sounded. " 'One fine day,' Vincent. She's singing about how she thinks this jamoke is going to come back to her and her baby and make her happy. . . ."

The voice was really pretty, and the melody was so pretty. You could tell it was Japanese because of the tune, but it was even prettier than regular Japanese music, which Vincent had heard in school, and which sounded to him like skim milk tasted, like they didn't have enough instruments to go around. He lay back against Grandpa, and listened to the lady's heavenly voice, and tried to let his sadness float on it.

But all he could think of was that his hunger was all gone, and of the way the mama's voice sounded before, when she was talking to her little boy, who wasn't even lost yet, but it was as if he was already a million miles away from her, so far she could never hug him again.

Chapter 13

May 1990

Under the mangy grape arbor in the backyard, which Vincent's dad never paid any attention to, though he always said he was going to and yelled if you goofed around with it, Vincent and Alex Shore were starting to set up this whole twig town for the little Playmobil guys to live in. They were big now, almost twelve, and they didn't really play with that kind of stuff much anymore; mostly, they rode bikes to Radio Shack or goofed around with the hoops at the park. Last night on the phone, they'd cooked up this big plan to use the spool of utility wire Vincent had found. They were going to string it from Vincent's window to Alex's, three houses down and across the street, and try to rig up a phone that really worked. But when Vincent's dad caught him taking out his bedroom screen and found the hammer and nails, he put a stop to the whole thing right away:

"Are you stupid?" he asked Vincent. "You want to clothesline some kid in a convertible?"

Which didn't sound so bad to Vincent, actually.

But the wire idea going bust kind of meant needing something to do. And it was hot, real hot for the last week of school. The pool wasn't even open

yet. Alex's mom wouldn't let them in the house because his brother Max had chicken pox.

At first they were just going to make some dirt barricades and stuff so the guys could have a war; but Vincent found some twine his father had cut off the tomatoes and showed Alex how Indians used to build wickiup—by tying a whole bunch of same-size sticks together at the top and then bending them out. Then you had a frame. Alex had the idea of using tissue to cover it; but Vincent said, "No, let's use that plastic wrap stuff, because then we can see what they're doing in there."

"They won't be doing anything," Alex said. "Unless we reach in there and move them around."

"No, you don't get what I mean. It'll be like we can set up little scenes, like one can be the deer-skinning hut or something. It'll be like a diorama at the Field Museum." Alex had never been at the Field Museum. "Well, it's where they have a lot of mummies and stuff, and they have all these dioramas of the hunter-gatherers and the Incas. Like models."

"I don't want to do it," Alex grumbled. "I just want to have a war is all."

"Well, that's boring and stupid," Vincent told him. "And anyhow, they're my guys." That didn't sound too good, Vincent thought, and he'd better be careful. Alex was his best friend—pretty much his only friend. On the other hand, he didn't want to do something really baby and boring like war. "Come on, Al. It'll be cool," he said. As Alex thought it over, Kerry came out into the yard, wearing her velvet American Girl dress (she wore it all the time, and it cost like a hundred bucks; it drove Vincent nuts to see her, like, wear it to gymnastics under her jersey; but nobody ever stopped her). Kerry was lugging a big bucket, filled to the top. Vincent caught the high, hottish smell of it right away.

"Wait a minute," he told Alex. "Kerry, what's in that?"

"The stuff under the sink," she said, smiling. "I'm going to kill the bugs in the sandbox." Vincent went over and took the bucket away from her; she started to kick him right away—she was only four, so this really shouldn't have hurt too much. But she was a good kicker. Vincent had to stand on one of her feet to stop her.

"Kerry," he told her, "this is ammonia. It's poison. You can't play with it. Where's mom?"

"On the telephone."

"Did she let you have this?"

"Yes," Kerry said. Vincent thought, Well, maybe she did. Oh, well.

"You can kill box elder bugs better with just plain old dish soap and water in a squirter. And it's funner." He dumped the ammonia under Mr. Aberg's poplars, which Vincent's dad said were really about half trees of heaven and the other half eyesore. "Do you want me to get you some of that?"

"Uh-huh, uh-huh!" cried Kerry delightedly.

"I'm going to go get her something and get some of that clear wrap, okay, Al?" Vincent went back to the grape arbor. "You want a Coke, too?"

"You're so damn bossy," Alex said.

"Cut it out," Vincent warned. His hands were balling up; they always did, he couldn't help it—even teachers knew it.

"My mom says you're so bossy because your mom never pays no attention to you."

"*Any* attention to me, Al. She never pays *any* attention to me."

"Well, that's what she says. And I think she's right. Your dad is at work all the time and your mom never pays no attention to you."

"You know, your mom is dumb, Al."

"Yeah," Alex said. "So?"

"Adults aren't supposed to say that stuff where kids can hear them. Your mom would kill you if she knew you told me that."

"So?"

"So, let's just get this game going, okay? We can have a war and a village of hunters, okay? We can do both." Alex shrugged. That was okay. He wouldn't leave if Vincent hurried up.

He went into the kitchen to snag two Cokes, and right away, even though he couldn't see her, he noticed how his mother was talking on the phone. Because she was really *talking*, saying, "Get out of here! How long have you known this? . . . But when did you really decide?" And then, "But will you even enjoy it? . . . You have? How many times?" She was laughing. His mother was laughing. He followed the telephone cord around the edge of the breakfast-room wall, and there she was, all coiled up in a chair, twiddling her hair with one finger. When she saw him, she waved at him.

His mother waved and ... grinned.

Vincent brought the Cokes back outside. Damn it. He had forgotten Kerry's bug spray. His mother was off the phone, but she was dialing it again. She called to Vincent, "Guess who's getting married?"

Vincent was so stunned he dropped the nearly full spritz bottle into the sink; it started to spill down the drain. His mother never spoke to him or anyone else first. He'd done, like, experiments, measuring how long it would take her to say anything if the phone didn't ring or Kerry didn't ask her for a cookie or something. And she could go hours, whole days probably. He had personally seen her go a whole day, once when his dad was out of town. She made beds and junk, like a regular person, except she never said one word, didn't even hum. It wasn't like she wasn't paying attention to him; she just didn't even see him.

Vincent didn't believe she was really thinking nothing; you couldn't. He and his cousin Moira had tried a whole bunch of times, once, to run around the house just one time without thinking of a pig. You couldn't do it. A person always thought; you couldn't drain your brain. In his humble opinion, it was really too much thinking—like static on the radio—getting in his mother's way. Aunt Tree had once said, when she thought Vincent was asleep, "The light's on but nobody's home," about his mother's head. But Vincent disagreed. Vincent picture his mother's head more like a beehive, sometimes.

But now she was looking right at him.

"Candy," his mom said, and he thought, Does she want some? But then he realized she meant her friend the police lady, the one who sometimes came up for the weekend and let Vincent touch her unloaded gun for just a second, and let him play with her gold shield. "Candy's going to get married. Can you believe that?"

Vincent knew something was expected of him. "Well," he said. "She is pretty old."

"Oh, she's not so old, Vincent," said his mother. "She's what ... forty, I guess maybe. She wants ... she wants a baby before it's too late."

"Too late?" Vincent asked, feigning more interest than he felt, desperate to keep her looking at him this way.

"Well, women can only have babies for a while. Then they get too old and their bodies don't work that way anymore." You mean menopause, Vincent thought—they told them about it in school. He always thought, why was it a pause? Didn't it really just stop altogether?

"But that's when you're real old, right?" he asked, urgently, feeling his mother start to slip away.

"Well, but sometimes if you have a baby when you're old, the baby isn't right. It has birth defects." He saw then that she was gone. He could pop out one of his eyeballs right now and she'd say, "Vincent, take that outside." She turned back to the phone. "I want Laurie to take Kerry for me. Do you want to stay with Daddy? Are you big enough to stay alone till he gets home from work?" She frowned. "I wish Jilly was still around." Mom was always wishing Jill didn't get out of school and get married. But Vincent knew this wasn't one of those questions parents asked that they'd already worked out the answers to. His mother didn't do that. When she asked whether they had long division in fifth grade, she really had no idea whether he knew what long division was. She had no idea that he'd placed second out of the whole school in the spelling bee, and that the word his missed was "withdrawal."

"Take Kerry when?" he asked now.

"Next weekend, next weekend," said his mother. "Oh." She looked at him again then. "Candy wants me to take pictures. Of her wedding reception. In Chicago. And I said I would."

Vincent had to sit down. Alex was probably disgusted by now; he'd probably gone home. To tell the truth, Vincent should be outside, making sure Kerry didn't run into the street or something.

But he had to take this in. He could not believe this.

In the last few years, she'd gone on planes to New York for work, on planes to Florida. But she never, ever went to Chicago—not when Aunt Tree's babies were born, not when Grandpa Angelo had a heart rhythm, not even for Christmas or to look at bodies the cops thought were Ben.

"Are you going to go with Dad?" he asked.

"Well, maybe," said his mom. "No. I don't think so. I mean, Dad has to

work. I guess . . ." She stared at Vincent as if they were both discovering secret buried doubloons. "I guess I'll just go by myself and stay at Aunt Ellen's.
It's only one night. Right?"

"I guess. Will you be okay?"

"I think so. Will you be okay?"

"Sure." What would be different, thought Vincent; it wasn't like she told
him when to go to bed or something. He scanned his mother's face as she
stared off into the yard—he could see Kerry out there, gravely squirting the
hose into the sandbox. It was almost as if his mother were trying to think
about what she was doing; he could *see* her thoughts walk back and forth like
puppets. Her hand fluttered toward the phone again. Dropped to her lap.
"Do you think Dad will let you go?" he asked, worried.

She didn't answer for so long that Vincent thought she was purely gone.
But then she said, "Uh, *let* me? Your father's not my boss, Vincent. I can go
somewhere if I want."

But he was still astonished when, a week later, she actually did go, putting
her duffel bag in the trunk with three of her cameras and her lights, even
bringing up the black hood thing that made her look like one of those guys
who took pictures in a big puff of smoke in silent movies. They stood
around on the porch, waiting for Dad to get back from the hardware store.

"Do you want me to call you tonight, when Dad's at work?"

"I'm going with him," Vincent said.

"Oh. Good."

Dad backed the Toyota into the driveway and started lifting out the bags
of turf builder he always bought, even though, as far as Vincent could tell,
they never had anything but the worst, knottiest lawn on the block. His dad
dropped the last bag, splitting it open slightly, and leaned his head against
the open trunk.

"You okay?" Vincent asked him. His mom just stood there.

"Just getting ancient," said his dad, wiping off his face on the sleeve of the
ratty flannel shirt he wore.

His mom leaned down to hug the air around him, and she squeezed his
dad's arm. Vincent wondered, as he always did, whether his mom would kiss

his dad; she didn't. Probably it was something you didn't like to do in front of a kid before puberty.

"Are you sure you don't need me to drive you?" his dad asked.

"I'm fine, Pat," said his mother. "I owe her. She never stopped."

"I think she's crazy. It's a crazy thing to do. This guy, he's crazy, too."

"Like she says, people have been fools for lesser things."

"I suppose." His dad smiled. "Kiss the bride for me. But not too hard." Dad always made these kinds of jokes about Candy, which Vincent had privately decided meant his dad thought Candy was a lesbian, a girl who married girls. But she wasn't. He knew that for sure. She smelled too good. He personally thought Candy would be a great mother—just for all the equipment she had in her car alone. He would love to be Candy's kid.

That night during the rush, Uncle Augie was in a take-no-prisoners mood, yelling at everybody, right up to the chef, Enzo, who even Augie was normally scared of. "People are starving out there, Enzo!" he yelled. "People want to starve, they can go to Ethiopia, they don't have to sit in my dining room!"

Finally, Enzo pointed the end of his biggest knife at Uncle Augie and said, "You say one more thing and I'm going to stick this up your fat nose, Augusto. You crazy old sonofabitch. You ever hire anybody else who got the IQ of my mailbox and maybe somebody would get to eat after all!" Vincent's dad had to break them up. Vincent loved it when this happened, even though his dad didn't. He hated fights. Linda, the big red-haired waitress, took Vincent to one side of the kitchen, near the open back door where the Mexican kids were cowering in their white shirts with "Cappadora's" embroidered on the pockets, and held his head right between her boobs.

"Shut up in front of the kid," she said, "Paddy, make them shut up."

Linda steered him out of the kitchen and gave him a plate of angel hair with white clam sauce, his favorite, which he had just started to eat at the bar, talking to Mickey, the carpet wholesaler, and Tory, the bartender, when Tory got a phone call for his dad.

"Go get Papa, sport," he told Vincent, and said into the phone, "Bethie, wait up, baby. I can't hear you. I'm getting him."

Uncle Augie was sitting on a wooden chair in the kitchen, mopping his face with a big handkerchief and drinking ice water. "Why would anyone ever drink anything but ice water, eh, Vincenzo?" he asked the boy.

"Where's Dad?"

"Outside. Smoking another coffin nail." Like Grandpa Angelo, Uncle Augie was a reformed smoker; he didn't even allow smoking in the bar. Their younger brother, Cosimo, had died from lung cancer.

"Dad," Vincent called out the door. "Mom is on the phone." His dad tossed the butt over the fence and picked up the phone. It was hot, so hot in the kitchen Enzo was working in his undershirt, which sort of made Vincent sick to his stomach to see. His dad pulled the cord out into the alley. He motioned for Vincent to come and stand next to him, and Vincent did, watching the pale ribbons of light he used to think, when he was little, were the aurora borealis, but which were really spots from Vanland across the belt-line. He was so tired and sort of hypnotized by the lights he didn't notice how tight his dad's fingers were around the back of his neck; his dad was actually hurting him. When Vincent pulled away, the neck of his T-shirt was soaking.

"What else did they find?" his dad was saying. And then, "Where the hell is that? Which Hyatt? ... Oh, Elmbrook, sure, sure.... Candy what? I thought she was getting married...." Vincent watched the sweat drip like melting icicles off his dad's upper lip. His dad looked funny; his eyes looked too deep in. "I'm leaving now, sure.... Why? What are you going to do? Is Ellen with you?" He covered the phone and said to Vincent, "Get Daddy a glass of water, pal." Vincent went inside to the ice machine. He filled the glass three-quarters with ice, the way his dad liked it, and then carried it slowly back, pushing open the kitchen door with his behind. That's when he saw his dad kneeling—he thought for a minute, He's praying. Why is he praying? But the phone was on the ground, and a squawky little voice was coming out: "Pat? Pat? Are you there?" His father's hands were pressed, one over the other, against his chest, and his too-deep eyes looked up at Vincent like one of those saints in museums who've seen God.

"I think I'm sick, buddy," he said to Vincent. "I think there's an elephant standing on me." He tried to smile.

Vincent reached over his father, picked up the telephone, lowered the hook long enough to make sure his mother's voice was gone and he had a dial tone, and called 911.

Chapter 14

By the time his mom came tearing out of the night into the intensive-care waiting room, Vincent already knew his dad was going to live.

Though the doctors had tried for hours to talk right over him to Dad's friend Rob Maltese and Uncle Augie, he mostly heard everything—and he decided the doctor with the cowboy boots to be the guy he believed. Cowboy Boots talked in normal language, and he didn't act like Rob and Augie were stupid. Everybody else who came in did. From Linda to Laurie's husband, Rick, to Laurie, they all kept saying to each other, "He's in the best hands," "This is the court of last resort," "Thank God we have the university hospital."

And then, as if remembering he was there, someone would turn to Vincent and say, "Your daddy's going to be fine. He's in the best hands."

But Vincent knew that was just the kind of thing you said to a kid. He'd heard it a lot of times before.

So he didn't speak at all; he just listened, and whenever he saw the beige lizard-skin boots come through the swinging doors out of the intensive-care ward, he turned up his listening and used the kind of concentration he used when he built a model motor. It was only about ten o'clock when Boots told Rob and Augie, "Well, in the simplest possible terms, what we were able to do here, I hope, and I think, is stop a heart attack from happening. Until we do an angiogram, we aren't going to be one hundred percent about the condition of the arteries and so on; but thank goodness we were able to start a TPA right away...."

"What's that?" Uncle Augie asked.

"A blood thinner, to dissolve any clots, get things moving again," said Cowboy Boots. "What we always have to assume, when we have a guy this young with this kind of trouble, is that there's blockage...."

"But he just got this awful news from Chicago," Augie said. "His wife just called and said they found the baby's—"

Cowboy Boots waved a hand, but nicely. "It's true, you always hear that people drop over with an infarct from what we call stress. But you can scare the pants off a guy with normal arteries all day and that guy may sweat or get sick to his stomach and feel lousy, but he's not going to have a heart attack. All stress does is pop the balloon, essentially—it exposes an underlying condition, probably the result of hereditary ... What did your father die from, Mr. Cappadora?"

"He died in the first war. He was a young man. In his twenties."

"Any other folks got heart disease in the family? Uncles?"

"Sure," said Augie. His voice seemed to say, Is this a big surprise or something? "Two of his brothers died real young from heart attacks. One was just maybe forty-five or something. But the fourth brother, he's still alive. He's ninety. And we had a brother die from lung cancer. And my brother Ange, he had to get a pacemaker. He's fine now, though."

"So there you see. And—" Boots glanced at his clipboard—"Pat has a history of smoking, not quite a twenty-twenty history, but he started really young, he says. What, thirteen, fourteen?"

"He's talking then? He's conscious?" Rob pleaded. "He told you this himself? He's not brain-dead?"

"Oh, no, not at all. He's quite alert. He hasn't lost consciousness. He's very, very anxious, naturally. We had to give home something to quiet him down...."

"Are you going to operate?"

Boots pursed his lips. "Well, let's just take one world at a time here. Our job right now is to get Pat nice and stable, and then, as soon as we can, take a real good movie inside that chest. But I can tell you, his cardiogram doesn't look very bad at all. We aren't seeing Q waves, which often means we headed off the most serious—"

And then his mom burst in through the door, her eyes all smeary with makeup running down under them. She had on her ordinary jeans, and gym shoes unlaced, with no socks, but this really fancy satin blouse that looped way down in front, and one, just one, big dangly pearl earring.

"Where's Pat?" she asked Boots, grabbing his forearm. He didn't jerk it away—Vincent liked that—he just put his hand over hers and told her what he'd been saying all night, like, "The first thing you need to know is that your husband is out of immediate danger," that the prospects for recovery, cautiously, at least, were quite good. . . . Mom didn't listen, of course. "I want to see Pat," she said.

That was Vincent's cue. He could say stuff now. So he spoke up: "I want to see my father. I want to see Dad, too."

Both Boots and his mother looked down at Vincent. "Have you had anything to eat?" Beth asked.

Eat? "Yes," Vincent said.

"We want to see Pat," his mom told the doctor.

"Well, I suppose, just for a minute or two . . ."

They were ushered into a lane of tile between curtained cubicles. Somebody—it sounded like an old man—was yelling about "nigger nurses." A baby was wailing out in the waiting room. The nurse, who reminded Vincent of the sisters at his school, Mount Mary, motioned to a cubicle right in the middle; the curtain was drawn back, and there was his dad. He looked a lot worse even than he had on his knees in the alley. His skin was blue around the mouth, and two tubes forked up his nose that ran to a metal plate in the wall. One of his dad's arms was tied down to a board and a bag of water hung above it, dripping, dripping; Vincent timed it, exactly two seconds per drip.

"Pal," he said softly. "Come here." Vincent walked up to the bed, sideways. He wanted to hold his dad, and was afraid that his dad would touch him. "You saved my life, pally. I think you saved your old man's life. You're a brave kid."

Vincent felt tears pull at the bottom lids of his eyes, and he got busy trying to see his dad's chest, to see if his heart was beating under the flowered hospital dress. He barely noticed his mother get down on her knees next to the high bed and put her face down on his father's arm. But he started to pay more attention as the black makeup ran all over the gauze. What a mess, Vincent thought. That junk is probably not very sterile.

"Bethie," said Pat. "Oh baby. I feel like shit."

"Paddy, you look like shit. I'm so sorry, I'm so sorry I wasn't here. If I had known, anything, anything, my God, Paddy, I'd have been here...."

With an enormous tug, like he was lifting Vincent up to change the light bulb in the garage, Pat put his hand on Vincent's mother's hair, which was normal in front but all matted up in back, the way Kerry's was when she got out of bed in the morning—tangles and knots, like she hadn't brushed it in days. It gave him the creeps.

"You're my girl," said his father, and his mother started to cry, so hoarsely Vincent first thought she was puking, but then it was embarrassing. The nurse looked in, sucked her lips in one of those sad smiles, and then drew the drape closed.

"Bethie, tell me," his dad said. "Tell me now."

She turned her big, dripping-black eyes on Vincent. "Not now."

"Listen, Beth, he called 911 tonight. He can hear."

And that's when she told them both about the shoe. About how she'd been having lunch or dinner or something at a hotel with Aunt Ellen, and all of a sudden Candy showed up in her beige silk wedding dress, and she had Ben's red baby tennis shoe. Vincent was puzzled; big deal, they had Ben's shoe a hundred years ago. But it wasn't that. It was, as far as the police could tell, Ben's *other* shoe, or one just like it, and it was left on a desk in the dining room of the hotel where Beth's class, that very day, that very weekend, was holding her twentieth high-school reunion. A big Hyatt out by the golf course where Grandpa Bill played. Not the Tremont. Not the hotel Vincent dreamed about sometimes when he had the running dream; he could picture those tiles, the color of meatballs, any time he wanted to, if he just closed his eyes. Sometimes, when he lay in bed at night, he tried to think about the tiles and the smell and standing on the luggage trolley first, so he wouldn't have the running dream. But it hardly ever worked. The dream came any time it wanted to.

"So this means," his dad gasped, "they're going to reopen the—"

"Shhhhh," said Vincent's mother. "Rest now. They never really closed the case, Pat."

"What do they think, that whoever—?"

"Candy says maybe someone found it a long time ago, and it's a sick joke. Or maybe it was a different shoe, and some crazy just thought it would be a thrill, you know...."

"Did Ellen stay with you?"

His mother didn't answer right away. Didn't she know? Vincent wondered.

"Ellen didn't even tell me the reunion was that night. She told me, but not until I got there. I guess she thought I wouldn't come. And Candy didn't even get to go to her own wedding reception. I never took any pictures for her. Her husband seems very nice...."

"So what are they going to do now?"

"Candy?"

"No, Jesus, Bethie—the cops. Bender."

"We'll talk when you're better, baby."

"Beth."

"They're going to try to figure out if someone who came to the first reunion, or was there that day, brought the shoe back this time. Candy says they can get good prints off the rubber this time; they already did."

"And if they did, it could mean that Ben is—"

"It could mean anything, Paddy. It could mean that it's the person who took Ben and that they were trying to leave a message—"

Vincent jumped when the little beeper on the TV screen over his dad's bed began to shrill; the nurse appeared instantly. "No problem," she said cheerfully. "No change. Doesn't mean a thing. Just a little malfunction." No one spoke as the nurse ran her hands over his dad's tubing and put a little probe in his ear that immediately beeped. "Everything's going just fine, Mr. Cappadora. But you have to rest soon."

"A minute. My wife just got here . . . Bethie, listen. 'A message'?"

"Maybe even like, to comfort us. . . .'"

"Beth! To comfort us?"

"We'll go now," his mom said. Where? thought Vincent. Where would they go? Would they leave his dad alone here? What if the machines all went off at once? What if there was a power failure?

"Where are we going, Mom?"

"Well, home, I guess. I mean, I guess I'll take you to Laurie's and then I'll come back here and sit with Daddy. You can't stay up all night. . . .'"

Vincent began to cry. "I want to stay here with Dad. I don't want to go to Laurie's. I have to take care of Dad. . . .'"

"Shhhh," said Beth, as the old person's voice began quavering. "What's that? What's the goddamned racket?"

"I'll take care of Dad," said Beth, pulling Vincent to her for an instant. He pulled back. His mother smelled, she really smelled like . . . he could almost remember the smell, like the kind of cologne Grandpa Angelo used to use, maybe he still did, the kind that reminded Vincent of an old jewelry-box lining. She smelled as though she'd dipped her head in it, and it was weird, because his mother only ever smelled of Noxzema. She didn't even have any perfume that Vincent knew of. But before he could sniff her again, Laurie's husband, Rick, appeared and took him by the arm.

"Let's go with Laurie, okay, big buddy?" Rick said, winking over Vincent's shoulder at his dad. As Rick pulled him away toward the doors, Vincent saw his mother kneel down by the bed again and heard her whisper, "Paddy. I'll go anywhere. I'll do anything. The restaurant with your Dad. We can do that. I . . . want you to. Just get better, Paddy. Don't die on me. Don't die."

Now she's sorry, Vincent thought. She always wanted to kill him, and now she's sorry she almost killed him. Or maybe just pretending she's sorry. That's nuts, he thought. But what if she really had done it on purpose, like a curse? What if his dad had died right there in the alley, and Vincent had to go home alone with her, forever, and his dad was never going to come back, never be with him?

And what if one day she found out? About stuff? He felt the tap again in his tummy, the scratch, scratch of fear as he stared at the black back of his mother's matted curls, almost purple in the underwater hospital light. He had to tell himself that even when she squeezed him, or yanked on the back of his neck, she wasn't trying to hurt him, just her hands were. Her hands were rough. Sometimes she looked at him as if she wanted to lie on top of him, like a blanket. At those times, her hands were as gentle as a dental hygienist's, feather hands.

But if she knew ... For a long instant, he had no doubt that if that ever happened, she would kill him, too. She would have no choice.

$Beth$

$Chapter\ 15$

It was not possible.

The first time she'd walked into the derelict bindery that was to become Wedding in the Old Neighborhood, Beth had thought, This is a pit, this is a hole, so dank and forbidding it could drive Pollyanna to Prozac. Pat and his dad are going to undertake a slow double suicide to distract themselves from the reality of a family diminished by lost fathers and lost sons. It was nothing but a useless barn with graffiti-savaged tin walls in the middle of the west side's toughest frontier, a neighborhood in which only a few bold gay men had begun to stake claims on crumbling brownstones.

One of those men was the designer Beth had met that day months ago— a set designer of national reputation who also "did" theme bars and restaurants.

Did he "do" illusions, like David Copperfield? Beth had wanted to ask. She'd swallowed the remark; since Pat's heart attack, she'd swallowed so many unspeakables that one day they would probably rise up and choke her. Nevertheless, magic was what this transformation was going to require.

And there was no other word for it. Magic. In six weeks.

Beth had never seen anything quite like what had happened to the old warehouse. It was like a dream tour of the Italian imagination. Room opened upon room—one fashioned to resemble a wine cellar, with casks running wall to ceiling, labeled "Ruffino," "Conterno," "Catello di Amma," cunning droplets of paint to represent spilled wine trailing down the walls. Elaborate plaster scrollwork framed the alcoves, with mottoes painted in colors of putty and sky blue. The tables in this room were rough cypress, spread with shawls and abutted by barrel-cask seats. In an alcove, a polished bar was nearly concealed, and a passage to the kitchen. It would be open for lunches, Pat explained, and for overflow on the three nights each week that the actual "weddings" took place.

Pat led Beth next to the more formal bar, where a ceramic model of the Fontana di Trevi, coated in marbleized paint and more than five feet tall, took up the length of one whole wall. Each booth in the bar was made to look like a rose-trellised gazebo; each seated six. Behind the bar, bolts of satin in dove gray and rose were draped and caught with silk roses. Actual petals—Angelo got them for pennies from his buddy Armando, a funeral director—would be scattered like a carpet on the floor each night.

The real triumph was the banquet room itself. Vaulted beams of polished pine made the ceiling look like the Duomo in Florence, and the painting that would cover the whole thing (a painter was up there now, Michelangelo-like, on his back on a suspended platform) would be on the theme of the seasons—marriage being, after all, the commencement of a wheel of birth and harvest.

"What are those for?" Beth asked, pointing to black wrought-iron balconies, six of them, tucked in at the corners of the beams.

"They're for people," Pat began, throwing up his hands at her look. "Don't ask me. It's my father's idea that there should be goddesses or something in them. This is what I really want you to see." He strode over to one wall and pulled a protective tarp. Beth literally jumped. She was looking at her own face.

"You're Mimì," Pat said, with the kind of uncorked delight she hadn't seen in him since he played Colt league. "And I'm Rodolfo." Slowly, he led her through the rest of the frescoes—some were not yet completed. Besides

La Bohème, there were depictions of scenes from *Carmen*, *Madama Butterfly*, and more, each character a Cappadora family face. They were painted with a diaphanous technique that made not just the opera paintings but the walls themselves look hundreds of years old.

"How did he manage this, in so short a time? It looks like years of work. Oh, Paddy, it's gorgeous!"

Pat was shining. "It is, isn't it? We were so right to get Kip. This place is going to knock their socks off ... And wait till you see the brides and the bandstand and this—and this, Beth...." He tugged up a corner of the dropcloth that covered the floor. Beth gasped. The entire floor was parquet inlaid in a mosaic, deep burgundy around the edges radiating in to the twenty-four-foot face of a woman in profile. Her forehead and crown, above her olive cheek, was draped folds of cloth, created of varying shades of blond and yellow oak, so sinuous they seemed to move.

"Oh, Pat," Beth whispered. "The hood of gold."

"This is where we'll have the tables at first. And then, when it's time to dance, see, the tables just roll back ... into this alcove thing. When Kip brought up putting the mosaic on here, I thought, This is too much. I thought it would be so garish it would be a joke."

"No, it's lovely. Lovely. But how will you ever let anyone walk on it?"

"No problem," Pat said with breezy delight. "We had a guy who does gym floors coat it. There's so much polyurethane on it you could drive a Zamboni over it."

"And will everything be ready for the opening?"

"It kind of depends on Dad." Pat hooked a finger at a table shrouded with plastic near the entrance, where Angelo sat in animated discussion with the designer. "They can't get together on the foyer. It's a big deal to Dad." In his baseball cap and cutoff shorts, Pat looked, Beth thought, maybe twenty. He looked not just rejuvenated but reborn, as if his life had a pure, unclouded focus, for once his very own, into which he could pour all his energy and creativity and tenderness. The idea for Wedding in the Old Neighborhood had been born the night of Jill's wedding, late at night, after most of the guests had left the back banquet room at Cappadora's in Madison.

Jill's wedding had been held not very many months after Beth had returned, after a fashion, to work. Returning to work had been so monumentally consuming for her that she could barely face Jill's moving out. Jill knew things Beth didn't know, like the names of Vincent's teachers and the parents of his friends; she was the one who made it possible for Beth to do what little she could with the children and still spend hours dabbling in the solitude of her darkroom, laboring to finish things she'd once been able to do with her mind on autopilot.

The whole family, in fact, had begged Jilly to hold off on marrying Mumit, a mahogany darling from Bangladesh she'd met only four months before. She was too young; they were too poor. Jill shrugged them all off; and that night at Cappadora's, truly radiant, she'd swept off with her groom to a brief honeymoon in Door County before Mumit started graduate studies in chemistry.

"You have to admit, they're happy," Tree had said a few moments later. "It was a beautiful wedding. Don't you wish you could go to a wedding like this every week? The dancing and the ice sculptures? The dresses? I wish I could have gotten married four times." She'd looked at Joey then. "To the same guy, of course."

That's when Angelo had begun to scribble on the leftover napkins, scrolled with the young couple's names in gold leaf. He had been telling Pat for years that he was sick of the run-and-hustle of Golden Hat Gourmet. He wanted to preside over a place in his last years—to work beside his son and son-in-law in a crown jewel of a restaurant. Theme restaurants—part eatery, part theater—were springing up all over Chicago: fish joints with swimming mermaids behind glass built into the walls; rib houses housed in old filling stations, where the corn and garlic bread were delivered on trays fashioned from old hubcaps.

Why not an Italian wedding? he'd asked Pat, then Joey. Why not an Italian wedding, maybe three, four nights a week, with a bride and groom as the host and hostess? "With family style at each table, mostaccioli and meatballs, big loaves of bread—you'd save a ton on plating," Joey put in, excited.

"And a band—you'd have a band and a dance floor!" Pat cried. "The bride and groom, we could hire these kids who are trying to break into show business, you know, like kids who work at Steppenwolf or Second City, really beautiful kids. And they'd do the first dance...."

"*Bellissimo!*" cried Angelo. "Imagine it!"

"It'll never work," Augie grumped. "Too much overhead. What'll you do when she tears the dress the first night?"

"We could work out stuff," Pat shot back. "Arrangements with the tux and gown rental places. Free advertising. Stuff that's going out anyhow. Who cares about the style? It might even be better if they were a little vintage. We could buy up the bridesmaids' dresses you see for cheap in the paper—Dad! All the wait staff could be the bridesmaids and the ushers...."

When Beth, limp with exhaustion, took Vincent and Kerry home at two a.m., the men and Tree were still talking, pounding the table, making fresh coffee and pouring shots of anisette. In the car, Rosie said, "There is no fool like an old fool." But she was smiling.

Even so, deep down Beth had never truly believed the battle to move back to Chicago would really be engaged. And once engaged, she'd never believed it could be won. As she saw it, Pat was lucky they had established a fragile ecosystem in Madison. The press hounding had died down; Beth was bringing in money with her portraiture and photo editing. From what she could observe, the children seemed healthy: Kerry had learned to talk and walk more or less on schedule; from the light that burned under the crack in his door late at night, Beth discerned that Vincent had learned to read chapter books to himself. She and Pat even had a semblance of a social life, occasional decorous dinners with Rob and Annie Maltese, and she still went to Compassionate Circle meetings with Laurie almost every other month.

Beth mentally dug in her heels. Pat would no more be able to convince her to move back to Chicago than he would be able to get her to dance topless in the Capitol rotunda. She would move to Chicago over her own dead body.

She had not counted on the prospect of refusing over Pat's.

She had not counted on what had happened the weekend of Candy's wedding. The weekend of her lunch with Ellen and Nick. The weekend of the second red shoe at the twentieth reunion. The weekend of Pat's heart attack. The weekend of Beth's sin.

Looking back, Beth could see that it had really all been decided, in the few seconds it took Candy when she had called to tell her that the alarm on her biological clock had sounded, and she and her old pal Chris had picked the first Saturday they could find open on their mutual calendars. There would be a blowout party afterward, and they wanted wonderful pictures. Imagine me a June bride, Candy hooted, and Beth, to her own surprise, caught the spirit, started razzing Candy about whether she and Chris had tried the bed voyage, and had it been rough sailing? No, Candy had screamed, laughing—she'd just closed her eyes and pretended he was Jessica Lange!

Beth drifted through raw-smelling piles of green wood and unassembled white-laminated slabs that would be tables in the soon-to-be-completed restaurant. Given everything that happened the weekend of Candy's wedding, moving had almost been an anticlimax. Really, not bad at all.

Even the house, which Tree had chosen for them (Beth refused to even go and look), was not so bad, though located not five minutes from the Tremont Hotel, smack in the middle of the neighborhood where all of them had grown up. Even the children were better than they should be. After Pat told him the "good news," Vincent had disappeared for three hours. Pat had been sick with fear, but Beth was calm. She did not think anything serious would ever happen to Vincent. He had a tough hide. Once he'd thrown a bowling ball out a window and caved in the porch roof when Beth made him go to bed; he'd set off fireworks in the shell of a house under construction, and started more playground fights than Beth could count on both hands. And yet, she thought, if not thriving, Vincent was more or less okay. Maybe being around Angelo would help tame him. Joey had been a wild kid when he started working at Golden Hat; Angelo had turned him into a good kid.

Now with the men still deep in debate over the foyer, Beth drifted back outside and sat down on the ornate stone steps that had first caught Pat's eye. The rest of the battered brick exterior had been stuccoed in cream; wrought-iron grillwork and a sign were to go up next. She watched a gaggle of little black girls performing fast-footed double-dutch tricks on top of a carpet of shattered glass in the parking lot across the street.

Turning her face up to the hazy sunlight, she let herself drift back, five months—just five months—to the weekend of Candy's wedding, the weekend that had resulted in Beth's mortgaged vow to come back to Chicago forever.

Not half an hour after Beth had arrived, Ellen had suggested the lunch. Her husband and Nick Palladino were working together on rehabbing an old women's college in Hyde Park, turning it into a sort of cluster mall and day spa; Ellen had been gabbing on the phone with Nick when Beth arrived.

"Three guesses who's here," she trilled into the telephone. And then Beth, all unprepared, was talking with Nick, asking about his children, laughing about his running into Wayne on a casino boat in Indiana. Ellen interrupted to ask why they didn't just talk in person; they could have lunch and then Beth could see the site at the college. It was gorgeous, what Nick was doing marbling the interiors. Beth found herself agreeing to plan a brochure.

Why not? Beth wasn't due to show up at Chris's South Shore penthouse for the wedding reception until eight that night, and she'd given herself so much time to get to Chicago—fearful that she could no longer read road signs and remember how to pay tolls—she'd arrived before ten in the morning.

"We'll goof around all afternoon and you'll still be a few minutes from the reception. You could even change in Dan's house trailer. Come on, let's make it a giggle, Bethie," Ellen had said. "It'll be fun. We'll go to Isabella on the Drive."

Beth had taken leave of her senses. She'd agreed.

But when she and Ellen pulled up in front of the cafe's discreet sign, Beth felt the thump and shift of the avalanche, heard its creak. "It's in a hotel," she'd whispered to Ellen. Ellen looked genuinely panicked.

"I didn't think ..." she began. "Oh, Bethie, I didn't even think of it! Haven't you been in a hotel, ever? Ever since?"

"No," Beth breathed.

"Not even when you go to New York?"

"Bed-and-breakfast places," Beth said, measuring out her syllables. "Always."

"We'll just leave then," Ellen said reassuringly, starting the car. "I thought if it wasn't anywhere near where the reunion is ..."

"The reunion," Beth said.

"You know, the twentieth reunion. It's this weekend. Didn't they mail you ... oh shit, I guess they wouldn't."

"It's this weekend?"

"Yes, but Beth, that doesn't make any difference at all. I wouldn't go. Wayne, nobody would go. It just happened to be this weekend."

"Where?"

"In Elmbrook."

Beth put her hand over her mouth. "Oh God, Bethie," said Ellen. "Just forget it. I'll run in and see if Nick's there and we'll grab some deli and eat in a park. Okay? Will that be okay?"

But then, Nick appeared around the corner of the old hotel, his tightly curled black hair dusted with gray now, his suit as crisp as a silhouette cut from gray paper, and something in Beth's abdomen uncurled like a lazy cat.

"My God," she said to Ellen. "Look at him."

"He never gets old," Ellen agreed.

"What ... what the hell." Beth suddenly got out of the car and ran into Nick's welcoming arms, kissing his mouth, which smelled of cloves, for just a millisecond too long.

Had she known, at that moment? Looked back upon, it all seemed choreographed, an elaborate series of steps and movements that all led into a single cul-de-sac, a loop with no exit.

Beth leaned her head against the pebbled ledge of stonework and prepared to let herself remember that day. She had to be alone, and she had to do it exactly the same way each time. She loathed herself when she did; but a hundred times over the months since that day, she had replayed that afternoon and evening, right up to the knock at the door, with filmic exactitude.

The three of them shared a bottle of wine at lunch—Ellen abstemiously denying herself more than one glass as designated chauffeur. They talked about ... dumb stuff. The night they'd all piled into Nick's father's old Electra and crept up to the gates of the monastery once too often, and how the monks had let the Dobermans loose on them, costing Wayne the back of his leather jacket. The time some rogue from Cine Club had opened the wrong side of the treble curtains during the variety show, revealing Cecil Lockhart changing costumes between numbers, wearing nothing but a bra and tights, and how Cecil had simply struck a pose in the blue spot, while the audience sat frozen in horrified admiration. About smuggling Beth back from her job as a camp counselor in Lake Geneva one summer night so she could attend the wedding of Cherry and Tony; Cherry was seventeen and pregnant, and Bill and Evie had forbidden Beth to go.

She remembered, then, Ellen's beeper going off. Ellen bitching that Dan wanted her to run over to some goddamned glazier's office a few miles away and roust the guy out to the site; all the glass was cut short and the carpenter was giving birth. Could Nick run Beth over to the site when they finished eating? Sure he could. Then Nick and Ellen going out to switch Beth's camera bags and duffel to Nick's car in case Ellen got stuck in traffic, while Beth snuggled back into the deep red leather banquette and drank and drank from a second bottle of Pinot Noir, wondering how she would manage to close one eye to shoot Candy's wedding photos.

Nick returning, a halo of sunlight around his dark head as he opened the door into the dark bar. Sitting down, not across but beside her. The talk shifting then to something smoky and late-night, in spite of the daylight burning outside the awnings. Talk about the covered bridge in Lake County, where they had lain, exposed to the summer night in Beth's convertible, Nick with nothing left on but one of those angelic-colored peach or pink Ban-Lon shirts that would've made any other guy look effeminate, but that only emphasized Nick's construction-crew tan, his Tuscan perfection. Beth, shorts and halter top rolled to a tangle around her thighs and neck, urging Nick to go ahead and do it, Nick holding back, holding his bronzed hips just away from her, then swaying forward to let her grip him, crushing his mouth against her breast, then stopping, saying, No, we can't, we're going to be married, it's wrong. That no, all those rumors, even about Lisa Rizzo, were just that—rumors; he'd never done it before. He loved only Beth. He wanted only Beth.

She remembered Nick putting his arm along the back of the booth at Isabella, not quite touching her, and reminding Beth how he'd told her at his own wedding that he adored Trisha, he would be grateful for the rest of his life to her and Pat for introducing them, he couldn't be happier that she and Pat were getting married too, but the only regret he'd ever have was that he'd never made love to Beth.

And then—this was the part Beth hated herself for loving to remember the most—Nick bending forward and murmuring, "I still regret it, Bethie."

She hadn't said a word to him, only gone into the washroom to brush her hair, looking at her face in the gilded old mirror and seeing herself as Nick must have seen her, not as the gaunt scarecrow Beth who glared back at her from under fluorescent bulbs in Madison every morning, but as a slender, delicate woman worth desiring, the hollows under her eyes and cheekbones not pitiful but dramatic, her hair a tousled dark cloud, her lips puffed with arousal, knowing that when she came back, he would already have a key and would know the way to the elevator, to a room down a badly lit hall that hid the worn spots in the once-expensive wool carpeting—a room called the Violet Room, all done in antiques, with a marble washstand where Beth carefully hung her clothes, turning to Nick utterly without shame or even caution, knowing there was nothing to discuss or pledge or doubt. Nick telling her only, "Andante, Bethie. Andante. We waited a long time for this." Her nodding.

They had lain on top of the lavender coverlet for ninety minutes by the clock Beth glimpsed over Nick's head, touching and tasting each other slowly, until her every limb was shuddering, beyond her control, until the insides of her thighs were so slippery her leg slid off Nick's when she tried to roll onto him, until the moan at the back of her throat was constant, like a motor idling. Then Nick pulling back the sheets and—she thought of Pat once, when Nick entered her, not as long as Pat but thicker, more thoroughly filling her side to side, as she had always imagined him, beginning to move, slowly, slowly, shushing her when she began, frantically, to grab him and pull him closer, her mind emptied of everything but the feel of his golden, nearly hairless chest against her cheek, her treacherous body feeling pleasure for what seemed the first time since she had known such things were possible to feel, and then, when she could no more have stopped herself from coming than she could have stopped herself from exhaling, hearing the knock.

Hearing the knock and thinking, The hotel is on fire. Thinking, Well, so the hotel is on fire, we'll still have five minutes. Five minutes is all I need, this five minutes, for the rest of my life. The knock again, sharper. Her name. Loud. A voice, a woman's, not Ellen's, a voice she knew.

Stumbling up, realizing she was still half-drunk, staggering as she dragged her jeans on over the bucking nerves between her legs. Buttoning her shirt. Her name again. Another, louder knock.

The rest Beth knew as if she'd read about it in a newspaper. The flower wreath in Candy's hair as Candy stood outside the door in her champagne-colored sheath.

The absurd exchange.

"I thought you were getting married," Beth had said.

Candy's reply: "I did get married." Candy glancing at her watch. "I've been married for an hour."

Candy had never asked Beth who was in the room with her. She had not apologized, except to explain that Ellen's housekeeper had told her where Ellen and Beth were having lunch. Nick had disappeared into the bathroom; Beth had gone back into the room only for her purse, leaving behind her underwear, getting into the squad car parked in front, next to its driver, the blond bride with the French braid, as the cafe manager stared in astonishment from under the portico. Some time later, at the Parkside station, Ellen had shown up with Beth's bags, and, in the first-floor bathroom, Beth had changed into the top of her evening outfit; her tie-dyed shirt had been drenched in layers of sweat, sex sweat and then panic sweat. For the first couple of hours, as Candy and Calvin Taylor popped in and out to brief her on the events at the Hyatt in Elmbrook, where state cops and Elmbrook cops and Parkside cops were questioning guests at the twentieth reunion of the 1970 class of Immaculata High School, Beth had not even thought to call Pat.

It was getting dark when Candy, extricating the elaborate little wreath of vines and gardenias from her hair, had asked Beth if Pat was on his way. Ellen had gotten up to call him; but Beth had run after her, a surge of guilt giving her legs power, and so it had been she who told her husband that when the doors to the ballroom were opened before the dinner, a tiny Red Parrot tennis shoe had been found on a speakers' podium. Told him that it had been, of all people, Barbara Kelliher who saw it, Barbara who nearly passed out and went running, screaming for Jimmy. That at first Jimmy and Karl Kelliher had thought it was somebody's sick idea of a joke, but that Jimmy had the presence of mind to make sure nobody touched it, and that he had overcome all his misgivings and called Candy, knowing she was probably clinking glasses with her groom at that very moment, knowing she would never forgive him if it turned out not to be a joke. It was Beth who told her husband that she had known from the minute she saw the shoe, in a sealed bag in Candy's hand, known from the tiny green plastic "B" shoved on the laces to keep little fingers from untying them, that it was real—that it was Ben's.

It was Beth who had told Pat, heard him reply, then gasp, then heard the phone drop and finally disconnect. Beth who finally reached Augie and found out about Pat, and then rode with Calvin Taylor through the night, going over ninety, as he radioed the state squads they passed on the interstate. Who crouched at his bedside for three days, only vaguely aware of Rob's periodic relays of messages from Chicago. The shoe was authentically made in 1985. The shoe had prints. But the prints were somehow ruined. The interviewed alumni, fewer by many than five years before, were whistle-clean. The staff had seen no one even slightly odd or out of place.

The press were baying at the moon, Rob said. The way he'd heard it, some rookie cop or other started talking about the shoe as if it were common public knowledge that the first Red Parrot was the link to the kidnapping. Candy, who'd successfully suppressed that detail, was fulminating; overnight, Ben's face was again on the front of every Sunday edition in America. Since the media learned that Pat had been rushed to intensive care in Wisconsin, the hospital parking lot, Rob said, looked like the scene outside the prison when Gary Gilmore was executed.

All Beth wanted to do was watch Pat's face, watch its color slowly deepen from gray to a hint of rose. All she wanted to do was lean against his bed and pray for her husband, whom she thought of as her children's only surviving parent, to live. She sat, helplessly hearing Pat's goofy laughter when she'd told him that somehow, in spite of their best efforts, she was pregnant again, with Kerry—heard him singing the sleepy song to Kerry on the morning of her birth. Saw him drawing a heart with marker on her stomach when she was pregnant with Ben. Watched him playing shortstop in Colt League when they were kids, she licking Fudgsicles with a crowd of twelve-year-olds, Pat just enough older and more glamorous that the way he hiked his belt up over his palm-flat hips made the hair on her arms stand up. Beth sat there, stinking of infidelity, and she had promised Pat—God, fate—anything in those first few days.

And Pat, God, and fate had collected.

Beth had not spoken to Nick again. After he left repeated messages on her answering machine at home, about how was Pat doing and then about Ben, which Beth didn't return, she'd gotten a one-line note. "I'm sorry," it read, "but I'm not sorry."

Unsigned.

She'd wanted badly to call him then. She had fantasized about the sheer romantic rectitude of it—twenty-year journeys ending in lovers meeting. But not for her. Pat had lived. That was the end of it.

She and Candy had never discussed Candy's wedding day. But since she and Pat had arrived in Chicago, Candy had been over to the new house twice. She'd brought bread and salt, knowing Pat would appreciate it, and news on the "new" investigation. The trail was colder than a witch's heart. The Feebies were fucking around with the shoe prints; the reopened phone lines had sparked only a trickle of tips, most of frankly lunar quality. Barbara Kelliher had talked a handful of Immaculata volunteers into a small revival of the Find Ben center out of her house, but the turnout was feeble. Most of the old schoolmates were frankly aghast at the double curse on the reunions and shied away. Even Wayne only sent a check, for a thousand dollars.

There was, however, a new, computer-generated age-progression sketch of Ben being prepared. Something would pop, Candy said. Something. With the same certainty she knew that Rosie, riding in a car, would never forget to reach up to hold a button on her coat if they passed a funeral procession, Beth knew that nothing would pop, now or ever. But she thanked Candy anyway.

The second time Candy came over, the visit had just been social. They sat on the porch, Beth drinking coffee with brandy in it, Candy drinking seltzer because she thought she might be pregnant. ("I'm nauseated, but then I'm always nauseated," she'd sighed. "I probably have ulcers.") Beth nattered about Vincent. By September, Vincent had established a school record for missed homework assignments. The school counselor was evaluating him for an attention disorder, though Beth was sure he didn't have one: he spent long hours every night poring over the newspapers and watching TV, writing down game scores and filing them away in notebooks color-coded by sport. When Candy got up to leave, she'd half-turned and told Beth, "If you ever want to tell me what's wrong . . ."

Guiltily, Beth had broken in, "I hate being here is all. . . ."

But Candy had shaken her head. "I factored that in, and I meant that if you ever want to tell me what's *really* wrong . . ."

But Beth would never tell. Not Ellen. Not Candy. It was part of the pact she'd made, to have to carry this final betrayal of Ben, of Pat, inside her, alone.

She was almost drowsing in the sun when Pat came out and sat down beside her. "Dad and Kip the designer are having a fight now. So they're happy. Everything's going to be okay, though this bitch is going to cost an arm, a leg, and a torso."

He was worried. Beth breathed in softly through her nose; he was worried, so he was fine.

"That's good, Paddy," Beth said. And they got up to drive back to their new home.

Reese

Chapter 16

"They keep the stuff in gallon containers, plastic, like it was milk or something."

"But it's a solid."

"Yeah, it's like a cake, it's made of compressed crystals, and you just chip off as many of the granules as you need."

"How many did you need?"

"Well, we needed a lot. A hell—" Reese measured the shrink across the table; what would he think if a thirteen-year-old kid cussed? He'd probably think it was evidence of his mental illness. So that could work; Dad ought to get something for his money. "A hell of a lot. Almost a whole gallon."

"Where do you get . . . uh . . . ?"

"Calcium carbide."

"Where do you get this? Did you, like, have to lift it?"

"Lift it?"

"You know—steal it, Vincent."

This guy, thought Reese, was a very clue-free guy. "No," he said. "We did not steal it, partly because you can't steal it, they don't sell it anywhere anymore—except like a construction or a building place. Or a mining place."

"Mining?"

"Yeah, like copper mining or coal mining or something?" Reese glanced at the clock with the fat, red liquid-crystal numbers displayed behind the shrink. This had already taken twenty minutes. Reese immediately felt more hopeful. At this rate, he could spend the next forty minutes spinning out this yarn about the explosion; and, if Leadoff Man was on at one o'clock, and if he figured on Dad's customary twenty minutes to say goodbye to his pool buddy, Deuce—and the drive, the drive was, like, ten minutes on a Saturday—hey! he would be home by the bottom of the second, top of the third, no problem. Not only his favorite match (the Milwaukee Brewers, his old team, and the White Sox, his dad's team) but a game on which a lot was riding—quite a lot. He hated to miss a game he had money on, especially his own. If you had an operation the size of Reese's, you would miss some games. It figured. He wasn't, like, Tom Boswell or somebody. He didn't write about it for a living, being, basically, a kid. There were Stanley Cup playoffs on past his bedtime. And games during the day when he was at school. He kept up—with the papers and the radio and ESPN—you had to keep up—but it took a lot of organization, and he sometimes felt like he wasn't really watching the game for the fun of it. But this would be excellent. Quite precisely cold, it would be, if he could wrap up this little interview here and head on home.

"Coal mining?" said the clue-free one. He looked about the age of Reese's cousin Jill, whom Reese could easily make cry.

"Yeah, they used to use what they would call carbon lanterns, this little light, and then there was a water tank thing, and you'd put a few grains of this stuff in there, and the reaction would, you know, power the light a really long time."

"Why didn't they just use batteries?" the guy asked, a long curl of his hair falling forward right between his eyes in a way Reese found disturbing.

"Well, duh, you should pardon the expression, they didn't *have* batteries at first, and then, you know, batteries are real expensive. If you have to have this helmet light burning, like, twelve hours, you go through them pretty fast.

And if you got a whole bunch of guys, and every one of them has to have one of these helmets."

"Sure, I see, Vincent—economics." The shrink leaned back in his chair, comfortable-like.

"Right."

But the comfortable stuff was a wrong number, because right away the guy bored in again. "Okay, so, how did you get these chemicals?"

"They used to sell it in camping stores."

"But they don't now."

"No. They have Coleman gas and stuff."

"So, how did you get it?"

Reese looked at the clock. Very good, very, very good. Thirty minutes gone now.

"My friend Jordie's grandpa had it. He's an engineer."

"Did he know you took it?"

"No."

"And what did he do when he found out about . . . the incident? I mean, it's a pretty creative use of chemicals, but you can see how Jordie's grandfather might—"

"He was definitely unpleased. He was real unpleased."

"And your parents? Bet they were unpleased, too."

Reese gazed into the young man's eyes. He had practiced this, trained himself not to blink, lying awake in the dark until his eyes felt like they were coated with gum. It was worth it, though; it was a very excellent maneuver on teachers, for example, when they said, "Vincent. Can you explain this?"

"My parents were also unpleased. That's, uh, why I'm here."

"Your parents weren't satisfied with your explanation. . . ."

"Uhhhh, no."

"And they wanted you to talk to someone?"

"Well, yes, they think I'm crazy. That is, my dad does. My mom . . . "

"Your mother?"

"Well, my mother didn't pay much attention to it."

"Why?"

"Well, she's pretty busy with my little sister and stuff."

"Well, sure. But I think, you know, it's possible that she was very concerned about this and simply didn't . . ."

"Anything's possible."

"So, you took the initial manhole cover off. . . . How did you do that?"

"Well, you know, we lifted it."

"They're pretty heavy. You just lifted it up?"

"Yeah, but we had this long piece of pipe. I mean a very long piece, like five feet, and it was metal, not PVC. So we put it in the hole in there. . . ."

"And you pried up the manhole cover?"

"Yeah."

"Wasn't that really difficult?"

"Well, you know what they say—'Give me a lever and a place to stand and I can move the world.' Or something."

"They?"

"Well, he. Archimedes."

"Oh."

"Yeah." The guy looked a little concerned that a kid would know about Archimedes; adults had this idea of you and what you knew and the limits of it, and they got real hostile if you got outside it—they said you were showing off or being an asshole or whatever. So Reese said, "I saw that on TV."

"I see." The guy looked down at his file, and made a note, and pushed his glasses up on his hair. Now he looked even younger, like sixteen. Piece of cake, thought Reese. "So what do you think, Vincent? Is there any other reason, besides the explosion, that your parents wanted you to talk to me?"

Reese winced.

"Vincent." It sounded like getting stung by a wasp. "Vincent." It was just a wimpy, doofus name, a foot short of "Vinnie." He didn't care so much when his grandma Rosie called him "Cenzo," that wasn't so bad. But "Vincent"—hiss.

"Is something the matter?" Reese glanced at the clock . . . slowly now . . .

"Uh, just the name."

"Your name?"

"It's just that, it's not my name. Vincent."

"Oh. I see here, from your doctor—"

"Yeah, but see, what they call me is Reese."

"Oh. Why? Is that a nickname for Vincent?"

Utterly and completely clue-free, this guy. This guy didn't know whether he was in town or not.

"No," Reese said carefully, as if he were talking with one of the Wongs at school, the kids he tutored in math, who learned how to make clam chowder in biology instead of doing the regular stuff; they were all called Wong after the guy who wrote the biology book for simples. "My name is really Vincent Paul. But the guys . . . see, when I came to Chicago, this was last year, they heard them read my name off in the class, and somebody goes, 'Vincent Paul? Saint Vincent de Paul? He's named after the resale store!' And they all laughed, not real mean-like, but afterward, because I dress . . . I mean, I like my clothes real comfortable . . . they would call me 'Resale! Hey, Resale!' and then, 'Reese.' "

"That's a pretty neat conversion. I mean, if you like it. But maybe you *didn't* like it. Was that painful for you? Did you feel they were making fun of your clothes?"

"Shit no!" said Reese, and then caught himself. The "hell" was one thing. He could tell from the guy's face, which suddenly got very still, that "shit" was another. "Pardon me. But no. It didn't bother me."

"Why not?"

"What's your name?"

"Dr. Kilgore."

"No, I mean your *name* name."

"Oh . . . Thomas. Tom."

"Well, Tom, imagine being named Vincent." Reese glanced at the fat red lighted letter. "Look, Dr. Kilgore, the time's up. I think my dad's waiting for me. . . ."

"Oh, you're right, I guess. I was just thinking about those manhole covers. Sure. Well, next time we can talk more about . . ."

Absolutely, Reese thought. Totally. He figured his dad was paying this guy, like, fifty dollars an hour or something. The next time he saw this guy they'd be roller-skating on the el tracks.

"Sure," said Reese. And then he looked up, and goddamn his lousy luck and timing, there stood his dad, in the little kind of arched door to this guy's office, which didn't have a door—it didn't need one, because his office was the whole first floor, and people waited in a kind of porch thing. His dad had walked right in, which was very Dad-like.

"Mr. Cappadora," said the shrink, suddenly all smiles and hands. Reese had seen his dad have this effect on people before. His mom, with her big witch eyes and her skinny face—people backed off from his mom, not that she noticed (talk about people who didn't know whether they were in town or not). Point is, she creeped people out. But people wanted to give his dad a doughnut or something. Grandma Rosie's friends, they were all over him, like he was Reese's age, or Kerry's. And whenever he met Grandpa Angelo's friends, or even Grandpa Bill's, for that matter, they were, like, "Paddy! Paddy, my boy!" and they were giving him stuff. Everybody knew before they even met him, like Dad was their long-lost brother or something.

"Mr. Cappadora, I wanted to go over a couple of things with you, a little background. . . . I just didn't get a whole picture on the phone, because this was sort of in the nature of an emergency and all."

And Reese's dad was, like, smiling, sure, no problem, though Reese knew he had to be at the restaurant in, like, an hour to set up. Reese glanced at the clock. Bottom of the first now, for sure.

"Vincent," said his dad. "You can go sit in the car and turn the radio on." Vincent trotted out the door. Their big old boat of a Chevy was sitting at the curb, actually not right at the curb, about a foot off it, because his dad was not a very godly driver, though he always said, when they goofed around, "Italians are the best drivers, you know. Parnelli Jones. And Mario Andretti. All those guys are Italian."

"And the best singers," Reese would say. His dad was such a sap, but he was a good sap.

"Oh, absolutely. Frank. And Pavarotti."

"And Madonna. Trevor Ricci."

"Trevor Ricci?" his dad had asked, that once.

"From On the Rag," Reese told him.

"That's a band?"

"Yeah, dad, like Smashing Pumpkins. Or Nine Inch Nails. Or whatever."

And his dad would tell him this shit was not music—kids today didn't have any idea of what melody was—and Reese would say, yeah, for real, Dad, like those tapes in the restaurant, those two-thousand-year-old tenors singing "Santa Lucia" over and over and over till you snapped. Now that was music!

The frigging car was locked. Reese took a long breath. He turned around and slumped back into the guy's office, and was about to throw himself down on this kind of swing thing outside the door, when he heard his dad say, " . . . that his brother was three years old?"

Oh, terrific, thought Reese, and edged closer.

"I knew . . . you'd said on the telephone that there had been another child." The shrink seemed to be apologizing now. He had heard that tone, that hushed, church tone, like someone was hugging you with his voice, whenever a teacher found out at the beginning of a term about Ben. It was the magic ticket, at first. They gave you soft looks, their heads tilted, and smiled at you no matter what you did, but it didn't last. By November, he was always riding the bench in the principal's office, and listening to extreme, rational lectures about how no matter how severe the grief we had to endure was, we needed to keep priorities straight, we needed to be strong, and try to accept responsibility, because the world wasn't going to cut you slack, you had to make the grade, and you know you have the ability, Vincent. . . .

"So, Vincent was . . . seven when his brother died?"

Bastard, thought Reese. He could hear the collapse in his dad's voice. Dad couldn't handle much talk about Ben. The dumb bastard was going to drag Dad down a flight of stairs right now.

Vincent slid behind one end of a bookcase; it only stuck out about a foot from the wall, but he was small and thin for thirteen, so he could stand erect and eavesdrop without being seen. There was a fringe of soft dust along the back of the bookcase; Reese wiped it with his finger.

"He didn't die. That is, I guess, yes, he died. But we are not sure. Because Ben was . . . we believe Ben was kidnapped. In fact, the police are pretty much sure that happened, because of clues they found."

"Ahhh," said the bastard. Guaranteed shocker. "And you never found . . . ?"

"The case is still officially open, and the police still get leads sometimes.

Last year, in fact, well . . . the thing is, there's not much hope, but I pray to God we'll at least find out someday."

"Oh, man. Oh, you must . . . it must . . ."

"And Vincent was right next to Ben when it happened. I'm amazed you never read about this."

"I don't read much. You say he saw the boy being abducted?"

"No . . . he—Ben—was just a baby, he was three that spring, and he wandered off. . . . They were in a hotel lobby. We lived in Wisconsin then, and Beth had the children with her here for her high-school reunion."

"I see, I see. . . ."

"Did he talk about Ben? About how he feels about what happened to Ben? Because I think, it makes sense, doesn't it, if a kid is like this, the way Vincent is, that there's a link?"

"Well, we have to presume that something that utterly traumatic . . . But no, Mr. Cappadora, he didn't bring it up. And that's not necessarily bad, especially at a first meeting. Kids aren't like us in a therapeutic setting. An adult will try to go straight for the problem. You know, 'I want to leave my wife' . . . 'I hate my boss.' We're aware that we need to consider issues, and we have the economics of the situation on our minds. But with a child . . . a child might not come out and say, 'I have a problem with this.' And adolescent child, particularly, and he's what? . . . nearly thirteen . . . will approach things in an oblique way, and the importance is establishing trust. . . ."

"Yeah, that makes sense."

Frigging shit, though Reese. He's going for it.

And then his dad asked, "So, when he talked about the explosion? Did he tell you people were hurt?"

"No."

"Well, that's good, because nobody was hurt. Though this old lady fell off a chair in her kitchen and got an egg on her head the size of . . . fortunately, she knows Beth's dad. But I hope Vincent gave you some idea of the . . . scope of this."

"He told me about the calcium carbide."

"What they did, him and this Jordie Cassady kid, they poured a whole bunch of those crystals down the storm sewer. And they waited a long time.

If they hadn't waited a long time, it might not have been so big ... but see, Vincent knows about this stuff. It wasn't Jordie Cassady, though his father or his grandfather or whatever had the chemicals—in the garage, for Christ's sake. But Jordie's a good kid. I'm not saying my son is bad, I mean. But it was Vincent who knew how long to wait. He waited until the crystals were sufficiently mixed with the water in the main so that they could really ... and then they lit this fatwood log—you know, the kind of thing you use to start a fire in a fireplace...."

"He told you all this?"

"The police told me all this. And he told the police. I guess. They had to look down at the paper for the name of the gas it creates. Acetylene gas. When they lit it, you never heard anything like it. It was like ... ten percussion grenades. Windows broke. Stuff fell off people's shelves. The goddamn ground shook. Beth and I are like ... 'The furnace blew up!' And the manhole covers for three blocks—boom! Up in the air. It's one a.m. we're talking about."

Reese could hear his dad get up, and though he couldn't see him, he knew his dad was reaching for a bone, realizing he couldn't smoke in the guy's office, putting the pack back in his side pocket, and then pacing. He went on, "Thirty feet up, and these are big, heavy cast-iron mothers. We're lucky somebody's cat didn't get flattened—and if it had been daytime, Jesus, somebody would've been killed." Reese's dad sighed, hard, like he did at the end of a Saturday night, when he came in the door, in the dark, smelling of smoke and garlic. Reese would hear him; no one else was ever awake. He would hear his dad sigh, loudly, and then start rummaging through the drawers, and he would want to run down to him and jump him from behind, like he did when he was a really little kid. Back then, his dad would never put him back to bed. He'd make him cinnamon toast.

"The thing is," Reese's dad was saying now, "Beth, his mother, and I ... we've had a ... it's been very, very hard. And the kid, the kid is this outlaw. He does, so far as I know, no homework. I mean, he'll write a twenty-page report on something like the Monty Hall problem...."

"The Monty Hall problem?"

"It's this probability deal. If you have three doors, and there's a big prize behind one, and you first choose number one, and it's not there, I think they ask, is there any greater statistical likelihood that the prize is behind number two or number three?"

"Is there?" said the shrink, sounding as dumb as Kevin Flanner, whom Reese had once had to punch.

"Hell if I know. I run a restaurant. And these mathematicians all over the country, they write to each other on the computer and debate this thing . . . And anyway, once Vincent wrote a whole paper on this; he even called this guy in California in the middle of the night."

"That's very impressive. This is clearly a really bright kid."

"But the thing is, it wasn't assigned! It wasn't his homework; he had long division to do, and he totally blew that off, and didn't turn it in. So the school calls. They call ten times a week. They must have us on the speed dial by now, and I know, I know, we've all been through hell, but my God, the kid is going to go to the pen. . . . "

"I don't think there's any danger of that, really. But the thing is, next time, we really need to get the rest of the family in here—your wife and—"

"Beth won't come."

"I'm sure she's as troubled as you are."

"Well, of course Beth cares about what's happening to Vincent. But since Ben's been . . . since this happened, she's not that willing to open up anymore. She went to a grief group, and we've gone to counseling, Beth and me, right after I was sick, last year. Once. There's been a lot of pressure. She's just . . . she won't deal with it anymore. . . ."

"Why don't you let me talk to her? I'm sure we can work something out. And . . . are your parents alive? And Beth's?"

"My folks are. And Beth's dad."

"Well, this is a whole family thing, Mr. Cappadora. There's been a lot of pain here, and maybe not enough of a chance for everyone to sort it out."

"I can't imagine my parents in a psychologist's office."

Kilgore laughed. "Nobody can ever imagine it. But it grows on you. So why don't we try to set something up?" Kilgore ruffled some papers. "You know, I can't stop thinking about this. Manhole covers went thirty feet in the air? Somebody saw it?"

"Yeah. Two people actually saw it. And Jordie and Vincent, of course."

"Cool."

"What?"

"I mean, I'm sorry, Mr. Cappadora. Pat. What I should be saying is that this is definitely dangerous, oppositional behavior, in a sense, risk-taking to the point of self-endangerment. Of course it is." Vincent strained to hear the shrink. He had gotten up, was moving away, out of earshot. Vincent leaned forward a fraction of an inch, and the guy said, "But thirty feet in the air? Boom?"

Reese heard his dad laugh, softly, very softly. "Did he tell you he's a bookie?"

"Get out of here!"

"Yeah, he's a bookie . . . football, baseball, hockey. Not the ponies. He just handicaps those for my buddies."

"This is some kid you have here." They laughed together, louder this time. They were laughing about a kid blowing up a neighborhood.

Jesus, thought Reese. I'm fucked.

Chapter 17

Though in his opinion Kilgore had missed his calling as a vet (he had more horse pictures on his wall than they had at Churchill Downs), Reese didn't entirely mind going back a second time.

It was partly the look on his dad's face when Reese agreed to try seeing the shrink again.

It was the same look Pat got when he'd finished raking the oak leaves for the third time in the fall. Like he could pretend that during the winter, some magic thing would change and it would never be fall again and he would never have to do the same job. It was a look that in Reese's mind was accompanied by the sound of someone dusting his hands together—there, that's done. On the whole, Reese would have preferred scraping paint off the Sears Tower to another little get-together with Clue-Free Kilgore ("Call me Tom, or even Doctor Tom, if you want"—Reese couldn't believe it). But he liked that it smoothed some of the wrinkles off his dad's forehead, made his dad's eyes open a little wider, like eyes that weren't always trying to read little print. He knew that his dad had been after his mom, and Rosie and Angelo and

Bill, to go to a meeting with Kilgore, too. Rosie didn't care, but Bill wasn't too cool on the idea (or so Reese could gather from the one side of phone conversations he was usually able to get, because his dad had this, like, sixth sense about someone being on the extension, even if you put a handkerchief over it and held your breath).

The real reason Reese didn't mind going back to Kilgore had to do with Kilgore being a psychiatrist instead of a school social worker or something. Which Reese could easily tell, having spent a lot of time with school counselors when he was little over some goddamn school thing or other. Was he clinically depressed? Did he have (Reese's favorite; it made him sound like the reverse-vitamin-enriched kid) underachiever syndrome? Reese could tell Kilgore wasn't like the others because his office was decorated so cool, skinny white panels of handmade paper lined up with only one, the second to the last, violet, which went with some pillows Kilgore had on his couches. Now, if there had been two panels with purple, one on each end, it would not necessarily mean the guy had money. But the one, just the one, sort of thrown in there, was classy.

And sure enough, before he went back, Reese looked Kilgore up in the phone book and there he was, Thomas K. Kilgore, M.D.

So that meant Reese could tell him about the heart thing. Which he couldn't tell his dad. Since Dad had the heart attack, Reese didn't even feel like telling him when he had a sore throat. The heart thing—which had been going on for a while—would be a good way to use up time when he saw Kilgore again. It would distract Kilgore from Reese's eye—which he knew Kilgore would bring up; in fact, he knew his father had told Kilgore about it in advance. But not just that. Because it was getting concerning. The heart thing was happening almost every night now, not just once in a while, and sometimes in school, too. His heart would just take off, like a flapping seagull getting up steam to rise off the water, *bash, bash, bash.* The first time it happened, Reese thought, I'm fucking dying. And he tried to get up out of bed, but he was out of breath, so he lay back down. And gradually it slowed, until it felt like a regular heart again, which is to say it felt like nothing, like you didn't notice it. At first, because it didn't start happening until after the fight, he thought Asshole Kramer had broken a rib or something when he decked him. But it didn't hurt other times, like, at all.

So Reese figured it was inherited heart disease, getting started early. And when he went to the office, when Dad was talking to Kilgore in the sort of porch place outside, he got one of Kilgore's green books down—*Growing Up: Bio-Emotional Aspects of the Adolescent*—and tried looking up early-onset heart disease. He didn't get the book back in fast enough, though, because Kilgore had shoes like Mister Rogers (probably to keep from knocking up that lovely polished maple floor) and he was standing right there before Reese could do anything. Reese almost shed a skin.

"I'm sorry if I scared you," said Kilgore, all nice.

"It's okay." Reese was sweating. He took a deep breath. "Actually, I don't care, because there was this one thing I wanted to ask you about since I was going to be here anyway."

Kilgore sat down on the chair opposite Reese. "Ask away," he said.

"Where's my dad?"

"We're done."

"Okay, you're a doctor, right?"

"I'm a psychiatrist." Shit, thought Reese, okay. Let's make this as prissy as possible.

"But you have to be a regular doctor to be a psychiatrist? So you were a doctor once, right?"

"Yep, and I still am. I can prescribe antibiotics and everything." Kilgore smiled. "What happened to your eye?"

"You already know. I heard my dad tell you I got jumped by some asshole."

"I just wanted to see if you got the license plate."

"The what?"

"Of the truck that hit you." Oh, what a riot, thought Reese.

"Well, actually, yeah, I know the guy. He's a sort of professional jerk."

"Jerk-about-town."

"Yeah," Reese said. He liked that phrase. Jerk-about-town. "But whatever. I'm having this problem at night ... when I'm in bed. ..."

"Most guys your age have—"

Oh, Christ, thought Reese. "I don't mean *that!* I think I'm having a heart attack is what, and I don't want my dad to know, because he'll go totally crazy."

"Why do you think you're having a heart attack?"

Reese told him about the seagull in his chest. Kilgore got up for a minute and looked at a horse. Then he picked up a little spiral notebook and made a note, just like shrinks in the movies.

"Vincent, has this been a problem for a real long time?"

"Reese."

"Reese, of course. I'm sorry. It's just . . . you know, it's actually kind of weird. Not bad weird. Kind of neat. You don't meet that many kids who changed their own name. Just adults. Mostly ex-cons."

"I guess."

"But about your heart, Reese—how long have you been noticing this?"

"I figured you'd ask, so I actually thought about it. For months, off and on. But all the time since the fight."

"Was the fight a really bad experience? I mean, your eye looks like an undercooked Big Mac, but even so . . ."

"It wasn't any worse than any other fight."

"Been in a lot of fights?"

Reese sniffed, unconsciously. "My share."

"But this time you got hurt."

"I get hurt a lot."

Kilgore laughed. He fucking laughed! "Has anybody ever told you the meaning of the word 'counterintuitive'?"

"No." Reese bristled.

"I mean, if you get hurt a lot, are you the kind of guy who never makes the same mistake once?"

"Listen, Dr. Kilgore—"

"Tom."

"Tom—the reason I got beat is 'cause I wasn't ready for him, and also, the guy is like, five-ten, one eighty. . . ."

"So why'd you piss him off?"

Why? thought Reese. Why is a good question. He knew why. He'd set out to find Kramer and piss him off, he knew that. Picked Jordie up on the way. They had to look two places: in the conservation park, where Kramer normally smoked like a big boy, and at the playground near the hoops, which was where they finally did find him. Kramer and his sensational friend, the rubber dick, Angotti. "I don't know," Reese said. "He annoys me."

"More that day than any other time?"

"No."

"So why that day?" Reese thought hard. And as he did, Kilgore said, "Did you have trouble with your mom? Your dad? Something going on at school?"

"No," Reese said. "Honestly. It was an ordinary Saturday morning. I didn't have to get back for any games or sports scores until like two or three. So I was just riding my bike."

"Riding your bike . . ."

"I was riding my bike around the neighborhood. I went down to where these younger kids play street hockey, at this one kid's house. . . . "

"Do you play, too?"

"No," Reese laughed. "They're like nine."

"So why'd you go there?"

"I like to . . ." Reese looked up at Kilgore. He felt a single wing beat in his chest, subside. "I just like to watch this one kid play. He's really good."

"He a friend?"

"I told you, no, he's like eight. I don't even know him." Kilgore looked puzzled. "I just saw him in the neighborhood this one time and then I went past his house and he was playing street hockey. So I watched."

"How long ago was this?"

"Months. A few months."

"Months ago?"

"Yeah."

"So, when you go over there and watch, do you talk to this kid?"

"No, I just sit there on my bike and watch."

"Have you done this more than a couple of times?"

"What's the point?"

"Just curious."

"Well, like a dozen times. Maybe more. He's a really good street hockey player. And you know, I'm interested in sports."

"Does he remind you of somebody?"

What? thought Reese. "Like who?"

"Like maybe you, when you were younger."

Reese said, slowly, "No. He's really big for his age, for example No, he doesn't look like me at all." The gulls, suddenly, gathered with determination. Reese leaned forward on the couch and hugged his arms to his chest.

"Reese? Reese?" Kilgore was on his feet.

"It's happening right now."

"The heart thing."

"Yeah."

"Reese." Kilgore sat down on the couch beside him. "I'm going to tell you exactly what's happening to you. You're not dying. You're not having a heart attack. You're having a panic attack, and though it feels very frightening and very real—and it *is* very real—it's not dangerous. It's not going to kill you."

"I didn't really think ..." Reese gasped.

"But maybe you did. I know it feels like it's going to kill you because I had some once."

Kilgore put his hand on the middle of Reese's back. He pushed. Not like he was hugging Reese or anything. He just sort of pushed like Reese was a bicycle pump—press, release, press. "Blow gently and slowly out through your mouth, Reese. But keep it steady. Pretend you're blowing up a balloon." Reese did it, and as he did, he could sense the topping of the hill, the change that meant that, although the gulls kept beating, it was going to end, it was going to settle down. He gulped, waiting for the sensation of stopping. And as soon as it came, Kilgore didn't keep sitting there; he got right up and acted like nothing out of the ordinary had happened.

"So it was after the street hockey game?"

Reese still felt kind of sick, but he figured, if Kilgore was going to blow it off—actually, kind of a relief—he would play along. "Yeah. I went to get Jordie and we went to the playground."

"And you ran into ...?"

"I ran into Kevin Kramer."

"Jerk-about-town."

"Yeah."

"And what started the fight?"

"Well, they were playing basketball, and I sort of rode past."

"And that was it? Just right then, you were having at it?"

"No. Because I rode in between them."

"Ahhhhh."

"And this guy, his friend, Angotti, this guy with, like, gray hair, he's been held back so many times, had to jump out of the way."

"Oh."

"And they're like, 'Cappadora, you little freak' ..."

"And you didn't want to put up with that."

"Would you?"

"No."

"It wasn't so much that they were making jokes about ... my height. ..."

"No crime to be short. You know, Reese, it doesn't mean you're going to be short all your life, either."

"What they were saying was, I was, you know, stunted ... all over."

"I see."

"This guy is like a sophomore. Kramer."

"I see."

"So I just said some thing, some ordinary thing, like ... 'Don't talk about your old man like that,' and he goes out of his mind. ... "

"Is this the first fight you've had with Kramer?"

"Yeah. Well ..." Reese considered it. "Not really the first *verbal* fight."

"First physical fight."

"Well, he just moved here."

"I see."

"Right."

"But your other fights?"

"Look, people just can't keep their mouths shut."

Reese got up off the couch and went to stand in front of one of the horse pictures—he realized that the man holding the horse's bridle was Kilgore, and there was a little girl sitting on it, a little girl with blond hair like

Kerry's. She had on this miniature-sized riding hat, a black thing with a big brim. You could hardly see her face. "Is that your kid?"

"My little sister."

"Your sister?"

"She's ten now. Big Irish family. There are eight kids. I'm the oldest and she's the youngest. I was already in medical school when she was born."

"What's her name?"

"Tess."

"They're not all T's, are they?"

"Yeah. Unfortunately, they are," said Kilgore. "Terrance. Tracey. Tara."

"You got pretty lucky."

"Don't I know it." He got up. "Reese, we're pretty much out of time. I want you to remember the balloon-blowing thing, because that kind of breathing helps bring a panic attack to a close sooner, if you can concentrate on it. Okay?"

"Okay."

"And next time we'll talk more about how you can stop having them. And why you're having them."

"Okay."

"And there's one other thing I want to show you." Kilgore reached out one hand and Reese cringed—Here comes the hug, he thought in disgust. But all of a sudden he was down on one knee; it was as if the guy had dug a piece out of his neck with the lit end of a sparkler.

"Jesus Christ!" Reese screamed. He was nearly crying.

"It won't hurt long," said Kilgore, and he was right. The place, the hollow just behind Reese's earlobe, which had felt electrified a minute before, was now simply limp. Reese pressed it gently. It felt pretty normal. "I'm sorry. But you had to understand how this depends on surprise."

"What'd you do?" asked Reese, rubbing his neck.

"We used to call them pressure points," said Kilgore, taking Reese's hand and putting his thumb against a place between two of his fingers? "See? You push ..." And *bam!* Reese pulled his hand away.

"How'd you learn that?"

"Medical school. There are nerve bundles all over the human body. See?"

Kilgore showed Reese a point behind the elbow, one near the small of his back. "You can look in an anatomy book and see where a lot of them are. Here—you can borrow mine ... And you can tell when you find one, because you can make that place start to tingle if you press it just a little. And if you press hard, it will hurt like anything. You don't usually press that hard on yourself, of course."

"What're you ...?"

"It's just, Reese, you can bring down an ox if you know the pressure points, and if you're going to keep on getting in fights, I just thought you might ..."

"Well," said Reese. "Thanks. I guess."

"I'm a short guy, too," Kilgore said. "See you next Saturday."

Chapter 18

The so-called family session lasted longer than double overtime, as far as Reese was concerned. It wasn't just that he was embarrassed by all of them (Grandpa Bill in aqua-and-green golf pants and Grandpa Angelo dressed like a pallbearer); he just had a feeling that getting them all together in one room was going to lead to ignition and liftoff. When his dad told his mom about the session—didn't ask her, just told her—she got that wild-horse look in her eyes that Reese recognized only too well.

Go slow, Dad, he thought. There be dragons here.

In those agonizing, dull minutes in the waiting room before it all started, Kerry (who also looked just great, because she'd insisted on wearing her purple net tutu) had really humiliated him. She'd had all five of her Red Riding Hood finger puppets on one hand. "Be the wolf, Vincent," she said all of a sudden. He took the wolf-head puppet and put it on his index finger and waggled it at Red Riding Hood. "I eat little girls like you for breakfast," he growled.

"You suck," Kerry said sweetly.

Great.

And then, of course, Grandma Rosie had clicked her tongue, once, so softly Reese knew it was an extra-special click just for him, like *he* taught Kerry to swear, which he didn't; Kerry was able to cuss from birth. Just at that moment, Tom came out and herded them all in, and they spent another eternity getting all shifted around on Tom's couches and chairs.

Reese felt sorry for Tom. Talk about having your work cut out for you. Reese had never, not once in his life, heard Grandma Rosie say anything, a single sentence that began with the words "I feel." She just gave commands; she sized up stuff. He had never, on the other hand, heard Grandpa Bill say a single sentence that wasn't in the form of a question; Uncle Bick said talking to his dad was like being the host on *Jeopardy.*

And true to form, right away Grandpa Bill had said, "What can we do you for, Doctor?"

And old Tom didn't waste time then, he jumped right in. "I don't want all of you folks to think we're here only to help out the master criminal here," he gestured at Reese, like he was pointing a pistol and firing. "It's my hope that you'll all get something out of this, or I wouldn't have put you all through arranging your lives to get down here. But I also know none of you wants to see a kid you love in this much pain, and Vincent—our buddy Reese—is definitely in a lot of pain."

Everybody, even Kerry, nodded. "But what I've been hearing about, I'm just guessing, but I think it's that this is a whole family in a lot of pain, for a lot of years, and Reese can't get out in front of this until, basically, we open it up and let a little fresh air get to it. You know what I'm saying?"

Grandma Rosie looked at Tom as if he had just told her she should shave her head, put on bells, and become a Buddhist nun.

"I do not see," she said softly, "how we can talk in this room and help Vincenzo be good."

"There's no guarantees we can, Mrs. . . . uh, Mrs. . . ." Tom was waiting for Reese's grandma to say, "Call me Rose." Wait on, Tom, wait on, Reese thought. "Mrs. Cappadora, there's no proof that in this situation, the healing going to come from talk. But this kid you love is a real angry kid. And you he people he loves. He might not act like that all the time, but that's the fact. And with a kid this angry, there's a whole world out there with its hands out, and the stuff in those hands is stuff you don't want for Reese. Next time it might not be sewer covers."

"You mean drugs," said Grandpa Bill.

"Bill," Tom said, not taking any chances on the old cozy first-name front this time. "Yes. There's certainly that, and other kinds of acting out. So what I want to know, while I've got you all here, is, is this new? I mean, was Reese always kind of the angry young man . . . ?" Tom smiled, right at Reese.

Nobody said anything.

"You've got a great kid here," Tom went on. "A kid with a mind that just doesn't quit. You all know it. And with a kid like this, the waste could be big."

"He came out angry," said his mom. A hundred years of silence, and then *boom*—this. Good old reliably nuts Mom. Everybody, even Kerry again, turned to look at her. "He was always hard. I mean, since he was a baby, he had his own ideas of how he wanted to do things. Not all bad ones. I'm not saying Vincent is bad."

"Okay, Beth, okay. But when you say he was 'hard,' was he difficult, like this?"

"No," she said. "He would only get mad at me when he was little. But after Ben died—"

Grandma Rosie gasped. "Beth," she said. "Benjamin is not dead."

"Oh, Rosie," said his mother. "He is dead. He's dead. If he wasn't dead, I would know it."

Here we go, thought Reese, let's talk about Ben for . . . like our whole lives.

"Beth," Grandpa Angelo said gently, "The children . . ."

"But I can't stand it! Everyone keeps pretending he's going to come back. I think that's half of what makes Vincent crazy. It makes me crazy. I don't care, Pat. I came here and why waste the money? I'm going to say this. I'm sick of it. 'Never give up hope.' 'Pray, pray, pray.' Well, why *don't* we give up hope? And just let whatever happens happen?"

"Because you can't just bury him, Beth." His dad spoke up. "You want to just bury him before we even know. I know why you feel that way, but . . ."

I'm here, thought Reese. I'm here.

"It sounds like there are a couple of camps in this," Tom put in, "and Reese is right in the middle of them. Reese, what do you think?"

Reese said, "Nothing. I don't think about it that much."

"Come on," Tom urged him. "Have you ever heard of the big purple elephant in the living room? There's this elephant right in the middle of the living room, and the whole family walks around it and pretends it isn't there. . . . You've got to think about it, Reese. It's right in front of you."

"I don't, though."

"I don't, either," said his mother, and a warm pulse in Reese beat toward her. "I don't think about it ever. What does thinking about it do?"

"Well, in my experience, it sometimes, sometimes gives you some peace," Tom suggested, and then they were off, his mom pointing out that the family did not put Easter eggs on Ben's grave at Easter now or in the past. "He doesn't have a grave to begin with," she'd snapped—or hang a stocking for him, or buy him birthday clothes one size larger each year . . . and his grandmother putting in that she *did* pray for Ben every day, and so did her daughters. . . .

Tom struggled to keep up, asking, "Does it bother you that Beth doesn't do that, Mrs. Cappadora? If you think she's given up, how does that make you feel?"

Grandma Rosie reached down and fingered her locket. "I am sorry for Beth. I have known Beth all her life. I love Beth like she is my own child. I am sorry for her, because she . . . she has lost her heart. She has lost her faith. . . ." His mom snorted. Reese couldn't believe it; it was like she'd jumped up on the uneven parallel bars. But Grandma Rosie wasn't about to give up: "Bethie, dear one, you know you have gone away from God. . . ."

"Oh, no, Rosie. No, Rosie. It was God who took the powder, Rosie. A long time ago. No offense, but . . ."

Gak and gak. Back and forth. Reese realized that, although he had never heard these words spoken, they were as familiar to him as the national anthem. He covered his ears. Finally, from the white throw pillow on the floor where he'd taken refuge, he could see the forest of their legs lengthen as Tom ushered them from the room. An instant later, Kerry's little purple twigs bounded out from behind the sofa. At last, Tom leaned down and said, "Hey, buddy, you got a minute to spare here?"

"I got five minutes, no more. In five minutes, I'm trying out for the White Sox."

"What position?"

"Center field."

"I don't want to interfere with a career in the show."

"They waited this long," Reese told him, "they can wait five more minutes."

"Actually, we've got maybe fifteen good minutes here."

Reese got up. "Maybe I should get down on the couch here, Tom, like in the movies. I never did that. You could say, 'So, Mister Cappadora, why do you think you look like a sheep?'"

"I think you'd fall asleep."

"Why?"

"You look like your candle burns at both ends, 'bro. Are you putting in enough sack time? Is it the business?"

Tom meant the betting. "No," Reese said. "That's just . . . I do that mostly on the weekends."

"It drives your father nuts, you know, Reese." Reese knew it didn't, not at all. His dad was as proud of his business as he was ashamed of it. It was the same way Grandpa Angelo felt about gangsters. "Most kids your age, they have a paper route."

"I can't have a paper route."

"Too strenuous, huh?"

"No." He hated to do this to Tom. "Kids . . . a kid once got kidnapped on his paper route. It was very famous. Johnny Gosch? They never found him. In my family, it's just not a thing . . . My father . . . my parents would freak. . . ." Tom wasn't like other adults, though. His face didn't get all waxy and soft, like he didn't know where to put his cheek muscles, when Reese said it. He just shook himself a little—like, as Grandma Rosie said, when a goose walked over your grave—and plowed right on.

"And what about you? Would you freak?"

Stiffly, Reese told him, "It wouldn't scare me."

"Not even a little?"

"I don't know. Anyway, who wants to get up at goddamn three o'clock in the morning?"

"Not me," said Tom. "Or you. Especially if you get to bed pretty late. Do you go to bed at a reasonable hour? Ten?"

"Yeah, I go to bed." Reese shifted. "But then I have to wake up and change the tapes, and it takes me a while to settle down again."

"The tapes?"

"I sleep with music on."

"Must be very restful for your parents."

"I use earphones."

"What d'you listen to?"

"Mostly classical stuff at night. And opera. Italiano. You know. It's a birth defect, like you being a Red Sox fan."

"Pardon me, Reese, but getting up to change the tape deck all night doesn't exactly sound like healthy slumber to me."

"It works."

"So this is why you look like death on a cracker."

"Well, it's not the music. . . ."

"What is it?"

Now. Reese thought. Now he was going to have to talk about it. He'd mentioned the running dream last session, just before they ran out of time. In fact, Tom had accused him of doing it on purpose, knowing perfectly well the time was up and the family was coming this time. Old Tom felt cheated; shrinks cranked up on dreams.

"Okay. It's the dream I started to tell you about."

"The running dream."

"Yeah."

"Where are you in it?"

"I'm in this big room, and the tiles on the floor are what I'm looking at. They're like . . . they look like meatballs. It's nutty. They're pretty ugly."

"Are you alone?"

"Shit, no!" Reese looked up. "I'm sorry. No. There's a zillion people there, and they're all talking."

"What are they saying?"

"Well, that's the thing. They're not saying anything."

"You said they're talking."

"I can tell they're talking because I can see their mouths move. But I can't hear anything. I'm just standing there, but I'm *not* just standing there." Reese frowned. "I'm running."

"But you can't move."

"Is that how everybody feels?"

"It's a common thing that happens in anxiety dreams. What matters is, who's chasing you? What are you running from?"

Reese strained. He tried to take himself back—the gulls flapped again, as if they were getting pissed, but it was okay, he knew how to breathe it down. He tried to look behind him. "There's nobody behind me. I'm running . . . *after* somebody."

"After who?"

"Uh . . . I don't know."

"You do know."

"I don't know. I mean, if I knew, why wouldn't I tell you?"

"You tell me why you wouldn't tell me."

Because I'll die, Reese thought. I'll die here on your couch if I tell you. Or maybe it'll be worse than that. Maybe I'll just shit all over your couch. Reese lay down on the couch, folding his elbows over his eyes. It wasn't the crying he minded, or even Tom seeing him; it was that he felt so damn worn out, so hauled down by anchors.

"I'm running after . . . somebody on the other side of the room."

"Who?"

"I don't know who."

"Listen, buddy," said Tom, getting up and tapping on the frame of one of the thousand horse pictures. "You know what I make an hour?"

"What?"

"A hundred and twenty bucks an hour is what I make."

"Well, congratulations," Reese said, sitting up. "Maybe you can buy some more horse pictures."

"And you know who pays me that hundred and twenty bucks?"

"Who?"

"Your dad."

BFD, thought Reese. It was, after all, his dad's idea, this whole head-shrinking party, in the first place. "So?"

"So, do you think your dad is a complete fool?"

"No, I don't think my dad is a complete fool."

"Well, you must. Because, if your dad wants to pay a hundred and twenty bucks an hour for you to sit here and jerk around every Saturday, and sometimes during the week, if he's so rich that that doesn't even matter to him, that's jake with me. I'll take his money...."

"You would, too," Reese shot back. "You'd take it, even if you knew it wasn't going to do me any good...."

"Sure, for a while. Why shouldn't I? I make money; your dad feels like you're talking to someone, everybody's happy. Except there's this kid who's on the way to first-offender boot camp, which is you, but that's your choice, buddy. I'm not your mommy. I see plenty of tough guys come and go. They're all losers." Reese felt his fists begin to curl. Different from the rest, he thought. You preppy prick. "But pretty soon, at some point, ethics dictate that I'm going to have to say, 'Well, listen, your kid's got his head up his butt, and he isn't going to say jack to me—' "

"I'm going," Reese said.

"So go," said Kilgore. "I still get my hundred and twenty bucks."

Reese got up. His face was itching, crawling with ants. Air. He needed some air. Then he whirled around. "You know exactly who it is," Reese told him then, his voice snake-flat, the voice he knew scared the hell even out of the two Renaldo brothers, the twins who were juniors and had necks the size of Reese's waist. The voice Reese didn't even know where it came from, that sounded like some freaking Damien voice, even to him.

"Okay. Who is it? If you don't mind my asking."

"It's my brother."

"Oh. Your brother. Which brother?"

"Fuck you," said Reese. "Fuck you sincerely."

"Thank you very much, I'm sure. Which brother?"

"I only got one brother. Which is to say I have no brother. It's Ben. It's Ben."

"And what's he doing? Come on, Reese, what's he doing?"

"He's walking out the door."

"Where?"

Reese thought he might puke. His throat tasted like acute Slim Jim poisoning. He thought he didn't dare open his mouth. But he made it split, pried it like a hinge, and moved his tongue. Finally, he fetched a voice. "He's walking out the door of the hotel."

"Did you see him, Reese?"

Reese shouted, "I don't know! I don't know! I'm running, and I'm running. But I can't move...."

"Did you move, Reese, in real life?"

"I don't know! I was just a kid...."

"Look at him, Reese. Look at Ben."

"I can't even see him; his back is to me. And so is hers...."

"Hers? Your mother?"

"No.... No." Reese struggled to breathe.

"Ellen? Your aunt Ellen?"

"No. No. The little old lady. The little skinny old lady."

"What's she doing?"

"She's walking behind Ben. She's following Ben. She's ... opening the door for him."

"Reese," said Tom, gently, so soft, sitting down next to him on the edge of the sofa. "Do you think this really happened? Or is this part of the dream?"

"I think it's part of the dream," said Reese, "because it really happened." And in a moment he would remember with hot shame for years, even after it all came down, he reached out and took Tom's hand. And Tom, thank God, acted like he didn't even notice.

Part Two

$Beth$

$Chapter$ 19

Kerry was screaming with such earsplitting might that Beth barely heard the doorbell.

"Stop, Kerry!" she ordered, in the military voice she hardly ever used anymore.

But once Kerry stopped, Beth wanted to join her in a few righteous screams herself. The bell was ringing with the kind of persistence that told Beth she would not be able to pretend not to be home—it was ringing, in fact, as if someone outside were on fire.

"Wait!" she yelled. "Coming!" The bell fell silent. Then it rang again.

If she let go now, Beth could kiss all hope of untangling Kerry's hair goodbye; the child would not let her mother come near her again with a brush in hand for three days, minimum. But because Beth so rarely remembered to brush Kerry's fine reddish-blond hair—which Ellen insisted was an inheritance from her godmother—it was a welter of rats and snarls under a soft veneer. Kerry simply ran a wet brush over the top every morning before school. To Kerry, smooth on top was combed, just as under-the-bed was

clean. "My teacher thinks my hair has a lot of natural body, Mama," she told Beth. "She says it's like Rapunzel."

Christ, Beth thought, the teacher's a twit and she must think I clean toilets at a trailer park. "That was nice of her," she'd told Kerry. "But she really thinks that because your hair is so full of tangles it sticks out from your head three inches. If you don't brush it, Kerry, it's going to break off and you'll have little cowlicks all over. Real ugly." Beth had risen this morning with a small, unexpended premium of energy; she had learned to make use of these, because she knew the drill of her ordinary days—all the other days she had nothing but minimum motion to give. She intended to buy Vincent some cleats today as well. But first she wanted to set Kerry to rights.

"I do brush it. Every day," Kerry told Beth, her voice skating along the midline edge of whining and aggression. "It looks good."

"But once in a while *I* have to," Beth answered. And everything that came next was choreographed. All Beth had to do was wave the brush in any of the air space around Kerry's skull and Kerry, the most docile of children, would transform herself into a rabid wolverine, kicking and squirming and letting out yowls that made Beth want to bite her.

Distracted by the thought of some Jehovah's Witness standing on the porch, his eyes raised in a prayer for strength to minister to the occupants of a house from which such screams issued, Beth attacked one more particularly horrific clump. As she did, the hairbrush snapped, and Kerry tore off, out the door of Beth's bedroom and down the hall stairs for the front door, while Beth slowly picked up the shards of shattered plastic, and then followed her daughter, swearing softly.

"Are you in sixth?" she heard Kerry say as she rounded the last curve of the staircase. The door swung half-open between Kerry and the visitor.

". . . in third? Were you the soybean?" She heard a child's voice, older, ungendered, say.

"Actually," said Kerry, "I was the feed corn." The spring festival, thought Beth. Had Pat gone?

"Who do you have?" the voice asked.

"Cook," said Kerry.

"I had Cook!" said the voice. "She's really nice!"

Beth jumped down the last two steps and put her arm around Kerry.

The bright noon sunlight, after the dark upstairs hall, had the effect of backlighting with a hard spot; Beth held up her hand to shield her eyes, but the kid was still a shape cut of black paper, a sun-shot halo around his head. He was big, though, big and heavyset, she thought, for a sixth-grader, but then Vincent was so small. She bumped her hip against the screen door to open it.

Years before, Ellen's mother had suffered a petit stroke. And long after, she would tell Beth it was possible for such brain events to happen in an instant, the time it took to speak a word; you could have them in your sleep and wake with nothing more than the sensation of having weathered a headache. But though the cadenza of sound Beth heard was as loud as a ripsaw and sent her staggering against the opening door, she did not lose an instant of consciousness. And she realized just as quickly that though the noise filled the street, the world, no one else could hear it. She reached up for her temple; the sound pounded, but now with a transparent quality; she could hear everything around it; the wind in the maples like water rushing from a pipe, crows clucking at each other like castanets. Bile sloshed over her tongue. But she gripped both sides of the door frame and bent nearly double, trying to measure her breathing and muster enough oxygen to fight the gathering pitchy dots that licked at the space in front of her eyes.

"Are you all right?" said the kid, backing off.

"Mommy!" cried Kerry in a tinny voice.

"I'm ... all ... right," Beth gasped.

"Mommy, are you going to puke? Should I get Georgia?"

The kid was backing down the three front steps. With real fear in his voice, he told Beth, "I mow lawns. I was just dropping off this thing with my phone number. I can do it later. I'll come back."

But Beth was now getting breaths she believed were restorative. How much time had passed? A minute? Ten? She couldn't stand upright, but she waved her hand at the kid, and at Kerry, in a gesture she meant to mean, No problem, right with ya. She did not want to terrify him. She tried to think of a plan, pitchforking options aside like sodden leaves. "Actually, I really need the lawn mowed," she said. "Could you do it today?"

The kid was astounded. "All right, sure! I just have to get . . . get my stuff. We live, like, two blocks."

"You don't need a mower. We have a mower," said Kerry helpfully. "And my big brother is supposed to do it. He's in high school. But he's lazy like a snake." The boy was already running down the walk, in high gear. Beth grabbed Kerry's arm, too roughly.

"Mommy, are you still sick?" Kerry said, looking up.

"No, I just . . . Do you know that boy?"

Kerry blushed; her skin was a video of emotional responses. Pat called her "the Visible Woman."

"Mom," she said seriously. "I was in my own house. That's not the same as stranger danger. He's a big kid in school."

"Oh," said Beth, her heart now beginning to slow. Okay, she said to herself, okay, okay. "What's his name?"

"Jason," said Kerry. "He's on patrol. . . . No, Mom, no, I'm wrong. Jason is the kid with the Gameboy, and you know, Mom, he got reported, because he was standing there playing Mortal Kombat when he was supposed to be watching the little kids go—"

"So you don't know his name?"

"It's Sam. He's Sam Kero—Kero-something."

Kerry followed Beth through the back of the house. Beth ran for the basement stairs, shoving their sleeping dog, Beowulf, aside with one foot; he coughed irritably and moved into the family room. Down into the basement, throwing open the door of the darkroom, fumbling for the light switch—the bulb was out, she knew that, had meant to replace it, the safe light would have to do. Searching in the eerie redness for her biggest bag, Beth pulled out her work camera, her Nikon F-90, brand-new, and rummaged in the mini-fridge for film. She thought as she pulled out the film carton and ripped it open with shaking fingers, 200 should be okay, and the color is absolutely essential, and the yard has patches of light; it's only dark under the trees.

"Are you going to work, Mommy?" asked Kerry.

"Kerry!" Beth shouted. Her daughter jumped. "Kerry—yes, you know what? I forgot I have to take some leaf pictures. So, it's okay if you want to go play with Blythe, okay? Go ahead."

Beth snapped open the camera back and pulled the film leader, fitting it to the sprockets. She slapped the back closed and heard the whirr of the automatic winding. Her hands were slick with sweat. Line up, she thought, line up. I will use a telephoto; and I will switch to manual focus. So I can control ... Kerry, as if from very far away, over mountains, was calling her. Kerry stood at the top of the basement steps.

"My hair is still a mess," she said, bored. "And you always say you have to watch me cross at rush hour."

Beth bounded up the stairs, cradling her camera against her breasts; sweat pasted her T-shirt to her sternum. "Just put your band on, okay, Kerry?" Kerry languidly pawed through her backpack, which lay on the hall floor, and found her rubberized band with glitter ladybugs on it. She wound her hair into an askew ponytail while Beth watched her, panting, with a hunger for her to be gone that Beth later realized must have horrified Kerry.

Georgia was pulling heads off her geraniums across the street. She waved to Beth, breezily, and pointed with exaggerated welcome to the door of her own house; that meant, Beth thought (line up, line up), that Blythe was home; Kerry could play. Line up, Beth thought, and made her own large gesture, pointing to her camera. Georgia made a big okay sign. They traded daughters back and forth all week.

Her fingers now actually slimy on the camera's surface, Beth slowly closed the door behind her. She let her eyes skim the line of family Christmas photos that marched along the walls, level with her chin. She leaned against the door. And then she was up, running for the second floor, pawing through Pat's drawers where he kept his cartons, hidden from her since his surgery, under his baseball programs and the collection of crayon drawings Vincent had once made, and the large paper cap he kept in a flat box, which he had worn during Kerry's Cesarean birth. Beth ripped the top of a package of Merits—tearing off not just the foil but an inch of the pack, so that the cigarettes tumbled and scattered on the carpet. She pulled open the closet and stuck her free hand deep into one of Pat's coat pockets. He had matches. He always had matches, though he refused either to lie to her or admit he still smoked outside the house.

Beth lit the cigarette, pulling in deeply, unaccustomed, choking. And then she walked into Kerry's room and out onto the little porch that overlooked the backyard. She sat down against the wall, nudging aside the hell of Barbies that Kerry customarily left lying outside in desolate nudity under the dusting of September leaves.

She smoked.

The sweat dried on her shirt, stiffened. The sun burned on her face, but her body was icy, trembling. Adrenaline made her fingers needle and itch. She set the camera down gingerly, afraid she would drop it.

She heard the kid open the back gate. That was all right. She could tell him that the mower was ... but then, no, she saw him trundling it around the side of the house, he'd already found it. He waved to her, looking straight up at her with round gray eyes, eyes that still looked almost lashless. Shielding the camera with her arms like a secret, Beth stood up and yelled to the kid, "I'm taking some pictures of the leaves. It's my job. I take pictures."

He nodded and leaned over, expertly starting the balky Toro on the first tug. And then he squared his shoulders and began to move, cleanly, starting from the back and making lines the length of the yard.

Beth leaned on the railing to steady her elbows and adjusted the zoom. No time for a tripod. She shot his face in profile as he moved out from the shade of the willow and worked his way past the swing set. When he rounded the patio, she shot him full on, as he lifted his head to wipe a sheen of sweat off with the arm of his flannel shirt. Letting the automatic advance roll, Beth shot at the rate of an exposure every few seconds. And in minutes, long before the kid had finished half of the backyard, she had shot the whole roll of thirty-six. She ran downstairs and searched for her dark bag. She couldn't find it. Line up, Beth thought, line up. You can do this. You've changed film by touch alone in a dozen dark places. She flipped off the lights, closed the door, and reached for her spool, winding the film to dry it.

And then she kneeled on the floor in the red light, her head pressed against the front of her handmade sink, which Vincent had painted with black marine paint, and said, "Domine Deus, Agnus Dei, Filius Patris; qui tollis peccata mundi, miserere nobis ... miserere nobis."

She heard Vincent open the door upstairs, heard it swing back and crash against the wall.

"Vincent," she whispered, imagining herself summoning him to find her purse, give the kid ten bucks. But her voice was less than a whisper. She dragged herself to her feet and went up the stairs on all fours. The yard was silent. Beth panicked, jerking open the front door.

He was gone, but there—a note. The kid had left a note, saying the mower had run out of gas. He would come back tomorrow. She ran to the garage. He had stowed the lawn mower neatly in the garage, in the space between the bikes.

Beth walked wearily up the stairs. Fifteen minutes more and she could print. "Vincent," she said, outside his door. She could feel the music from his boom box with her feet, throbbing. "Vincent." She tried to turn the knob. The door was locked. She tapped. No reply. The music wailed and thumped.

Beth stood back against the opposite wall, raised both feet, and kicked the door with all her force. The music collapsed into silence. Vincent opened the door. Beth saw, but did not analyze, the way his eyes streamed. He was crying.

"I want you to go downstairs and order a pizza," she told him. "I want you to do that first. Then, I want you to go get Kerry at Blythe's and put a tape on for her. Take the money for the pizza out of my purse." Vincent nodded dumbly. "I have to do some work in the darkroom, right now, and I have to do it all at once. So I want you to give Kerry some pizza, okay? Will you do that?"

He nodded again, furtively scrubbing at his eyes with the back of his hands. Then he slouched toward the stairs.

"Vincent," Beth said sharply. "Did you see the boy who was mowing the lawn?"

"*What* boy?" He scowled.

Checking her watch, Beth clattered down the stairs to the darkroom. Line up, she thought. They're only pictures. You make pictures twice a week. She made the motions mechanical, deciding to print each shot separately, eight by ten, though it would take forever. A contact sheet would be too small, too torturous. Enlarger. Stop bath. Fixer. Take your time.

She leaned over the bath. A drop of sweat fell from her chin, plinked on the mirror of the surface, and bloomed like the shape of an atom, widening, shimmying, finally disappearing.

And then, the edges of a face, growing more distinct, looking up at her, reaching up to her from darkness.

Chapter 20

Beth left the prints strung on the line with clips.

Even from the open door of her darkroom, a distance of no more than four feet, many of them looked like copies, or a sequence in which the shutter had opened and closed, opened and closed, on the same subject in the same position. But when you came closer, you could see that each of the angles was subtly different, each a discrete variation of the boy's fair face with its sharp chin and raccoon's mask of light freckles beneath the eyes. Others, a few, captured his whole body. His legs were long—most of his length was right there—but grooved with the kind of effortless musculature he would have all his life.

The kind he had, indeed, had all his life.

By the time she came upstairs, Vincent was back in his room, and Kerry, red-eyed, has just completed her second straight hour of cartoon gluttony.

Beth flicked off the set, and Kerry prepared to launch herself into her bedtime routine.

But Beth caught her and pulled Kerry gently down with her on the deeply sunken end of the much-used pillow sofa. She held Kerry wordlessly, stroking the child's feathery globe of cheek with her own, rougher skin, and finally rocking her with a motion so small and slight it could have fooled a passing glance into calling it stillness. Kerry didn't object, but Beth could feel her arranging herself carefully on the brace of her mother's arms—Beth's hugs were not usually so indulgent.

But no matter what else happened during the rest of this day, what Beth had already seen gave her, for the first time in nine years, sufficient courage to let herself experience the yielding body of her youngest child. Kerry's fingers were spangled with marker dots; she smelled of fruit and dish soap, and something warmer beneath—down, innocence. Beth looked up over Kerry's tangled hair at the crest of the avalanche, the mountain of memory and half-memory, of rerun, regret, poignancy, and outrage, poised to hurtle down and paralyze her.

Nothing moved. Not a grumble. Not a single cold stone dislodged.

Beth led Kerry up to her room and listened while Kerry read from *Little House on the Prairie.* She was not a gifted reader, but she was a dogged plodder; her determination blazed from her like a scent. "I'm getting better every day, and I am nine now. Eighteen kids in class are still eight," sighed Kerry, and Beth wondered where Kerry found a child's confidence from the scraps of attention she had been fed while growing up.

"Night-night," Beth told Kerry, switching off the overhead light.

"You're not sick anymore, are you, Mommy?" Kerry asked.

"No, I'm peachy keen, peachy," Beth said.

She passed by Vincent's door and tapped it. "'Night," she called. "Thanks for watching Kerry." There was no answer but a vague growl under the pulse of the music; it was classical now—Perlman playing Mozart. Beth didn't try the door. She knew it would be locked.

She glanced at the clock. It was after nine. Pat would be home in an hour.

Ordinarily, Beth devoted this last hour of the day, the last interval before she could take refuge in a cold glass of water and three Trazodone, with reading English novels. The English didn't seem to have many children or care much about them when they did. What roused the English breast was a good water spaniel, a gentleman with a stick who'd come back from India to rejoin his ruddy-cheeked wife called Bea who gardened. The best books for Beth were those in which one day varied from the day before only in the variety of sandwiches at tea, in which vicars called on the sick, in which people went out for a drive to look at old button sets or used volumes of Thackeray.

But tonight, she could not release herself into a village just off the Montford road or a shop in Hastings Crossing.

She sat in the living room, the taste of cigarettes (she'd smoked three) acrid in her mouth. Pat was late. Then he came through the door humming, carrying an old double-sided cardboard that advertised the winter specials at Wedding in the Old Neighborhood. It would soon be time to put up a summer board, and Kerry liked to draw on the used ones.

Beth heard him put down his keys and turn on the kettle for his nightly cup of tea. She felt him check once, around the dark first floor, to see if he dared open a window and have a smoke before bed.

She said then, "Pat."

He jumped. "Bethie!" he said. "What are you doing up?"

Beth walked into the yellow glare of the kitchen and put her arms around Pat. Gratefully he rubbed her back. "What's up? Is Kerry sick?"

"No," she said, wanting to draw out this last stable moment, the last moment of snow bridge she had built and packed hard, so that it felt almost like concrete, you could walk on it. Their fragile suppositions were an ache, but at least they were used to them. Now, what would happen? What would give way?

Beth said, "I have to show you something."

Pat took off his sport coat and followed her down the stairs. Beth remembered the spent light. "Paddy," she said, "Get a light bulb for me, okay?" He turned and left the room. Beth could see the pictures in the faint wash of light from the upstairs hall—his hair now darker, almost maroon in the sun. He would call it brown, she supposed.

This boy.

Sam.

Pat came back with the light bulb and snatched out the old one, tossed it in Beth's huge rubber trash can. Replaced it in the dark. The light flickered, then shone steadily. Pat looked at the pictures. He stepped forward and tore one down, then two.

He said, "Beth."

She said, "It is, isn't it?"

They sat down side by side on the bench that ran along one wall in Beth's darkroom. Pat pulled down another fistful of pictures. They moved into her office. Beth sat at the desk, Pat on the overstuffed chair.

"Is this possible?" he said, his voice strangled in a way that made Beth wonder if he should have a tranquilizer or a nitroglycerin. She could almost feel the flutter of his toiling heart.

"He came to the door," Beth told Pat softly. "To mow lawns. I let him mow the lawn. He's coming back tomorrow. Because we ran out of gas for the mower."

Tears filled Pat's eyes and streamed down his jaw, dripping onto the front of his shirt. In every other respect except the tears, he did not seem to be crying; his breath was measured, even.

"Where does this boy live?"

"Two blocks, he said."

"Two blocks?" Pat cried. "Two blocks? Did they just move here?"

"Pat. I don't know how long they've lived here. But Kerry knew him, and she's been in school at Sandburg four years."

"Did she . . . ?"

"No, Pat, for God's sake. I would have never known unless . . . well, maybe I would have. But he looked just like the aging projection Morris made. And I shot in color so that we could see . . . His hair is so dark. . . . It's possible, Pat, that it's just a kid who looks that way."

"Yeah," he breathed.

"And I wanted to show you, to ask you, before we called Candy or . . . or anyone."

"Let's call them now," said Pat. "Let's get up there and call, and get down to that house."

"No," Beth said. "It's late night, Pat. He's asleep. And we don't even know his last name."

"His last name? Christ, Beth, his last name?" He yanked off his tie, fumbled at his shirt pocket for the place he once kept his cigarettes, before the surgery, before he began hiding them from Beth. "But what if they're . . . doing things to him right now?"

"He didn't look or talk like an abused kid, Pat. And if he is, Pat, it's been nine years. . . ."

"Oh, Bethie—oh, Bethie—two blocks. When he saw you, did he . . . ?"

"Nothing, Pat. Nothing. He had no idea. Pat, he was three."

"And he wouldn't know this house."

"No."

"Maybe he'd know me."

Beth felt a sudden, powerful splash of rage rise; she wanted to slap Pat hard, in the face. But she breathed in and out, slowly, taking her time.

Pat said, "I gotta have a cigarette, Bethie. I'm sorry." He grabbed a sheaf of the photos.

They sat on the porch, with the lights off. The sweat from Pat's hands had already smudged the prints.

"Two blocks," Pat said. "Two blocks. I never saw him."

"You're never around. And I never go anywhere walking. Just school. The drugstore. There are probably fifty kids in this neighborhood I've never seen in four years living here."

Beth leaned against her husband. Be a rock for me now, Patrick, she thought. I don't even want to see tomorrow, because even if it is Ben, we might have to know things that could bury us. Looked back upon, her nine years of quiet avoidance seemed . . . almost peaceful. Not like this clammy present fear.

But she felt Pat's fragility through his wet shirt, felt the slender rasp of his damaged breaths as he smoked.

Okay, Candy, she thought. Be my rock Candy.

"I think we should call Bliss now. Or Bender. Or Jimmy."

"Not tonight, Pat."

"Beth," he told her with desperate urgency. "What if he's not there to-morrow? What if whoever . . . And why would they still be here? What if they take him and get out of Dodge?"

"They live here."

"*They* live here?"

"He's not going anywhere, Pat. Like he told Kerry, he's in sixth."

And then, possessed with a lust to touch him, to praise his body for planting the seed in her that became Ben, for not dying yet, Beth took the prints from Pat's hands and kissed him, releasing her tongue deep into his mouth. He responded weakly, softly cupping one of her breasts, exploring the nipple with hands that barely seemed robust enough to grasp. Beth pulled her shirt over her head and tossed it onto the porch. She unbuckled Pat's belt and lay back, wiggling out of her tattered jeans, centering him over her, drawing him inside her. She rocked to start him. "Please, Pat," she whispered. "It won't hurt anything." And finally Pat took hold, and gripped her arms and plunged into her hard on the hard step, hurting her, making her feel sore and open and new. In a minute he said, "Shouldn't we get ... ?"

"I'm not going to get pregnant, Pat," she said. "Forget that. Just go ahead, go ahead, go ahead...."

Pat buried his tear-wet face against her breast and finished, in a shudder that came up his throat like a groan.

Just then they heard a voice, a neighbor calling in his cat. They lay still in the dark, cold as sculpture, as Beth felt Pat subside and shrink within her, and her own muscles contract, contract and relax.

"I'm going to call Dad," Pat said, when they heard the neighbor's door snap shut.

"Don't tell him. Not until we know."

"I won't. I just ... I don't want to work tomorrow."

"Right."

Pat got up and arranged his clothing, using his thumbs to straighten his shirt collar as if he were headed for the bank, or for work. He buckled his belt carefully and put the change that had scattered on the porch back in his pockets. Last, he picked up the prints and held them to his chest. "I'm going in," he said.

Beth didn't answer. She drew on her jeans, retrieved her shirt, and lay curled with her hips on the mat, the pebbled cement under her pillowed arms, and strained to see the streetlight beyond the streetlight at their corner—the one two blocks down. She pretended that she knew she was looking at the right one. Call it the intersection of Menard and Downer, she thought. And she began to watch. I will have to make coffee, she thought, so I can be sure to watch until morning. And then she thought, No, I don't need coffee. The cold will keep me awake.

She drew up her legs and wrapped her arms around her knees, scanning her mind like a cookbook for a lovely antiseptic thought. Paint colors, tulip bulbs, low-cholesterol chicken Tetrazzini, tables of contents ... yes. She would index the book of Sister Kathleen Noonan's oils for the exhibit catalog.

Page one, she thought, the bell at the Franciscan House in Saint Francis.

Page two, the doors of the Baptistery in Florence.

Page three, three angels above the door frame at a tea shop in the East Village in New York City.

Beth stared at the orb of radiant light, two blocks away.

Chapter 21

There was no interval at all that Beth could later recognize as a period of sleep. She was awake, and looking at the light, her forearms prickled with the cold fall air, her eyes burning; and then she was awake, looking for the light, which was off.

It was morning. She scanned the street quickly for evidence of cars backing out of driveways to be at work by eight. There were none. It was early morning, before seven.

Beth rose and felt the cold wetness in the crotch of her jeans, looked up at her bedroom window, which faced the street. Was Pat awake?

Line up, thought Beth. I will wake Kerry; I will wake Vincent. I will measure coffee and put it in the drip. Then I will call Candy. While it's quiet, I'll call her. She pushed open the screen door, the moment when she could call Candy fluttering ahead of her like the tail of a kite.

Pat was at the table, reading to Kerry from the back of the Cheerios box. Vincent was eating toast, standing with his back to Beth. The lines in Pat's face looked carved in wax; he was ghastly, pouches larger than Angelo's, reddened bruises beneath his eyes.

"Kerry's having breakfast," he told Beth.

"I see, I see," Beth replied, catching a glimpse of her own stained and rumpled self in the bathroom mirror.

"What were you doing on the porch, Mommy?" asked Kerry.

"Watching the sun come up," said Beth, and then asked her son, "Vincent, do you need a ride?"

"Jordie's dad," he said quietly.

"Okay, that's good, that's fine." Beth walked into the kitchen and began to measure coffee into a filter. But Pat had already made coffee. Lots of coffee. She dumped the fresh grounds into the sink. She heard Pat tell Kerry to *mangia, mangia,* soon it would be time to walk to school.

"I'm going to ride my bike," Kerry told him. "I'm nine now. I'm older than eighteen of the kids in third."

"You can't ride your bike," Pat told her gently. "Kids in walking distance can't ride their bikes. And you don't have a bike lock."

"Will you get me a bike lock just in case, Daddy?"

"Yes, I will."

"Today."

"Yeah, sure," said Pat. "I'll get it right after you go to school, and you can put it on when you get home."

Beth listened, amazed. By the time Kerry got home from school, who among the people around this table—whatever happened, whatever the magnitude—would be able to think of bike locks and chains and combinations? Pat, she realized. Pat would. Pat would do it, beforehand, in penance, in petition. And so she wasn't surprised when he followed Kerry out the door, kissing the child lightly and calling her "Chicòria," the name in Italian for a wildflower. Beth heard him start the car, heard him pull away. . . .

Line up, she thought. Line up. Now what? She poured her coffee, raising it recklessly to her lips, burning the soft skin so badly that she felt a welt rise. Vincent was leaving. She caught up with him at the door and, suddenly, fearfully, laid her head against his shoulder, which was exactly at the level of her own shoulder. He stopped, shrugging his knapsack onto the other shoulder, looking out into the street with forceful intensity.

"Goodbye, Mom," he said, not looking. She saw his jaw jump and writhe, as though the muscles were being stimulated by jolts.

"Vincent," said Beth. "Wait." She needed urgently to tell him. She had to tell him, but what could she say?

"It's possible that a kid two blocks away is your brother, that Ben isn't dead anymore"? "And we still don't know anything more about the way we lost him than we did that day you lay on the luggage trolley at the Tremont and slept with Ben's blanket across your chest"?

She said instead, "Vincent. I love you. I want you to know I love you."

He said, "Right. Thanks." Not a trace of surprise. He still didn't look at her.

Beth said, "Have a good time today."

"You too," he said.

Beth heard the crunch of gravel as Jordie's dad wheeled his immense cherry-colored Chevy van into the apron of their drive. As the door closed behind Vincent, Beth saw something lying on the chair where he had stood, eating his toast. Half the chewed bit still lay on the edge of the table, next to Kerry's empty cereal bowl. There was a slip, no, a sheet of paper, in the chair. She picked it up.

It was one of the full-face shots of the boy mowing the lawn. It was not one that Beth had given Pat. This shot had been strung on the line last night. It was one of the best. Beth had meant to give it to Candy.

Beth ran to the door and yanked it open. The van was just turning the corner, lights winking. Still, she yelled, "Vincent, wait!" The brake lights seemed to come on for an instant, but then the van kept going. "No!" Beth cried. Fool. She should have kept him home. He was not a child of seven anymore. To send him off to school today was a mortal insult.

But it was past eight. She picked up the telephone and looked at it. She called Candy at home.

"Girlfriend!" Candy cried happily. "I'm running more than one thousand percent late. Can you eat lunch one of the weekdays?"

"Candy," Beth said. "There's something I need to tell you."

"What's wrong, Beth?" said Candy, instantly tensing. "Is Pat sick?"

"Candy, listen." She paused for breath. "I think I found Ben."

Because Beth had seen her do it so often, she could now watch the silence on the other end of the line as if it were film, watch Candy Bliss let her gargantuan bag slide down her arm like a weary cat, see her raise one perfect finger to the place just between her eyes and press, press, press hard.

"Beth, do you mean that you got a letter or a phone call?"

"I saw him, Candy. He came to my door."

"He came ... he came to your door? Here? He found you here? Ben would be ... what ... he'd be twelve, Beth. You're saying he came home?"

"No. He didn't know me. He lives here. They ... whoever it is that took him, lives in this neighborhood, I guess."

"That's impossible."

"Well, he's here. Except I don't know it's him. For sure."

"You do know."

"I don't know. He looks like the age projection. His eyes were always a weird shade of gray, without any blue, and they still are. The shape of his lips and eyes—yes, I would say with ninety-percent certainty that this is my son. He has two cowlicks."

"The birthmark?"

"I didn't pull his pants down, Candy." As she said it, a revulsive thing squirmed under her heart. Who had ... who had? Which scenario was it? Come on, Mrs. Cappadora, choose door one, two, or three? The con artist, the yearner, the molester?

Was this *Ben*?

Nine years had telescoped into a day and a night and a day. Was it over?

"I'll be right there," Candy was telling her.

Because it was one of her arts, Beth knew precisely how long it would take for Candy to drive from her own apartment to Beth's house, depending on the time of day. She glanced at the clock. She had twenty-five minutes.

Running upstairs, she stripped off her gummy jeans and shirt, which still stank of developing chemicals. She showered and carefully pulled on middle-level work clothes—cotton trousers, a tunic. She dried her hair instead of merely combing it with her fingers. She put on mascara. She sat down on the bed and forcibly tried to still herself. Dead legs, limp arms, hands that felt animate only around the edges of a camera, dead stomach that had learned to receive food as a matter-of-factly as a supermarket scanner, dead heart with its battened receptors, all surged and tingled.

Could he be her Ben—her freckled babe, her rain-eyed darling, folded so long in death, silent as his baptismal gown lying in the cedar chest—come miraculously alive?

It was stupefying. Wonderful beyond imagining. It was terrifying.

And then, Beth thought, oh, God, my God, I will be able to touch Ben's hair. If she could do that, she would not care if her hand was then set on fire.

The doorbell rang; but before Beth could answer it, Candy walked in and took Beth into her arms without greeting. They stood in the fractured sunlight of the lower hall, where Pat found them when he came home, dutifully carrying Kerry's bike lock and chain.

"Are you scared to death?" Candy asked.

"To death, to death," Beth told her.

"Scared?" asked Pat. "Scared of what? Let's go. I can't wait, Candy—we have to go there, right now."

"Go where?" Beth asked him irritably. "We don't know what house he's in, or if he's really in a house two blocks away. And anyway, he'd be in school."

"It's the short day," said Pat. School ended at 1:30 p.m. on Mondays.

All three of them looked at their watches. It was just after nine. Candy silently picked up the print Vincent had left behind and studied it, as Pat shifted the bike chain and lock from hand to hand.

"He said he'd come back," Beth said. "To finish the lawn. He ran out of gas."

"I didn't get gas!" Pat nearly screamed.

"He's not really going to mow the lawn, Pat," Beth told him, nearly laughing before she could stop herself.

"Of course, no one thinks we're going to sit here and wait for this kid to remember to show up and mow the lawn," Candy said softly. "You're just not thinking clearly. I can't imagine how you would. Or how I will. But I'm going to try, and the first thing we have to is—Beth, you said he goes to Kerry's school?"

"She says he's in sixth. At Sandburg."

"And they're two separate buildings, the elementary and the middle."

"Yep. Connected. There's one gym and all."

"Okay, so that's where we'll start. I'll call . . . well, I guess I'll call Jimmy Daugherty, though strictly speaking, this isn't what he does anymore, but I know how much he'll want to be involved if . . . if this is it. And we'll go down there and find out the kid's name and the identity of whoever's listed as his parent or guardian." She got up, pouring herself coffee no one had thought to offer her, and went on, as if dictating a list to an assistant. "Might need a subpoena. If the school isn't sufficiently impressed with the necessity of cooperating with the release of this information. Not a problem. Harry Brainard will help. . . ."

Beth looked at Pat. "Circuit court judge," she said.

"But if we start with school pictures, yearbooks, this shouldn't be too much trouble. I would want to cooperate with helping solve one of the most intractable missing-persons cases in recent history, wouldn't you?" Candy tapped her teeth with her nail. "But first, I need to see the rest of the pictures."

Beth said, "On the hall table."

"Did Reese see them?" Candy asked rummaging in her bag for paper and a pen.

"I think he did," Beth told her. "One, at least." Pat looked up horrified. "You showed Vincent?"

"I didn't show him. He looked."

Candy asked, "Can I see them now?"

Beth laid them all out, except the one Candy still held, end to end on the kitchen table, in lines like the child's game called Memory. Candy put her glasses on and stood over them. As Beth watched her concentration, she realized Candy was crying—prettily, quietly, without either pretense or fuss, the way Candy did everything. "I'm sorry," she told Beth.

Beth said, "I can make more."

"This face . . . this face." And Beth thought of the side-by-side photos of Ben that Candy kept above her desk, tacked to her bulletin board, not dog-eared, not wrinkled, carefully smoothed. All of them: his baseball-mitt picture; the first Missing poster; the second; the computer projection of Ben's face at six, at eight. "This face. When I went . . . Philadelphia, Santa Fe, Jersey. The child in Palo Alto. The little Grainger boy in Michigan. And then afterward, when we all presumed, even I presumed, that he had died, wherever I went—conferences, vacations, to see my mother in Tampa—I carried those copies. I still have them." She extracted a manila envelope from her purse and spilled the contents on the table. "And I realized, after the first few years, that I could no more stop looking for that face than I could stop breathing in and breathing out. It was like the fantasy of the perfect lover. 'Be there, Ben,' I would say. 'In this park. At this fair. Let me see you on the street. Let me bring you home to Beth.'"

Candy scrubbed at her eyes with the back of her hand. "And then there'd come a time, when I knew it was only a day or a few hours before I would have to leave, and I'd call and say I was in town. 'There was this kid. . . . Right, you remember, the Cappadora kid. . . .' And I would ask about their unidentifieds. Their Baby Does. Autopsy pictures and graves. Potter's fields and beautiful plots. Wanting and hoping it would be Ben. Terrified it would be Ben. But mostly hoping. That Ben would be found. Done. Even if I had to tell you he was dead, that he'd been dead for years."

She reached out for Pat's hand. "I wanted to see this face. I wanted to have Ben back. For you. And me."

Then, shaking herself visibly, she stood up to find the phone. "I'm going to call my lieutenant and the chief and tell them, and we'll get things started."

"What should *we* do?" Pat asked. "Should we go down to the school?"

Candy paused. "Paddy, until we can ID this kid—I mean, prove for absolutely one-hundred-percent-beyond-the-remotest-shadow-of-a-doubt that this is Ben—you can't start calling the shots. And right now, this kid is the legal responsibility of whomever we learn are his parents. . . ."

"His parents?" Pat cried.

"I mean, until we're sure it's Ben, we can't just go and grab some kid who might have gotten that red hair from his uncle Harold and take him to Wedding in the Old Neighborhood for braciole."

"So how are we going to find out for sure?"

"The whole routine. Blood tests. Identifying marks. The fingerprints, of course, of course. Dental charts . . ."

"He was three, Candy. He didn't have charts," Beth said. "We went through all that a million times when it happened. You remember."

"Well, right. I'm not all there. Could you folks excuse me for a few moments?"

"You folks"? It shocked Beth.

Wasn't Candy family? Or nearly? Hadn't she shared nights of too many beers, picnics in a humid field, Candy and Chris's second anniversary at Wedding in the Old Neighborhood, a barbecue at Rosie's, Candy taking Kerry horseback riding for the first time—all of these had telescoped on a dime, as had the span of Ben's absence. It was the day after the night of the day.

Candy was still a detective. They were civilians.

"Now I'm going to go down to the school with—" Candy scanned the table—"with this picture. And the others, of course. You guys stay here and listen for the phone. Jimmy will be calling as soon as they can find him. He knows to come here first. Sit tight now. Sit tight." She left, trailing her bag.

Beth left Pat in the kitchen and went upstairs, where she lay down on her neatly made bed. A few moments later, Pat came up and lay beside her. They did not speak or touch. The telephone startled both of them, but neither reached to pick it up. When the answering machine clicked on, they could hear Jimmy shouting, "Jesus Christ, Bethie! We're going crazy over here. Bethie? Pat? Are you there? Well, I don't know if you're there or not, but I'm on my way." He seemed to speak for a moment to someone else: "I know. Can you believe this shit?" And then, "I'm on my way. Hang in there, Beth, Pat, Vincent."

How long they lay there, Beth would not later remember. Perhaps only minutes. Then the front door opened and closed, and she heard Candy pick up the kitchen phone. Beth raised herself and rolled off the bed; Pat had fallen, with automatic grace, asleep. She sat on the bottom step until Candy saw her.

"They want a fucking subpoena," she said. "I'm on hold for Brainard." Beth said nothing.

When Candy finally finished, she turned back to Beth and said tersely, "I have no patience for this. I'm sweating like a pig. They did let me look at the yearbooks. He's been there since kindergarten. His name is Sam Karras. We couldn't get the parents' names, but Beth . . ." Candy came and sat beside her on the step. "He's an only child."

Chapter 22

At Parkside, the longtime chief's last name was Bastokovitch. Over the years, Candy had often told Pat and Beth, the troops had created a whole dictionary of obscenities based on it. But Beth had never met him before his unmarked slid up the driveway next to Candy's.

He'd come, Candy warned, to counsel caution. "There was a belief," she said, flicking back the curtain and watching the big man's slow progress up the drive, "that if he ever got up, he'd learn his butt had got stuck to the chair. This is evidently a fallacy." She opened the door.

"Chief."

"Detective." Then, "Candace."

"I'm glad you came. It's time to proceed. I know you agree."

"Bliss, the kid is in protective custody; he's not going anywhere," Bastokovitch said softly, accepting Beth's offer of coffee with a sad smile.

"But that construction van is in the driveway, Ed," Candy pleaded. "That probably means the parents—forgive me, Pat—the suspects are there. You know me, Ed. I don't arrest first and talk later. But who can figure what the

goddamn principal has done already? Called them? You have to know he's called them. They could be getting out the passports right now."

"There's an unmarked sitting right in front of the driveway, Candace," Bastokovitch sighed. "They'd have to tunnel out. We've looked up the people, Candace. They've lived in that house for seven years. Man, his wife, the kid. The wife's got . . . she's got cancer or something. Sick all the time. The husband works this business out of the house, every day. This case is big and long, Candace. We don't want to go off half-cocked. Every move we make is going to be scrutinized. You know it. So I say, let's go down there nice and quiet, one car of uniforms, maybe, and us, and we say, 'We need to ask you some questions. Sir. Madam.'"

Bender walked in the front door then, without even ringing the bell. "It's a house, Bender," Candy said, disrespectfully. "You know—knock, knock?"

He ignored her and nodded to Pat. "Is it true?"

"We don't know," Candy said. "How very solicitous of you to come."

"You are a very hostile woman, Detective Bliss."

"Yes, I am, Agent Bender. I have grown hostiler with age. By the time I'm sixty, I'll be spitting tobacco on your shoes."

Pat went out into the garage to get more chairs, the aquamarine folding chairs they used at the Wedding in the Old Neighborhood when there were real weddings or overflow Saturday nights.

"Where'd you get folding chairs that color?" asked Bender.

"There wouldn't be any harm in having a warrant," Bastokovitch mused then. "Can you get something?"

"I already talked to the DA's office. I talked to Kelly Clark. He's ready."

Bastokovitch looked long at Beth and Pat. "Good grief, you folks . . . you poor folks. Are you ready for this?"

Beth said, "You don't get to be ready for it." She sounded, to herself, coplike; she had a weakness for falling into Candy's rhythms whenever she spent more than fifteen minutes in her light.

"We're going to do this right." The chief sighed again. Beth heard Candy make a sound, hoped Bastokovitch hadn't. "We're going to take them," he said, again, this time holding out his hands, as if wishing for Pat or Beth to drop the flag and let the games begin. Then the front door banged open, and Vincent slouched into the hall.

"This is my son," Pat said quickly, jumping up. "This is Vincent. Vincent, you know Candy. This is Chief Bastokovitch."

Vincent looked straight at his mother. "Does Kerry have Girl Scouts?"

Beth thought a moment, ruffling a card file that had fallen all over the floor of her head, facedown. "Uh . . . I think."

"So she won't be home until after five."

"Right."

Vincent whipped his head once around the breakfast room, taking in the folding chairs, the stacks of photos still littered among the coffee cups on the table, the murmurs and bursts of laughter from the kitchen where the uniforms were traipsing in and out the back door to smoke among the roses.

"The picture," Vincent said then.

Beth led her son out into the hall. "You saw the picture, and you know that I think it's Ben," she said softly.

"You think. Yeah. Well, it's Ben," Vincent said. "You know it is."

"Did you recognize him?"

"When?"

"When he came here to mow. You said you didn't see him." Vincent looked out the window, up the block; he could easily see over Beth's head, though he was no more than an inch taller than she.

"Is he the kid in the red house?"

Beth's hand flew up before she reckoned what she intended to do with it, which was slap Vincent's face. She had never—not in all the vicious fumblings, the hair pullings, the time she'd pushed him down on the lawn after he casually lobbed not one but two baseballs through two glass windows, or the times she'd locked the door and gone to bed, forgetting he was in the library or at a basketball game, all those manifest atrocities, significant and negligible, neglects and abuses—for all those, never had she slapped his face. She didn't now, but Vincent's head jerked sideways. It was just as if she had.

"You saw him? You *saw* Ben?"

"I didn't . . . know it was Ben." He dropped his knapsack, anvil-heavy, in the middle of the floor, where it would lie unopened all night, as it did every night. "I just used to see this kid goofing around, and I thought he looked like Ben. I mean, I *guess* I thought he looked like Ben. I never really thought about it much." Beth watched his face reconfigure then, as if a front were passing over Lake Michigan, watching the restoration of his bored, cocky sneer, his Reese face.

"Why didn't you tell me?"

He started to turn, to go for the stairs. Beth asked again, "Why didn't you tell me? Or, for God's sake, your father?"

"I told Tom."

"You told Tom. Why didn't Tom tell us?"

"I don't think he got it. I don't know if *I* got it. He will now, I guess. I didn't make a big deal out of it."

"But why didn't you say something?"

"I don't know."

"Vincent, our whole life was . . ." He gave her a murderous look, and Beth tried to back-pedal. "You knew what was at stake! Why didn't you say something? Why didn't you tell me yourself?"

"Say something? Tell you? Tell you what, Mom?" he spat it out then. "That I'd found my long-lost brother down the street? Would you have believed me? Would you have even goddamn *heard* me?"

"I would have believed you. I would have listened."

He smirked.

"Vincent." Her voice stopped him, one foot on the bottom stair. "When did you first see him?"

"How long have we lived here?"

No, God, Beth thought, no. Her finger ends pounded, one, two, three, four years.

"It doesn't matter now, Vincent," she said, thinking, Of course it matters, nothing else but this matters, and why, what, how he could have been possessed to keep it a secret? Or was it possible, even remotely, that her son to whom computers sang and chemistry released its riddles had truly believed it wasn't worth mentioning? It was too un-Vincent. There was something else. There had to be.

But, struggling to breathe evenly, she said, "There isn't anything we can do about it. And ... I should have told you this morning. It was stupid that I didn't." She stopped. "I'm sorry for it. But they took this boy out of school without knowing for sure. They think it's Ben. The boy you ... saw in the picture. They think it's your brother. That he's alive." She added, fumbling. "That's why all the cops are here."

"Oh, thanks," Vincent said. "I thought it was, like, a fire drill or something." He shook his head. "Jesus. May I please go upstairs now and go to the bathroom? Mom?"

"Wait," Beth told him. She didn't know how to do it; she almost had, this morning, when she laid her head on his shoulder. "Vincent, I ... it could be all right, Vincent." She took his hand, marveling at its clean warmth, its huge size—how long since she had really held his hand? Not to scrub chocolate from it or snatch from it a hammer or an Exacto knife, not to grip it to cross a street, but really *felt* it, felt the supple palms, the emergent man's knuckles that had, outside her notice, replaced the indented dimples of childhood—long, tapered fingers exactly like her own, the "piano hands" her mother had cherished such admiring hopes for, even when Beth bashed away at the keyboard with all the grace of a drill-press operator.

She raised his hand; he let her, neither yielding nor withdrawing, and laid it against her cheek. "Vincent, we've all been through so much. You've been through so much. Oh, Vincent, please forgive me."

She heard him say, "Don't," and imagined him looking up the hall, humiliated; they were not twenty feet away from the group in the breakfast room. She should have stopped, right then.

But she said, once more, "Can you ever forgive me?"

"Forgive you?" he asked. "What the hell did *you* do?"

She couldn't help it. A flute of anger.

She looked up and saw then, in her son's eyes, plain as the exquisitely backlit detail in a Karsh portrait, not anger, not affection. Pity. Unalloyed pity. No other thing.

"I'll call you ... when ... they ... I'll tell you," she blurted.

"Fine," Vincent told her, slowly pulling away his hand.

Candy was calling her. Beth turned back into the kitchen.

"Is he all right?" Candy asked, and Beth, not trusting her mouth, nodded.

Pat spoke up: "I have to call my mom and dad," and it had the gratefully galvanic effect of restoring Beth's attention.

"No!" she and Candy nearly shouted at the same time—but, Beth would think later, for vastly different reasons.

"Pat, we need to go down there as quietly and unobtrusively as we can. This guy could have . . . anything in there. Another kid. An arsenal. We have no idea what's happening in that house," Candy said.

"She's right," said Bastokovitch.

A young officer bounded up the front steps and in the open door, placing a sheaf of papers, embedded with carbons, in Candy's hands. She thanked him.

"I'm going to go up with my buddy Bender here," Candy said. "Righto, Bob?" Bender got up, actually adjusting his muted paisley tie. Beth watched Candy take her gun out of her satchel and stick it carefully in the belt of her slacks, behind her back, just over her right hip. "You got?" she asked Bender, and he tapped his breast pocket. "Okay, then." Candy stopped, and briefly hugged Beth, hard. "Now we go."

Beth saw the brake lights of Candy's car blink to a full stop at the corner, and then she began to run. She didn't look back to see if Pat was following; she simply ate the blocks, forgetting to breathe, arriving at the turn to the red house just as Candy and Bender were crossing the parkway to the front stoop. Behind the van neatly stenciled with the words "Karras Construction," two officers crouched with drawn guns.

Jimmy grabbed Beth's arms. "Don't," he hissed, surprised. She shook him off and bounded across the lawn after Candy, who shot her a look of unvarnished fury.

"I'm coming."

"Bullshit," said Candy. "I told you we don't know . . . shit, Beth, go back down there. He could be aiming a rifle at your head right now. Don't be an ass."

"Mrs. Cappadora—" Bender began.

"I want to see him."

"No."

"What are you going to do, arrest me?" Beth asked.

"Oh, fuck," Candy said. She turned her back, shoving Beth slightly behind her, and rang the doorbell.

He was little. A handsome, slender-hipped man with smooth Mediterranean skin, almost teen-looking except for two identical wings of white hair that framed his face. It was good hair, Beth thought; it was a vanity.

"Are you George Karras?" Candy asked.

"Yes," he said, smiling, opening the door wider. "What's wrong?"

"I am Detective Candace Bliss and this is Agent Robert Bender of the Federal Bureau of Investigation. Mr. Karras, do you have a twelve-year-old boy named Sam who lives in this house?"

"I . . . my son," he said, and then stumbled, sagging against the outer frame of the door. "What's happened to my boy? Is Sam hurt? Are you the police?"

"Mr. Karras, Sam is unhurt, and he is in custody of protective services of Cook County."

"He's at school," Karras said. "How did he get hurt?"

"Mr. Karras, you are under arrest for aggravated kidnapping in connection with the June 3, 1985, abduction of Benjamin Cappadora," Candy said evenly. "You have the right to remain silent. If you give up the right to remain silent, anything you say can and will be used against you in a court of law . . ."

"What?" Karras said, turning to Beth. "My son's at school. Who's Benjamin—?"

"If you give up the right to remain silent, anything you say can and will be used against you in a court of law. You have the right to have an attorney present at any time you choose. If you cannot afford an attorney, one will be appointed to represent you. Do you understand these things, Mr. Karras?"

He said, then, "I get it. You got the wrong house. The people who lost the little boy, that kidnap case a long time ago, they live down over there. You can ask my neighbor lady—she knows the dad."

"Mr. Karras," Candy said, "may we please come inside?"

"Sure," said the man, smoothing his flannel shirt. "I was just doing the bills. But I don't think I can help you much. Because I don't know the family. You got the wrong house is all."

"They're not arresting us," Beth said.

"Huh?" Karras stared at her. "Are you a cop?"

"No," Beth said.

"We're his parents," Pat said then, puffing, dragging himself up the steps behind Beth. "We're Ben's parents, you sonofabitch."

"That's enough," Bender said.

"What?" Karras asked again. "Where is this kid? Is my boy hurt?"

Candy moved into the living room, where a large card table was set up next to a low corduroy-covered couch. There were stacks of invoices piled on one end next to an adding machine with a long tail of tape. "Mr. Karras," she said, "please slowly raise your hands—"

"What?"

"Raise your hands so that the officer can make sure—"

"I don't have a gun." The small man smiled, then, at Beth. "I was doing the bills. I don't have a computer." One of the younger patrolmen quickly patted Karras's sides, the inside and outside of his trouser legs. "Please, I don't know what's going on. This is my house. I didn't do anything."

Beth wanted to get down on her hands and knees and examine the fiber of the carpet, where a tiny pile of ground-in potato chips dotted a corner, to untie and explore the two huge pairs of boys' tennis shoes she saw neatly standing side by side just inside the door, put her fingers in the pockets of the Bulls jacket tossed on a hook. A well-oiled mitt snuggled deep into the cushion of a fat maroon chair, near the fireplace; on the television, a photo of a boy, crouched grinning in a green silk baseball uniform, was framed in wood and gold. There were a pair of ceramic candlesticks at each end of the mantel. Only one had a candle. There was a vase with silk gladioli, white. And above that, a painting—no, Beth thought, in quick correction, a re-touched photograph. The woman looked straight into the camera with an antelope's shy grace and wide-eyed intensity; she wore a high-necked gray dress, a gown nearly, with a line of pearl buttons at the throat, and her pale hair haloed away from her forehead as if it were being lifted by invisible fingers. Blown, thought Beth; they had used a fan in the shoot. She reached for the edge of the couch, missed it, and sat down hard on the floor.

"Beth!" Candy turned, distracted, one eye still on Karras as he instinctively reached out a hand to help Beth.

"That's Cecil," Beth gasped. "That's Cecil Lockhart."

"Oh," Karras said, "Cecil. Sure. She's an actress. Did you see her on TV?"

Beth fought for a normal breath. She began to get up, settled for kneeling. "Why," she asked then, "do you have a picture of Cecil Lockhart?"

George Karras drew himself up, nearly proudly, then nodded, his lips pursed with a wistfulness, a sorry rue Beth would never forget.

He said, "That's my wife."

Chapter 23

They could not make Candy stop apologizing.

When she thought about that first week, years later, it was Candy's utter despair that Beth remembered most, the coruscating blame she heaped on herself and Bender and even the devoted officers from her Parkside staff, blame in fistfuls, even after Beth begged her to stop, even after Rosie, for God's sake, put her hands on Candy's shoulders and said, "This is not right. You did everything. This family owes you its life."

It started the moment the three of them stepped out onto George Karras's porch and stood blinking in the late-afternoon sun—after Karras had told them, and Chief Bastokovitch had confirmed by phone, that his wife, Cecilia, had been a patient at Silvercrest in Elgin, a private hospital for the mentally ill, for the past four years. That he, George, was essentially a single parent of their only son—Sam, Cecil's child from her previous marriage, whom George had legally adopted not long after his own marriage to her, seven years ago.

Beth had tried, and to an extent had been successful, to make a blur of the moment George Karras said that, to blot out the remembrance of her nausea when the vein in Pat's forehead began to flutter, and sweat beaded at the neck

of his shirt. "Legally adopted?" he'd said softly, dangerously, that I'll-break-anything-here Vincent-look in his eyes. "Legally adopted?"

Candy urging, "Pat, wait. . . ."

And George continuing, fervently, anxiously, "No, no, it's fine, it's okay. You can check. I got the legal document right in my safe. With his birth certificate. Go ahead. Let's clear this up, okay?"

Jimmy showing up in the living room then, and he and Candy leading a rigid Pat outside, while Bastokovitch flipped open a steno pad and sat down heavily on George's couch, asking, in low tones, if Mr. Karras would like an attorney present before he answered some questions. Sighing, as he began, while even outside, Pat, Beth, and Candy could still hear George's voice piping up, "You just got to look at the papers. That's all. He's my son. He's my wife's child. It's a mixup. Just let me get them."

Outside the door, Candy had turned to Beth and Pat abruptly. "Please, please," she said, for the first time of what would turn out to be dozens, as it began to break over all of them, the thing that had somehow actually happened, and gone on happening, for long years, two blocks from the Cappadoras' front porch. "Please forgive me."

"What?" Beth cried. "Forgive you? What?"

"Please, please . . . No, don't forgive me. This is the worst fucking abortion in history. He was here all the time. I don't deserve you to forgive me."

And even Pat, ashen, raised his head and told her, "Candy, no. You couldn't have known. . . ."

But Candy would not be stopped. For the first time since Beth had known her, the ever-composed Candy indulged, those early days, in a virtual orgy of emotionalism—berating herself with curses even more fluent than her usual fare as fact after fact emerged.

It was Jimmy who told Beth how Candy slammed down her office phone and pulled a window shade off its cord when she heard that Cecil had cooperated fully with officers in an interview at her parents' house, just months after the kidnapping, even cracking a bedroom door so they could peek at her sleeping son, whom she described as four years old, not much older than Ben. "That," she had told Jimmy, "will make me wake up screaming the rest of my life." And after Candy learned that a clear set of Cecil's finger-prints, taken during a mass arrest at a nuclear-weapons demonstration in Champaign-Urbana years before, existed in FBI files, she'd run up three flights to shout into the phone at Bender that she didn't care if the fucking bungling dirtbag lived in Budapest now, that Bender had better find him, be-cause the Cappadoras were going to sue the government for millions; it was going to cost the government millions of bucks because some asshole FBI tech had been given prints on rubber, for Christ's sake, on the bottom of Ben's second tennis shoe, prints probably as clear as the dummy sets they gave you to study in the academy, and still managed to screw up lifting them. "And you guys had a matched set!" Candy screamed. "Cecil Lockhart did ev-erything but call you on a bullhorn on the night of the second reunion—'I'm still here! I did it!' This could have been five fucking years ago! . . . Yeah, the kid is okay. Well, *maybe* he's okay. We don't know everything yet. . . . Does that justify it, Bob? All's well that ends well? And if I find out that this kid was touched, that a hair on his head was harmed, I'll personally get you then, Bob. Take it to the bank."

Beth had listened, terrified, then ventured helplessly, "You're taking too much on yourself, you're too close."

"Oh, really, Beth?" Candy snapped. "How about the fact that even I fucking spaced the Minneapolis connection? She only moved back and forth about fifty times." She stopped, then, and apologized for her sarcasm.

But even long afterward, when the whole sorry unraveling of nine years of near misses and sheer mishaps was pieced together as best it could be with-out the keystone information that only Cecil herself could have provided, Beth could not accept the intensity of Candy's guilt, the determination with which she turned away all of their comfort, their thanks. "*You* found him," she told Beth a dozen times. "Don't thank me. I didn't earn it." That the me-dia, and almost every other official source connected with the case, seemed determined to laud her anyway (she was, if anything, even more elegant and glamorous than she'd been nine years before, even more irresistible as copy)—this only deepened Candy's frustrations. She told Beth, one night the following fall, that the only forgiving moment of the whole spring had been on the night of the "arrest," which had, of course, quickly turned out to be nothing of the sort—the moment when she and Jimmy had the chance to see Pat see Ben.

Beth was able to summon that part herself, entire, play it back almost like a time-lapse film of a rose opening: All of them standing outside the emergency foster-care home in Wheaton, aware of two kids hanging out a second-story window to try to see them under the roof of the porch; George, his eyes and nose reddened, but his handkerchief neatly folded in his sportcoat pocket, arriving with Bastokovitch in the chief's car, passing the Cappadoras with a silent gesture, elbows in, palms up, something midway between a shrug and a plea, as he went inside. Then more waiting, Vincent plowing the soft dirt of a flowerbed with his toe, Kerry sitting on the ground, holding the whining, squirming Beowulf on his lead, Beth wondering why she'd given in when Kerry insisted on bringing the dog. Waiting for impossible minutes as the curtains on the inner door were drawn back, then dropped again; George finally emerging, blowing his nose, then the foster mother, gray and formidable even in a fuchsia sweat suit, already protective of her charge, flicking on the outside light in the gathering dusk. She'd come out onto the step and stood to one side, holding the screen door open behind her.

And then Ben.

It was Pat's gathered energy Beth could still feel when she thought of that instant—his coil; she thought he would leap up onto the step, leaving her behind, numbed, her arms hanging thick and useless. He had, instead, raked his hair, once, and then walked up to the step slowly, cautiously, the way a field biologist would approach a newborn antelope, and extended his palm, made as if to shake hands. And when the child only stared at him, as Beth held her breath, Pat had lifted his hand, run one thumb down the side of Ben's face, from his hairline to his chin, and asked, "How are you?"

"I'm good," the boy had answered automatically, and then, "Dad ... ?" And when both George and Pat answered him, Beth began first to cry, then to breathe. Behind her, she could hear an enormous chorus of coughing and shuffling, as assembled masses of Parkside and state officers, who'd materialized from nowhere, let go. It was she who leapt onto the steps then, she and

Kerry and Beowulf, Beth inhaling his smell as eagerly as the dog did, engulfing the child, nearly knocking him down as he stiffened and finally backed away, reaching for George.

"I know," the foster mother said then, freighting the two words with supreme kindness. "But he's just stunned."

Pat had told Ben, then, to get some sleep. George, calling Ben "Spiro," which Beth learned later was George's Greek name for Sam, hugged him and propelled him back inside.

And that was when Candy said again, "I'm so sorry."

But Pat had turned to her, his face smoothed, flushed, the shortstop's face Beth had yearned for a hundred summers ago, and said, "Sorry? Candy, this is the best day of my life."

And to underline it, Pat, for whom working at Wedding was respiration, had barely gone in to work over the next few weeks. Between supervised hour-long visits, every other day, with the child they soon learned to call "Sam," Pat and Beth consumed dozens of quarts of coffee and absorbed the information in reports Candy brought them, almost daily, of police interviews with Cecil at Silvercrest, interviews that hardly merited the name. Michele Perrault, the little lawyer George had hired, had almost gotten in trouble at the arraignment, Candy told them, when Judge Sakura asked whether the defendant had chosen to stand mute, and Perrault shot back, "Your Honor, that's the only way she can stand."

But it was dead accurate. The diagnosis, in lay terms, was catatonic depression. When she entered Silvercrest, years before, Cecil had, Candy said, showed some animation—spoken occasionally in the trained, spheric actor's voice that took the staff by surprise, especially when what she said was senseless. Now she was still as a well, making no noise even when she yawned or scraped her leg on a piece of furniture. At Silvercrest, in Cecil's room, in the dayroom, in her supervising physician's office, Candy and, after her, Robert Bender, Calvin Taylor, others, had spent hours with Cecil.

They had shown Cecil pictures, pictures that George, in a fumbling open gesture that made Pat cry, had duplicated for the Cappadoras—pictures of Cecil on her mother's porch with Ben on a brand-new red bike with training wheels, pictures of George with Ben sitting on his shoulders on a mountain path. A picture of Ben on Santa's lap, with his hair still dyed Vincent-brown, no more than six months after . . . How had she dared? Beth thought, and then thought, Of course, what else would she have done—was Cecil, after all, stupid or just crazy? That picture, the one that attracted Beth most, had to have been taken the fall after the police interviewed Cecil, after she had moved back to Chicago from Minneapolis. Candy said Cecil's mother had confirmed the move, that Cecil had showed up with a grandson Mrs. Lockhart had never even met before. Beth pressed Candy: Why had Mrs. Lockhart believed Cecil? Didn't she connect the sudden grandson with Ben's much-publicized loss?

"If she did, she's not saying," Candy replied.

In the meantime, after the Ben pictures failed, the police, with the help of Cecil's psychiatrist, had tried evoking responses with other stimuli: hippie music from high-school times—Cream and Jimi Hendrix and Donovan. They had brought her mints, which her nurses said Cecil loved, and watched Cecil reach out and gobble them, the only movement she ever made voluntarily. They had brought in a videotape machine and showed Cecil long excerpts of herself in the *Hallmark Hall of Fame* production of *Major Barbara*. They had brought in a big poster of Cecil, her platinum hair upswept in a magnificent Gibson pouf, in her one-woman show *Jane Addams of Hull House*, the performance that had won her the Grace Dory Arts Achievement Award just the summer before the reunion. They brought out front pages, old headlines ("Mom Blasts Kidnapper: You Heartless Bastard!").

And, as her doctor predicted up front, they had elicited . . . nothing. Less than nothing. Cecil was more than vacant, Candy told Beth; she was bottomless. She ate her mints; she got up when her angel-faced nurse, Mary, put pressure on her elbow. Whatever she knew, if she any longer knew anything at all, walked in her alone.

George was pitifully eager to help fill in blanks. He came to the Cappadoras' house more than once, unbidden, and then chafed miserably at their kitchen table, his eyes drawn again and again to the baby pictures of Ben on the walls. He brought his son's growth charts from the pediatrician, his dental records; the description of the broken wrist Sam had suffered in a soccer match at age nine. Beth brought him coffee, with cloth napkins she had to go upstairs into a dresser to find, brought cream in a pitcher, things she never did, to soothe him.

And finally, one night, when Ben was still in transitional care, George had blurted, "You guys probably think I should feel more guilty. And I do feel guilty. I do. But how can I blame myself? It's probably impossible for you to believe how little I knew about any of this. All I know is my boy—God forgive me, he's my boy, too. I mean, Beth, Pat, look at it from his point of view. He's already a kid whose mother's in the loony bin. God bless her. Poor Cecilia, she was the most gorgeous . . . You know, Beth, when I met her, I didn't think she was a day over twenty-five, and she was really in her midthirties by then. She was so delicate and so sweet, like a flower." George tapped his chest. "We were running this promotion deal; you got tickets to that theater out there by the airport. She had just moved back from Minneapolis, and she was in *My Fair Lady*. And here am I, this dummy who builds decks. That she would look at me . . . that woman, this girl, would look at me . . . I couldn't believe it."

He sipped his coffee, his pinkie delicately extended. "And then, you know all this, there was the boy. He was—well, Beth, he was just like . . . like he is still, even now. So happy and game. So smart and strong. I fell in love with him as much as Cecilia. It was Cecilia who wanted to get married, right away, almost like she could tell she was going to . . . oh, Jesus God. Before she was hospitalized the last time, she . . . she got his hair cut all short, in a buzz, not an eighth of an inch long. And it grew in all reddish. Brownish red. I noticed. God, I thought, kids change. I never knew the father. Irish, I thought. I build garages. Pat, I just build decks and garages. He's my boy. I adopted him as my own boy. But even before that, he was my boy."

George ran his hands though his perfect hair—Was it whiter, in only weeks? thought Beth. Was this just a myth, or did it actually happen to people? George said, "I figured, of course, Cecilia and me, we'd have more; but she got so sick, so fast, and then I found out she really wasn't so young. And Jesus, the shock treatments. Times I'd come there, they'd have her bound up in belts. She'd bite at the . . . And then, later, when she didn't even know me anymore. Didn't even know her mother or the boy. But I had Sam. My Spiro. I had my little all-star. See?"

Beth could feel the dampness at her neck; her shirt collar was soaking with unwiped tears. Her nose was running; she'd hadn't even been aware she'd cried. "George," she said. "You don't have to tell us."

Despite the ache of sympathy they felt, Pat and Beth agreed to stand firm. Whatever George would be to Sam, he was not going to be another father. And yet, they never turned him away—he was their only window into the cocoon from which Ben had emerged Sam.

Charges were issued. The state of Illinois had charged Cecilia Lockhart Karras with aggravated kidnapping and stood prepared, depending on what was learned about the conditions under which Ben had lived for nine years, to tack on everything except the abduction of Patty Hearst: false imprisonment, child abuse and endangerment, interference with custody, secreting a child, civil rights violations. Candy smiled when she read the complaint: "They left out forgery and possession with intent. . . ."

But Candy knew, as everyone knew, as Beth knew, from the first moments of dawning comprehension in George's living room, that the whole legal process would turn out to be mostly theater, an elaborate pantomime intended for no purpose but completion, like binding up the newspapers, corner to corner, with twine, and setting them at the curb. All the hearing would accomplish, Candy predicted, would be to make a public witnessing of tying that knot, securing it, snipping the cord.

Cecil would be led down the steps of the courthouse at Twenty-seventh and California just as she would come up, with lights she probably didn't see panning her face, and words she didn't hear burbling in her ears, go back to Silvercrest as free a woman as she had been when she was taken to Cook County Jail in the hospital van. She would go back to the room no one knew for sure whether she recognized, to be ministered to by rough or gentle hands no one could tell whether she felt; to stare at television if it was turned on in front of her; to sit with her fingers interlaced until someone took her hand and raised her to her feet; to soil herself raw without any apparent discomfort. Sending Cecil to prison would be redundant; no one had any lust for it, Beth, even Pat, least of all.

Chapter 24

June 1994

All five of them in the social worker's office felt like a crowd. Nobody knew where to go. Reese finally flopped on one end of the couch—one of those nubbly orange numbers that show up in places Reese had frequented, public-bucks places, like school social workers' offices. Tom, now, Reese thought, Tom wouldn't have put a couch like this one in his garage. He concentrated on watching a spider pick delicately in and out of the canyons of the acoustical tile. The murmur of his parents' voices blended with the social worker's drone, until, if he tried, Reese could pretend he could hear a fly buzzing, running from the spider through miles of tiles.

He swung his feet down and stood up.

The kid was staring out the window, with his back to Beth and Pat.

". . . certain adjustments," said the social worker, looking up, startled, at Reese. His parents were staring at him, Dad looking particularly annoyed, but the social worker was prepared to go right on, apparently even if Reese stood on his head and peed on the floor. "We have a list of agencies, here, and you can choose to access—"

"Can I go outside?" Reese asked then, and thought, Damn, I sound like Mommy's little boy. "I'm going outside. It's getting hot in here."

"I can open a window," the social worker suggested thinly.

"It's all right," said Pat. "There's no real reason that ... they ..."

"Of course not," said the social worker.

"Wanta go?" Reese asked the kid, who blinked as if he wasn't sure he got the dialect. "Wanta go outside?"

The kid shrugged. Reese opened the door. There was a kind of playground outside, with a couple of basketball courts; some other disadvantaged deefs were swinging on the swings or kicking around an old tetherball, still on its string. Wonder what they're in for, Reese thought, holding the door open for the kid, who passed through quickly, head down, fists jammed in his jeans pockets.

"Vincent," said Beth, then. "You *will* keep an ..." Reese saw the look his dad gave her then, as if even he couldn't believe she could be that stupid. But it was already almost out; Reese knew what she was going to say. He shrugged and let the door bang shut behind them.

It was colder outside than it looked. Especially for late spring. The kid was wearing just a flannel; Reese was glad he had his leather. He shrugged it up onto his shoulders, as always feeling the momentary surge of joy it gave him. It moved like another, tougher skin. He took out a butt, examined the angle of the view from the window—he could see his dad, but his dad had his back to him. Not worth it.

"So," he said to the kid, carefully replacing his cigarette and folding the pack. "Was the guy here this morning?"

"The guy?" said the kid, not tracking.

"The guy, the guy—the guy who was your stepfather—George What's-His-Name," Reese said.

"He came to the foster-parent place real early," said the kid. "He didn't want to come here."

"So how does it feel to be a celebrity, Ben?" Reese asked. "Mug on the front page. Major miracle on Menard Street ..." The kid gave Reese another measuring look. He thinks I really want to know, Reese thought. What a deef.

"Actually, it's kind of sickening," said the kid. "I mean, all these days, the past two weeks, the psychologist is saying, 'So, you must be having a lot of feelings about all this.' ... How can you have feelings about something you didn't even know was going on?"

"Is this, like, your permanent counselor now?"

"Permanent?" They walked over onto the concrete and Reese propped his foot on one of the baby swings.

"Take a clue here, Ben," he said. "You have now entered the counseling zone. This is the champion mental-health consumer family you will be living with here. My mom and dad off and on go to marriage counseling, and she used to go to grief counseling, and Kerry goes to, like, drawing counseling, and I myself hold the world's record in my age cohort for consecutive visits to a shrink...."

"Why? What's wrong with you?"

Reese kicked the swing.

"Nothing. Nothing has to be wrong with you. It's just ... school shit. And so forth. It's mainly my dad who thinks I'm this major fuckoff."

"And what about your mom?"

"You've met my mom."

"Well ..." said the kid, turning away, which Reese didn't want.

"No, my mom isn't like this bad person or anything. She's just like ... 'Ground control to Beth Cappadora,' you know? She doesn't get stuff half the time, or you think she doesn't." Reese sighed. "Anyhoo, I wish we had a car."

"You don't have a car?" said the kid.

"No, but a car is a thing you can always have if you want."

"What do you mean?" the kid asked him.

"I mean, a car is just there ... for you...."

"You steal cars?"

"No, I don't *steal cars*. But you can borrow a car, no harm, not much foul, you know what I mean."

"That's just a kind of stealing."

"Well, I want to know that I flourished in my youth," said Reese. The kid looked around him, like he was trying to find a cop or something. Shit, thought Reese, next topic.

"So what do you do?" he asked the kid.

"Do? I don't do anything," said the kid.

"I mean, like, what do you *do*?" The kid's gray eyes widened then, and Reese, staring at him, almost lost his train of thought, the kid looked—

"I play ball."

"B-ball?" The kid nodded, and walked over onto one of the scarred concrete courts where two black Bulls signature balls nodded together under a bush. The other deefs kept kicking the tetherball, shuffling away from Reese's approach like herd animals.

"You any good?" Reese called, going after one of the balls.

"I play city league," said the kid. "Traveling squad. First string."

"Traveling squad?" cooed Reese. "Oh, my goodness."

"Look, I'm in sixth grade. The other kids are in ninth, okay? It's the height."

"Though where you got that . . ."

"Whatever."

"Wanta shoot some. Play Horse?" The kid shrugged. His hands were big; Reese watched him spin and fondle the ball, like it was a pet, before he dribbled—then, release, drop, release, drop. The kid had seriously big hands, and—Reese looked down—feet to match.

They took positions, pretty far back—After all, Reese thought, he's first string *traveling squad.* He watched the kid shoot—looked like an old Olympic basketball video—squared up, with the follow-through down the wrists to a fingertip flip. Good little kiddie, thought Reese, plays by the book.

Size didn't matter much here; the kid was as heavy as Reese was, and all but an inch as tall. Reese took a step back, one-armed it. "Nothing but net," he said.

The kid stepped back, took the ball, and matched it, no problem.

"Free-throw line," said Reese, and bricked one off the back of the iron. It went wide.

"My turn," said the kid happily. He stood up in that old-fashioned way, and Reese saw his face change: he had one of those faces that told you he was only doing what he was doing—not revising the names of people on his permanent shit list or anything else. He was right there. Reese could tell before the ball left the kid's fingertips that it was good.

And so Reese zipped his jacket to get rid of the flapping pockets, balanced the ball on one hand, and zeroed in. He missed again.

"That's *h*," yelled the kid, who stood beside Reese and drained one without seeming to even set it up.

Reese heard that fat bastard Teeter, the basketball coach at school, who also taught P.E., saying, "It's a mental thing with you, Cappadora. You're about one taco short of a combination plate about half the time. If you could just think about what you're doing . . ." He tried to look through the shot, but he could feel it go wrong the minute it took flight.

"That's *o*," the kid said again, with pure joy.

"I let you," said Reese, dribbling down the lane—he leapt and finger-rolled it in. "Net this, bozo."

"We're playing Horse."

"You did okay standing still, huh, First String?"

"I can take you," the kid said evenly.

Reese drove for the basket again, skipping onto the paint, looking for the sweet spot of his driveway nights—boom. "Okay, buddy, ready to go downtown?"

The kid was confused. "What are the rules?"

"I don't play in city rec, my man." Reese drove again, missed his lay-up, and spun as the ball flirted off the far side of the hoop.

"Is this Make It—Take It or what?"

"Your ball, rookie," said Reese. He didn't have to name the game, though clearly the game would have been Make It—Take It if he'd nailed the last shot.

"To what? To what?" said the kid, dribbling absently. "To eleven?"

"Just play," Reese told him. And the kid checked the ball, then made as if to dribble left, but instead dropped right three steps and set up for a shot off the board. "Count it!" he cried, and tossed the ball to Reese, murmuring, "Check."

Reese ignored him and lined up at the top of the key. The kid seemed to be measuring him, wondering how to slide, avoiding Reese's eyes. Then Reese cut right, leading with his dominant hand and bouncing the ball slightly too high. Reese thought he could anticipate the kid, so he kept on coming. He knocked the ball off the kid's thigh, recovered it at the top of the key, shot, and missed, with the ball bouncing off the rim. But Reese slipped for the board, got his balance, and tipped it in easily over the kid's extended arm.

"Who are you?" Reese asked him then, dribbling, panting.

"I'm Grant Hill."

"I'm Pippen."

"Okay." They played in earnest then, with Reese holding on to the lead, the kid repeating the score after each basket. Then Reese aired one and the kid boxed out, grabbed the rebound, took it back, and drove for the lay-up. "That's evens up," said the kid. Reese lined up. When the kid came in, he turned, feinted, and raised an elbow. The kid stumbled.

"Sor-ree," Reese said, grabbing the ball.

"You fouled," said the kid.

"This ain't the YWCA, Ben," Reese said.

"It's not Ben."

"Okay . . . Ben," Reese mumbled, driving past the kid toward the baseline. But the kid shifted his position—he had a way of sliding more than running, it was hard to follow—stepping in to take the charge. Reese struggled for concentration; he was chasing the ball, not moving with it, damn it, so he drove hard right at the kid, leading with his left arm and whacking the kid across the bridge of his nose. The kid kept his head, but Reese could see his eyes water, and then, as Reese went up for the shot, his eyes still on the kid's face, this look, this look of fear . . . he looked like Ben, who would not even slide down the plastic slide into the six-inch-deep wading pool unless he, his brother, stood there with open arms. That same wide-open look, right across the bones of his cheeks. Scared. Game. Coming. Ben, Reese thought . . . and in the instant of lost concentration, the kid batted the ball away; and both of them ran for the corner where the ball bounced. If he went for it, Reese saw the kid would fall out of bounds. The kid had no options. He had to just dive. The ball hit Reese's leg hard and out of bounds.

"Christ!" Reese winced. It hadn't nicked him where it mattered, but groin was groin; it was close enough. "You dumb shit."

"You did it," said the kid. "And it's my ball."

He took it, went left, and laid it in with a reverse lay-up that put his body between Reese's arms and the ball. Two. "I'm up now," said the kid to Reese, who was bent over, sucking air, while the kid was breathing like he was sleep. "What's it to? Twenty-one now?" The kid was excited. He almost laughed.

"Just play," said Reese.

"Go to twenty-one . . . Vinnie?" said the kid. He said it way soft, but Reese heard it and drew back, gathering, the way he had in the moments before a dozen fights, a hundred. He took the ball and dribbled around the back court, giving himself some time, raising up for a long jump shot. Sweetness.

"You see that in rec league, Ben?"

"Yep," said the kid. "In girls'." And the kid took the ball, driving right, but Reese knew his moves now, and simply spun on his heel left and stiffed him with both arms. The kid was caught under the chin and went down, off the court and into the trampled dirt, his leg doubled under him, his lip bloody.

"Shit," Reese said. "I didn't mean—" But at that moment his father barreled into him like a snowplow, knocking Reese flat on his can on the concrete, with a pain that shot up his tailbone and would have made him scream if he hadn't bit down.

"You little shit!" said Pat. He reached up and yanked off his tie. "You bully!"

"Jesus Christ, Dad!" Reese said, struggling to stand.

"I'm all right," said the kid.

"Are you hurt . . . Sam?" Pat asked him, pulling out his handkerchief. The kid waved him away, staring over Pat's shoulder at Reese.

"I'm okay, I'm okay."

"Can you go a day—this one day—without trying to hurt something?" Reese saw his dad's eyes crinkle in pain. Oh, shit. Was that sad pain or heart pain? Oh, shit, Reese thought.

Beth came out of the growing shadows under the overhang of the county building. "What happened?" she asked. "What happened to him?"

"We were playing ball is all," Reese muttered.

"It's okay," Sam said desperately. But Beth gave Reese the look she gave him once a year, like she was really seeing him or something, before she reached out to touch Sam's arm. She ran her hands over him as if she was patting him down for weapons.

"Nothing broken?" she said in her little metal voice, her I'm-just-so-fine voice, her school voice.

They put Reese in the front seat with Beth. Dad sat in back with the kid. Nobody even mentioned going to get Kerry from Grandma's place. At Benno's the pizza they ordered sat there, grease hardening in ridges like a relief map. The kid ate two pieces, carefully picking off the pepperoni, which Reese's father absently speared off the plate with a fork and ate himself. Reese watched his dad; Pat was sweating heavily, as if he'd been running. He hoovered the Coke in.

"Eat something, Vincent," said Beth. She should get a T-shirt that said this, Reese thought. So he made a game of seeing how long he could chew a single bite, watching Beth watch him, her own mouth moving in synchrony. If Reese made a monkey face, would his mother do it, too? The thought made him grin.

The kid looked up then, and asked, "Can I have some milk?"

As his father waved for the waiter, Reese asked, "You drink milk with pizza?"

They all stared at him, as if he'd told the kid to go fuck a tree. Reese got up and went into the john, where he messed with his hair and washed his face. He was drying off when Pat stuck his head in and said, "Let's go."

Dvořák, thought Reese, lying back on his bed—his lumpy good bed; they'd bought a new one for young Sam, didn't even attempt to take this one back. The Largo from the "New World." Excellent choice for a slight case of jits. He cranked it, wondering if he could levitate soundlessly simply from the vibrations out of the headphones. When he got up to get a glass of water and to change to his oldest Metallica CD, he heard Beth down the hall in the kid's room.

"Do you want a light?" she asked.

"No, I don't sleep with a light," said the kid.

"This must feel very strange to you." The kid didn't answer. "You want a blanket?" Wow, Mom, thought Reese, it's only frigging May. Right through the bathroom wall, when he went in, Reese could feel Beth touching the kid; she couldn't keep her hands off him, though he noticed, every time they saw Sam in the last week, she always drew back before she touched, as if the kid was hot.

"Saturday tomorrow," called his dad, coming up the hall. "You want to take in a game?"

"Okay," said the kid.

Father city, thought Reese. Yep. Going to take a lot of games, though, Dad. Lot of catch-up to play this season. He ran into Pat when he opened the bathroom door. His dad looked as if he were ready to have a talk; Reese tensed. But Pat only leaned against the frame of the door.

"Vincenzo," Dad said, and Reese felt his throat close. "Please, please . . ."

He heard their bedroom door shut. Mom would be in tranquo-land now; he could drive a front-loader up on the porch and she'd maybe turn over. His dad, he wasn't sure; his dad might stalk around some. And sure enough, Reese heard his parents' mattress sigh and the jingle of Pat's change as he put his pants back on. The Metallica was making Reese even more jumpy. He got up and rummaged around until he found the African sax guy whose name he could never remember. There, he thought, laying one hand exactly parallel with the other along the sides of his hips. Nothing strenuous. Drift. . . .

Didn't work. Needed Puccini maybe. He rummaged again.

Reese woke up in the dark. His father must have turned out the light. Turning, he felt under his back the familiar lump. Over the years, Reese had occasionally tried to figure out what the constant body pressure was morphing Ben's red bunny into looking exactly like. He thought sometimes it looked like a tadpole now, except for the one remaining ear. Easing up, careful not to press his groaning bladder, Reese pulled it out from under the bottom sheet. One eye. A humped, fat shape, in places its red plush worn nearly transparent pink. Embryo, though Reese now. That's it. Igor the Embryo.

Still carrying the formless thing, Reese got up to pee, and put the red bunny down on the sink. His father was snoring, the strangled choke that drove Reese nuts. The one that made him breathe along with Pat until sleep drove him under. It was after he shut off the water that he heard the sound.

Kerry? But Kerry was at Grandma Rosie's. Reese walked down the hall, keeping close to the wall, and toed open the door where the kid, Sam, slept.

He was asleep, or at least his eyes were shut. Reese stepped closer. Sam was lying on his back with his arms thrown out, sleeping that kid-sleep where you go down so hard you drool. Reese looked for eye movements. The kid was zonked. Then, Reese opened his hand and let the chafed red shape of the bunny Igor fall next to the bed. But as he turned to walk out, he heard the kid groan. Sam's arm came up over his face and he said, "No. I just don't ... no ..."

Did he mean "I don't know"? Or was he trying to stop something? The kid moaned again.

Reese sprinted for the door—what if the kid woke up? But Sam rolled over and again, this time softly, he said, "Oh, no."

There was a space between the door and the opening to the closet. Reese leaned against the wall and slid down soundlessly. He folded his arms over his raised knees and adjusted his eyes to the dark. If he strained, he could see the hands on the clock face above Sam's dresser.

It was three a.m. So. Maybe three hours. Reese had gone without blinking longer. Anyone with training could watch that long. It was just ... Reese leaned forward, his chin on his arms. You couldn't tell. . . . But then the kid tossed once again, the upper part of his body shifting into a shaft of light from the street lamp on the corner. There.

Reese relaxed. He could see his face.

Reese

Chapter 25

June 1994

For a dime, Reese would have bagged the last couple of weeks of school. But he figured that all he needed to do was get his dad on edge, and his brand-new driver's license would be folded six ways and stuck where the sun didn't shine in about five minutes flat. Dad was still Dad—in fact, he was extra-jovial Dad now that the sainted Sam was actually living under his roof—but he wasn't going to tolerate anything that would kick back on "the family." Reese could picture the headlines: "Miracle on Menard Street: Regaining a Son and Losing Another?"

Fuck that. He had two lousy weeks to keep his nose clean, and he was determined to do it. Though the strain was getting to him. He had two term papers due, and he'd been using the books he needed to write them to prop up the broken leg on the old bed that had been Ben's. Jordie had accused him of thinking he could absorb all the facts about multiple personalities (his chosen topic for psychology) by sleeping on them.

Reese figured he knew everything about multiple personalities by osmosis, from living with his mother. But he had to settle down, and with his house the Grand Central of the universe, that was pretty hard to do.

He couldn't get away from it. Everywhere he went in school, some teacher had a copy of the *People* magazine, the one with Sam dribbling in the driveway on the cover—the one with the headline that said, "Back ... But Not Ben," and underneath, "The Incredible Odyssey of a Lost Boy." Some dildo in fourth-hour study hall even asked Reese to fucking autograph it. He did. Taking pity on the kid, he wrote, "Best Wishes, Daffy Dick," when he by rights should have written something much more blistering. His mom had had a veritable shit hemorrhage when she'd seen Sam's picture on the cover— even more than she'd had over the first *People* cover, which Reese still remembered vividly.

He'd heard her yelling downstairs, "What do these people think? That we have no life?"

And his father answering, "Beth, that's what you used to do for a living. . . ."

Tom, being Mr. Detective Psychiatrist, had of course asked him, a couple of times, "Are you *sure* you didn't know it was Ben?" And Reese couldn't believe it—like, why wouldn't he have said something? If he had been really sure? Knowing the only thing his parents wanted on the entire earth was to find Ben?

And Tom had said, "Because maybe it wasn't the only thing you wanted on the entire earth."

Which was what was frustrating about Tom; he always thought he could trick you into revealing some deep subconscious longing by bringing up something so far out of the ballpark it was on top of a bus heading up Waveland Avenue. Reese, in fact, had thought about it himself, and the only real reason he hadn't mentioned the red-haired kid to his mother was because it was just too damned ridiculous to think that his long-lost brother lived around the corner. The kid didn't even really look like he remembered Ben; in fact, he didn't even remember Ben, not that much.

"I was seven years old, for Christ's sake," he'd told Tom in disgust. "What do you remember from when you were seven?"

"I remember that I had a little brother who was three months old, who died of SIDS, and I was the one who found him, and it took me ten years to figure out why I was afraid of going to sleep," Tom told him.

Trust old Tom to have a big, dramatic answer. Well, that's why they said shrinks had to be crazy themselves.

And then Tom had started asking him a whole bunch of stuff about how he felt about Cecilia Lockhart, which Reese totally had nothing to say about—I mean, how could you be mad at a crazy lady for something she didn't even know was wrong?

And when that didn't get anywhere, Tom had gakked on about how was he feeling about Sam, was he mad at Sam? Reese couldn't figure why Tom would even ask. Mad? Mad for what?

"For getting all the attention," Tom said.

"I'm not a kid, Tom," Reese told him. "I mean, if you lost a kid and hadn't seen him for nine years, wouldn't you sort of want to spend all your time with him, and be sort of obsessed with him? It's pretty natural. Especially if you had this other kid that was—"

Tom had really zeroed in on that. "Another kid who was what, Reese? What?" Reese had shrugged. "What, Reese? Another kid who wasn't worth being obsessed with?"

"Dr. Kilgore, this psycho crap can get really tedious."

Tom had laughed then, and asked Reese how he thought it would be if he had to listen to it forty hours a week, coming from his own mouth. And Reese had sort of loosened up then. He'd told Tom he was thinking of becoming a psychologist himself—you didn't have to get dirty, you didn't just bury your mistakes like other doctors. Plus, Reese figured that Tom could have paid for a strip mall just with what he'd made off the Cappadoras alone over the years.

They talked about sports, about this idea Reese had that maybe he'd try out for basketball in the fall, finally, junior year being his last chance and all. Tom thought it was a pretty good idea, but Reese wasn't sure. He wasn't much of a joiner, and though he did love the game, and had some pretty heavy fantasies about suiting up and actually showing he could do it, he just didn't know if he could take the boredom of drills and shit.

Nonetheless, he'd been doing a lot of stuff in the driveway, putting up folding chairs from Wedding and dribbling around them until he was sweating like a warthog. Sam would come out there and do it, too. Reese had to admit, the kid was fast in spite of how big he was, and he already knew things it had taken Reese years to learn, like never really letting your palm touch the ball: Sam could dribble so low a snake couldn't ease under, with those hard, long fingers, just the tips tapping, all control.

Dad would come out, in this suit, and try to play a few points with them—it was just like Grandma Rosie used to say about Grandpa: he looked like an immigrant, mowing the lawn in a sport coat. Dad always tried to get in on it when Sam and Reese were doing something; it never failed to stiffen Sam up, Reese noticed.

But Sam played baseball, too, and practice was starting, so most of the nights Reese dribbled and lobbed and dribbled on his own.

The last few days before school ended, Reese began taking a pumpkin into the deserted gym and trying some things in there. Mostly seeing if his fadeaway jump shot was really as good as it felt in the driveway and on the playground. He'd been lifting weights a little bit, to build up his arms. People didn't know it, but it took a lot more strength than a regular shot from midcourt, because you were rearing back from the guard, basically weakening your stance, instead of putting all your weight forward. But it could get a much bigger guy off you, and Reese knew that with his size, he was going to have to be able to be dead solid perfect with that and the free throws or he'd have no chance at all. Until he'd started trying to perfect the fadeaway, he'd never understood just how incredible Jordan's shot really was. And Jordan didn't have that much height, either. I mean, he had ten inches on Reese, but by NBA standards six feet six was no giant. Some nights, by the time Reese got home, his arms ached. He'd watch Sam and think, *That kid's going to go right up and stuff 'em if he keeps growing like he is now.* Was he jealous of Sam's size? He didn't think so. It just would have been a whole lot easier if he'd gotten a few more of Mom's big-Irish genes than Dad's scrawny wop ones. Look at Uncle Paul. You could float a cat in one of his shoes.

Jealousy. Nervousness. Half the time, Reese realized, he was hanging around after school trying to figure out what he was really feeling about Sam. If nothing else, his years with Tom had taught him that no matter how smart you were, when it came to how you felt about things, you were pretty much always the last to know. The first time he saw Sam, and knew it was Ben, in the counselor's office while Sam was still in foster care, Reese had almost started to cry, he was so glad. It was like Ben had this light all around him, and he couldn't believe that if he walked right up to the kid, Ben wouldn't just grab his arm and start talking about the time the squirrel got stuck in the car engine or the time Ben fell off the end of the long pier at Lake Delavan, or about the tree house in Madison. Even if he remembered the day in the lobby, fuck, he was just so glad Ben wasn't dead. . . .

But Ben—that is, Sam—had looked Reese right in the face. And he couldn't have been faking it. He looked like he'd never seen Reese before in his life. "This is your brother," said the social worker. "This is Vincent."

The kid had offered to shake hands. "Hi, Vincent," he'd said, and god-damn if his voice didn't sound like Ben, that funny, deep, hoarse voice that used to sound so weird out of a little kid. That was when Reese had wanted to run, to just get away from all of them, this fucked-up unlucky bunch of people who didn't even recognize each other, any of them. He could be like Horace Greeley or Thoreau or somebody and just head out, and work on the railroad or something. Did people still work on the railroad?

But he'd known, even then, he would never do it. He was too lazy and scared, and that was when he'd started getting irritated with the kid, with his "Yes, ma'ams," and his table manners and his phobia about germs. It hadn't taken Reese—or Kerry, for that matter—long to realize that Sam had this psycho-thing that if you breathed on his food, he wouldn't eat it. And so Vincent got so he could just exhale a little at the dinner table, just as Mom passed Sam his plate, and then Sam would sit there, looking all sick, swallow-ing like the food was old socks that stuck in his throat. But then Kerry had started doing it, too, and Dad lowered the boom.

The kid was never anything but nice and polite to Reese. Nice and polite and just . . . in himself. It drove Reese nuts. He had no idea what to do to get to Sam. Sam just didn't talk.

One time, the kid had come down while Reese was watching *Hell Is for He-roes* about one o'clock in the morning. Sam sat down, and after about half an hour he had said, suddenly, "So, is that where you got it?"

"What?" Reese had asked.

"Your name." There was a guy in the movie called Reese. But that didn't have anything to do with *his* name, Reese told Sam, and explained the "re-sale" thing, and the kid was like, well, Vincent's a good name, too—like Vincent van Gogh. Reese had been pretty shocked, a little kid knowing about Vincent van Gogh.

But what he had said, and he sort of regretted it, was, "Yeah, and he was nuts, too."

Sam, though, hadn't seemed to mind. All he'd said was, "But you didn't cut your ear off. At least not yet."

A pretty decent kid, in some ways. He never got in your way. It made Reese wonder what it would have been like, having a kid brother; Kerry had always been so little, he couldn't remember a time he didn't have to take care of her. Though Tom said that when they grew up, that would "bond" them closer. Like they were covered with some kind of rubber cement.

Go out, reverse, imagine the big blocker, fade back, shoot. Reese did it over and over. Sometimes for an hour or more. He got so he was making it about ninety percent of the time; of course, there was no real defense there, so he was probably giving himself breaks. Between concentrating on the shot and thinking about Sam, he didn't notice Teeter the day the coach came up behind him, reached over his head, and slapped the ball away.

Reese's heart felt like he'd been filled with helium. "What . . . ?" he yelled, whirling around. Teeter was built like a mastodon; they said he'd guarded Pistol Pete Maravich back in college, but that was twenty years ago, and now he looked like he'd eaten Pistol Pete and his brother for breakfast. Coach Teeter had to go three hundred pounds dry.

"If it ain't Cappadora, the terror on the playground," Teeter said, in that weasly sort of southern voice Reese always associated with drill sergeants in movies. "I been watching you in here, Vince. Going to drop out junior year and try to make the draft?"

"No," Reese told him, recovering his ball. "I'm just goofing around."

"Pretty famous guy now," Teeter said. "Huh?"

"You got me confused with my brother," Reese told him. What the hell, why piss the guy off? He still hadn't formally decided not to try out next year.

"All you Cappadoras are famous, right? Maybe that's why you don't think you have to show up for school except on alternating Tuesdays during the full moon, eh, Vince?"

Reese said nothing.

"Oh, I forgot," Teeter went on. "It ain't Vince. It's Reeeese. That's right. Reeeese. Pardon me. So, Reese, you like basketball?"

"I like the game," Reese said evenly.

"They say you take 'em pretty well out there in the street."

"I do okay."

"Wanta try with me?"

"I don't care," Reese said. They played a little Make It—Take It. Teeter was still fast, in spite of the poundage, and Reese had to hustle him; the coach also had natural size, so the lay-up was easy for him. But he couldn't get around Reese's fadeaway.

Finally, puffing, Teeter said, "You got a pretty fake there."

Reese was caught off guard. He smiled. "I work hard at it," he said.

"You thinking of coming out for the team next year?"

"I've been thinking about it."

"You think you could make it?"

"I might try," Reese said evenly.

"Do you think that the other guys would be willing to put up with all your shit, just because you got one shot?"

Reese felt all the blood pound into his face. The fat fuck. He'd drawn him out, right into the water, and then let him go.

Teeter went on. "I been watching you, Cappadora. Not just in here. You got a chip on your shoulder the size of Mount Rushmore, and you ain't got the size or the heart to back it up."

Feeling the curling of his hands, the telltale signal Reese had come to fear, he answered, "I do okay."

"You do okay, huh?" Teeter stuck his pork face right up next to Reese's. "You do okay because everybody feels sorry for you. I knew your father growing up, Vince. Nicer guy never walked the earth. Everybody felt like hell, all the shit he went through, and then, what does he get? This runt who thinks his shit don't stink."

Teeter waved one broad finger under Reese's nose. "You got speed and moves. But you come out for my team, you gotta know right then you ain't no special case. You'll be the same as the rest of them, maybe a little lower on the scale because you been living your whole life on getting the breaks. . . ."

"I've never——" Reese began.

"Come on, Cappadora! You think you're such a big man, how about acting like it? *Are* you a big man? Or just a bully?" He scooped up the ball, Reese's own ball, balancing it in his big ham hands, and bounced it once off Reese's forehead. Then again. The bridge of Reese's nose stung like a sonofabitch. His eyes began to run. But he didn't put up his hands to block Teeter's attack. Teeter did it again. And again. "Big man, Reese, huh? Wanta go? What're you going to do now? Can you take it, Cappadora? Or are you just a pussy, deep down?" And he drew back to give the ball a little more punch, but then Reese's fist came up and he snatched the ball down, almost pulling Teeter off balance.

The big man's face slackened. And he took a step back. Oh shit, Reese thought, that was the way they all acted. When they saw the look. What did I ever do to you, you fuck? All I was doing was messing around. Maybe trying to do the ordinary thing, just once. And even that got him in the shitter. Reese felt again that ferocious urge to take off, to smash Teeter's meat nose into his brain and then run, forever, to a place where he didn't have to carry around every fucking thing he'd ever done or thought like a load of bricks on his back.

"Look," Reese said, then. "Look, I just——"

"Forget it," Teeter said, whirling and slouching away. "Your kind of attitude, nobody needs."

And Reese just stood there, both arms wrapped around his ball, holding it to his chest as tightly as he could, while Teeter flipped off the light switch to the overheads, leaving him in the dark.

Beth

Chapter 26

What it seemed like to Beth was watching a tiger in the zoo.

There were times when the animal's eyes locked on yours, but there was nothing in the contact. You could never be sure whether the tiger was aware of you, individually or at all, or whether you were simply scenery, an unremarkable figment of the landscape. Did a tiger recognize a human being as distant kin, even as alive?

As she watched Sam pace, from the front porch to the back window, followed ceaselessly by Beowulf, she wondered whether he recognized her even as a member of the same species. His motion was constant, from the moment he got home from school (it took him two weeks to walk in without ringing the doorbell) until he politely, promptly closed his door at night. Even when he sat doing his homework at the kitchen table, his legs bobbed and jittered. Beth wondered if he needed . . . something—vitamins, sedatives, more milk. In his laboriously printed eight-page dossier on Sam's traits, George had indicated that his son always displayed a surplus of energy. "He's like a half-grown puppy," George had written. "He'll run and run and run and then he'll just fall down and sleep, wherever he is." Beth had seen no evidence of that. Sam's eyes were puffy, mornings; his sleep was not like that of an eager, healthy little hound.

The social worker called nearly daily. ("It's probably the first time in her life she ever did anything interesting that didn't involve five adults having sex with the kid," Candy had explained.) Sam's anxiety was natural, she explained. He was experiencing, on some level, the stages of mourning—shock, denial, anger, alienation.

"How do you know?" Beth asked her one afternoon.

"I . . . I don't," the case worker admitted. "I just . . . guess a kid in that situation would feel that way."

Beth remembered the kinds of questions the reporters used to ask the myriad experts whose headshots she took for Sunday specials. "What does the research say?" she asked.

"There isn't any."

"What do you mean?"

"I don't think this ever happened before," said the social worker. "Kids, if they're kidnapped, either are found right away or pretty much never found. Alive, I should say. I'm sorry, Beth."

The social worker described the case of a little girl mistakenly given to the wrong parents at the hospital, literally switched at birth. There had been a lot of publicity; hadn't Beth read about it? Beth made polite noises; she hadn't read anything about a missing child in more years than she could recall. This child, the social worker went on, was quite well-adjusted in most ways. Good grades. Popular. The way the natural parents found out was that the daughter they believed to be their biological child died from a congenital heart ailment, and blood tests proved she could not have been their child. There was a big probe into hospital records, and it all came out.

"And did she ever see the father she thought was her real father again? The man she grew up with?" asked Beth. "Do they have contact?"

"Er . . . yes," said the social worker. "Actually, she still lives with him. She didn't want to return to the natural parents, and a judge ruled in her favor. But then she . . ."

"What?"

"Changed her mind."

"Oh."

"And went back to her real . . . er . . . first family."

"Oh," said Beth.

"But she was much older, a teenager, and the circumstances . . . ," the social worker's voice trailed off.

The circumstances in their house were so different, Beth sometimes felt they were all strangers brought together to act in a play without rehearsal.

As vigorously as Beth resisted it on the first Saturday, the family began arriving before any of them were even awake. Angelo. How could she close the door on Angelo? And he could not have done better; he didn't leap on Sam and crush him, though Beth knew he must have wanted with every beat of his straining, mechanically charged old heart to do just that. He sat, tears streaming down his face, and told Sam about the frescoes at Wedding in the Old Neighborhood. "They look down on the *matrimonio*, the wedding. Each one of them is one of the operas, Ben," he said.

"It's Sam, Ange," Beth reminded him softly.

"Sam, of course. This is a good, strong name, Sam. I am an old man, Sam, and foolish," said Angelo. "But let me tell you. In the one, it is *La Bohème*, the face of Rodolfo, the artist made the face from a picture of your papa, of my son, Patrick. And do you know Menotti? *Amahl and the Night Visitors?*"

Sam, to Beth's astonishment, nodded. "I saw it at school, on the big TV," he said.

"The little boy? With the crutch?"

"Yes?"

"That is you, Ben . . . Sam. That is you. The little boy is you."

"Cool," said Sam. "Can I see it?" Angelo looked up at Beth, his faded eyes brimming.

"Soon," said Beth. "Let him settle down a little, Ange." She hadn't insisted for nothing that no one except her, Pat and the kids visit Sam at first. Now, on his first real full day home, she could feel Sam's fragile shell giving way, feel his confusion. She wanted to stand and motion for everyone to leave. But it would have been like trying to divert a river.

"Who's Reese?" Sam asked then.

"Reese," Angelo said. "Ah. Of course. He is Pinkerton, in *Madama But-terfly*. A bad man, unfortunately. I told Vincent, make another choice. So he chose Don Giovanni, a worse man! So, we left it be Pinkerton."

"Lot of walls," Sam commented.

"Lot of walls?" Angelo bellowed. "You should see it. This is a big place, Sam!" He turned his head as Tree came in. "And your auntie, she is the mama in *Amahl*. She is your mama on the walls."

"Ben," Tree said, kneeling, holding out her arms. Looking at Beth all the while, Sam walked into them, uncertainly, and Tree burst into tears. "Oh, Ben. Oh my God." Poor kid, thought Beth; she wanted to hang a sign around his neck that said "The Name Is Sam."

And so it went, the same scene, over and over, all weekend and into the week. By the simple sight of him, everyone, Paul, Bick, her father, seemed driven to attitudes of penance, of worship, as if he were a vision in a grotto instead of a twelve-year-old with badly scabbed knees.

After hugging him, holding him at arm's length and hugging him again, Bill thanked Sam for coming home while his grandfather was still alive to see it.

"You're welcome," Sam replied gently. "Are you sick?"

"No, no," Bill told him, heartily. "No, I'm not sick. Don't you worry. I'm just so happy, son."

"I'm your uncle," Bick told Sam eagerly. "And you were named after me. They call me Bick, but my real name is Benjamin." And without waiting for Sam to open his mouth, Bick asked, "Do you remember me? Do you remember the time I pulled you out of Lake Delavan . . . ?"

If anything was accomplished by all of it, Beth thought later, it was the fact that Sam, hopelessly confused and exhausted, desperate to give appropriate responses to questions for which he had no answers, began to hang close to Beth's side or, if she was out of the room, to follow Reese wherever he went. As the living room filled with a teeming crowd of neighbors and family, police, and the occasional reporter who slipped in grinning brilliantly and continued to grin, protesting innocence, while being ejected, Beth watched Sam and Reese dig mitts out of the garage, lock the gate, and word-lessly begin fastball catch in the yard.

They would get to maybe three apiece and then another pilgrim would arrive. Another blessing, another profession of amazement, another pronun-ciation. Rachelle. Aunt Angela. Charley Two's daughter and his son. The Bonaventuras. The Rooneys and the Reillys. Recently retired Chief Bastokovitch from Parkside. Paul's best friend, Hank.

Barbara Kelliher and her two daughters.

Barbara, who for some reason was the only face that caused Beth to blub-ber like a fool—Barbara, her neat cheerleader's haircut still pert and suspi-ciously chestnut-brown against over-pink cheeks, her Chanel still preceding her into a room, who had known Beth only slightly in high school but who had decided, on the basis of something Beth could only understand as the same quality of resolve that once made Barbara able to smile and raise a fist cheerfully while doing Chinese splits, to simply suspend her own life and rush chivalrously to the defense of Beth's. Beth caught her around the waist and would not let go; and after a moment of shocked resistance, Barbara re-turned Beth's embrace, and began to rock her, rocking her as a mother rocks a baby on her hip.

When Beth's sobs subsided to hiccoughs, Barbara asked to see Ben. Beth went to the window to call him.

"No," Barbara told her. "Just let him be. Just let me watch him a mo-ment." She turned to Beth as Ben spun to grab a high fly. "It's you he looks like," she said.

Sam fell asleep on a lawn chair, still holding a rubbery slice of pizza about eight o'clock that night. Beth had to help him up to bed and at nine the next morning was still heavily, soddenly asleep. Beth hated to haul him out, but Rosie and Angelo had arranged and paid for a special mass at Immaculata. Pat insisted all of them go, and go humbly, and was already arguing with Vincent about the condition of his chinos before Beth had had her first cup of coffee.

Blocks from the church, Beth already noticed a kind of electricity in the streets, an extra stillness only enhanced by the presence of more than the usual number of cars, nose to tail, even blocking driveways. It felt like an Easter or Fourth of July morning, a concealed and unaccustomed bustle belied by the absence of workday traffic. When they turned off Suffolk Avenue onto the boulevard, even Vincent gasped. The street in front of the church was blocked at both ends and clogged with satellite trucks and a welter of police squads—from a dozen villages and the city of Chicago, from the state—all with hood lights flashing, the concussion of rotating spots and floods creating a sort of artificial sunrise. On both sides of the plastic-tape cordon, whole families stood craning over the heads of reporters, knocking over sawhorses. "There must be a thousand people," Vincent breathed, his voice almost childish with awe.

As it turned out, the Cappadoras could park nowhere near the entrance; and they had to fight their way to the door of the church as the bells tolled for eleven o'clock mass. None of the assembled crowds seemed even to recognize them until they were on the threshold of the foyer door. Beth was almost disappointed on behalf of the press; something in the nature of this was making them expect to see a little red-haired boy, led by beatific young parents, instead of a bleary-eyed adolescent with his baseball cap ruefully turned backwards, flanked by short, dark, nearly identical men (one young, one middle-aged, neither beaming), a nondescript graying brunette in ill-fitting clothes, and a strawberry-blond girl in a miniskirt and tights. What truly stunned Beth was the fact that the church somehow was filled not with leakage from the curious throngs outside but with faces she recognized. Every face was lifted entire from her past and Pat's. What kind of screening process could have accounted for the uniformity of it? You rarely knew every face even at a family wedding. Who had been the arbiter? Who had known enough to let only the insiders pass? Beth later learned that, in fact, there had been no gatekeeper; somehow, those who knew they should enter had done so, and, with the exception of reporters, those who knew they should only look on had not tried to do more.

As Beth and Pat walked up the aisle with the children to where Rosie, Angelo, Bill, and Bick stood, with Paul and Sheilah behind them, dressed in night-class finery and holding open seats in the first pew, they passed dozens of outstretched hands and lifted, tearful faces. Classmates and neighbors;

Candy, of course, as well as cops Beth had never seen out of uniform, even many who'd long since transferred to other departments; a whole contingent of Madison friends: Laurie, of course, with her husband and children, and Rob and Annie Maltese, but others, too—the blind man on the corner who had given Ben and Vincent Life Savers when Beth strolled them around the block with their Big Wheels a generation ago, and Linda, the waitress from Cappadora's.

The opening hymn was "Amazing Grace," and Father Cleary, who had known Beth and Pat all their lives, lost no time in forging the link. "We meet today in the midst of what the Church calendar refers to as 'ordinary time,'" he said. "That is, we are not in the wake of or anticipating one of the great festivals of our liturgical tradition. But clearly, there are indications, including the fact that all the seats are filled"—self-conscious laughter—"that this is not an ordinary occasion; it is in fact a festival that celebrates not only the reaffirmation of our faith—and, as some of you may not recall, we do this every Sunday—" more laughter—"but of the power of faith and the mercy of God, which surpasses all our poor power to understand or estimate. Today, we celebrate, as we did in song, the mercy of God as symbolized by the homecoming of a child who was once lost, but now is found." Father Cleary coughed, once, nervously, and Beth forgave him for his obvious awareness of the cameras, and his ambivalence; she wondered if he'd set the VCR in the rectory to tape the noon news.

"We celebrate," Father Cleary continued, "the presence among us, in its wholeness, of the Cappadora and Kerry families, families with long roots in this Church, this school, this community, whose tragic loss nine years ago was a sorrow from afar for people all over the world, but a personal sorrow for those of us who have known Rose and Angelo and Bill and Evelyn, and Pat and Beth—children I baptized on a couple of fine Sundays some years ago. As you all know, their son Ben was taken from them nine years ago, when he was only three—and, by what can only be called a modern-day miracle, returned to them just weeks ago, not maimed, not torn, but healthy and whole.

"I will not ask the Cappadoras to stand, not only because you all know them well, but because they have already stood too much scrutiny, too much examination of their personal Calvary. But I will ask you to join with them today in their gratitude and their faith, faith that sustained them, which never wavered when the faith of those less strong would surely have collapsed, to welcome, with them, the return of Ben—" he stopped, glanced down, then looked up, straight into Beth's face—"of Sam Karras Cappadora"—Beth felt Sam, next to her, straighten his shoulders—"to his family and to our family of worship.

"Though not every celebration of the Eucharist at Immaculata is televised on worldwide TV," he continued, over yet another appreciative ripple, "we have made the decision to allow a certain level of media today in our sanctuary, because we wish to allow those who cannot be here to share today in this community of worship, in this festival that reaffirms the strength of a community, and its heart. . . . And we are asked to remind all of you that Angelo and Patrick Cappadora and their families invite you to a luncheon at Wedding in the Old Neighborhood, 628 Diversey Street, Chicago, Illinois, immediately following the service, and that it is the hope of the family that each and all of you will attend. Maps are available on a table in the baptistery. And now we wish to begin this festival, in ordinary time, by saying, The Lord is with you."

"And also with you," the crowd murmured as one.

"Lift up your hearts," Father Cleary commanded, in his old but still sonorous voice.

Beth did not know what made her look over her shoulder—a rustle of sound at the back of the church? Simple discomfort with the beginning of the liturgy, which she, lapsed and lacking, had to struggle to follow?

But she did look, and just to the left of the aisle, small in his pinstriped blue suit, stood George Karras. From a distance of thirty yards, Beth could feel his agonized unease, the effort it took for him to stand still, without straining at his tie or shooting his cuffs. She did not think about it very long. Had she stopped to think, she might have thought of a dozen things that would have stopped her from moving—the media possibilities, the imagined wrath of various Cappadoras, even the clutch of pity and dismay at her own stomach.

She got up, eyes turning speculatively to follow her, and walked quietly to the back of the church and extended her hand, which George, gulping in humiliation and relief, took. She led him back, toward the first pew, and it was only as she neared the family, the last few feet, that she dared to look up—and it was Sam's face she saw, turned on her and George, with a look she had never seen on it before.

It was, she later guessed, joy.

C h a p t e r   2 7

Pleading a sudden urge to spend a few hours alone, loosening up and prac-
ticing, Reese gave it his best try, getting out of going to the restaurant for the
big hooha lunch after church.

After all, he reasoned, his dad didn't know anything about what had happened at school with Teeter, that fat bastard; so in Dad's mind, Reese was
still toying with the idea of going out for the basketball team next fall. And
Reese was content to let Dad think that, as long as it lasted. Wherever the
hell he was really going, Dad seemed to assume he was at the rec center or
somewhere, doing drills. "Working on the free throws?" Dad would ask him
every so often, just to prove that, even thought no one else in North America
knew there was a kid in the whole Cappadora family besides Sam, his dad
at least still knew Reese existed.

"Sure, Dad," Reese would say. "Workin' on 'em."

" 'Cause you know, the team that gets the free throws wins the game," his
dad would say. "And height doesn't count for tick on the free-throw line."

"Right, Dad," Reese would agree. Dad would look all content then. Just the mention of Reese doing anything "constructive," as his dad put it, got everyone off Reese's case. Which was fine by him.

But he should have known better than to pull the old sports hole card today; it was actually fairly stupid, given that tryouts were a half-season away anyhow. There was no way he was going to get out of playing his part in the goddamned manger scene. When Reese brought it up, Dad gave him one look, and it wasn't a "Please, Vincenzo," look, either. It was a "Don't screw with me" look, and there was no use arguing. Dad could be as stubborn as a pit bull when it came to some things, and it was for damn sure that one of them was the full-out "Aren't we happy" treatment for the benefit of the masses.

In fact, Reese felt damned sorry for Sam, who looked like his underwear was about six sizes too small, and he only looked worse outside the church after that poor little guy George gave him a kiss on the forehead and told him he wouldn't "bother the family" at the party. Dumb shit. Didn't he know the kid already felt like a piece of crap for leaving his father? George was an adult, and he could have managed to come down there and have a sausage sandwich if it would make Sam feel better.

On the other hand, Uncle Joey and a couple of the others had been standing around outside the church doing the Italian hand-jive, and that could only mean they were talking about the nerve of that guy showing up at the mass at all—they were the Cappadoras! Whatever else he was, George was that bitch's husband! Probably George had a good idea of what might happen if Joey got a few Seven and Sevens in him downtown. Uncle Joey was pretty decent, generally, but he was a hothead—as were, Reese realized, about sixty-five percent of all the adult men he knew.

As they all piled into the car, dodging yelling reporters, Reese reflected that some of it, to tell the truth, wasn't all bad. The media thing was ultra-boring, though some of the guys, even Jordie, had this totally kidlike idea that being in the newspaper would make you feel important or something. The good part was that Heather Bergman and about five of her equally foxticular friends had decided to become his mother hens over the past couple of weeks. The other girls were okay, but the way Heather's blunt-cut blond hair moved at the exact level of her lips when she turned her head could transform Reese into one giant bulge in about fifteen seconds. And be-fore all this, she'd been like, "Cappadora, that little hood." Now it was, "I never knew you were so sensitive, I never knew you went through all this. . . ." Where had she been living, Zaire? Last week, as they'd walked home from the library, after what had been for Reese a fairly agonizing two hours of trying to remember Civil War dates while inhaling the smell that seemed to come from the hollow directly below the scooped neck of Heather's jersey, he'd managed to back her (and she wasn't protesting) against the wall of the un-finished library addition, and in the course of making out for maybe twenty minutes, he had not exactly felt her up, but his forearms had made definite contact when she'd thought he was just touching her cheek with his hands.

At least, he figured she just thought that. Or did girls know exactly what you were doing, too? And just pretend they had no idea? And she was like, "Reese, you're sweet," afterward, instead of looking like she wanted to belt him, which was okay, too, as long as it lasted.

But this. Shit. When they got there, the parking lot at Wedding and the street in front looked like the biggest concession for used Eldorados in Chicago.

They managed to get through another press gang, and went inside. It never failed; Reese was always surprised at the sheer goofy magnificence of Wedding, every time he walked in. This time, he got a kind of kick out of watching Sam, who'd never seen it before—watching him look up and take in the stained-glass rose windows and the replica women (even Reese thought they were beautiful, although nuts), Juliet and Santa Lucia and the one he always thought of as the Tuscan Goddess of Sexual Intercourse. He had no idea why there were women in balconies in the eaves of Wedding in the Old Neighborhood, and he always thought it made the place kind of look like the Pirates of the Caribbean ride at Disney World; but everyone seemed to either love them or get a chuckle out of them, or both. He fol-lowed the kid around the banks of linen-covered tables, as Sam goggled the frescoes, stopping particularly long in front of the Gian Carlo Menotti one—was it possible that he actually recognized his own face? And then Reese took Sam by the arm and brought him out to the bar area, where the model of the Fontana di Trevi gushed Champagne out of a jug in the arms of the sea god. They got Scottie to give them a glass and each had a sip. It was cheapie stuff—Angelo always insisted that he wasn't going to run Moët et Chandon through plastic pipes. But Sam seemed to like it.

And then, of course, Mom caught up and nabbed the glass, and then they sort of hung around the cloak room while ten thousand relatives streamed past. The place was all set up as if it were the "big" night at Wedding, Saturday night, when people brought their out-of-town relatives to visit the restaurant. There was usually just one bride and groom, but today there were two: the sweet, pretty bride, who looked like his cousin Moira would look when she grew up, and the hot one, who looked like she belonged in the swimsuit issue of *Sports Illustrated*. He remembered that one's name, Claudia. There were two others, but he could never keep them straight. He was fairly certain that two of the three grooms were gay—one was a dancer, even—but they were all great-looking and big. The two here today, one was the one Grandpa Angelo called "the Nazi" behind his back, because the guy looked like something out of *The Sound of Music.*

By the time Mom actually got herself calmed down enough to walk into the banquet room, the tables were all filled. People were eating.

"Vincent," she said, "come over here. I want us all to walk in together." Big production, Mom, Reese thought. Shit. Oh well. He looked behind him for Sam, who was goofing around running under the coat racks with Kerry. His size fooled you: he was only this little twelve-year-old. Reese's stomach felt another tug of pity.

When they came out of the bar area into the room, the band leader caught sight of them and struck up that old song about "I'll be loving you always," which Reese thought was intended for nothing except to get everyone chewing on their sausage to start bawling; even Father Cleary was in tears.

What it did, though, was make everyone stand up, and as soon as they stood up, they started to applaud. And once they started to applaud, it seemed like they would never stop.

Sam sort of hid his head against Mom's shoulder, and Reese tried unobtrusively to move over a little so that he was shielding Sam from most of the faces in the crowd. But everybody kept on applauding and yelling for about six hours, and the band kept playing cheesy songs, like "Danny Boy," and everybody cried harder. Reese thought he was going to puke. Even he felt like he might start bawling.

But at last, the bandleader, Billy, got everybody to quiet down and said, just, "Welcome home." Not the name, thank God. Nobody really knew exactly what to call Sam. And Sam kind of waved, and everybody clapped a little more then, and finally they sat down to eat. Which was good, because Reese, who normally didn't eat much of anything, was starving. And Sam was eating like they were going to outlaw ravioli tomorrow.

By the time they set up the table with tiramisu and cannoli, the busboys were moving the front tables back a little to clear the dance floor—boy, thought Reese, they're going to do the whole deal. The first bride, the one who looked like his cousin, had bustled the back of her dress and was getting ready to dance with the fag groom. What they did first, on a regular night at Wedding, was dim all the lights and have the bride and groom dance to "Sunrise, Sunset," usually with Grandpa Angelo cutting in at some point to represent the father. Reese's dad even cut in sometimes, even though he didn't like to dance. So they did that now, and then the lights came up, and the bride picked up her skirts. The sweet bride just picked them up a little; but Claudia, Reese recalled, hiked them up way high, so you could see her garter on her thigh—tough luck it wasn't her. He knew then that they were going to do the tarantella, and sure enough, pretty soon half the joint was up dancing, too.

It always killed Reese to see people who weren't Italian do the tarantella; it was like watching people who weren't really Polish or married to Polish wives trying to polka. They thought all you had to do was stand there and kick your feet, one after the other—boomba boomba boomba boom—when in fact there were steps to it. Vincent knew them, had since he was a kid, but would rather have been burned at the stake than actually do them. To his surprise, though, his father got out there and put his hands palms-up on the back of his hips, the way you were supposed to, instead of just putting your hands on your waist, the way Grandma Rosie did when she was mad—which was the way people usually did it. Back when the place first started, in fact, Grandpa had to demote a really beautiful bride to waitress because she couldn't get the hang of doing the tarantella like what Grandpa called "a real madonna."

Today, though, the Cousin Moira bride was in top form, her satin shoes flying like little pistons, and when everybody was out of breath, the band started playing it faster, and Dad started motioning for Sam to get up and dance too. Reese thought he'd pee from shame for the kid. But Sam, affable the way he was, he got up, and he started talking to Dad, and Dad motioned to the bandleader. Billy stopped right away. "My son doesn't know the tarantella, but he knows the miserlu." He stopped and bent down to hear what Sam was saying. "The sertu—it means 'the tail.' Do you know that?"

"But of course," Billy smiled, and he started playing, real slow, "Never on Sunday." Grandpa Angelo came over and gave Sam one of his great big linen handkerchiefs with the A and the C embroidered on them in red. Reese figured this was part of the dance; he'd seen it once, at a Greek wedding on TV. Sam stood there, holding the handkerchief and looking around him, until— My God, Reese thought, no way—Mom got up and walked over and put out her hand. And Sam started to show her the steps, which were slow, right foot over left, then behind, then a little hop and a turn. Mom wasn't much of a dancer, but she looked dreamy, like she was drunk; she looked almost beautiful. And then Dad took Mom's hand, and Sam pointed out how you had to hold your arm up, in an arch, and Grandpa Bill got Grandma Rosie up ... it was enough to gag you.

In a while, his mom had the hang of it. She was weaving and dipping gracefully, her shoulders swaying, smiling up at his dad, and there must have been fifty people in concentric rings, Sam right at the middle, still leading, still holding the handkerchief, kind of laughing even, his reddish hair a little plastered up with sweat. He caught Reese watching and rolled his eyes.

Oh, Ben, Reese thought. He looked away from the kid and up, away from the kid, at the frescoes on the walls. At Ben's face, the wise and wondering angel face of a little crippled boy seeing God, and then at himself, his face proud and probably better-looking then he actually was, but painted to represent some bastard whose biggest contribution to history was getting some pretty Japanese chick to off herself.

He went out to the bar to see if Scottie could be talked into letting him have another glass of Champagne.

Beth

Chapter 28

Even after the nurse and the bailiff brought Cecilia in and settled her in the enclosure beside her attorneys, Beth forgot to sit down.

She felt Pat pulling on her arm and twitched her wrist away in irritation, only then recognizing that the press, the officers, and Judge Sakura were already seated. A young Asian man, the judge was regarding her with a waiting glance, an endless and mild dispassion. Beth sat down then with a thud, wincing as she knocked her tailbone on the edge of the bench, aware of the zipping sound of a seam in her skirt splitting.

If she craned her neck slightly, though, she could still see the angelic wide face of the nurse, and just beyond her, Cecil. Had she not had the foreknowledge of Cecil's identity, Beth would have picked her out only because she wore jail-orange cottons, like a doctor's scrub suit, the only person in the courtroom not dressed in Sunday-like finery.

Cecil was not only changed. She was buried.

Crammed into the pants and tunic, the swanlike girl Beth remembered now was frankly fat, packed with rolls of flesh, odd protuberances where the skin was simply pushed beyond containing. You could still spot, in the point of her chin, in her wrists, the tiny, still-perfect bones. Cecil looked like a funhouse mirror image, a stuffed-toy Cecil, watching her nurse with rapt attention.

Beth had half-expected to feel a spurt of pity for Cecil, or rage, or something. She felt only a ravening curiosity. She wanted to crack Cecil open like a matrushka doll, opening shell after shell, searching for the woman who had stolen her baby, and beneath that the talented, patrician, disdainful teenage hotbox, and then the sharp-elbowed neighbor kid always glomming onto Ellen.

But Cecil's attorney, Michele Perrault, stood up now—small as a child, with feathers of short dark hair, dressed in jewelly colors like a medieval troubadour—and so did the DA, both with words slung on their hips like six-guns. It was the chief deputy DA, Candy pointed out, only because this was the Ben Cappadora case, and press from Boston to Brisbane were sardined into the courtroom, watching on closed circuit in two other rooms down the hall, and flowing down the steps outside, onto the curbs, onto the lawns, a human waterfall in the hazy summer sunlight.

"Your Honor," began Michele Perrault, "I have done this work for a very long time...."

Judge Sakura smiled. "We are all aware of your longevity as a litigator, Ms. Perrault," he said with immense sweetness.

Perrault softened then, too, and glanced around her almost girlishly, as if suddenly aware of all the cameras and poised pens, the sketch artists busily drawing.

"I've done this work for a very long time, relatively speaking," Perrault began again. "And I have spent many hours with my client, Mrs. Karras, over many days."

"And?" asked Sakura, scribbling.

"And I have been able to get nothing, nothing out of her that gives me reason to believe that my client can understand the charges she faces. I have the gravest doubts about whether she can assist in her own defense. Usually I can get some kind of response from virtually anyone, no matter how impaired. But my client shows no indication she knows there is someone talking to her at all."

"While I can understand your conviction, Counsel," Sakura said, "I'd like to know if you have any documentation about Mrs. Karras's mental-health history that can support your opinion."

"I do, Your Honor," Perrault said quickly. "May I approach?" The judge nodded, and Perrault brought him a sheaf of papers. "These were obtained from the psychiatrists who have treated Mrs. Karras at Silvercrest."

"For the past four years?"

"And previously, Your Honor. Mrs. Karras has been hospitalized on eight occasions, for periods of several days to several months, and has undergone a wide range of drug treatments and other therapies intended to address her condition."

"Which is?"

The DA spoke up then, as if, Candy would tell Beth later, he simply needed to pee on the tree and prove he'd been there. "With all due respect to Ms. Perrault, Your Honor, she is not a medical doctor, and not qualified to describe—"

"It's all in the documents, sir," Perrault told him. "In lay terms, Mrs. Karras is catatonic."

Perrault read from her copy. "Mrs. Karras has a long history of mood disorders, going back to her teens, and immobilizing depression that has persisted, off and on, for the past six years, becoming total four years ago. She has not"—Perrault waved at Cecil's blank presence—"been any better or worse than this since then."

"I need to study these records, of course," Sakura said. "I'm sorry if I interrupted you, Ms. Perrault. Did I? But I need to know if the attending physician is present today, and if he can explain to us Mrs. Karras's condition at the time the alleged abduction took place."

"He is," Perrault said. "But he was not treating Mrs. Karras at that time. Her physician at that time was a psychotherapist in Minneapolis, where Mrs. Karras lived on and off before her marriage to Mr. Karras, after her divorce from Mr.—" she sprinted back to her files and consulted a clipboard— "from Adam Samuel Hill, a theatrical writer, to whom Mrs. Karras was married for ... well, a total of three years. That therapist was a woman in her sixties, and died two years ago, Your Honor. Mrs. Karras was not hospitalized during that period of her second marriage. And Mrs. Karras's former husband—"

"Is he here?"

"Mr. Hill is disabled, he suffers from multiple sclerosis, Your Honor. But I have a sworn affidavit from him about Cecilia's intransigent emotional problems during their marriage. He is extremely apologetic that his condition makes it very difficult for him to travel."

"Do we have other—?"

"Mrs. Karras's mother, Sarah Lockhart, is here today. With your permission, I'd like to ask her to describe her daughter's emotional state at the time of the kidnapping."

Sakura nodded at the DA. "Is this okay with you?"

"Again, sir," the DA said, "I have to point out that I am not aware that Cecilia Lockhart Karras's mother has any credentials that qualify her as an expert medical witness."

"You know that this court is not going to regard her as such."

"Thank you, sir. The state is appreciative."

"Not at all." The judge nodded to Perrault, who asked to call Sarah Lockhart.

As the trim older woman walked rapidly and silently from the back rows of the huge room, the bailiff Beth had heard Candy call "Elvis," though his bronze tag said something else, turned to the clerk for the swearing-in. They didn't use a Bible, Beth noticed. She supposed that was out of fashion.

She still recognized Mrs. Lockhart; she had not seen her in twenty years. Beth studied the older woman's face carefully as Perrault explained how cooperative Sarah had been, how shocked, how horrified she had been to learn that her grandson was another family's purloined child. How she had helped, as Cecil's legal guardian, to obtain medical histories from Cecil's hospitalization. How bitterly sorry she felt for the Cappadoras—

"We all understand," the DA put in, with a tick of annoyance, "how Mrs. Lockhart must feel."

Perrault then burrowed right in, asking Mrs. Lockhart how well she knew the little boy known as Sam Karras.

"Very well indeed," the old woman whispered. "He was my grandson."

And she looked point-blank into Beth's eyes, Beth thinking, This is how Cecil would have looked one day—sweetly rounded and Yankee and just the least bit arty, like a matron who'd started the town's most active book group—had Cecil been spared the hot injection of madness. Sarah Lockhart's eyes begged Beth. "I never had any idea that he wasn't Cecilia's child. Cecilia's own child by birth."

"But you were not present for the birth of the child your daughter presented to you as your grandson."

"No. She and I ... Cecilia had a great deal of difficulty in her relationships with her father and me. When she was little, we considered her high-strung ... She had tantrums and then blackouts ... we thought, an artistic temperament ..."

It was not until Sarah Lockhart's recitation actually began—told Rosie-fashion, with whorls and wings of wee, irrelevant detail—that Beth realized it: There was to be no flash of illumination. Ever.

Over the long summer of the investigation, Beth had herself come to know Cecil as well as the family who had raised her.

That is to say ... not at all.

So, half-lulled by the heat of the hundreds of bodies around her in the room, Beth listened to the scant facts of Cecil's life as her mother, the D.A., and Perrault understood them: her first three marriages, all to theater types, none of which lasted longer than two years. And the pitiful truth that, of all those husbands, the Lockharts had actually met only one: George.

Beth heard about the friends the police had tried to find from Cecil's flighty periods in Minneapolis, California, and New York. Friends? None of them had ever even shared a meal with Cecil, though a few apartment neighbors in Minneapolis thought they remembered seeing Cecil with a little boy. They seemed to remember that she referred to him as her "nephew." The one true hope, a designer Cecil had stayed in touch with since college, had died the previous year from AIDS, as had his lover.

Beth could barely rouse herself even when Mrs. Lockhart began to cry, as she described Cecil's reaction when Adam Hill—"a drama critic, quite well-respected, much older"—abruptly took up with a younger woman, a dancer.

"It was one of the few times that I felt Cecilia really opened up to me," said Sarah Lockhart. "She was heartbroken. She said she felt used up. Adam never wanted her to grow old, or even to grow up, and she wasn't even thirty at the time. Of course everyone thought she was years younger." Mrs. Lockhart began to frankly sob. "And I tried to comfort her, assured her that there were compensations for getting older. She would find a good man and have a child . . . but of course, she couldn't." She looked suddenly at Beth and Pat and said slowly, "We were talking about it last night, her father and I. I'm the only one who can understand Charles very well since the stroke, and we realized that was why she did it, because of the miscarriage . . ."

Beth leaned forward in her seat, her arms stabbing with adrenaline prickles, aware only of Candy sitting up sharply, adjacent, reaching forward to curl her hand around the back of the bench in front of her.

"The miscarriage," said the D.A., looking up at Perrault, whose neck was flushed as deeply as her rosy scarf.

"I don't know this," Perrault said. "Your Honor, I . . ."

Sakura slipped his wire-rimmed glasses off and massaged his eyes. "Was Mrs. Karras given a routine physical exam in custody?" The lawyers scrabbled through their papers.

"A battery of neurological tests; we have the results right here, which counsel also has," the D.A. said quickly.

"A physical exam?" the judge asked again, patiently.

"We were concerned with the patient's mental and emotional state . . . " the D.A. replied softly.

"Which can, of course, be affected by her physical afflictions," the judge said with a sigh. "Mrs. Lockhart, did you forget to tell the police that your daughter had suffered a miscarriage?"

"No."

"Then, why does Ms. Perrault seem shocked by this knowledge?"

"I didn't tell them."

"Why was that?" the judge asked softly.

"Because I wasn't sure. I still don't know. Perhaps Charles and I should have brought it up, but we thought better of it."

"Then, I'm sorry, Mrs. Lockhart, I'm not following you."

"I'm not following either, Your Honor," Perrault put in, but he silenced her with a measuring look.

"You have to understand," Sarah Lockhart pleaded. "We saw our daughter perhaps, oh, three times before she moved back to Chicago with Sam. She didn't even come home when her father had his first stroke, and was expected to die, though he did recover fully that time ..." Sarah Lockhart breathed heavily, and Beth found herself straining to lend the old woman composure across the few feet of air that separated them. "Though I did try, I only spoke with her at any length one other time after the night she told me that Adam was leaving her."

"And then?"

"And then, she said that the reason he left her was because she was pregnant, and that she was going to get ... old and fat."

"So you went to her?"

"No, because all at once she said the pregnancy was all over; she'd had a miscarriage! And then I didn't see her again until the authorities contacted us and told us she was in Bellevue; have you ever been there?" Mrs. Lockhart winced; it was long ago, Beth thought, but perhaps not long enough. "Cecilia was just about like she is now, except that she seemed to know me, she would squeeze my hand a little. And the nurses couldn't get anything out of her. They'd kept trying to find someone to help her, but she ... she kept closing like a shell." Mrs. Lockhart's dainty hands made a small clam shell, slowly meeting. "It was the police who finally found us, found our address, because Cecilia had been fingerprinted when she was a young woman, arrested in some rally or something, not a crime."

Beth heard Candy's rapid snort, and saw, from the corner of her eye, FBI agent Bender stiffen.

"So when you talked with police and investigators from the district attorney's office, you didn't think to bring up this miscarriage ... "

"I didn't know if she'd had a miscarriage! You didn't ever know whether what Cecilia said was true or a dream!" Sarah Lockhart burst out, for the first time angry. "I just knew that my child was slipping into this darkness, and I had to make all kinds of decisions with my husband about whether they should attach electrodes to her head and put her in an icewater bath ..."

"Mrs. Lockhart," the judge put in gently. "Do you need a moment?"

"No," she said firmly.

Perrault, dazed, seemed to recover herself and said, "Well. Then. Mrs. Lockhart, then, as you told police, you believed when Cecilia showed up in 1985 with ... Sam, that he was her child. How is that possible if you thought she'd lost her baby?"

"Please!" Sarah Lockhart pleaded. "I loved her dearly, I love her still. Don't you understand? If I asked Cecilia a question she didn't like, she would threaten to kill herself, or never to speak to us again ... and we knew that she meant it." She glanced down at her hands. "When she said she and Adam had actually gotten back together and had a child, but then split up, it seemed possible. When she said the court had given custody to Adam because she was too ill to care for him ... well, what was I to believe? She seemed so ashamed."

"But if she was too ill to care for him?" Perrault ventured.

"Then, well, she got better! She seemed fine, and she seemed to be a good mother, even though the child was shy with her ... well, I assumed that was because he was only getting to know her all over again after spending so much time with his father."

"And why didn't you confirm all this with Adam?"

Sarah Lockhart looked at the attorney with pure scorn. "Miss Perrault, I had never even met the man. He had left my daughter alone, and ... and expecting, and then taken her child from her. Why would I have talked to him?"

"To know," Perrault fumbled helplessly. "To be sure ..."

"Cecilia said Adam was ill, that he had multiple sclerosis. Which I now know is really true. He actually does. You don't understand. She could be very convincing. And ... then, I just ... I didn't dare."

"Why?"

"Because Cecilia said that if I called Adam, ever, she'd never let me see the boy again. And I ... I wanted a grandchild. I wanted a healthy, loving child who loved me. I wanted to ... believe her. And he was so big, I believed he was four, not three...." She turned her gaze on Beth, and Beth felt her own eyes tug and itch in response. "Beth, I swear to you on my honor, he was always such a big boy. And not red-haired. We all saw in the papers that Ben was red-haired. His hair got reddish when he got big, of course—and when Cecilia married George, of course, we saw Sam all the time."

Sarah Lockhart leaned forward, gripping the polished rail. "Beth, she never spanked him. She never hurt his feelings. When Cecilia was well, she was gentle and tender to Sam; she always read to him; she taught him songs. They played this little game where she taught Sam to pretend he was the echo from the well in the wishing song from *Snow White*, and he knew all the words. . . ."

Beth was nodding, nodding, transfixed, when she felt Pat bury his face roughly against her shoulder; she turned almost casually to cradle his head and felt, rather than heard, the whirr of cameras that would make the big color shot that would splash above the fold next morning. What Pat was thinking, of course Beth understood—his beloved baby in the arms of the serpent, Ben's lips forming words the witch pronounced for him. But what, Beth thought angrily, suddenly, was the difference? Would it have been better to hear that Cecil was a bad, absent, crazy mother, who smacked Sam or called him stupid, as she, Beth, had done to Vincent, and even Kerry—and more than once? Would Pat feel more righteous had he known that Cecil had forgotten to wipe Sam's nose or give him Triaminic when he coughed? If Sam were not strong, healthy, bonny, would that further authenticate their grief?

Then Beth noticed Candy, turned in her seat as if studying Beth's face for a lost coin or a dropped stitch. What, Candy, Beth thought, what? She glanced at her watch—wouldn't court break soon?

"Then George and Cecilia were divorced," Mrs. Lockhart murmured.

"Cecilia and Adam?" Perrault asked.

"No, Cecilia and George—George Karras. They are legally divorced."

"Right. Yes. Was this because George wished to pursue other relationships?" asked Perrault, who knew better.

"No, oh my goodness, no," said Mrs. Lockhart. "He loved Cecilia with his whole heart. No one could have put up with . . . well . . ." George's small construction business did well, explained Mrs. Lockhart, but the insurance he had could not begin to cover the magnitude of costs associated with Cecilia's long hospitalization. And disability programs were limited if a woman had a healthy, working husband. "George was afraid her illness, if it went on forever, would eat up everything. That he'd have to sell the house and not be able to take care of Sam." She glanced again at Beth. "I'm sorry, Beth."

To her shock, Beth said, clearly, "That's all right."

When Sakura called a recess, reporters crouched all around Beth and Pat like elves, as they rose to leave the room—Pat was genially telling them, "I never really knew Cecilia but now, God, she's pitiful. You can't hate someone so absolutely pathetic." ("Ben's Father Forgives," Beth imagined the headline, inwardly smiling as she recalled the way Ellen had begun calling Pat "the quotable saint.")

Candy motioned to Beth then, and with that unearthly ability to part the press like the Red Sea, led her out the door into the corridor of the jail, where the bailiff stood sucking a Tootsie Pop just beyond the door.

"Elvis, baby," Candy said to him in her best flirty growl, "don't make me want you. . . ." Beth saw his name now, clearly: Elmer. He moved aside to let them pass.

"This is probably against some law," Candy explained in a whisper. "But I want to see her. You want to see her. Perrault is with her. You want to come in?"

Beth nodded. She could feel all her pulses, the backs of her knees, the underside of her chin. In a pen of what looked like chicken wire, Cecil was alone with her nurse and her lawyer.

"Cecilia," the nurse said, with the kind of respect Beth knew she could never summon over and over again, in the face of a clay figure, "Chief Bliss is here to see you. Is that okay?" Cecil didn't even blink. When a stray bottle fly lighted on her upper arm, the muscles didn't quiver. Candy knelt down in front of Cecil's beefy knees.

"Cecil," she said. "Listen. Cecil. Please tell me. Where is the baby's grave? Where is the baby buried?"

The baby? Beth's unease erupted in a flutter—another child? A murdered child?

"Have you checked?" Candy asked Michele Perrault. "Did you find a death certificate?"

Flustered, Perrault replied, "A death certificate? How could I check for something I didn't even ... listen, Detective, you have to know that this came from left field for me. My client's mother never said one word about a pregnancy, though I can't imagine what she was thinking ... I mean, in keeping it back."

Musingly, Candy said, "I don't think she needed a reason, Michele. Or at least, a reason that would make sense to you and me."

"But to lie!" Perrault caught herself, with a guilty look, as if hearing how she sounded for the first time. "I mean, to forget such a seemingly important detail. Of course, Sarah Lockhart has been under enormous strain. It's not entirely unexpected."

"It's not at all unexpected," Candy replied, wryly. "I fully expect people to try to protect their children. They do it all the time. They do it in much more outrageous ways. In her mind, Mrs. Lockhart was clinging to the fact that with Cecil, she could never be sure."

"You know," Perrault said, "a miscarriage sometimes triggers an abduction. I mean, no one disputes the facts of what took place here. We're talking ... what, four years after the fact, probably, but it still might have given us something to go after. Something in the way of a cause for Cecil's actions."

"Oh, Mrs. Lockhart probably understood that, somewhere deep down."

"So, are you saying then that she really did suspect Cecilia's child was Ben? Maybe without realizing it? Because I never got the impression she was being deliberately untruthful," Perrault said.

"Nor did I."

"Then why not talk about this miscarriage thing?"

"She probably told herself it was a long time ago. And that it didn't matter ..." Candy paused, pressing her finger against the line between her eyes. "Or maybe ... maybe, she sensed something about the whole thing," she went on, more slowly. "The way I do."

"What?" Perrault asked.

"I mean, it isn't as though I've never heard of people who got knocked off their pins by a miscarriage—or even by thinking they had a miscarriage. And this isn't a normal woman. But something . . . maybe there really wasn't a miscarriage. Maybe there was actually a baby."

Beth broke in then, "What baby? Her baby?"

"Wouldn't that even be more of a reason to be absolutely forthcoming?" Perrault fumed. "Her having a grandchild out there somewhere? Dead or alive? Or is that what you're saying at all?"

"It's probably nothing," Candy said, kneeling, putting her hand on Cecil's leg. "I just . . . I don't know." Cecil's eyes began to dart down then, down and up, over and over. Her head began to follow the eye movements, as if a string were being jerked ever more vigorously.

"Don't think she really heard anything," the nurse said smoothly. "She's perseverating. She'll do the same movement over and over sometimes, unless you stop her. There, there, now, Cecilia . . ." She caught Cecil's bobbing chin in her hand. "That's good."

"Cecil. Help me find your baby's grave," Candy murmured again.

Beth was sure, later, that she imagined it. After all, Candy, utterly fastened on Cecil's face, said she never saw a thing. But Beth heard a tiny shushing sound and believed she saw Cecil's lips draw back and her teeth align the way an ordinary person's would before she made the sibilant sound of an *s*.

Candy got up off her knees. "Bethie," she asked, "you want to take a ride with me?"

"Now?"

"Tomorrow. Maybe, you know, maybe even tonight if this all goes down as fast as I think it will. All Sakura's going to do is ask for another independent psychiatric evaluation and a physical, with periodic reviews of her condition . . . After all, this is a serious charge. But I think he'll basically dismiss, you know that, don't you?" Beth nodded. "Because even if she knew what she was doing nine years ago, she clearly doesn't know what she's doing now. And she probably never will. So, you want to take a ride?"

"Sure," said Beth. "Where?"

"Well, there are really two things I'm concerned with. You remember way back when I called Bender the first time, the coupon shopper who spotted Ben in the mall with the old lady?"

"In Minneapolis."

"Yeah," Candy said, her finger pressed against her forehead line. "I want to go see that little old lady. I think she wants to talk to me."

"I thought you wanted to find out about a baby."

"That, too," Candy replied, suddenly straightening up, and surprising Beth by smiling. "Try to keep up with me here."

Pat was only mildly miffed when Beth asked him, outside the courthouse, about going up north with Candy.

"What am I going to do with the kids?" he asked.

"Oh Pat, don't be tedious," Candy said. "Take them to the Six Flags of Italian restaurants—isn't that what *Bon Appetit* called it? We'll be back by to-morrow afternoon."

"Why don't you take your own husband instead of my wife if you want company?" Pat mock-whined, but smiling now.

"Chris is a babe," Candy admitted, "but would you want to drive nine hours in a car with a corporate lawyer?" She glanced at Beth. "Me and Beth, we'll sing the country Top Forty, okay?" Her voice dropped, suddenly directed, serious. "This is a thing that I just think I want Beth to see too. Okay?"

They drove in Candy's own car, a sleek new black Toyota Beth had never seen, not the chief's squad Beth could still not get used to seeing her drive. Chief Bliss. Crackerjacker cracker of the Cappadora case. Beth sighed. If those Florida bartenders could see her now. Candy swilled Coke and sang along with dirges about faithless men and woebegone women, doomed to meet when everything but the light of their love was extinguished by circumstance.

"No wonder they drink," Beth said after two hours of unrelieved longing in two-part harmony.

"Don't you like?" Candy asked, giving Beth a half-elbow to the ribs. "Aren't you a romantic?"

No, thought Beth, that I am assuredly not. "Are you?" she asked.

"Yes, I think I am. I think that all the bad things in the world, including wars and religion, and all the good things in the world, including Shakespeare and country music, come from love. That's what I think."

"I'd have to agree, especially with the first bit. But I also think there'd be electric cars and a cure for AIDS and I don't know what all else if people didn't have to crack up over love about six times a lifetime or feel like they were missing out on something."

"Not you," Candy said. "At least not you. Not over that."

Not me, thought Beth, oh my goodness no, not faithful little Elizabeth Kerry Cappadora. And Beth almost told her, then, about the day at the hotel, which had softened for Beth, become a kind of little romantic shrine she went to tenderly, without the scalding splash of guilt, now that Sam was home. Even when she woke wet from dreams of Nick, she was grateful for Pat's untainted presence beside her.

Sam, she thought, had raised them all up, and for all her anguishes and regrets, Beth liked to think that he might lead them all to a higher place where they could stand.

As if privy to her thoughts, Candy asked about Sam. "How's he fitting in?"

"Pat thinks he's going to be fine," Beth told her. "But he's still so ... silent. We're going to Madison next week, for the Fourth. It'll be the first time he's been there since ... well, since. He seems worried about it. I've asked him what's going on, but he just shrugs. I'm thinking of asking if Tom Kilgore will talk to him...."

"He's got a lot on his mind."

"Kerry thinks he's a celebrity, like someone whose face would be on a cereal box instead of a milk carton. And she's such a little chatterbox, asking him all the time how it feels to be kidnapped, asking him if he'll sign Blythe's soccer ball. But he doesn't get mad at her. I think maybe he's missed having brothers and sisters. He follows Vincent around all the time."

"And how does Reese treat Sam?"

"He ignores him."

Candy laughed. "Well, that's normal, right?"

Was it? Wearily, Beth decided to accept that it was. She sometimes felt as though she were studying Vincent like a tropical disease, trying to read the variations in his generally impassive expressions as if they were mutations in an exotic strain. But there had not been a school incident in months, and weren't all teenagers morose? At least the pierced-navel crew he'd started to hang with had been less in evidence of late, and Jordan had been showing up more often, probably drawn back by the sudden Cappadora celebrity.

Maybe, Beth thought, she was simply waiting for other shoes to drop that weren't even hanging in the balance. If she could spend some time with Sam, some time alone, Beth thought, growing sleepy. Maybe we can take a day together, he and I. I can explain Vincent to him. Or something.

When she woke, it was dark, Tammy Wynette was still warbling, and they were in front of the gates of a cemetery called Saint John of the Cross, in White Bear Lake, just outside Minneapolis.

"Why . . . what are we here for?"

"I have this hunch," Candy said. "Cecil was crazy, but she was a cradle Catholic, like you. And we know she lived less than two miles from here, in a rooming-house sort of place, after she left that guy Hill. I'm assuming she was still pregnant then." Stiffly, Beth unfolded herself from the bucket seat and followed Candy up to the gatehouse of the cemetery. A light burned in a window. "And if you had a baby who died, maybe who you killed . . . I'm not saying she did, but wouldn't you want that baby buried in consecrated ground? That would sort of be logical, wouldn't it?"

She isn't even talking to me, Beth thought. She'd doing what my grandmother Kerry used to call talking out loud. But it was Beth who spotted the sign on the gatehouse door, Will Return, and a clock face set at 9:00 a.m.

"It figures," Candy fumed. "Don't people visit their dead at night? So, what do we do, Beth? Wanta go get a room someplace and sleep? Wanta go to a disco and pick up guys?" She glanced sidelong at Beth. "Want to go to a show at the Guthrie? Want to go see Cecil's landlady? Maybe that tipster, our anonymous concerned lady citizen, maybe it was someone who recognized Cecil from before. And knew her kid. Knew Ben wasn't her kid. Huh? It's possible."

Candy started the car. "But that's ridiculous," she continued. "She said on the phone the kid was with an old lady, an old gray-haired lady in a big picture hat and sunglasses. Not Cecil. Well, maybe the landlady was a babysitter. Not Sarah Lockhart. Unless she was lying, she didn't even know Ben existed that summer."

"And she's not scrawny. She's plump. Not skinny like Cecil," Beth said.

Candy dug through her bag to root out the copy of the earliest timeline for Cecil's whereabouts during the first years after the kidnapping. The apartment complex in Minneapolis—the periodic long stints at her parents' house. "Here," she said finally. "The rooming house."

She scanned the one-way street they were driving on, looking for the address. "F. Scott Fitzgerald lived in this suburb with Zelda," Candy said suddenly.

Beth huffed, "I knew that."

"What I meant is, this must be a mecca for the wild at heart."

"Doesn't look like it."

Apple Orchard Court was only a half-step down from the manicured suburban middle-density expanses that surrounded it; the houses were older, wooden gingerbread in good repair. Twice in three blocks, Beth saw signs for bed-and-breakfast inns. "We could stay at one of those," she told Candy. "It's probably cheaper."

"I hate the locks on regular houses," Candy said. "Give me a Best Western anytime." She inched the car forward and glided into the drive of a white two-story frame number with tiny topiary shrubs sculpted all along the massive front verandah. "This is it. This is where Cecil lived after she left Hubby Number Three."

The old man who came to the door had no idea who Cecilia Lockhart was. "My brother's the one you want. But he's playing gin at the church tonight. And he won't be home until after ten. They go late. But even then I don't know if he could really help because Rosie ran most of that show."

"Rosie?" Beth cried.

"Rosemary," said the old man. "My sister-in-law. She ran the rentals. And there were a score of young women and men who lived here—some of the men you couldn't tell if they were men or women, you take my meaning."

Candy flipped her shield out then, and the old comedian settled right down. "You're police," he said.

"I am, and all the way from Chicago, and though I hate to bother you at this time of night, I have to ask, is Rosie home now? Rosemary?"

"Oh my, no," the old man said earnestly. "That's even more difficult. She's ill. That's why we've been batching it, Herb and me. My Lydia died in eighty-nine, and now with Rosie so ill ..."

"Too ill to talk to me?"

"Well, she's living up at the nursing home. Prairie View."

"Where's that?"

"Other side of town. By the new mall."

"Do you think I could use your telephone? Call her and see if I might visit her?"

"Well, you could," said the old man. "But that's the thing. Rosie's real sick."

"Is she dying?"

"No."

"Then?"

"She's not right. She's got this Alzheimer's disease. She don't remember anything except from the past."

"This was in the past," Candy said hopefully.

"I mean, real past, ma'am. From when she was a little girl in Sioux Falls."

Candy nodded sharply and reached out to grab one of the old man's gesticulating hands, to shove one of her business cards into it.

"Please tell your brother we'll be at the downtown Best Western," she said. "We'll be there tonight, if he'd give us a call. We'll come right over, no matter what time it is. This is extremely urgent business."

"Oh my," said the old man, glancing at Candy's card. "I will do that."

But at that moment, a huge, ornate old Lincoln Town Car pulled slowly up in front of the house, and an erect, smaller edition of the brother from Tampa, dapper in a seersucker sport coat, bounded out of the front seat and up the walk. Candy turned to face him. Yes, he said, he was Herbert Fox, and his wife, Rosemary, had indeed rented rooms to young people. Candy produced one of the glossy photos of Cecil in her heyday as an actor, and Herbert Fox studied it carefully.

"Well," he said. "This looks a lot like her. Like a girl I remember for one reason. But she had red hair, you know."

"Did Cecil have red hair?" Candy asked Beth.

"She had every color," Beth said.

"A tiny little thing," Herbert Fox went on. "Sick in bed a great deal. My wife was very fond of her. Mother-henned her a bit. And of course, you know, we didn't realize when she moved in, but she was ... expecting."

"That's the one, then," Candy said. "Mr. Fox, did Cecilia have the baby while she lived here?"

"Well, yes she did ... that is, not right here in the house, but I know that my wife drove her to the doctor when her time came," said Herbert Fox. "And that was the funny part. She insisted Rosemary go back home and leave her there. And afterward, Rosemary went to Little Company of Mary, and they'd never heard of Cecilia ... Hill. That was her name. Cecilia Hill. Apparently, it was a false alarm, and she didn't have the baby that time. But she didn't come back, either. Rosie was worried sick for a while. She was getting bad then, my Rosie, and every little thing really set her off. She'd go on about stuff for hours. Of course, we didn't know at the time how serious what Rosie had was ..."

"Mr. Fox," Candy persisted. "Didn't Cecilia ... Hill come back for her things?"

"No, she didn't."

"Are they still here?"

"No, no. There was no unpaid rent. So we just boxed up the clothes and things. The room was furnished. A year later, after Rosie was real sick, a lovely woman, an older lady, came and got the girl's things. And this woman was very nice. She insisted on paying a month's rent, just for our keeping the things."

"And did she ask about Cecilia's baby? About the false alarm? Did she tell you about her grandchild?"

"Oh dear, no. She was a very quiet, polite lady."

"And did you tell her about what happened that night?"

"Well, she was the girl's mother, wasn't she? She'd know all about a girl's ... delicate things, wouldn't she? I didn't think it was my business to meddle, and poor Rosie was way past understanding, so even if I'd found anything out, I couldn't have told her. Doesn't pay to be nosy just for the sake of it."

"And did you tell the police about this, when they interviewed you about Cecilia?"

The old man was honestly stunned.

"Police?" he whispered. "What? Did that little girl come to some harm?"

"No. No, she's . . . alive and well. But you haven't talked with police about Cecilia Hill? Cecilia Hill or Cecilia Karras?"

"Not before you."

Candy sighed. Gently, she took Herb Fox's limp hand and thanked him, and courteously began to explain the basic facts of Ben's abduction; but the old man suddenly looked drained of breath. "If you don't need anything else," he said, "I think I'll just turn in, officer."

"That's just fine, Mr. Fox. You've been more than helpful. Don't spend any more time worrying about this. It's all over."

In the car, she turned to Beth. Her face, already drawn, was further bleached by a shard of late moonlight through the front window. "You're thinking, aren't you, why didn't they ever talk with Herb Fox? And I'm thinking the same thing." Beth opened her mouth and Candy held up a warning hand. "But Bethie, wait. At the same time that I'm thinking why didn't they ever talk to Fox, I'm thinking, why should they have? There was no reason to think Cecilia had a child. We weren't trying to find a kidnapper, we already had her in custody. We already had good witnesses to her movements since the kidnapping. All this," she waved at the neat hedge around the rooming house, "happened before Ben was even born, years before the reunion."

Beth turned away, and Candy said, to her back, "You can call that sloppy work. I might even agree with you. But people don't know what they don't know."

"Police do," Beth said.

"Police especially don't," Candy murmured. "They've been in so many forests they sometimes don't see a tree unless it falls on them."

"What if," Beth asked, struggling with tears, "what if she did it before? What if she tried it before? And did she kill her baby?"

"Do you have an idea of how we could find that out, Beth? Because if you do, I'd like to hear it. We'll go to those cemeteries in the morning. Or to the coroner and look for a death certificate, in case it wasn't a late-term miscarriage after all."

"The cemetery," Beth said abruptly.

Candy gave her a measuring look. "Okay," she said.

"And maybe I can think of someone else we might ask," Candy mused aloud. "But really, to say that your old pal Cecil wasn't much for enduring relationships is really an understatement, huh?"

"She wasn't my old pal," Beth shot back, thinking then, unbidden, just one enduring relationship. Just one.

"I'm sorry," Candy said then. "I'm just tired. I'm so tired I feel like I'm a hundred."

"Me, too," Beth sighed.

"And I, for one, could use several drinks."

Beth said meekly, "Me, too."

By the time they checked in at the hotel, there was only a double room left—"a first-floor corner," said the young man at the counter.

"Nothing on the third floor? I can't imagine every room—what do you have here, two hundred?—" Candy began.

"We'll take that," Beth told him exasperatedly.

"It's a very nice room," he huffed. "It's just that the twirlers are in town, and everything else. . . ."

For the balance of the night, Beth and Candy, each lying gritty and fully clothed on her own queen-sized bed, listened to the stampede of high-school drum majorettes as they squealed and rampaged up and down the halls. At midnight, Candy sent down for cheeseburgers and pitcher Bloody Marys. She drank two, leaving most of her burger. Beth nibbled, but finally gave up and simply drank, too.

"I hate loose ends," she told Beth. "And I'm celebrating yet another month of perfectly planned sex with perfectly timed ovulation and perfectly awful results."

"I'm sorry," Beth said.

"Me, too." Candy flipped the card listing the pay-per-view attractions. "Most women spend most of their lives trying not to get pregnant. I never used any of the high-tech kinds of birth control in my life. Naturally, I thought I'd be an instant fertility goddess. I was thinking maybe we'd get two kids in before I ran out of steam." She slugged her Bloody Mary and turned her attention to the program card. "Want to watch Arnold? A sensitive Japanese flick about doomed love among serfs? At least now I can drink for the next week. Before my next appointment with Dr. Clomid. Now, here's a possibility. *Vixens After Dark*—how about that, Beth? See how the other half lives?"

"I'm afraid I've always been a failure as a vixen." Beth smiled.

"You are the original one-man woman," Candy agreed.

"No," Beth protested. "I had my adventure period." Candy made a face. "No, for real. Before Pat, when I was in college."

"I thought you got together in college."

"Not the minute I got to college. What I mostly did was try to pick out guys to sleep with who looked like they understood the big mystery. And it took me a long time to figure out that they were probably thinking the same thing about me. I didn't really appreciate sex until I was probably thirty, you know?"

"All the wasted years," Candy said, leaning back on her elbows. Beth realized both of them were more than a little drunk.

"What about you?" Beth asked then, noticing the belligerent edge in her voice. "You say you're this big romantic, but the way you talk, you've spent most of your life trying to convince the boys that your pistol was as big as theirs."

"And don't think I don't regret it," Candy said. "I've had maybe two serious lovers in my life, not counting Chris."

"Which you don't exactly count."

"Beth, come on."

"I'm sorry about that, too."

"You are. You're a very sorry person." But Candy smiled. "Two serious lovers, and then the whole gamut of stuff you think you're supposed to do because you're a free-to-be-lesbian-feminist chick ... which is mostly just boring."

"Is it?" Beth asked. "Is it boring?" She wondered if she was seriously drunk. "I mean, I've always wondered, and I've never asked you . . . I just assumed that it would be better between women, the sex part, because you would know what the person wanted. . . ."

"And be really sensitive and tender, right?"

"Well, yeah."

"Actually, I hate to let you down, Bethie, but there are just as many selfish and demanding gay women as there are straight men."

Candy smiled, a sort of private smile that made Beth feel, suddenly, very alone. "You know," Candy said. "It's not awful with Chris at all. It's nicer than I thought it would be, and I was determined to grit my teeth and bear it even if it wasn't nice."

"But you still . . . you've had other relationships anyway, right? I mean, you couldn't just . . ."

"I'm married, Beth," Candy said.

"I just meant . . ."

"Is it a marriage of convenience, a rather more goal-directed marriage than most? Sure it is. Or maybe it isn't. I mean, shit, don't half the people in the world marry people they're not exactly madly in love with because they want security, or children, or whatever? We just didn't pretend about it. And so why would I have cheated on him?"

"Well, Chris knows that you . . ."

"Do you cheat on Pat?"

Beth hesitated. "Of course not," she said.

Candy sighed. "I'm being hard on you, probably because I'm such a bitch today. I know exactly what you mean, and probably, Chris truly wouldn't even consider it a huge, huge deal. He's a man of the world, as he often reminds me. He's very proud of how PC he is about my past." She grinned. "It would be me that I was letting down, Beth. It's just a cheesy thing to do, in my opinion." She looked hard at Beth, who made a show of stirring the celery stalk in her tall glass. "Don't you think it is? Don't you think it's sort of the ultimate in dull, predictable behavior?"

She knows, thought Beth. *I always knew she knew, but now I'm sure.*

"I don't know," Beth stammered, trying to recover. "There could be reasons that people—not me, maybe, but . . . don't you ever think that maybe the great love of your life is still out there?" And maybe, she thought but didn't say, you met him once and gave him up, because while he was sweet and sexy and basic you were afraid you wouldn't be able to discuss Russian novels together?

Candy said then, sighing, "I guess. What do they call it? That 'lifelong passionate conversation.' But I'm never going to have that. Probably. Chris and I . . . it's not like that." She raised herself up on one elbow. "You know, Bethie, there were times, at the start, when I thought that you and Pat would split. What you went through . . ."

Eighty percent of us divorce, Beth thought, eighty percent. But Candy was continuing. "But later, I saw that you and Pat could weather anything. You can tell when people have . . . what you have."

In the morning, they drove to the cemetery against the early-morning traffic streaming into the city and Beth waited in the car while Candy went in to interview the caretaker. After about twenty minutes, Candy returned, a slip of paper in one hand. She got into the car and sat for a moment, looking straight ahead, gripping the wheel. Beth thought she would burst.

"What?" she finally asked.

"It was a four-corner bingo, Bethie," Candy said. "Look here." She held up the paper. "Hill, Samuel Seth. A–14. Out of all the Catholic cemeteries in all the cities in all the world, she walked into this one."

Beth had not expected to feel so near tears. But neither she nor Candy spoke as they picked among the simple stones to the flat marker that read, after the name, "April 6, 1983–April 14, 1983." And below it, "Tomorrow and tomorrow and tomorrow."

"That's weird," Candy said. Beth's voice wouldn't come. "So. He died in a week."

"But of what?"

"Of complications of prematurity," Candy said, and to Beth's look, added, "I saw the death certificate, Beth. They had it on file here. It was the county hospital. And remember, our old buddy Herb didn't even know she was pregnant when she moved in."

"Forget it," Beth said. "Let's just forget it."

"And what do you think the inscription means?"

"It's Shakespeare. *Macbeth*, where he talks about how life creeps in its petty pace from day to day. It's very famous."

"I guess I didn't go to that school," Candy sighed. "But it's not what you would imagine for a child. She was already probably not entirely there, Beth."

"It doesn't seem that strange to me," Beth said. "I guess because I wasn't entirely there, either, when I felt like that."

Beth drove on the way home, and Candy dozed restlessly. They were past Rockford when Beth suddenly sat erect and jammed the brakes.

"What?" Candy yelled. "What's wrong?"

"Her hair was white," Beth said.

"Whose hair was white?"

"Cecil's. I just remembered. The day of the reunion—I never think of it, I haven't thought about it in years. But Ellen said Cecil's hair was white. Dyed platinum. And Herb Fox said she was sick. She was always skinny. And even later, when she was well again and met George, he said she wore her hair up most of the time, in a bun. So she could have looked like a little old lady, even though she was young I mean, in a hat and everything."

"Detective Cappadora, that is very good work," Candy said. "That could be it. It very well could be. I thank you. Now, I'll just go home and relax, like Dr. Clomid says. I'll be pregnant by Friday."

Chapter 29

Beth woke the next morning to the sounds of voices raised, arguing, below her window. She'd fallen into bed the night before, waving away Pat's urgent questions, not even bothering to brush her teeth, pausing only long enough to shuck her jeans.

Now, as she tried to bring herself to full consciousness—her head felt like a heavy flower on a stalk, likely to snap at a movement—she was shocked to realize that the angrier voice was Sam's.

"I already told you!" Sam was saying. "This is what I always do!"

And Pat's voice responded, "Look. Those kinds of fireworks are illegal. We'll go out on Rick and Laurie's boat and we'll see real fireworks. You can see them all over the whole city...."

"I'd rather stay with my dad, though," said Sam. "I don't remember Madison. And we have fireworks my uncle Pete brings from Missouri, and they're really cool, and only the grownups do the punks, so it's real safe...."

Beth sat up, settling her elbows on the windowsill to see the two of them. Vincent was down there, too, fiddling with stuff in the trunk of the car, but Pat and Sam were facing each other squarely in the middle of the driveway.

The way they stood, Beth noticed with a pang, with their fists planted on their hips in confrontation, was exactly the same.

Beth had believed the hardest thing that she would have to face today would be to try to interpret for Pat not only the facts she and Candy had learned but their import. She had almost decided that the facts would have to be sufficient ... at least until she'd had time to sort through all the empathy she couldn't help feeling about Cecil and her lonely, useless week of motherhood, followed by the later, even more lonely and ultimately useless years.

Beth jumped out of bed and into her jeans. She would sooner have tried to break up a three-dog fight than explain all that to Pat. He would call it Beth's crazy yen to ferret out the dark cloud behind every silver lining. It would enrage him, he would say her musings were the kind of stuff that filled up the second hour of made-for-TV movies. The tiff below was a welcome obstacle. Who knew, maybe Pat was right—that all they needed to do was give Sam time. There was no other alternative.

She bolted down the stairs and out the door. Sam and Pat were still bickering, and even Vincent was getting in on the act.

"Sam, it's actually pretty fun," he was saying. "All the other boats are out on Lake Mendota, and people are cheering and stuff. It's neat. You'll like it. And Rick and Laurie have this big pool in their backyard. . . ."

"I'm not going," said Sam.

"Well," Pat told him gently, "you are going. You are going when the rest of us go, because that's what we planned. I'm going to go into the house and get the cooler, and when your mother is dressed and Kerry is ready, we're all going to get into the car and we're going to go."

"Maybe we can show you the house," Vincent suggested, then. Beth felt a spurt of pride surprise her; he sounded so reasonable, so nearly parental. "Don't you want to see the house where we lived?"

Still sulky, Sam said, "Why would I want to see where you lived? I don't remember being born."

"Aren't you a little curious? Lincoln didn't remember being born, either, but I bet he liked going back and looking at the little log cabin," Vincent said.

Sam said, "You're not curious about my life. You never came over to see my room or anything. You don't even like my dad."

Beth broke in, "Of course we like George, Sam." Sam looked at her, just noticing she was there. "It's not that we don't like him—"

"You don't even care about what he thinks."

"Not that much," Vincent agreed, cheerfully.

"Vincent," Beth warned.

"I don't think you like him, or you'd let me go and spend Fourth of July with him the way I want to."

"The fact is," Pat said, breathing harder. "You're our son. Not George's. We're doing our best, Sam, but some things we're goddamn well going to do as a family. That's how it is. There are some things that just aren't negotiable."

"You just want to show me off!" Sam cried then, and turned to Beth, stricken. "I didn't mean that."

"I know," she told him. "Go get your mitt now, or whatever else you want to take, and let's go." Sam slumped into the house, Beowulf following him, chuffing hopefully.

Beth turned to Pat. "You know what?" she told him, suddenly inspired. "Let's take two cars. I want to run up to Peshtigo tomorrow and shoot some stock. And I was thinking I'd take him. Sam. Just him and me. Spend some time with him."

She noticed Vincent slowing down, suddenly concentrating on her, and felt like whispering under the force of his gaze.

Pat didn't notice. He griped, "Now? Why in the hell now?"

"Don't get all juiced, Paddy. I just thought, since I'd be halfway there . . . I've been wanting to do this anyhow, and I think it could help, if he just gets a chance to talk to one of us alone. It's okay, right? This is a good time, because he seems to be opening up, doesn't he?"

Pat stalked up onto the porch and hefted the cooler. "I don't care, Bethie," he said. "Though I can tell you, don't expect some big mother-and-child confession. I've spent a ton of time with him, between here and the ball field and the stadium and the restaurant and stuff, and the kid is completely cut off. He's so self-possessed I envy it."

"Maybe he's just scared to say things," Beth offered. "He didn't seem so in control this morning."

Pat smiled wearily. "Do what you want." Sam walked out onto the porch. Pat turned to him. " 'Sgo, buddy. You can ride with your mom, okay?"

But Sam, with a last-ditch effort to save face, insisted on riding with Vincent, even though Kerry begged him to come with her in Beth's old Volvo and play Car Bingo.

He did cheer up at Laurie and Rick's, paddling amiably in their pool, eating not one but three burgers with everything, Rick's special recipe. Just before dark, they launched Rick's boat from the Robertson Pier, Rick deviling Laurie the whole time about all the years she'd teased him for taking the *Queen Mary* out on a lake the size of a postage stamp. "Bet you're glad it seats nine now, right?" Rick kept asking, while Laurie threw life jackets at his head.

They rocked gently on the dark water in the middle of the lake, and after a while the rockets began, to the north and east, washing the children's faces in green and blue and violet streaks of light. Covertly, Beth watched Sam and thought, once, she could see tears in his eyes. But when he caught her looking at him, he deliberately smiled, showing his big, even teeth, a smile that seemed intended to tell her that he was a good boy, after all, and not spoiled. She wanted to scoop him up then, and hold him bundled against her. Tomorrow, Beth thought then, tomorrow and tomorrow.

The next morning's start was held up until past noon by a long, late breakfast and a torrential flurry of goodbyes—of switching bags and bundles back and forth between the two cars four times to get it right, and the momentary loss of Vincent, who took off unannounced with his brand-new license to pay a surprise visit to old Alex Shore. After all that, Sam and Beth were content to sit spent in the front seat for the first hour, listening to Tom Petty sing about good girls who loved Elvis. Beth headed up Highway 151 toward Fond du Lac, where already a few trees were starting to turn, then onto 41, past Green Bay, near but not quite on the hip of Lake Michigan. She was feeling corky for some reason, renewed and released, and she laughed appreciatively when Sam suddenly started to sing along with her.

"How'd you learn how to harmonize?" she asked him.

"My mom could sing," Sam said happily, then slipped a glance at her. "I'm sorry."

"Honey," Beth told him. "I know she could sing. She had a beautiful voice. I think it's neat that you do, too."

"You knew my mother." It was not a question. "I mean, you knew Cecilia."

"Sure," Beth said, her heart quickening. It was the most he'd ever asked of her. "Everybody knew her. She was hot. Cute and talented. I was jealous of her, because she was friends with Aunt Ellen—with my best friend, Ellen."

"Why?"

"Because Cecil was so ... grownup. And I thought Ellen would like her better. She didn't, though."

My God, thought Beth, why the hell would I say that?

"Was she nice?"

"She was ... everybody was drawn to her. She was like a movie star, sort of."

"Not to me."

Beth's stomach fluttered. Slowly, she thought. Line up. "You mean, she wasn't nice to you?"

Sam laughed. He laughed! "No, I mean I didn't think she was like a movie star. She was just my mom. Even when I saw her on TV, when I was little, my dad says I would just go, 'Oh, there's Mom.'" Beth tried to laugh, and instead croaked. Oh, help, she thought—"She was just my mom"—oh, help. But Sam went on, "Was my mom ... mentally ill, back then?"

Beth winced. "No. She was different...." Beth felt Sam stiffen and tried to backtrack. "Not in a bad way. She was just ... an actress."

"I think sometimes she got mental because of what she did."

Beth almost swerved, but then recovered the wheel. Was he trying to tell her that he'd been aware, when he was small, that Cecil had stolen him? "Because of what she did? What do you mean?"

"I mean, stealing a kid. I started thinking after I met you guys, maybe she didn't get mental because I was too ... you know, hard for her to handle on her own. She got mental because she did this thing a long time ago."

"Sam," Beth said slowly, "you weren't hard to handle. You were the easiest kid in the world. Ask Dad. And Sarah . . . your grandma Lockhart said she was sick sometimes even when she was a little girl."

Sam nodded, and Beth thought, You wanted this, too, didn't you? Should I go on, risk spoiling what feels delicate and new? But I could lose the moment, too. I've lost more than my share.

"Sam, you make me wonder," Beth said, "if you knew that Cecil wasn't your . . . real mom."

"No. I thought she was."

"So you mean, you just started thinking about why she got sick since you came back, just this spring."

"Right. Do you have any other CDs?"

Beth was caught short. "What?"

"Any other ones. Because this one started over. Do you have any old Beatles or something?"

"All I want you to know, Sam, was that it wasn't . . ." But he was rummaging in the glove box, virtually holding up a semaphore that signaled "End of Chat." So Beth found him an Animals disc, and started nattering about Peshtigo, praying to draw him out, get him talking again.

"Do you know what the Great Chicago Fire is?" she asked.

Sam gave her a pitying look. "Uh, yes," he said.

"Well, did you know that there was an even worse fire, in Peshtigo, in this little town we're going to, and it was in the same year, in 1871, and on the same *day?*"

"Get out," said Sam.

And having snagged him, Beth pulled up next to the fire museum, in an old church just off 41. "We could go in here. It's cool. There's all this stuff that was found after the fire, like farm tools all twisted from the heat. They called it 'the great tornado of fire.' Want to?"

"Is that what you're going to take pictures of?"

"No. I was going to take some pictures in this little cemetery down the road, where a lot of people who died in it are buried."

"Why?"

"Well, I like cemeteries." Tomorrow, she thought. Tomorrow and tomorrow and tomorrow. "And, it's . . . you know . . . it was a great tragedy. Every single building in this whole town burned. Every one."

"And people . . . ?"

"Hundreds of people died. I mean, you know, lots more than died in the Chicago fire, Sam, but that was a big city, so that was what everybody paid attention to."

"We could go to the cemetery then."

"Okay."

Now, Beth thought, can I remember where it is? She turned the car around—the last time she'd been in Peshtigo had been . . . when? . . . in '91? She'd made pictures for *Midwest Living*, for a section on historical observances and ghost towns. But she barely recalled that shoot—it was like so many of the things she did the first years after the reunion, a gauzy dream. Today, she could look at whole contact sheets of pictures from those years and have no memory of ever having framed those images in her lens, or laid eyes on the people she must have spoken to and spent time with.

She remembered earlier times in Peshtigo, before Ben was lost, with much more clarity. The town had always been one of Beth's favorite photographic shrines. Once, newly pregnant with Kerry, she had photographed the graves of a family in the little cemetery outside the museum, where they lay under a huge tree that had long outlived them: Sarah, Beloved Wife; Alvey, Age One; Maria, Age Two; Arthur, Husband and Father. She had lain down on the grass above those bones, and thought—as she used to think, in her newspaper days, every time she made a picture of a stretcher burdened by a blanketed form so small it seemed to have no topography at all, if I feel this entire, if I let this wound me, my own will be spared. I will be absolved, by lent and prior pain, from destruction in the first person. The scythe will whicker blindly all around, but miss Vincent, miss Ben.

The memory of the self who actually believed such prevention possible touched Beth today with a kind of abashed pity, like a ten-year-old still believing in Santa Claus.

Wandering with that more innocent Beth, she missed the modest iron arch that marked Rock of Ages, and had to turn around in a farmer's stupendously green field. She remembered, then, that the incursion of road repairs had forced the moving of the cemetery's oldest graves up onto a hill more than a block away.

"That's where I want to go," she told Sam, "up on the hill. That's where the people from the fire are."

She pulled into the cemetery over a graveled rise, parked, and hurriedly began unpacking her equipment. The afternoon was getting old; and the late light, with its low color temperature, its orangeness, was what she wanted for compositions of the rectangular and rounded shapes of the headstones. She took out her little flash unit, for backup, the case with the Hasselblad, a fold-up reflector so new it still felt stiff and funny under her hand.

"What do you want me to take?" Ben asked, and Beth realized it still caught her off guard, how easily, naturally helpful he was—well raised, well-bred.

She gave Sam her bag and they began to hike up a narrow, stony path. Beth watched her son, only half-aware of the building drama of the late light. There was a crowned tomb with smaller headstones ringing it like pupils around a teacher's desk. "Let's take that," she told him; and Sam watched her as she squatted, shooting up from the base of the tallest monument.

"What do you see?" Sam asked her.

"What I'm looking at," Beth said, "is the way the big tombstone sits against the sky, almost like it's protecting the little ones. Here ..." She unlooped the strap from around her neck and put the viewer in front of Sam's eyes. "See?"

He peered. "Yeah."

"Do you want to take it?"

"I never used this kind of camera."

"It's easy," Beth told him, putting her fingers on top of his, feeling the jolt that still accompanied her contact with his downy skin, showing him the buttons. "I'm going to stand up now, and you shoot it."

She stood up and, backing off a step, collided with something hard; she whirled, nearly topping an old man. Beth yipped in surprise, and to her relief, the stranger pushed his striped railroader's hat back on his sunburned forehead and began to laugh.

"Think I was a ghost?" he asked. Then, noticing Sam, who had continued to click the shutter, not even turning at his mother's shriek, he asked, "Who's the photographer?"

"My son," Beth said, adding, "Actually, I am. I take pictures for my job. But we're just playing around here." Sam stood up then, and extended his hand, carefully settling the camera on its strap around his neck first.

"Hello," he said, and the old man, taking the boy's hand, smiled at Beth, a conspiratorial smile of shared pride in Sam's almost antique politeness.

"I'm Will Holt," the old man said.

"I'm Beth. I'm from Chicago. This is Sam. Do you work here?"

"Work here, live here." He smiled, a farmer's face with permanent river-beds along the margins of his jaw. "Not *here*, I mean. At least not yet, though I suspect the time will come. But live in Peshtigo. Always have."

"I'm looking for the graves of the fire survivors."

He laughed again, harder. "Got none of them, I'm afraid, young lady."

"The victims, I mean, of course." Beth blushed.

Beth noticed that behind him, Holt had a little wheeled cart, shaped like a wheelbarrow, but really more like a wagon. It was filled, as nearly as Beth could tell, with masses of red and blue flowers and piles of tiny American flags. Following her eyes, Holt told her, "Fourth of July. Wanted to get them cleaned off before it rains and they fade. That saddens people. The Christmas wreaths sat here until February. I felt bad about it. Had flu for a couple of weeks and was weak as a kitten most of the winter. Better start jogging, eh?"

"Better," said Beth. "Can I take a picture of that wagon?"

Hold gestured at the cart. "Well, sure, why not?" he said. Sam handed her the camera.

"Are all those from soldiers?" he asked Holt.

"No, not all, son," the old man said. "Some. But most are just from the graves of ordinary people. Their folks miss them, on the holidays." He turned to Beth, who'd finished her shooting, and continued, "Now, most of the fire graves are up there—not in the middle, over there, just under the aspens. Of course, that's not where they originally were; parts of this cemetery were moved a few years back."

"I know. I've been here before," Beth said.

"Ah," said Holt. "Live up here?"

"Chicago," Beth repeated. "I used to live in Madison."

"Madison," said Holt. "I went to college in Madison. Ag school. I was the Langlade County extension agent for more years than Ollie's cows have legs." He walked stiffly toward the cart and lifted its handle. "Then I retired and all. And now I do this, just whenever I want to. Little money. A little peace. I used to dig the graves with some boys, but now they have a backhoe for that."

Holt began to walk, and Sam followed him. Beth caught up. They walked along a wide, glimmering, flat swatch of green that led to the foot of the ridge. They passed a grave that looked too new for the rest of its companions. "Caron Anne, Our Youngest," it read. "1985–1988."

"Now that's the Willards' youngest. The funniest thing—died of an ear infection. Seems that my grandkids get one of those a week, and it hasn't killed one of them yet. Her mother wanted her up here, though most people prefer all the landscaping in the new cemetery by the church. We all felt so bad, we wouldn't have suggested otherwise, and of course, there are generations of Willards up here, so she's among her people."

They walked on.

"That's a kid, too," Sam said, pointing.

"Right you are." Holt nodded, taking off his hat. "Places like this should be reserved for old folks like me, but it don't always run that way. Now, Grace Culver was the age of my older boy, Bill. Her brother told her on the school bus he was going to shoot her with his daddy's gun when they got home, and that's just what he did. That was in '56. Yes, that's right—'56."

"My God in heaven," Beth breathed.

"Oh, ma'am, I'm sorry," Holt said, gesturing at Sam. "I never meant to scare him."

"I'm not scared," Sam said, his eyes level. "I was kidnapped once."

Holt shot a glance at Beth. She nodded. "He was," she said.

"Were you afraid?" Holt asked Sam.

"No," Sam replied. "I was little. And my mom, she . . . Well, I just got back before school let out."

"You were away for months?"

"Years. My whole life," Sam said.

Beth squirmed, adjusting her cameras. "It was . . . you probably read about him . . . we lived in Madison then. Benjamin Cappadora."

"Oh my yes, oh my yes," said Holt. "Goodness yes." He looked Sam up and down. "Still, you seem to have survived it." Then, to Beth, "And you, too. Things okay now?"

"Yes, mostly," Beth said, struggling with a sudden longing to tell this gentle ghost encountered in the graveyard, "You should know better than to believe everything you think you see; our son was stolen, and we never really got him back, though you may have read otherwise in *People* magazine." She wanted to ask, "Now, Mr. Holt, you have long experience of human nature, does this polite and curious young fellow seem at home in the world to you? Like the prodigal son of one of the luckiest and happiest of families? And me? Do I seem like his mother? Or an actor? Actually, it was his other mother who was the actor—"

Then Sam asked Holt if the graves neares him were people from the fire. "They all have the same name," Sam said.

"Well, Sam, that's another one of those stories. Carrie Moss and her four children. Oldest was eleven, the youngest one three." Beth looked down at the neat gray stones, all exactly matched, then at Sam. Should she stop Holt? This was damned gruesome. Sam was transfixed. "Fellow was a railroad worker. Hailed from all over, you know the kind. But born here. The way he said, when they got hold of him in Madison, was that he was in love with Carrie Moss from when they were children. One day while her husband was out harvesting—oh, not a half-mile from the house—he came to their house."

"The guy . . ." Sam's voice was low, choked. "He killed them?"

"He did," Holt said evenly. "That house is still there right out on the road near Keller Creek. Nicely built. But nobody ever bought it. Frank Moss moved to Des Moines. No, I'm wrong there. It was Dubuque. This was just before the war—'43. Not all the crime happens in Milwaukee—no, not by a long shot. Not all of it happens in Chicago."

They walked up a small footpath to the knee of the ridge. A single stone stood just to the left of the path, and Beth stopped. No, she thought. Maybe Sam won't notice it.

David Taylor Holt. No dates, simply the etching of a water lily on the marbled rose of the surface. Sam squatted down, touching the stone.

"Is this a relative of yours?" Beth asked softly.

"Yep," said the caretaker. "I'm sorry to say that this is my son."

"Did he die in the war?" Sam asked. "Was he a soldier?"

"Sam, wait," Beth rebuked him.

"Oh, no, it's all right. I like to have him here—better than if we had to go down to Beloit, his mother and me. That's where he was living. He wasn't a soldier, son, just a college kid."

"Was he . . . was he sick?" Sam asked.

"No, no," said Holt. "Though in a sense I guess you could say he was. We thought it was what a boy goes through—some of the drinking, the bad grades, missing classes. But I guess you could say he was suffering a case of depression. He was in love with a girl—you might say she never returned that. And one night, well, he drove home, he'd been drinking, and he parked his car in the garage at the house where he rented a room. And he just left it on. He had a full tank of gas. The landlady, poor woman, she nearly died as well."

"He was mentally ill," Sam said. "That's too bad."

"Sam!" Beth didn't know how to react.

"You're right, Sam. He was ill. We just didn't know." Holt reached down and brushed a clump of clotted leaves from the face of the stone. "His mother, now, she thinks Donnie fell asleep. And I must say, I tell her that I do, too. But the truth is, I know better. I found this part of something, a poem he was writing. It was as sad as one of those country songs. He wrote, 'I may be weak and I may be strong, but I've been in this wicked world too long.' So I knew then he just couldn't wait. And he wrote this, probably at the Christmas before, when he was home for break. Months before. Well, well. It's been ten years now."

"You miss him," Sam said.

"I sure do," Holt said. He gave himself a shake. "Now, right up there, to the left, there are your graves. I'm sorry. I have to shake a leg here."

"Of course," Beth agreed. But she didn't want to leave him. She wanted to take him someplace fragrant and homely, like the Pepper Pot in town, and buy vanilla Cokes and steak sandwiches for him and for Sam. They could sit and talk in a warm ring of yellow light until all of them felt full and strong.

"Good luck to you, Beth," Holt said, jolting his wagon onto the small path. "Sam, you take care of your mother."

"You, too," Sam said, kneeling down again near the pink marble tombstone. "Why do you think it's a water lily?" he asked Beth.

"I don't know. Maybe he loved those flowers."

"They smell awful. But he was a nice old guy."

"He was," Beth said. "It's very sad."

"Yeah." Sam paused. "For him, you mean, or his son?"

"Both of them."

"I don't know about him." Sam pointed at the rosy stone, which glowed in the last blades of sun. "For him, it's probably better."

Beth froze, her camera dangling. "What do you mean?"

"I mean, he was so sad and all, it's probably better for him to just . . . sleep. There could be worse things than being dead."

Beth grasped, gasped. Her camera knocked against her chest. Suddenly she wanted to shake Sam, or slap him. "Sam, he's dead. His life is completely over. He's not asleep. He took his whole life away from himself, from his parents. And all for something he would have gotten over if he'd given himself the time."

Sam stirred the loose earth stubbornly with one toe. "Maybe not. Maybe he was just too sad."

I could just fall, Beth thought. The very ground under her feet seemed to drag at her, draw her down with the seepage of its accumulation of mourning. Worse and worse, the bones warned her through the sound of shivering aspens above her head, there is worse and worse.

The scythe had whickered and swung; and it had indeed missed Ben. Ben, as Sam, had endured a middling-hard childhood, and yet, as Sam, he had thrived. And now he wasn't thriving anymore. He was surviving, and only because of a base coat of basically healthy nature.

Not because of having his family back. Not because of that at all. Their gain was his loss. Beth had been returned a child who was as remote from her as heaven.

And yet, and yet, wasn't she more fortunate and ungrateful than so many others she'd met at Compassionate Circle? She could see her child; she knew his favorite dinner was gyros and yogurt, that he was a fast, not altogether careful reader, that he could touch-type; she had seen how he transformed at bat from an oversized clown, pulling faces at his teammates, to a beautiful novice athlete with a clenched jaw and a level swing that made Pat's eyes tear up.

She knew where her son was, Beth thought, as the last of the sunlight drained from the band of sky over the ridge. And it was not here.

"Sam," she said then. "I want to ask you something."

"What?" he said, getting up, dusting off his hands.

"Do you ever wish you were dead?"

He said, quickly, "No."

"What do you wish?"

"I just said there might be things worse than being dead."

"Like what?"

"Like everybody always pulling at your life and making you stay at a place where everybody hates you."

"You think that . . . we hate you?"

"Not you."

"Who, then?"

"Well, Vincent." He picked up Beth's reflector, turning his head up toward the ridge. A light winked up there, and for a moment Beth thought it could be a shooting star; then she saw it was a blinking light on a radio tower, warning planes that it was safe to come only so close, no closer. "When I was at the home, my dad and I talked, and he said we should make a list of what wouldn't be so bad about going back. And one of the things I put on the list was that it might be fun to have brothers and sisters."

"And?"

"And then . . . I mean, Kerry's great, but he looks at me like . . . Jesus, you see how he looks at me!"

"Sam, I don't think he looks at you any differently from the way he looks at all of us. He's ... he's had a hard time."

"But it wasn't my fault! That's what I keep telling you guys!" She could not see him, just the outline of his bent shoulders, but Beth reached for him then, and folded him against her. He did not resist; perhaps she imagined it, but he seemed, momentarily, to cling.

"Oh, Ben ... Sam," she said into his hair. "Do you know how many million years it was that I could never hug you? That you had to be without me to hug you, too?"

He patted her back then, like a fond colleague, as Angelo might have done. "They hugged me," he said. "They hugged me all the time."

She was barely able to summon the words that naturally followed. They would seal something, and her throat was paralyzed with pity and conscience.

"What do you wish, Sam?" she finally asked.

"I don't know," he said. "Just that ... everything was like it was before. Except for that would hurt Pat and you. And I can't stand that, either. I just ... don't know."

Beth thought back then to the early questions Sam had asked, and how hard she had to resist to keep from turning every answer into a forty-minute lecture. Had Beowulf liked him when he was a baby? Did he see Kerry right after she was born? Did Beth remember if he was allergic to cinnamon? He was sure he was now, though George said that was just because he once threw up after eating a whole pound bag of sticky buns. After weeks of the little questions, little answers, Beth had taken the plunge: she'd called Sam in one lazy Sunday afternoon and told him that she wanted to show him something. The apprehension in his eyes almost stopped her; but she pressed ahead, taking him upstairs to her and Pat's room, to where the large hooped cedar chest Rob Maltese had built for them as a wedding gift still sat, used mostly by Pat as a clothes rack for piles of shirts destined for the dry cleaner. She swept the shirts aside.

As a filer, Beth considered herself a failure. It was one of the sinkholes in her motherhood resume. Vincent's baby book was a virtual anthropological study, recording, in the margins when the spaces gave out, not just the date of the eruption of each tooth, but the development of moods, gestures, intellectual milestones that Beth considered evidence of genius. By contrast, Ben's and then Kerry's albums were basically repositories for cards and photos. Beth hadn't even been sure that the words she scribbled in as "firsts" actually were, since the scribbling had so far postdated the actual events.

But she had done one thing carefully and well. Each of the children's christening gowns and "coming home" outfits was sealed in a plastic envelope Beth bought from Sears, with photos and mementos of each of those momentous days and placed reverently, impervious to time and shift, in the cedar chest.

She'd lifted out first Vincent's package, letting Sam sift through its contents—he was curious, even avid—and then the one marked "Benjamin Patrick Cappadora."

"They're so little," Sam had said, laughing. "Was I really ever this small? They look like Kerry's doll clothes." Some of Ben's clothes, Beth thought then, in fact were now Kerry's doll clothes; and she'd almost said that.

But it happened then. Ben lifted the lacy gown Rosie had so lovingly embroidered up to his nose, inhaling its sweet, hamster-cage scent.

"What's that smell?" he asked.

"Cedar. It's supposed to preserve clothes and keep moths away. Lots of closets are lined with it. Didn't you ever smell it before?"

"No," Sam said firmly. "It could be ... maybe it was that my yaya had a trunk like this. I think so. She brought it from Greece. Maybe I played with it when I was a kid." But his face didn't register confidence. "At least, I think so."

And then Beth had noticed, with growing excitement, that tears were welling in his eyes. She had never seen Sam cry, except for an instant at the intake center when he'd kissed George goodbye. Now, he was scrubbing at his eyes with twelve-year-old modesty, shaking his head.

"What? Sam?" she'd asked, daring to think, This is it. Something, some gear has engaged. He remembers. And then Sam had reached out and patted Beth on the shoulder. "I'm just so sorry," he said.

"For what, honey?"

"I'm sorry because this happened to you. I know you loved this . . . loved me so much when you did this. I'm so sorry."

"Sam, Sam . . . you don't have to feel that way."

He shook his head, more fiercely this time. "But I also think you believe that my mom and dad are bad people. And they're really not." He went on, Beth barely hearing him, her stomach gone icy. "Just because I'm really sorry that this happened doesn't mean I don't love my dad. And I love my mom, too, Beth. She doesn't mean to be sick." Numbly, Beth nodded, mechanically reaching for the christening gown, folding it against the creases so it wouldn't disintegrate. Sam was crying hard now, hiccuping. She wanted to hold him against her, stroke his broad back with its immature and jutting bones. "Beth," he finally gulped out, "can I see my dad today?"

When he'd gotten back, later, from George's, Sam was lighter, less antsy. He'd played a game of Sorry with Kerry. He'd come right out and asked Vincent to shoot some hoops. But Beth had never forgotten the supplication in his face as he knelt by the chest, the confusion in his voice about the right way to talk to kindly strangers to convince them to help you find your way home.

She had tried to tell Pat about the cedar chest. He'd brushed it away. "Bethie, do you remember being six weeks old?" he'd laughed. "Don't stew over it. He'll come around."

Pat would listen now. He would have no choice.

As the shadows blanketed Rock of Ages cemetery, Beth and Sam locked the cameras in the trunk, and Sam asked if he could lie down in the backseat. "Sure, baby," she said. "Sleep."

There was worse and worse, Beth thought; they had given him life, Beth thought, tilting the rearview mirror to look at her sleeping son; that was a covenant. No one would ask them to give their boy back the life he mourned, at the cost of the life that had been restored to him. But wasn't that part of the covenant, too?

She needed to talk to Pat. She hadn't the heart to talk to Pat, or the courage. He would turn from her words with all his might and with all justification, and what would be left for her then?

A phone call, Beth thought then—almost stopping, almost forgetting that she would wake Sam, that it was late. No, she would look the number up to-morrow. She knew it was in the book. She'd looked it up half a dozen times over the past few years, noted when the office moved, when the number changed.

With the thought of the phone call secure above her mind, like a strap in a swaying subway car, Beth headed through the dusk, south toward home.

Chapter 30

To call first thing the next morning, Beth decided, would seem desperate. That it had taken four years to get to the point of making the call—and that no one but she knew that—was of no consequence.

She would work first. For . . . an hour. Decency demanded it.

She took out the last proofs of the photo essay that would appear two months from now in *Life*—the children-walking-away portraits. *Life* was going to run them as a six-page spread for no other reason than the fact of them. It was an arrival, big-league. But she had to admit that not one of the pictures was really anything that would merit a gold star beside her name in God's notebook. She still used the same tricks and conceits in her work that she'd developed as a novice. Venturing in new directions would have required thought and concentration, study, the willingness to expend emotional capital. She had not had it to give—and she often thought that she was lucky that a fairly good ability to make pictures had become second nature to her long before she'd taken up residence under the avalanche. Her "new eyes" were as a kind of deformity born of that residence.

Beth recognized the truth that she could do most of her work with the

eyes of her mind closed; that meant admiring that the real reason people paid her handsomely was the conjuring power of her last name, the little italicized credit that appeared under every picture of hers someone published, the explanation of who she was. The reason Wedding in the Old Neighborhood was being featured in *Bon Appetit* only now, when the food and the theme had been a spectacular draw for years. The reason a book publisher had offered Beth and Pat an actual million dollars (it still made Beth wince to think of the crumpling of Pat's jaw when she insisted they reject it) for rights to their family's story. The Cappadora name had been dredged from a stale estuary of tears and rumor not only unstained, but no longer just golden: now it was platinum.

This *Life* layout, for example. The editors naturally assumed that the subject had sprung from Beth's joust with fate. In fact, Beth had always taken pictures of children walking away. Their backsides appealed to her—a kid's personality showed in his walk. Before Ben disappeared, it had been, for her, a metaphor for growing up. None of the pictures she'd chosen for *Life* were of her own children, and lots of them were old: toddlers waddling away through the lilac bowers in the University of Wisconsin arboretum; a boy carrying his skates slung over one finger, crossing Lake Wingra on a winter morning.

There was one picture for which the editors would have paid an even handsomer bundle. But it was too late to include that one. And Beth had washed her hands of the notion, anyway.

Looking up at her tack board, Beth turned her full eye, both her real and her photographers' eye, on the one walking-away picture she had taken of her own children. It had been at Ellen's house, after a barbecue a few weeks ago. All three of them were heading up the driveway to the car. She had told herself then that she was intent on the rose-quartz quality of the twilight; but the photo—Vincent elbowing Sam just a little over Kerry's strawberry blond head as she skipped between them—was beautifully composed, the boys like a bridge over their smaller sister. Last spring, when she'd sold the layout, just after Sam was found, one of the editors had asked, ever so delicately, whether any of the photos depicted "the boy." Beth understood; the layout wasn't just poignancy, it was news. She'd almost given in. Just one backshot of Sam.

Quickly, she'd told him no, there wasn't. And the temptation to give them this picture—was it to cash in? to confess?—was still strong. Even now, when she knew that the issue deadline would make changing the layout impossible.

Was she proud of her picture? Or, as she suspected Pat of being, proud of her wounds? Could she pick the two apart, ever? She did know that, whatever their origin, work and money provided satisfaction, however remote. She simply did not know how far that satisfaction went.

Would work sustain her? If everything else were gone?

Forty minutes had passed. She picked up the phone. The company was called Palladin Reconstructions—the yellow pages ad, which Beth thought was clever, said, "Have taste, will travel." When he was a kid, Nick had always made much of his last name, which he thought linked him with his legendary Sienese ancestors. The underline read, "Historical ruin in distress? We'll come to the rescue." That was going too far. But then, as Dan, Ellen's husband, said, you couldn't argue with four million bucks a year, which was what Nick turned over, appealing to the lucky convergence of twin trends toward architectural recycling and nostalgia.

The phone burred, and Beth felt her stomach grip.

To her chagrin—she had been counting, secretly, on a secretary, even hoping for an answering machine—he picked up himself.

"Nick," she said.

"This is Nick," he replied.

"Nick, this is Beth. Beth . . . Kerry."

"Uh . . . Bethie!" He didn't sound the way she'd planned he would, overjoyed, hushed with gratitude. He sounded . . . just surprised. "Wait. I got to get rid of a guy." He was back in a moment, his voice lower, more particularly pitched for her. "Bethie, it's good to hear you. Is anything wrong?"

"Nothing," she said. And then, "Everything."

"What do you mean? Is Pat sick?"

"No, he's fine. I just . . . Nick, I know I never called after we . . . It just seemed—I couldn't."

"Bethie, I understood. And then everything happened. I never got to tell you how happy I am. Your boy . . . I know Trisha called you. I wanted to."

"Thank you. It's a miracle. We're ... it's almost too much to understand. But the reason I called was, I think of you, often. And I was wondering if we could have lunch. I know it's abrupt."

He paused. Oh no, Beth thought. He's thinking that I'm asking him to sleep with me. *Am* I asking him to sleep with me? "I mean," she said stupidly, before he could reply. "Really lunch. Not ... that."

She could hear Nick smiling. "I must say, I'm struggling with disappointment," he offered gallantly. Beth sighed. "But really lunch is better than nothing. I can't wait. When? Today?"

They arranged to meet at some nowhere chain out by his office, near the airport, in two hours. Deliberately, Beth did not rush back to the shower to shave another layer off her legs; she didn't redo her hair. She simply put on slacks instead of the ripped jean shorts she was wearing, lipstick—and at the last minute, Rosie's mother's diamond studs in her ears.

Nick was slightly, ever so minutely, heavier, as if a child had drawn a crayon outline around him and shaded in a bit more. A prosperous man. When he put his arms around her, he still smelled better than anything human; it made Beth woozy.

It took a full hour just to fill Nick in on Sam's homecoming; he questioned her with the gentle patience of a good father, drawing out the painful liquor under the surface.

"And Pat? How's Pat handling this? How are you guys?"

"Pat's good," Beth said seriously, rearranging her lettuce under mounds of tuna salad. "He feels like ... blessed. I mean, he already had the restaurant, and that was more or less a new beginning for him. He never guessed he'd have this, too. He's got, you know, all these plans. He says he wants to travel and all that. Though I don't believe him. I mean, Pat gets nervous after five hours with Kerry's class at Six Flags and starts calling the restaurant to see if the edges of the ravioli have been crimped. . . ."

Nick laughed. "I can relate. I take a phone to the beach in Virgin Gorda. It's like you lose your eyes or something. You wait all year for the vacation and then you can't stand it."

She told Nick about the million dollars, and how Pat had argued when she refused to consider the offer. "He said that just because I won't talk about what happened to us doesn't mean it will go away. He kept reminding me of what I used to say when I took pictures of a guy who jumped off a building."

"And what was that?"

"I used to say, 'It happened.' "

"Well ..."

"But I told him this was different. It happened, but it happened to *us*. We didn't jump off a building. We were pushed." Without really meaning to go so far, Beth suddenly found herself telling Nick that it was more than question of style—that she had suspected her husband of coming close to saying that it was an ill wind that blew nobody good. That he had all but said that lemonade could be made from lemons, that prosperity could erase the sour taste of the past nine years.

"Is that so outrageous, Beth? I mean, you can't say you're owed, but you are owed. Pat, he's right. It's college and retirement and ... But it's not worth fighting over. Because you guys have to be doing okay, anyhow, moneywise. I see the restaurant all the time in the columns. And I see your stuff. So as long as Pat's health is good and stuff ..."

"It's good. I mean, Pat's never going to be mellow. He's always going to be fretting about the staff...."

Nick sighed, a businessman's sigh. "Tell me about it. You can't get a decent worker for any money."

"Yeah," Beth said. She had not pictured them discussing the shortage of good help. "But he's happy, as much as he could ever be happy." Would they never stop talking about Pat? "It's ... Nick, it's Sam I'm worried about. It's Sam and ... the other kids, because of Sam." She explained the trip to Minneapolis, the trip to Peshtigo, how it confirmed what she'd feared even before then. As Beth talked, she kept asking herself whether it was their history, or that Nick was just spectacularly easy to confide in, or that she wanted him, or that he comprised a fresh and objective panel of opinion. Even with Candy she wasn't as open. She couldn't tell him enough.

"It's not as though Sam's ever bad," she said. "He does just what you tell him to. But he's . . . eroding. It's almost like you can see him being chipped away." Beth told Nick about the long afternoon with Sam at the cedar chest. About the way his grades had plummeted from stalwart B's to C's and D's. About the way his hustle on the practice field had deteriorated to a shamble. About the day Sam had gotten up from a sickbed, in the midst of a serious bout with strep throat, so as not to miss his weekly two hours with George.

"The social worker says he's in transition, but if he's in transition, shouldn't there be some sign of progress?" Beth asked Nick, who was cutting his remaining half of Reuben neatly into fourths. Sam, she went on, was in their house but not of it; he kept his room as neatly as a guest, carrying his own shampoo and toothbrush back and forth as if their home was a boarding school. When he was late coming home from school, she knew he'd ridden his bike to one of George's construction sites, or spent long minutes sitting in front of his old house. Beth could liken him to nothing else but the foreign-exchange students Ellen used to take in—bright, helpful, polite, excruciatingly out of place and uncomfortable, mimicking rituals they didn't understand, quiet and given to long, late silences spent staring out of their neatly arranged rooms at the patterns of stars in the night sky.

"The only thing that keeps him going is the visits with George," she said, pushing her plate away. "And even Candy doesn't think that's such a good idea. I mean, people think we're giving him mixed messages about who his real parents are."

"Maybe she's right," Nick broke in. For a moment, Beth thought she'd imagined it; had he glanced, ever so delicately, at his watch? "Blood is blood, Bethie. And what else can you do but see him through it?"

"That's what Angelo says."

"Well, it's true. All those things, the grades and stuff—even normal kids go through that stage. I did. It sounds like he's just in a period of adjustment."

"That's what Pat thinks."

"I think Pat's right," Nick said. "Kids adapt. They're survivors."

"I hope so," she said. "Still, I wonder if—"

"Are you happy, Bethie?" he asked then, leaning forward and covering her jittering hand with his own—his small, blunt, perfectly manicured hand. Is this a pass? Beth thought.

"I'm relieved," she said carefully. "But I don't know if you could say I'm happy. I don't know if it's possible for me to be happy after all this. Or if I'm just expecting too much. Or if . . ." She looked up at him, reaching up for his fingers with her own. Is *this* a pass? she thought. "Maybe what I need to be happy has nothing to do with my children."

"I've missed you," Nick said. "I thought about you so many times."

"Oh, me too," Beth said. "Me too. A million times."

"Do you want to go . . . somewhere?"

"I don't know."

They drove to a small field where someone was building a landing strip for gliders. Beth let him take her in his arms, leisurely, gently open her mouth with his tongue. She let him lift her shirt and cup her breast, feeling the shivering begin in her waist and percolate up. But her potential for lust, Beth thought, taking hold of herself forcibly, wasn't what she'd come here to measure.

What was?

"Nick," she said, breaking off, kissing his neck as she sat up. "Did you ever do . . . this before?"

"Before today?"

"No, I mean, before we did."

"Not very often," he said.

"But before? Before we did?"

"A few times, maybe." She looked at him. He had removed his sport coat and now he smoothed it, tenderly laying it on the leather of the backseat, making sure every fold was just so. Don't, she thought. Don't self-destruct in front of me, Nick. Then she reversed, sternly telling herself, Don't look for it. Don't go prospecting for grief. He wants you. He's gorgeous. He's good and kind, and the history you have with him is sweet prehistory.

But she was unable to help herself. "When?" she asked.

"Oh, when the kids were little. I don't know. It didn't mean anything."

"And with me?"

"Well, of course, Bethie. It meant something with you. Bethie, you know how I felt about you that day. I even thought—" Okay, she breathed then, it will be okay now—"at that time, that we might ... see each other more. That maybe we could have—"

" 'See each other more'? You mean, behind people's backs?"

She couldn't believe her presumption. What had she expected him to say? "Found the meaning of life"?

"Well, I wouldn't have put it that way," Nick smiled. "We're going to talk now, I see. I think I need a smoke."

She itched with impatience as he got out his engraved lighter, his neatly folded pack of Lights. "Nick," she asked again, "did you think that after that day we'd start being lovers?"

"Was that such a bad thing to hope?"

"And never tell anyone?"

"I didn't know. I didn't think about it."

"Even after?"

"There was no point in thinking about it after." Nick drew in on his smoke and folded his hands. "Bethie," he said then, "did you want to leave Pat? Is that what you want now?"

"No," she said. "Well, I don't know."

"When you never called me, I thought, well, it was just one of those things that happen when you're under stress. But then, when you called me today, I thought, maybe she feels her life is missing something, too."

"Is that how you feel?"

"Sure," Nick smiled. "Doesn't everybody?" He reached for her, holding her not quite comfortably across the divider between the bucket seats. No wait, Beth thought. It's not just "Doesn't everybody?" It's more than "Doesn't everybody?"

But Nick was saying, "A long time ago, my brother Richie told me that if you put a jellybean in a jar for every time you made love during the first year of marriage, and then you took one out for everytime you made love after, you'd never empty out the jar."

"What's that got to do with it?"

"Well ..."

"So it was just sexual for you?"

"Wasn't it for you?"

"No!" she cried. "Yes, and no."

"Well, yes and no for me, too."

"And have you had other affairs, since?"

"What does it matter?"

"How often?"

"Beth, numbers are just numbers."

"No they're not."

"Okay, then. A couple of times. But not like this. Beth, they were just no big deal. I don't want you to think I'm some pig or something, Beth, but it's . . . Pat would say this . . . I mean, maybe not, because you're so . . . full of life. But for me, being bored, physically, in a marriage doesn't mean that it's not a good marriage."

Pat, thought Beth in a hot flush of loyalty, would never say that.

She asked Nick then, "Is it a good marriage? Your marriage?"

"Yes, it is," he said. "I think Trisha is happy, and the kids are great. We are good friends. We respect each other. Other people rely on us. She has a full life of her own."

Beth thought, Doesn't everybody? Nick slid his hand, comfortingly, erotically, across the back of her neck, letting his fingers probe her muscles. "That doesn't mean I don't want you. That I don't want us to spend time together. Beth, a part of me will always love you. And probably even more because you've been so brave. Nobody else could have gone through this like you did. You were always that way. My ma used to say, 'Elizabeth will always get what she wants.' I used to get mad at her for it. But she was right."

Beth disentangled herself from his arm and peered out the window. She wished she could teleport, deliver herself from this seat to her kitchen in one blinked motion, without the need to taper down this conversation, smile, comb her hair, drive. From the rim of her eyes, she caught Nick tilting the mirror to re-form his hair where she had mussed it. He did it well, with the deft assurance of a woman currying her perm.

She turned to him. "It would be easy for me to make love to you. It would always have been easy for me. But it wouldn't be enough."

"I'm not saying that would be all there is to it, Beth."

"What else would there be?"

"What else do you want? Do you want to marry me, Beth? Did something change in twenty years, other than I got older and more money?"

"Yes," Beth said then, tears forming. "I changed. I wanted . . ."

"Me? Or just something?"

"Something. I thought maybe it was you."

"And maybe it is. I'm not saying all the doors are closed, Beth. It's just . . . you call me after four years. We have lunch. You ask me if I've ever slept with anyone but my wife and you, and if I did, I'm this creep."

"Not a creep. Just not . . ."

Not Pat, she thought. Not Pat.

He was out in the yard when she got home. She had examined her face fully in the mirror; it was neither too flushed nor too wan.

It was just a little better than ordinary.

Pat was looking up at one of the bedroom windows. "Do you think a dormer would look like hell?" he asked her as she came up behind him. "I'd like to give the boys more space, but I don't want it to look like a trailer park." "The boys." She heard him roll the plural in his mouth, love it. She wanted to swaddle him gently, in a blanket, keep him from harm.

"Come upstairs," Beth said, surprising herself. "I want to show you something." He stared at her, then followed.

The house was hushed and cool. She locked the bedroom door behind them and walked out of the cotton pants, amazed at her own boldness— they didn't do things like this anymore. Leaning back with her palms on the wood of their dresser, planting her legs apart and rising up on her toes, she coaxed Pat out of his belt. Caught between puzzlement and excitement, he tried to figure out which way to move. He kissed her, with his lips trying to draw her to the bed. Sensible. But Beth leaned back farther, her hands up under his shirt, aligning the two of them so they stood ribcage to ribcage. This had always been easy for them, because they were nearly the same height; when they were kids, they had laughed about it. All we'd ever need would be a phone booth, Pat used to say. Obligingly, he slipped out of his pants and bent his knees—Beth was surprised, as always, at how ropy and strong he always emerged from his clothes. Dressed, he looked like a little ghost.

Pat raised his face to her then, and she saw his eyes grow hooded, his jaw tense, as they always had when another element walked into the room—the harshness and urgency of a man simply hot for a woman, any woman, not necessarily his familiar wife. Those had always been the best times, even before, times when they broke out of the tight threads of emotion that surrounded them, threads of weariness and responsibility and jealousy and even love, and the nakedness was more than physical, and a cold concrete floor or six neighbors watching from a window would not have stopped her from pulling him into her.

"For an old lady," Pat said, low, almost without moving his mouth, "you are some lady. You look twenty, Bethie. You look like you did on the grass behind the fieldhouse."

She pulled him under her, into her, with her hands along his hips, finding a place on his throat to plant her open lips and suck at him. "Paddy," she said, "Paddy. Do it. Just do it."

"Let me ... here ..." Pat cupped her breasts, awkwardly, diving between them, inhaling her.

"No, no," she shushed him, "just this way." The smell of Nick on her forearm, as it chanced to cross her face, confused her, drove her hips against Pat's with a bluntness that startled them both. "I just, I just ..."

It was infuriating. She could not dismiss Nick's movie-perfect eyes from her mind. Though she and Pat worked together gracefully, making love with the kind of concerted grace of long habit, Beth felt they were fumbling, wearing heavy gloves, taking turns at a campfire poking a single glowing coal with a stick, missing it, sending it rolling, finding it again, missing again.

They were both pouring sweat by the time Beth pushed Pat down on the bed, locking her legs around him, suddenly terrified he would let go before she caught up with him, and that this would mean something it had never meant before, not just an ordinary miss. "Wait for me," she whispered. "Wait."

He pulled her arms down then, and pinioned them with his own, so that

she lay on top of him but held fast, unable to move. There was no space between them except the space Pat created with the small coring movements of
his hips. And then, gratefully, Beth felt him strike the center of the coal with
patient, consistent friction, felt the beginning of the burn ... and Nick's face
stretched and faded and stretched until, at the instant she felt Pat buck and
spill, it vanished as if punctured, popped. She could see Nick, his beauty, his
style, outside her, a lovely memory. Pat, suddenly heavy and wet beneath her,
smelled like soap and salt and pine: the cleanest man she'd ever known. For
years, she now realized, the most she'd managed to feel was a surface sizzle
when they linked, the light off a sparkler that quickly sputtered. This time,
the burn had gone all through. She hadn't thought they had that left.

"You ... you are so fine, Paddy," she said then. "You would never leave
me, would you?"

Pat's voice, when it came, was remarkably calm, full of breath, not like her
own postsexual rasp. "I don't know," he said. "Are you going to make me
want to?"

Beth had not noticed the refrigerator chill of the air-conditioned room.
She pulled a corner of the quilt over her. Sounds came back: Kerry banging
in the kitchen downstairs, Vincent shouting at her to turn off the TV.

Without a word, Pat got up and began taking his suit and shirt for work
out of the closet, absently selecting a tie. Beth closed her eyes. In a moment,
she heard the rush of the shower across the hall. This should be the part
where I have a good, hard cry, she thought. And then I'd be cleansed, and I'd
know what to do. But I can never cry when I need to. Or faint when I need
to. Or sleep when I need to. She lay with her eyes open, remembering a feeling from girlhood, from days when she'd come out of a movie theater,
blinking into the ebbing light of a Friday afternoon, disoriented in time, sick
with the sense that something had been wasted. She pulled a pillow over her
face, willing the slams and muffled calls, the activity of the house, to recede.

The next sound she heard was Pat's voice, from far off, shouting to her
that Sam was gone.

Chapter 31

"He's outside," Beth, still fuddled with sleep, told Pat as she stumbled down the stairs. "What time is it? Is it morning? He went down to the school to shoot baskets." She glanced around the empty kitchen. "Is Beowulf here? Maybe he took the dog out."

Hearing his name, Beowulf obligingly slid out from under the dining room table and chuffed over to nose Beth's hand.

"It's five o'clock in the morning, Beth," said Pat. "He wouldn't go out to shoot baskets at five in the morning."

"Five o'clock in the morning?" But Pat was still dressed in creased and gravy-fragrant work clothes. "Where were you?"

He looked away. "I had a few drinks."

Ahhh, Beth thought then, her panic over Sam receding for a moment, like water off the hull of a rising submarine.

Had Pat been with ... someone else? How many people had there been in their bed yesterday afternoon? Three, four? Not only Nick, but some lovely Claudia or Roxanne of Pat's dreams? Maybe one of the three rotating

hostess-brides at Wedding, all actors or models and cute as Mediterranean buttons?

After what had happened between them yesterday?

Beth felt no stab of jealousy, only a consuming curiosity: Before yesterday, would she have cared? Or mourned? Now, she wondered if one last big, fat irony was in store: she had loved Pat all along, but thawed to the recognition of that love only just ... too late. Months late? Days? Despite all her own digressions and frank absences, in thought and deed, in spite of the terrible words both of them had spoken over the years, she had never even considered the possibility that it would be Pat who would turn away from her.

She looked at her husband's face, shadowed with overnight stubble, shorn of the restorative balm of sleep. Her biggest fear, yesterday, had been of the reckoning, of facing with Pat the possibility that by claiming Sam, they would destroy him, and by letting him go, they would destroy their family.

Now she felt again the sinking she'd dismissed with sleep the previous day. Pat might not go the distance. Perhaps whatever reckoning was to be faced, each of them would face alone.

"It was Joey and me," Pat said then, in a hurry, as if receiving her thoughts. "And the one bride and groom, Roxanne and Dustin. We went to that hippie place on Belmont."

Beth asked, "Until five in the morning?"

The room was icy. Beth reached into the hall closet and pulled out a sweater. Why did they have to keep the air at arctic levels, anyhow? She fumbled for the thermostat.

"Then back to Joey's. We watched *The Wild Bunch*. What the fuck do you care, anyhow, Bethie? You know how many times I don't come home until morning, and you don't even know? You think I was robbing a train or something? Were you waiting up or what? And where the hell is Sam?"

My God, she thought. Sam.

"He could be in the basement watching TV," she said. "Did you ask Vincent?"

"He's asleep. His door's locked. I knocked. Kerry's asleep—wasn't she going to stay over at Blythe's?"

"She got homesick. You know how she does. Georgia brought her home. I heard her come in."

"Anyhow, I looked everywhere. Jesus Christ, Beth. Jesus Christ, where is he?"

Beth reached automatically up over the coffee machine for his angina pills. "Stop now, Pat," she instructed, struggling to pop open the bottle. "Let's just think a moment. Maybe he's running. He started running. . . ."

"Beth, this house has been on the news, pictures, everywhere," Pat gasped. "You don't have to have the address to cruise by and see a kid out in front . . . a kid whose face had been on every front page in the country."

"You mean," Beth asked him then, incredulous, "you think someone took Sam? Kidnapped Sam?"

"It could happen!" Pat screamed. "All the fucking publicity! Some pervert could have . . ."

The doorbell rang. Beth watched as Pat's face literally leaked color, like an ink wash in a bath, down across his cheekbones, his neck. "Oh, Bethie, oh God, no."

It was Beth who crossed to open the door, her own heart now jerking like a cat in a sack. On the porch, in the first morning sunlight, stood Sam and George, George's arm gently propelling Sam forward. Sam's face was creased with tears and sleep. Beth could smell the milk on his breath. He half-turned back toward George, who nodded, urging him, and followed Sam inside.

"I'm sorry, Beth, Pat," George said. "I'm real sorry he did it again."

Pat was clawing at his hair. "Did what? Did what again, George?"

George looked, confused, from Beth to Pat, then back over his shoulder, where the newly risen sun's glare above the rock garden was brightest. Some-one was standing just at the turn of the drive. Someone . . . Beth shaded her eyes. It was Vincent.

"What?" she asked softly. "What?"

The first time Sam climbed out of his room in the middle of the night, climbed up the rose trellis outside his old room, knocked out the screen, and got into his bed, George explained, had been another of those nights when Beth had gone to bed early and Pat had been at the restaurant. And of course, he, George, was ready to bring Sam right back—"I mean, I love my son," he said. "I'm sorry, Beth, I love Sam is what I mean. But I knew you'd be out of your mind with worry, and you'd think that I, like, let him do this." But as soon as he'd given Sam some toast and a hug and taken him outside to the front porch, well, there was Reese, hunched in his jacket, astride his bike. Reese, who gave George a worldly shrug and assured him that he'd see the wanderer home and explain everything to the folks.

That same thing had happened the second time. And the third time. And this time, too.

"Vincent never told us," Beth said, mostly to Sam.

"I know," Sam muttered. "We agreed to not tell you."

Beth turned to Pat, absurdly pointing out, "I thought you said Vincent's door was locked."

"It *was* locked," Vincent said, elbowing past George and Sam and turning toward the stairs. "You can lock a pop lock just by closing it behind you if you're a mechanical genius. There's more than one way to leave a room. Ask Sam."

"Listen, Vincent. . . ." Pat clenched his teeth.

"Give it up, Dad." Vincent pulled off his slantwise Sox cap and tossed it on the banister. "I'm going to bed. He's home, right? He's home this time, anyhow."

Watching herself from without, understanding the poverty of the gesture at such a time, Beth offered George coffee. Eagerly, he accepted. Sam reached down and zipped up his jacket.

"Go up to your room, Sam," Pat said, so sternly everyone, including Sam, was visibly surprised.

"What did I do?" Sam asked, with sudden heat.

"You ran away! You scared the hell out of your mother and me, that's what you did! And you've done it before! You could have broken your neck, or gotten hit by a car, or worse!" Pat pushed his face close to Sam's. "Hasn't enough happened to this family? Hasn't there been enough hurt to go around for everyone?"

"Yeah," Sam answered, but as Beth watched, he seemed to gather himself, thrust forth his chest. He was nearly as tall as Pat, and broader. Oh, she thought, he is not going to back off now. He has a Cappadora's temper. He has a Kerry's stubbornness. He is going to say it. And then, ashamed of her glancing jolt of relief, she thought, Then at least I won't have to. "Yeah, there's been enough. I mean, I'm sick of this whole thing."

"What whole thing?" Pat asked quietly.

"This ... whole thing." Tears gathered in the corners of Sam's eyes, and slowly, beautifully spilled from the fan-shaped ends of his long lashes. "I'm sick of this. I want to go home. I want my dad. I can go to court and get you to give me to my dad. I read it at school."

"Look," said Pat, "whatever you read, you can't be serious thinking you could get us to give you to the husband of the woman who stole you, who kidnapped you?"

"It's not my dad's fault!" Sam said then. "Dad, you want me to come home, right? Tell him!"

George's misery was so overwhelming, so palpable, it was like another body in the room, a sweating, laboring presence. He looked from Sam to Pat, and then, beseechingly, at Beth, who mechanically measured out six spoons of coffee and carefully unfolded the brown paper filter.

"What?" Pat said finally. "What is he saying?"

George sat down heavily. "He's been asking me, over and over, Pat. Why he can't live with me. I keep telling him ... what his mother did, what Cecilia did, was so wrong, and what you folks have gone through—"

"But it wasn't really her fault, either," Sam trilled. "My mom is mentally ill, Beth. She's mentally ill. You said that when we went to that little town up there. I told you all about it. She didn't know what she was doing. She really thought I was her real little boy. Right?"

Beth said, "I know."

"And no offense, Beth," Sam said then, sensing an opening, measuring it. "It's not like I hate you. I mean, I tried for three months! Three months!"

"Sam, son, come on," George said, taking Sam's arm.

"No, Dad, listen! We talked it over. Beth knows." Beth could feel Pat's scouring look along her arm. She avoided his eyes. "I told her how I don't see why I have to live here, two blocks away from my own house, with people I don't even know, because of something that happened a long time ago that I didn't even do."

"Sam," Pat said. "Sit down." Sam sat down, careful to put George between the two of them. "Sam, listen. We know how hard this has been. We know how much you miss your . . . you miss George. But this is a fact we have to face: you're *our* son. You don't remember being our son, but the fact is, you are our son. We gave birth to you. And you belong with your own family."

"But that's just the thing!" Sam was sobbing now. "I was maybe born in your family, but I never, like, saw you before in my life. I didn't remember anything, except the . . . well, I didn't remember anything about your house or anything! You see?" Pat nodded, closing his eyes.

"But look," Sam went on, shaking, trying to smile, "it can be okay, after all. I read . . . I looked it up on the microfiche—I didn't tell you this, Beth, but there was this one kid who divorced his real parents because he wasn't happy with them, and he got to be with his foster parents from before . . . see? He was used to them, because he lived there, like, five years. Then, all of a sudden, his mom got a job or something and she's like, 'I'm taking him back.' Now, I don't think I would actually have to get a lawyer or anything— right, Dad?" He looked at George searchingly. "I could just . . . move home. And maybe sometimes, I would come over or something. Like I do with my dad now. See?"

"But that was a case where the child wasn't being taken care of," Pat said, wearily. "That mother was probably neglectful or bad to the boy. We didn't do anything wrong, Sam."

"Well, neither did I!" he shouted.

Pat continued, softer, "And, Sam, I don't think you could do this even if we wanted it and—"

"Yes you could," Sam told him urgently. "I read. You could do it if you wanted to. It's all legal and everything."

"But we don't. Sam. We love you. We wanted you back and we still want you and we'll always want you."

Sam put his head down on his folded arms, and both Pat and George reached for him instinctively. Beth bent over the coffee pot, feeling Kerry, for once silent, come up behind her and grab hold of the tail of her shirt.

"What's the matter with him, Mom?" she asked. "What's the matter with Sam?"

"He so sad, Ker Bear," Beth told the girl, stroking her silky, knotted hair. "He's just so sad."

"Go upstairs now, Sam," George said steadily. "Lie down for a while. I'll come and see you before I go. Okay? And ball tomorrow night? Huh? Okay?" Sam lurched from the table, nearly shoving George off-balance.

"I hate you!" he screamed. "I hate you—and I hate you, too, Dad! And I hate your dumb ugly house and your dumb freako son with the peanut-butter name! I'm never coming back!" Knocking over a chair, Sam ran for the stairs and up, two at a time. Beth could hear him strike the wall, three times, in the upper hall, and then the echo of his slamming door.

"I'm so sorry," George whispered. "The poor little sucker."

"George, nobody blames you," Beth said, rushing to finish making the coffee, bringing napkins, bringing cream in a pitcher, bringing matching spoons—all things she never did.

"I want to do right by him!" George cried then, slamming his palm down on the table. "I want him to be happy. And if you guys are the guys that can give him the family he deserves, goddamnit, then you give him that! But I got to tell you, Beth, Pat, this kid is the saddest kid in the world right now. I have never seen this kid sad more than twelve hours in his life. It's . . . it's not in Sam. I mean, even when Cecilia . . . he was *sorry* for her, Pat. He would hold her hand, and her hand was limp like a washrag, and say, "It's okay, Mom. It's okay.' And now . . . my God. Maybe it'll get better. . . ."

Pat said then, a gulp, almost a croak, "And maybe it won't."

"And maybe it won't," George said. "But I gotta tell you, it's killing me. To come in his room like I do every morning and then, once in a while, to see him curled up there in his bed. See him there, with the pillow my ma made for him tucked under his leg. Beth! Pat! Of all people on God's good earth, you know how I feel!"

Pat looked at Beth with a scalding stare. "What did he tell you, up north?"

"This, basically. But not so much," she said, lowering her eyes. "I wanted to talk to you about it. . . ."

George stood up hurriedly, knocking the chair over, catching it before it hit the floor. "I'm going, you guys," he said. "I'm sorry, again."

They both made as if to rise, but George waved them down with a weary motion of his hand.

Beth and Pat sat at the table, the fresh coffee in three mugs cooling between them. I will make breakfast, Beth thought. I will get up and do that.

"Paddy," she said. "Go get some sleep, huh?" He shrugged and headed for the stairs. Beth got out a bowl and began to beat eggs. French toast, she thought. It was still a bafflement to her, cooking, after years of Pat bringing home forage from the restaurant on his dinner break for him and the children—for herself, there was always a bagel, a yogurt, a handful of crackers and cheese. But Sam seemed to expect actual meals at predictable hours—salads, side dishes, desserts. George had followed the pyramid plan religiously; Sam weirdly liked such things as bran muffins and dried apricots. Beth peeled apples and oranges and mixed them with yogurt. Fruit salad. That was a good thing for a mother to make. Beowulf slapped his fat graying tail under the bench, the scattering hairs floating in the sun's spreading glow like little slivers of glass.

Vincent came down, drawn by the scent of cinnamon and butter. Pat, now in shirtsleeves followed. In silence, one by one, they came to the table and ate. Sam collected the dishes to stack in the dishwasher.

"I'll help you," Kerry said.

"It's my day," Sam told her, carefully stacking plates and placing the silverware on the top of the heap.

"You want to have a catch?" Pat called to Sam.

"I said I'd mow for the Silbergs," Sam said.

"But it's not even seven o'clock," Pat told him.

"Maybe sleep a while first," Sam replied. Pat hitched his chair back so he could watch Sam at the sink. He studied Sam's hands; Pat loved Sam's capable hands on a ball, any ball. Those masterful catcher's and shooter's hands were Pat's special joy, and Beth suspected, his guilt, too. Pat had been a shortstop, all bluster and speed. Sam's baseball was different, smart and slow, all thought.

Beth emptied the coffee grounds into the trash. Kerry turned on Looney Toons. Vincent disappeared into his cave. Now I'll sit on the porch, Beth thought.

When she went outside, she found Pat watering the roses.

"I can do it," she told him, with a spurt of irritation; hadn't Angelo reminded his son a million times you had to water the roots, not the leaves, or the leaves would mold? "I thought you were going to sleep."

"I can't sleep," he said. "Can you sleep?"

"Then Paddy, I guess we'd better talk."

"If you want," he said.

"He's not happy. What happened last night, that's just the tip of it."

"I knew you were going to say that, Beth. In a situation that's almost good, you have to find the all-bad. The social worker warned us about this. She said that it was going to take a long time. Remember? Confusion about his identity. All that stuff."

"That's just it, Pat. Do you think he has any confusion about his identity? I don't. He knows exactly who he is."

Pat turned his back on her and began scraping at the leaves with a hoe he found against the side of the house. "What are you getting at?"

Beth sat down on the grass. "Pat, remember when we'd read about those cases where the birth parents wanted the baby back after the adoptive parents had the kid for two or three years? And you always said that if you were the judge, you would rule in the best interests of the child? You were always the one who said it was a terrible thing to do to the child?"

"This is different."

"The effect is the same."

"The effect is not the same."

"Paddy, George is his father."

For an instant, Beth thought Pat would raise the hoe and strike her. What he did instead was drop the hoe, grab the hose and throw it hard against the trunk of a tree, so that it undulated in the air like a cobra, spraying droplets over both of them.

"Listen, Beth," he said quietly. "I'm going to say this once. I love you, Beth." He walked over to the spigot and switched off the water. "I love you, and I've probably loved you your whole life. We've been married twenty years, and I've known you your whole life. And you know what I've seen about you, your whole life?"

"What?" Beth asked.

"You have made a career out of being unhappy."

"That's not fair. When Ben was——"

"No, I mean even before Ben was kidnapped. You were always just waiting for an excuse to be miserable. I'm not a doctor, Bethie. Maybe you have some kind of head problem, a personality thing. But see, Beth, I'm not like that. If I get the chance, I'll be happy. Even before we got him back, I decided I was going to be happy. I was going to die if I didn't. And then we did get him back. My life is how I want it. I thank God for my life being how I want it. And nothing on this earth is going to make me want to change any part of it, not after what I've been through. Not after what Vincent's been through."

"You know I don't want to do anything to hurt Vincent."

"I don't think you do. I really think you believe that. But what are you suggesting, exactly? That we give Sam back to the people who stole him when he was a baby? Are you nuts, Beth? Can you imagine what people would think?"

"I don't care what people think. I care about Sam."

"Well, then be a mother to him, Beth. If you care about him, help him get better."

"I'm trying to."

"No, you're trying to figure out a way we can all be miserable again. So that you can take another nine-year powder. This is about you, Beth. It isn't about this kid."

"Pat, listen, I wasn't thinking of completely giving him up. Lots of families, when there's a divorce or something, they share custody. We only live two blocks apart. He could have two families."

"Beth, he *has* a family! By the mercy of God, he got his family back. He's my flesh and blood, Beth, my son. And if you think I am crazy enough to go along with anything that would take my son away from me again, after all that hell, I don't want anything to do with it, Beth. Or anything to do with you. I mean it."

Beth glanced around the yard and stood up. Pat was yelling now; she was sure the Beckers could hear him through their open windows; they didn't have air conditioning. "Paddy, we don't have to decide anything right now."

"Yes, we do, Beth. This is a pattern. The restaurant's a hit because people are ghouls. So what? Maybe they are. They'll forget in time. People forget everything. My sisters hate you because they think you gave up on Ben. Well, maybe they do—they'll get over it. People get over things, Beth. Sam will get over this. People have survived worse. We're lucky, Beth. We're lucky, do you get it?"

"Pat, I can't. If I love him, I can't ignore this. Let's talk to Tom Kilgore, huh?"

"I'm not going to change my mind, Beth," said Pat.

"It's not just your decision!" she shouted at him then. "You don't just say, 'I like my life, I've got my life!' He's got a life, too!"

"Yeah, he does! And it's right here! He's my kid!"

Tell him now, Beth thought. It's too late in the day for a coward's politeness. Tell him so he can't pretend he doesn't already know. Lay out the evidence, brick on brick, so that he can't say later he never really understood—never really knew that their baby, their Ben, had been right.

There was a deep end of the ocean. Ben had gone there, and he had not come back.

They could never go there with him, or know what he had experienced, or truly understand what had made him. They could only see the result.

Ben had walked out of the waves like a sturdier Venus springing from the foam, fully grown, transformed. He had walked out Sam Karras, a fine boy any parent would be proud to have raised; but Beth and Pat had not.

The smell he remembered as parental vigilance in the night was not her soap but George's cigars. Sam was a whole sediment of accumulated beliefs and impressions that had nothing to do with the Cappadoras: The red eggs of Orthodox Easter were the ones he had held in smaller hands; Alicia Karras, not Rosie, was Sam's yaya; his nana, the patrician Sarah Lockhart. He slept in pajamas, not underwear and t-shirts, as all the Cappadoras did.

Beth wanted to tell her husband how she'd scrutinized Sam for hopeful signs of breakthrough, for the merest hints. How she had seen Sam study Angelo and wondered, Is there some connection in this? Vague, but real? How she'd waited for results after Sam spent hours with the family photo albums, poring over details with the intensity of an adult at work on a difficult jigsaw puzzle, and grieved when none seemed to come.

Pat's face was shut, truculent. Could she tell him? Or would it be wasted breath? Didn't Pat know that all of Sam's memory molecules had been altered, and not with horrors? Didn't Pat remember the day that the county social worker told them that things might have been clearer, though far more harrowing, if Sam had grown up with sexual abusers or vagrants? That then, at least, he might see his biological parents as fairy-tale heroes? Instead, she said ruefully, "I hate to say this, but he probably feels like you were the ones who stole him, from his dad." Pat had been outraged, even after the worker apologized. He'd fumed for days.

Remind him, Beth thought.

And then said, "Pat, I think there are a lot of things going on you just don't want to see. And one of them is that I'm not the enemy here. Don't you think I want the same thing you want? If I could take a pill, or Sam could, and we would all forget this ever happened, don't you think I would?"

Pat paused before he answered, then said, with care, "I don't know whether you would, Beth."

"Jesus, that's cruel. You think I enjoy this?"

"Not enjoy it. No, I wouldn't accuse you of that. But you thrive on it. I mean, what would you have to keep you going if you didn't have your . . . your holy suffering?"

"Pat!"

"Well, there it is. It's like you finally found the big misery, Bethie. The thing that made it okay to be the bleak Irish. And now you're going to look for more. Losing just one kid one time wasn't enough." He stopped.

She said, "You mean, I could accept losing him again. It wouldn't hurt me as much as it did you."

And even though Pat stood silent, Beth heard him say it again, as if he'd spoken. The words he'd used. "Losing *just* one kid once."

" 'Just one,' " she said. "You think that I lost them both, don't you? Sam *and* Vincent? That it was all me?"

Pat said, "No. Christ, no. I'm sorry."

"That's what you meant, though."

"I didn't, Bethie, no, and I don't." Pat looked sincerely horrified.

I could hate him now, Beth thought, and it would probably help both of us. But the only feeling she could touch, rummaging inside, was regret as soft-edged and familiar as old flannel. Regret and guilt already worn by years of touching, long before the day of the reunion ever came, the day the long-simmering virus of her mother deficiency flared into frank symptoms.

Okay.

She hadn't been the best of mothers. In her affection as well as her wrath, rough-and-tumble. Impatient. Madly loyal, but not always sympathetic. Not always willing to make enough room.

Maybe, Beth thought, and almost said, even before the kidnapping, there were too many of them and not enough of me. I couldn't give them everything I had, the way really good mothers do, because I had to keep some for my work.

But what about you, Pat? You were in the restaurant business, for God's sake, a twenty-four-seven job your whole adult life. Why did you do it? Why didn't you sell computers instead? Did you maybe like the hours, and the life, in spite of all your bitching? Was that okay, just because you were the father? And that was how *your* father was? Because when you *were* home, you were naturally sweet, not like me?

Beth kneaded her forehead. Stop, she thought. Don't buy this. Don't use the past as a prelude to the day of the reunion and everything after as simply a reprise of the theme—Mom half-there, kids half-served, then, finally, the payoff.

No. She struggled for a single good, settling breath.

"The thing is, Pat," she said, "if it wouldn't have happened, everything would have turned out all right. For us and for the kids."

"What do you mean?"

"I mean, we'd have been happy. We were. You think Ben got lost because I was a sloppy mother. And I *was* a sloppy mother. . . ."

"That wasn't—"

"Yes, it was, Pat. It was what you meant. But that didn't bother you then. Not so much. And even if I had been worse, they would have turned out okay. You want to see things in terms of 'if this, then that.' That's how you are, Pat. If things go down, it's because there was a flaw in the structure. But there wasn't. Not really. When you were growing up, Angelo was always having his little phony Italian breakdowns, and Rosie was always at the shop, and you turned out. Maybe things were easier then. There was church and the Moose lodge and you lived in one place all your life. But what there wasn't when we were kids—" she paused, looking for the word—"was . . . awareness. The fact that we knew how hard it was for kids who had parents who have to hustle for everything. My parents just thought that was ordinary life. They sort of dressed you and fed you and hit you if you didn't do your homework. But *I* knew. I knew I was selfish to want lots of kids and work, too. So I tried to make it up to them, so they would understand, no matter how I failed them in little ways, I never failed them in the one big way." Beth stood up and took Pat's arms. "I knew I wanted them. They knew it, too. They knew that I was as good as I could be."

When Pat made as if to dismiss her, Beth gripped harder. "And if you want to, you can say that after Ben was lost, it was my fault that Vincent got lost, too. You can say that, because it makes it easier for you. But I was as good as I could be then, too. And the reason that my best wasn't very good wasn't just the grief. It was probably because I believed, just like you did, that it was my doing. I felt that I could easily let Vincent down simply by being his mom."

Pat was crying now. But Beth knew she could not afford to give in to either rage or pity. She could not, would not stop. She would talk until the window slammed shut. "And you know what the only thing we still have is? Awareness. We can be aware that we have two sons and they're both strangers in our house, and if we don't pretend this isn't true, maybe we can save something out of it. You've pretended long enough, and . . . you could say I have, too. How we got here doesn't matter."

Pat looked at her then: his eyes not knowing, or full of solace, as they had been so often in years past, but, like her father's, trusting and desolate and weak.

"What does, then?" he said. "What do you want from me?"

And if Beth had ever doubted it, she was sure at that instant that there was to be no shared responsibility for the consequences of whatever happened with Sam. Even if Pat didn't hate her—and she could see that he didn't any longer dare hate her—he would still be unable to say to his family, "We talked it over. We decided that Sam is too unhappy this way. We decided what was best for us to do." There would be no "we" about it. Pat would not be disloyal to her, but it would be salt plain that he was living with a choice that Beth had made.

And now she would have to make it.

Reese

Chapter 32

"So it's kind of like a joint-custody arrangement? One week here, one week there?" asked Tom, one leg thrown up over the arm of his overstuffed chair. Reese had observed that since his marriage, a few months earlier, old Tom had loosened up considerably. Perhaps getting all that regular . . . But no, he wasn't going to head down that particular path today.

"Actually, I don't know what they worked out exactly; it's only been like a few weeks. I know they went to see a judge and stuff," Reese said. "I guess there are rules about it. But he hasn't been around much." Which was overstating the case. That day when he saw Sam heading down the drive, Reese had just dived into the sounds from the luxe new CD player his father had finally allowed him to take money out of savings to buy. He didn't even go down. He could picture the scene on the porch: his dad all slumped over, probably crying, his mom standing there like she was watching the *Hindenburg* burn. And poor Kerry, holding Blythe's hand and asking, "When's Sam coming back?" Shit, you had to be a goddamn masochist to live in the Cappadora *Days of Our Lives*. The boom box, Reese figured, was sort of a lollipop to keep

Vincent from crying over the loss of his already long-lost brother; shit, this got redundant. Like he gave a damn.

The house was already about seventy percent quieter, which was fine with Reese. They had never really made it as the Cleavers, anyhow, and Mom somehow looked more normal with her eyes watching the planets spin than she'd ever looked trying to actually see what people were doing.

"... feel about that?" Tom was saying.

"Pardon?"

"Earth to Reese." Tom was such a card. His slang was about thirty-five years old—Reese expected him to say "groovy" any minute—but he did his best. "I was asking you how it felt to know that Sam had made that choice. Did it feel ... kind of tough on you?"

"On me?" Reese was surprised. "No. I thought it was kind of a kick in the butt, excuse the expression, to my parents."

"Yeah, I can see that," Tom said. "So. How'd summer go? Still training for going out for basketball?"

Reese sure as hell wasn't going to tell him about the sweet little meeting with Shit-for-Brains Teeter. "Yeah," he said. "But I might not. I mean, of course, I'm academically challenged and understimulated in the traditional high-school setting, as you know." Tom snorted with laughter. "But my dad has this idea that if I don't get into the UW I'll die young or something. So I have to book next year. Really book. I might not have the time to give to the game, you know?"

Tom made a little steeple of his fingers. After years of seeing it, Reese knew deep thoughts were on the way.

"You sleeping okay?"

"Yep, pretty fair. No problem." Actually, this was a damned lie, but there was, again, no sense getting into it. He'd been having his fucking little-kid nightmare, twice in the last week. It annoyed him to think he was probably going to always be more or less borderline nuts, over something he didn't even care about anymore, or even remember. Much, that is. He felt his heart skip and flutter. Oh, shit, no, shit no. Not that, too.

"What's wrong, Reese?" Tom swung his leg onto the floor, crouched forward in serious-shrink posture.

"Nothing, nothing. I think I'm getting the flu or something is all."

"Are you sure that's all it is? I mean, this is pretty heavy stuff, Reese. Getting him back. Figuring out that whole deal. Then having him go, and having to figure out *that* whole deal."

"I don't have to figure it out. It's got nothing to do with me."

"I think it has."

"That's your job, Tommaso. You always have to think it has, or you'd be out of work."

"True enough. But I know that shit has a way of catching up with you, too. What about your mom? You getting along?"

"Oh absolutely. With Sam gone, she has a new appreciation for my many talents. We played mixed doubles tennis on Thursdays, then there's bridge on Fridays. . . ."

"That gets old, Reese."

"Well, so does the question," Reese snapped. "I mean, my mom has spoken to me like ten times in nine years, and eight of those times were in the past couple of months. It's not, like, her fault or anything, but my mom sort of generally hates my guts."

"Whoa! Whoa! Wait a minute, buddy. I know your mom has her problems with intimacy, shall we say, but I've never once had the impression that—"

"Well, look at her face once. She looks at me like something you try to scrub off the bottom of the refrigerator."

"I don't think that's true. But it's important that you feel that way."

"Tom, I've been coming here, what, four years? A little more? How often have you met my mom?"

"Once or twice."

"Well, if you gave a fuck about your kid, wouldn't you think that maybe you'd like to check in more than once or twice? Tom, I don't give a damn. I got one more year in the bosom of my family. . . ."

"Make that two. At least, Reese. And what about your father, and Kerry? Are they just some kind of background scenery? Don't you care what they think?"

"Sure I do." Reese stopped for a moment and got up to look at his favorite horse picture, the one of Tom and his little sister. "Your sister, she still ride?"

"No," Tom said ruefully. "She's in middle school. And she wants to be a pompom girl. She looks like ... like some trashy backup singer in a garage band."

"Tom, Tom, Tom—she's just expressing herself, you know." Reese waved a finger. Tom grinned.

"Well, see, what Kerry does, she rides horses now. And swims. And plays flute. And plays soccer. Kerry is going to grow up to be this one-woman vaudeville show, like riding horses while tap-dancing and playing the flute. All she ever does is take lessons."

"Maybe she feels it's a way to get some attention for herself."

"I think it's a way to get out of the house. Which I totally understand. And which is why Dad virtually lives at Wedding in the Old Neighborhood. Especially now."

"So you feel pretty left out."

"Tom! I'm sixteen. I'm not in kindergarten. It's just that ... this isn't the family who goes bowling on Friday nights, you know? And thank God, because that would make me puke. But sure, my dad loves me and he loves Kerry."

"But your mom hates your guts. And she's the one you're around most."

"If you can call it that."

"What would you call it?"

"I'd call it, like, two people who have to live in an airport, the same airport...."

"And where are they going? From the airport?"

"I didn't mean they were going anywhere."

"But say they were." Tom was up to his old tricks.

"If they were, my mom would be going ... Jesus, I have no idea ... to Mars. And if she had her way, I'd be going to ... Siberia. Or hell. Or something."

"Why would your mother, who's already lost one kid, twice, want her other kid to go to hell?"

The flutter-beat in his chest returned again. "I have no idea," Reese said evenly. "She resents all the shit I've caused in school. I know that. It gets in her way."

"But you said she wants you to go to hell. That's not what most people want for a maladjusted teenager, if you want to call it that."

"Call it what you want." Reese glanced at the red numbers on the clock. "Hour's up."

"Don't give it a thought, Reese. My next appointment canceled. And your dad's loaded."

"Not to hear him talk."

"Well, don't worry about it. We were talking about going to hell." And, speaking of that, why don't you? Reese muttered to himself.

"It's obvious. She blames me."

"For what?"

"For *what*?"

"You heard the question."

"For the kid going back to George is what. She was like, always, 'Pay more attention to him,' 'Don't be so hard on him'...."

"Were you hard on him?"

"No. I shot some hoops with him. I didn't, whatever, read him bedtime stories...."

"He's too old for bedtime stories."

"I mean, I treated him perfectly normal, given that I don't have much in common with a sixth grader!"

"Even a sixth-grader who happens to be your brother you haven't seen in nine years? Don't you think that might call for a little more attention, Reese? Or would that be too much effort?"

"Tom," Reese pleaded. "I think I have a fever, is what I think. I'm going."

"I think you have a bad case of the poor-little-me's, is what I think. Your dad ignores you. Your mom hates you. Even your little sister takes too many riding lessons. Sound like Oliver Twist, you know, Reese?"

"So I give, okay? All I know is, she thinks the whole fucking thing is my fault, and you don't know, because you never see her except when she's acting all ... there, and all nice...."

" 'The whole fucking thing'? You mean what you said, him going back to George?"

"No!" Reese caught himself, ran his hands down his forearms, so he wouldn't scream.

"What, then?"

"Nothing."

"What, Reese? I can sit here all day."

"For fucking losing Ben in the first place. Happy now?"

"No. And she does not."

"She does so."

"No one would blame a seven-year-old kid for not watching his kid brother in a crowded lobby of a hotel, and anyway—"

"You don't know," Reese said miserably. "You weren't there!"

"Neither was she."

"But she knows! She knows!"

"What does she know?"

"She knows that I . . ."

It was as if he were having the running dream right then, having it awake. He started thinking of that smell, the day Ben was kidnapped, that bottle-gravy smell of that hotel kitchen, under the scent of all the woman's powder and cologne. And he wanted to puke on the rug, or get up and knock Tom's glasses right off his smug, pink-Irish face. The dick. "Look, Tom," Reese said with an effort. "I don't know what I meant by that. She just gives me the creeps."

"Maybe you give *her* the creeps."

"Maybe I do."

"Maybe she was right. Maybe you did drive the kid away. Maybe he could tell you didn't want him around. That if he was around, maybe you wouldn't be able to get everybody to sit up and pay attention every time you decided to pull some JD stunt, huh, Reese?"

Reese put his face in his hands. "Don't ask me. I don't know."

"I think you do know, Reese," Tom said. "I think you do know. I think you know, and you're afraid to tell me, because that would take you to a place you've managed to stay away from for a real long time, wouldn't it, Reese?

And it would take a lot to go there. A lot of effort. And you seem to like to take the easy way."

"The easy way?" I sound like a whistle, Reese thought. He wondered if whatever little bulimic or pyro was waiting in the outer room could hear him. Oh, right. Canceled. At least that. He lowered his voice. "If you think that living in the Addams Family has been easy, you're the one who ought to be sitting over here."

"I never said it was easy. I just said that maybe some people have enough guts to go there, and some don't."

"Guts? Look, nobody has ever called me afraid. They've called me a lot, but never chickenshit."

"I am."

"Go to hell, then."

"I thought that was your destination."

"Very cute, Tom. Highly professional."

"Reese, you might as well hang it up," Tom sighed. "You're going to be stuck where you are until you finally meet someone big enough and mean enough to beat it out of you. That's if you're lucky. I just wish you weren't so determined to take the whole family with you."

"I'm not," Reese said then. "I just want them to leave me alone."

"I thought that's what you *didn't* want. But it sounds like every time some-body tries to get close to you, you can't wait to find a way to piss in his face."

"Don't," Reese warned.

"Why, Reese? Gonna rumble with me, next? Not content with blaming your mother for all your troubles?"

"Blaming my mother? Christ, I've been trying to tell you. It's her! It's her! She knows what I did, and she hates me for it, and I don't blame her!"

"What you did? What did you do?"

"What did I do? What did I do? I let go of his hand! And you know what I said? To my sweet little kid brother? I said, 'Get lost.' I said, 'Get lost.'" Reese figured he'd cry then—it would have been a relief to cry then—but he didn't. He was boiling. Boiling dry. The top of his head would be rising like the lip of a tea kettle if Tom could see his insides.

"Reese," Tom said, far away. "Reese."

"What."

"Did you always know this? Did you remember it just now?"

"I don't know."

"You do know."

"I always knew it. And I didn't. That's the truth. It was, like it was in a box. But I remembered it when he came home. Like, first a little. Then some more. Then the words."

"Reese, think. Think a minute. There's no way on earth your mother could know you said that. And you didn't mean for him to literally get lost."

"But he did. He did."

"The fact is, you didn't mean it, and you didn't even know what it really meant. You were just a tired little kid sick of watching his little brother while your mom goofed around with all her friends. You were probably hungry, and bored. . . ."

"Yeah, so big deal. She still hates me."

"I don't think she hates you, Reese. I think she's scared of you."

"Scared . . . of me?"

"I think she's scared you're going to find out about her, the same way you were scared she'd find out about you."

"Find out about her? What did she ever do?"

"Think about it, Reese. Think about it and we'll talk next time. It's in there, Reese. You opened the box. That's a pretty brave thing to do, Reese. Now, we have to look at whatever flies out of there, and if we have to, we'll swat it down, like a bug. Okay?"

"Okay."

"It wasn't your fault, Reese. It wasn't your fault. You don't have to believe me now. Like, people didn't used to believe there were such things as atoms, because they couldn't see them. But there are." Reese shrugged. "Listen. I told you one time about my little brother. The baby who died of SIDS. I told you I was the one who found him. But I didn't tell you the rest. My mom sent me up there to get him out of his crib." Reese looked up. Tom was looking at one of the horse pictures, directly over Reese's head. "And I was mad. I was sick of carrying around babies. There were eight of us, and we all had to take care of the little ones, and it wore you out. So I went up there, and I reached for Taylor's arm. And it was cold. It felt . . . like a little cucumber from the refrigerator. Cold and hard. And so you know what I did? Reese?" Reese nodded. "I had been reading the comics, and my mom kept telling me, 'Go get the baby, go get the baby,' and all I wanted to do was finish the comics. So I did. And finally, when I went up there, and found him like that, I was still carrying that newspaper. And I spread it out, and I covered him all up with the comics. I'm sure I didn't know, or I didn't let myself know, that he was dead. But what I do know is, I wouldn't let my mother touch me for . . . really, for years. She thought it was because of what she'd done to me, exposing me to that awful thing, when I was just a little kid myself. She thought I was afraid of dying in my sleep. And I was. But that wasn't the big thing."

Reese jerked his head. "What was?"

"The big thing was, I didn't know until I was in high school, or even college . . . I thought I killed Taylor. That I messed around so long that he died from starving to death or something. That if I had just gone up there sooner, when my mom told me to, he would have been able to live, just a little longer. Reese, I thought that when I was older than you are. And you can see, I can tell by looking at you, you can already see, it simply wasn't true. It couldn't have been true."

Reese nodded again. His head was big, pulsing, like a balloon on a stick in the wind. He didn't think he'd ever had a headache this bad, so bad he almost asked Tom for some aspirin or something. But Tom would probably have had to write a prescription or some deal; doctors never just gave you anything to make you feel better. There had to be a big process.

Air, Reese thought, when Tom finally let him go, with a brotherly squeeze on his shoulder. He'd been in the fucking horse gallery for two hours. Jesus. He'd opened the box, and what for? He knew Tom was a decent guy, but that story about the dead baby—he didn't really get it; no one could really get it.

Reese steered his bike up Hollendale toward the school. It was getting dark already, summer ending, he thought. Thank Christ Dad hadn't insisted on driving him today. Maybe he would just sit in the outside bleachers for a little while. Suck some air. See if anybody was around and play a little pickup if somebody was. His neck felt like it was shrinking, pulling his head back into his shoulders.

He spun into the parking lot, pedaling hard, and then he saw it. The big old white Thunderbird, a restored '68. The vanity plates said BG COCH, which they all knew that fat bastard intended to mean "Big Coach," but to most of the kids—except, of course, the loyal storm troopers of the varsity A squad—it was "Big Cock" or "Big Crotch," depending on the mood they were in.

Teeter. That fat fuck. Probably in there right now planning ways to emasculate some ninth grader into peeing himself. An old fart, gone to fat, still trying to drive his Beach Boys car around town. Teeter, thought Reese, slowing down, carefully stowing his bike in the bushes, behind a stack of railroad pilings. He put his hands in his pockets. It was almost dark now.

Which suited Reese just fine.

Chapter 33

The guard pulled the metal-armed chair out for Reese and motioned for him to sit down.

And then he left, silently, as if vaporized. Reese wouldn't even have known the guy was gone except for the eddy of deflected air from the closing door. He stared at the smeared Plexiglas partition, with its distinct prints of hands, snail trails of . . . he didn't like to think what. Reflexively, he lifted his hands into his lap and held his arms tightly against his sides. He didn't want the furniture, with its hosts of prior bacterium, to touch his body and inhabit his skin. The room was rank; it stank of hair rinsed in cigarette smoke, of dirty insoles. It was a little, little room, a narrow closet. Reese tried not to breath, tried not to take the molecules of stink into his nose; whatever you breathed, dog fart or cinnamon bread baking, it became part of you. Oh God, I want to be clean, Reese thought. I want my bed. I want my toothbrush. He didn't have his watch anymore, and the room had no windows; but he knew it was morning. The sky had been lightening already when they drove him over from the hospital. And then it took about twelve hours to do

his fingerprints and take away his normal clothes; and then they told him to go to sleep—and he did fall asleep, in spite of all the noise and crying, but only slept for like a half-hour. Then they got him up and told him his parents were there. They had been at the hospital, but he'd been so high from the shot they'd given him he couldn't remember what his mom or his dad had said, or even whether they had touched him.

Now, he wasn't much improved. If anybody asked him, Reese could not have sworn whether four hours had passed or forty. But it had to be Saturday. Just later Saturday. When he saw his mom outside the door, he suddenly had a memory flash from the hospital emergency room. Red jeans. She still had on the same red jeans.

The no-contact visiting room was supposed to be soundproof. There was a vanilla-colored telephone on his side that he would use to speak to his mother when she came in. But he could watch her already, through the long rectangle of the window of the door opposite, standing in profile as if the window were a picture frame, her head hanging down, her fuzzy dark hair shadowing her face.

She was talking to someone, and when she shifted back to pick up her shoulder bag, that someone reached for her. Candy: the swan arms and frosted fingertips unmistakable, even in a blue blazer-type thing, the kind of thing he hardly ever saw Candy wear. Candy put her arms around Reese's mom and stroked Beth's hair. Reese would have given anything, at that moment, to hear ... He laid his head down on the Formica laminate of the counter, forcing himself not to cringe at the contact. Soundproof—ah, yes. Another triumph of technology—not. He could hear his mother say, "... better off home?"

But Candy's voice was louder, good ol' Candy. Hers was a voice accustomed to giving orders to people with voices lower than hers.

Mutter, mutter, she said, and then, "... could kick him today even, though technically, you know, there has to be a custody proceeding for a juvenile, and we can't do that until Monday afternoon at the earliest. But Bethie ..." They were leaning against the door now, as if they didn't realize he was sitting there at all, some three feet of air and an inch of plastic away, right there. Hello, Mom. Hello, Candy. They didn't look at him. "... a bad idea to let him stay the weekend." Reese could feel sweat snake down his breastbone. "There's a kind of kid you know is going to snuggle up to those little friends in there and learn some tricks ..." Reese lost her voice for a moment as she turned briefly away, but then, "... scare the hell out of him. I mean, the decisions going on in there are whether to cop to the rape charge in exchange for dropping the drug charge. They got the father shooters on one side and the mother shooters on the other. It's a gamble, Bethie, but this is a kid who wrecked a stolen car, drunk, and scuffled with a cop ... peanuts, Beth."

It's peanuts? Or not peanuts? Reese tried to slow down the thrum of his heart that interfered with his hearing. His heart rebelled, pummeling harder.

Outside, Reese's mom made a noise, tossed her head back.

"I don't mean to you," Candy went on, "but for all Reese has done in the past, you know ... a criminal kid. This isn't a pattern. This is his first major antisocial.... Beth, you know what I'm saying.... In this case, reform school for this, especially with his history ..."

Jesus God, thought Reese. Is that the best I can get, or the worst?

"... teach him the world doesn't owe him a living no matter how he screws up?" Mom asked then, louder.

"I don't think the world owes him a living, Beth," Candy said. "But the world owes him an apology."

"... to us all. And what about Sam?" True to form, Mom, Vincent thought. I'm in the can here, and we're going to find a way bring up the prodigal son. Who, like, wishes you were anywhere but here. Who literally jumped out a second-story window to get away from you. Who probably hates your guts. Yes, Mom, let's discuss Ben, alias Sam.

"Ben, too," said Candy. "That is, Sam, too. But Reese didn't do this thing because he was trying to throw his weight around...."

Reese heard another voice, muffled. Dad. Oh, good Christ. And Candy replied, "Well, yeah, Pat. You know all this shit. What kids do if they're hurting, kids like Reese. He's not going to come up to you and say, 'Well, Dad, I didn't really mean for Sam to leave, though I'm not entirely sorry he did. This is bothering me.' They can't do that—Reese especially—so he has to do something crazy, something so big it draws all the attention off how he feels about this...."

"... his fault?" It was his mother.

"Oh, Beth," said Candy, her voice tangy with irritation. "You know he thinks everything is his fault. And you know, Beth, I don't want to scare you—you've been scared enough for ten people in one life—but you know how many car accidents are suicide attempts for kids? You know that? I'm not trying to lay blame on top of this, but let's think about what he's going through...."

Whose fault? Not yours, Mom, no way. Reese rubbed his neck. His skin felt coated with syrup; he was accreting every piece of grit in this place.

And then, all of a sudden, his Dad was yelling, "... pay some attention to him once in a while, he'd know you gave a shit whether he was up in his room or wrapped around a fucking tree!"

"Well, Pat, they ate last night at Wedding in the Old Neighborhood, while your son was hot-wiring a teacher's car," Beth said evenly, shrilly.

"Why not be a mother, Beth?" Reese could hear his dad's voice, tiny, but he knew Pat was yelling. He could visualize him, throwing his chest out. He hated that little rooster posture, the one that sometimes ended with a fist through a hollow-core door. "Why not just try it?"

"Pat," Candy said. "Shut up."

The door behind him whispered again. The quiet guard. "They'll be with you in a minute, Vincent. They're talking to the chief."

The chief. A definite smile there. Reese still couldn't help it. Chief Bliss. The babe cop who found Ben Cappadora. Even though she didn't. Even though she couldn't find him, for nine years, a mile from the police station. Well, okay, Candy. Affirmative action. Go for it. He put his hands over his face. Fuck the bacteria. And then the door in front of him opened inward, and there was his mother, not much more deranged-looking than on any ordinary day, taking in the dirty window and the scummy phone and him in his lank green jail jump suit, as if all of it were furnishings, sitting down. He was so sick to his stomach, tasting the peach brandy, that looking at the raccoony way Mom rubbed the backs of her little strong hands against her cheeks as she sat down, it was so much something he could picture her doing in her robe in the kitchen or something, he almost started to cry, and then he thought he would puke. He looked away.

"Vincent," she said.

"Hi, Mom."

"How are you?"

"Okay."

They sat there. His mother breathed in through her nose and let the air escape her mouth with a long hiss. Vincent concentrated on swallowing, swallowing. Maybe, he thought, she'll give me hell. She'll tear a strip off me. Any other parent in the hemisphere would. This was, after all, a big-time jerk-off. He guessed he deserved it. Mom? He looked at her and coiled in preparation. But she just sat there Momishly. Finally, she seemed to think of something.

"Well, do you need anything? I mean, anything at all from home? Because I think that you're going to have to stay here a day or so more, because it's the weekend. . . ."

And learn my lesson like a good little boy, thought Reese, feeling better. Well, actually, Mom, yes, I need a couple of things. I need to get out of this shitty dump where the light's in your face no matter which way you turn and the guy in the next bed keeps looking at me as if I was a Big Mac and the little thirteen-year-old kid one room over is crying nonstop for his grandma. A little kid who cut his mother's boyfriend in the gut with a steak knife. Yeah, I need a couple of things, Mom.

"No, I'm fine," he said.

"Are you sure? You look green. Are you sick to your stomach or anything?"

Reese had to look away. It was like she could see the brandy-and-acid pluming up and down the sides of his stomach like one of those musical light fountains. Where did his goofy buddy Schaffer get that shit anyway? Did adults actually drink it? And why did he pick Schaffer up anyway? Why hadn't he just ditched the damn car and sat in a ditch to drink? No simple mistakes for you, Cappadora, he thought. He struggled again not to cry. Well, now I know. I know what people talk about to their kids in jail. Nausea. But before he could stop himself, he said, "My head aches."

"Candy says you should tell one of the officers if you feel bad in any way, and they can get you something."

"Well, they can't get me an aspirin. I already asked. They have to have, like, a nurse. They said not for a couple hours."

"I have an aspirin," said Beth, reaching for her purse. Reese smiled and reached up to pat the Plexiglas partition. "Oh, sure. I forgot. My God, Vincent. Is your head bleeding?"

"No."

"Oh, honey. Uh . . . do you want to see Dad?"

Exit stage left, Mom, thought Vincent, that's your bit. He was about to nod when he realized, abruptly, that he did not want to see his dad, maybe ever, especially not here, did not want to see the gray crescents under Pat's eyes, and the way Pat would rake his hair and reach for the partition as if he wanted to melt through it and lift Vincent up. If he saw his dad, that would be it. He had to keep himself low and slow, low and slow. So he said, "Not now, Mom. I just want to sleep."

She said, frightened-like, "Okay." He thought she would get up to leave then, but instead she placed both her hands flat on the counter on her side and cradled the telephone on her shoulder. She reached up and touched the partition. "Vincent. There's something I want to ask you."

He was intrigued. From Mom, this much conversational initiative was the equivalent of a film festival. Panic, he thought. She knows this is the big time. She's going to ask me why I did this—whether I was trying to kill myself or something. She's going to ask me what the hell I'm trying to do to her. . . .

"Yeah?"

"Ben is here." She shook her head. "Sam is here."

"Oh, shit." Figures. "What did you bring him here for?" Turn him away from a life of crime? The existent proof?

"He asked to come."

"How in the hell did he even find out?"

"Your dad told him."

"Why?"

"He thought . . . You can imagine, Vincent. The accident was on television news. The late news. They weren't supposed to use your name, you're just a kid, but because of Ben, you know, they said it was Ben Cappadora's brother. It was a piggy thing to do. And then, of course, they were all on the lawn fifteen minutes later. By this morning, Sam saw it. He called. Well, George called and put Sam on. He thought Sam would want to know if you were hurt...."

"Sam," said Reese, angry now, "*Sam* wouldn't want to know if I was on fire, Ma. What is this shit?" Reese had an inspiration. "I don't even think you can bring little kids in here. That is, the little kids who aren't already in here."

"Candy said it's okay."

"Is there, like, some big therapeutic reason 'Sam' has to come in and see me? Is it, like, healing?"

"I don't care if he does or not, Vincent." His mother's eyes were gone all black, no green. She laser-looked him. "I don't care if you see him or you don't. He wants to see you. I said I would tell you. He asked us to drive him over. We drove him over."

Reese thought, She knows when they say you can do whatever you want and that they couldn't care less, you always do what they want you to. There's no way out. He waved his hand at her.

"Okay," she said. "I'll go get him. He's downstairs."

"Whatever."

"Okay."

"Mom?"

"Yes?"

"Can I see Tom?"

"Tom ..."

"Tom Kilgore Tom ... you know, Mom?"

"Ummmm ... I don't know, Vincent. They said only immediate family."

"But I can see Sam."

The way she looked at him then, Reese thought, She really does hate me. I knew she hated me, but she really fucking hates me. He started to apologize, to say something, but then his mother said softly, "Sam is immediate family."

"Right. I wasn't thinking."

"Well, look. I'll ask Candy if I can call Tom."

"Forget it."

"No, I will.... And a lawyer, maybe, though I don't know if—"

" 'Cause I don't even know if he knows."

She looked blank, so Reese reminded her: "I mean Tom."

Beth sighed. "Oh, Vincent, he knows. I think everyone in four states knows." Reese thought, I'd like to paste her, just once.

Reese stood up and tapped on the door that led back to the detention. The guard was standing right there, but he did this elaborate yawning thing, like, Oh, is that a fly I hear? Reese closed his fist and banged harder.

"Problems?" asked the guard.

"I just want a drink of water, okay?"

"No water."

"No water?"

"We got no water. You want coffee?"

"I didn't mean like bottled water...."

"I can't get water from here. Want coffee?"

"I'm sixteen, man. I don't even drink coffee," Reese pleaded, and then added, "Much."

"I'll see if I can find you some pop."

When the guard let the door shut, Reese felt the room suck at him. It was so very small, so small. And the patterns of dirt on the walls and floor were the only variation in all the blond-and-cream-wood-and-plaster, the only decoration. He was not claustrophobic; he remembered the box on the landing of the stairs, where all of them would hide, and snow forts . . .

Reese didn't even notice the kid. But Sam was already holding his telephone. Reese picked up. "How long have you been here?" he asked.

"A minute." The kid looked scared to death, and he looked . . . little. Shrunken. He had on a Cubs shirt.

"Are you okay?" the kid asked.

Reese suddenly had this picture of one of the old Pat O'Brien movies his dad made him watch with him in the middle of the night, where Jimmy Cagney was this arch-criminal who was going to the chair, and Pat O'Brien was his old friend from when they were kids, a priest, and he came to the jail to beg Jimmy Cagney to act like a coward when he was going to the chair so all the little kids in the neighborhood wouldn't think this wrong guy was a hero or something. Reese started to laugh. He couldn't stop laughing.

"What's the matter?" Sam said. "What's so funny?"

"Nothing ... I'm ... nothing. Well, Sam man, fancy meeting you here."

"Are you okay?"

Reese automatically reached up to touch the bandage on the back of his head, where they'd stitched ... it stung. He still couldn't figure out how the hell he'd banged the back of his head running into a light pole with the front of Teeter's car.

"I'm okay. It doesn't hurt."

"Are you going to be in here for a long time?"

"Well, five to ten years," said Vincent, and then he looked at the kid and thought, That was a shitty thing to do. "No, I don't know, Sam. I guess ... I know guys who did stuff, and they had to go to one of these schools. . . ."

"Reform school. Beth said it's not for sure."

"Yeah, well, it's like a farm, I guess. For JDs. I don't know."

"What did you do?"

"I took Teeter's car. I wasn't going to keep it. I just was going to ride around. . . ."

"Teeter the coach at the high school?"

"Yeah, that asshole."

"And so why didn't you just bring it back?"

"I was going to, but this goon I know, Schaffer, and I, we were goofing around, and then when I saw the cops, I just went faster. . . ."

"Were you drunk? That's what Beth said."

"I was overserved ... yeah, Sam, I was drunk. But I never did anything this bad before. . . ."

"That you got caught for."

"That ... right. So, Sam, what do you want?"

"Nothing."

Reese could see his parents sort of scuffling to see in the skinny window, his dad waving a little. Reese waved back. He couldn't see whether his dad looked sick or not. At least Pat was wearing matching clothes; this was a sign he couldn't be too bad. Bad. Speaking of bad, he felt bad. Why am I baby-sitting this kid? Why wasn't one of them in here with Sam? Wasn't this against some law or something, letting a little kid go in to visit a felon?

"Well, then, why are you here? Is this, like, the alternative amusement for Saturday morning?"

"I wanted to see if you were okay."

"Well, I'm okay."

"Okay."

The kid looked around the booth.

"So? Sam?" Reese, all at once thinking he could maybe sleep, prodded the kid. The sooner this day could end, the better.

"This is pretty ugly, this place."

"It's ugly."

"How fast were you going?"

"I don't know ... like ninety...."

Sam's eyes blinked and fastened on Reese. He grinned. "Ninety?"

And it occurred to Reese that maybe he should go easier here. That Sam was probably not just ordinarily fucked up, but a little more than ordinarily, just barely back with George and all. A couple of weeks at his own house after the foray into Cappadoraland. And now this shit. He was such a kid.... Oh, Ben.

"Look, Sam. I don't know if you know ..." Reese dropped his voice. Soundproof, my ass. "I don't know if you know how incredibly stupid what I did was."

"Well ..." said the kid. "Yeah. I do."

"I mean really, monumentally stupid."

"Yeah?"

"Like, I'm a jerk, Sam."

"No," said Sam.

"I'm a fuck-up, and it's not funny, it's not cool." Reese was almost whispering now, leaning toward the partition.

"I just thought ..."

"What did you think, Sam?"

"I thought we could be ... friends."

"Friends?" Reese was glad he couldn't get his hands on the kid. "Look, you idiot. First of all, how would we be *friends*, Sam? I don't hang with twelve-year-olds. And second, you come back, you leave, and go in and out the window . . . I don't even know you, Sam. You're a concept, you follow me? And you don't know me!"

"That's not my fault!" The kid looked on the verge of tears. Reese could see Pat motioning for Candy to punch in the code and let him in. He quickly waved Dad off, to try to soothe him—I'm not instructing him in the finer points of car theft here, Dad. You don't have to save him.

"I know it's not your fault," he told the kid with what he thought was awesome patience, considering. "But I have a life of my own, you know? And it's unfun right at the moment. What do you want from me?"

"You're my brother. I haven't come around, because I didn't know if you guys would all be so mad at me you wouldn't want to see me. But . . . I missed you. There were even times when I thought I shouldn't have . . . whatever. You're my brother."

"I'm not your brother!" Reese gave up; the tears were running down his filthy face; he was just tired out, is all, and this fucking kid . . . "Look, if I were your brother, what would you want from me? I mean, I'm fucking going to some kind of penitentiary or something! Even Dad thinks I should be in a padded cell! I probably have, like, no future. I probably won't even graduate. . . ." Reese rubbed his eyes, trying to get himself to stop. His head was filled with that pool-water smell—that drained limpness he remembered from being a little kid, when you cried and cried until your chest was hollow.

"I just thought . . . It's okay," said Sam. "I'll leave."

"Yeah, leave," said Reese. Then he winced. "Sam, I'm sorry. I know you probably feel crummy. It was nice of you to come over here. But here's the thing . . . I have to get out of this somehow. . . ."

"I know, and I—"

"You don't know. Don't say you know because you don't. You never did anything wrong in your whole life! You're just a kid. And you're a real good kid. Look, when I come home, I'll come and get you and we'll go get something to eat, okay? Or shoot pool or something, okay?"

"Where?"

"What?"

"Where could we go?"

Reese sighed. "I don't know, buddy. Anywhere in walking distance. I may not be driving until, like, two thousand and ten."

"Can we go to Wedding?"

"Nah. Not there. I meant like a burger."

Then the kid sighed, too. "Okay. I just didn't want you to think I believe it when they say you're crazy."

"Well, I *am* crazy. Who says I'm crazy?"

"My dad."

"George."

"Yeah."

"He said so. In so many words?"

"Sort of."

"What do you mean 'sort of'?"

"Well, he said so."

"Okay. Come on. How?"

"He said . . . he said . . ."

"Yeah?"

"Yeah, when I was at your house, he would say, 'Watch out for that kid, Sam. Watch out for that kid. He ain't right.'"

"'Ain't right.'"

"Yeah, and I don't think . . . I mean, I love my dad, but he doesn't understand. . . . He thought you would hurt me or something."

And so I would, thought Reese, and raised his arm in motion for the guard, but the kid said, "Wait a minute. Reese?"

Reese sighed again. The room would inflate.

"I got to tell you something."

Reese made a weary circular motion with one hand. So? So?

"I remembered something."

"Yeah?"

"I remembered something from when I was a kid."

Reese stiffened. He thought, Christ, no. Not today. I don't want him to remember today. And anyhow, he couldn't, he was just a baby, he couldn't remember the words. . . .

"When I was at your house, Beth showed me this trunk. The trunk at the foot of your bed." The cedar chest, thought Reese. The big hope chest with the hoop top. "She took out all these baby clothes she said were mine. And she showed me some blankets and stuff. Some pictures."

"And? And?"

"And I didn't remember any of them."

"Oh." Reese's weariness was deafening. So long as the kid didn't remember the lobby, what the fuck did he care? How much, Reese thought, how much more? Isn't this enough, Mom?

"But I remembered the smell."

"The smell."

"I remembered the smell of the cedar chest. From being inside it."

Reese let the phone drop, almost. It was as if Mom, gesturing, shrugging her shoulders, outside the window, asking if Sam wanted to come out, was on film instead of real. He could feel his shorter self running up those stairs in Madison, into the little room half-made-over for baby Kerry, where they dumped everything, pulling over the boxes of diapers and clothes and whispering, "Ben, Ben, where are you, Ben?" Running back down. Thinking of the dryer. Thinking, Mommy will kill me if he's in the dryer again and turning blue. He wasn't in the dryer. A pulse thudding in his neck. He couldn't let his mother hear. She would screech. She would grab his hair.

". . . hide-and-seek," the kid said.

"I know," Reese said, adjusting the telephone, which had gone slimy in his wet hand.

"And there was this one time I got into the big chest? Did that really happen?"

"It really happened. You let the lid shut, and it caught."

"I knew it! I knew it!" said the kid. "I can really remember lying in there in the dark—there were these cracks of light, so it wasn't totally dark. I was just lying there on some clothes or something, and the top was so high, I couldn't even touch it unless I sat up. And at first I tapped on the top, but nobody came, and I thought I couldn't breathe, but I could. So I just stayed there."

"And I was running all over the house, looking for you, telling you to quit fooling around, it wasn't funny anymore—"

"But I didn't hear you—"

"Because I couldn't talk loud ... Mom would have heard me—"

"And finally you came and opened the top of the chest—"

"And you were there. You were just there. Not scared or anything. Just got up and got out."

"See, that's the thing. That's what I remember."

"What?"

"That I wasn't scared. I wasn't scared, because I knew ...'"

"Yeah?"

"I knew you would come and find me."

And Reese could see it, Ben's white freckled face, unexpected, staring up at him from the trunk, like a baby in a basket. And his relief, his huge relief, when Ben moved, sat up. He'd jerked Ben's arm, but not too hard, and called him a dork, and asked him why he didn't yell, told him to never go in the trunk again. But Ben just started jumping down the stairs, one at a time, saying he was a bunny. Reese could hear him: "Bunny. Bunny. Bunny. Hop. Hop. Hop. Can you do this, Vincent?"

He tried to erase the image, cover it with anything, any picture, even last night's gaudy wash of ambulance lights. Reese wondered if this was what Pat had done when he had the coronary, willed himself to die, squeezed himself so pitilessly that his heart burst. Tried to take himself out on purpose because he couldn't stand thinking of stuff anymore. I would do it now, Reese thought, shading his eyes with one hand. If I could just die now by wanting to, I would, I'd just disappear.... Shame was not a thought. Shame had mass and volume. Right now, thought Reese, I'd blow.

"So, Reese?"

Reese couldn't talk; he nodded.

"That's why I came. In case you were wondering. To tell you I remembered that. And see if it was real. Because then I'd know. That I was really there once. I didn't make it up or get it from pictures. And then I could figure stuff out better. Stuff I had to do, or whatever. It might not matter, but I wanted to know."

"Good," Reese mumbled, hoarse. "That's good."

"And one more thing. What did I call you?"

"What?"

"When I was a kid."

"Oh . . . uh . . . Vincent. You called me Vincent. And you could always say it right. Not like a baby."

"Vincent. So, okay. So, I'll see you, Reese, okay?"

"Okay." Reese motioned to his mother; she opened her mouth. She was telling someone to let Sam out. But as the knob turned, Reese said, quickly, "Sam?"

The kid had already put down the phone; but he grabbed it up. "Yeah?"

"You can call me it. Vincent. It's okay."

Beth

Chapter 34

Beth sat down one day in early fall and tried to think of a couple she knew well who'd been through a divorce. And after half an hour, she had to give up. She couldn't think of a single one. Surely for her age, her generation, the education level of her social circle, that was peculiar.

But unless she counted Candy—and she didn't really count Candy, that wasn't a real divorce—she didn't know anyone to compare things with. Candy's abrupt but tender parting from Chris had been more in the nature of a return to the organic nature of their friendship after an experimental grafting that had failed to take. It had been decided and was over with in a couple of weeks, decided and acted upon as suddenly, and to Beth, as surprisingly, as the marriage. Chris and Candy had dinner together after court. Surely that wasn't what most divorces were like. Beth had never seen a couple really sunder from the inside.

Eighty percent of us divorce, she remembered Penny telling the Circle meeting. Eighty percent. Penny's statistic, Beth reasoned, counted couples whose search ended in an unbearable truth. Or in an endless enigma. For what had happened to her and Pat, there were no predictors.

If people knew how estranged she and Pat were becoming, they would think, Why now? Wasn't it doubly bitter, doubly unfair, after having "been through" all that together, to split? Why not back then, if ever? Even Sam's leaving should not have accomplished what the hottest hell of fear had not managed.

But we didn't care enough to get divorced back then. Having a marriage didn't seem to matter when all you saw as a goal was staying upright for another hour.

She didn't blame Pat. When she looked at him, she felt the widest sinking. No one had decided on this. Things just happened. And once they happened, they were irrevocable. Two days after Sam "went home" (and that was how Beth forced them all to put it) Pat had taken to sleeping downstairs. He'd done that before—on hot nights, on nights when he'd worked especially late. But those other occasions had been accidental and sometimes a relief: Pat had always been a restless spoon sleeper, and more than once she'd shoved him away and he'd left in a huff. But this time, when he'd gathered up a pillow and a blanket from Sam's fresh, abandoned bed, Pat had not done it rancorously, or with show. Next morning, he'd simply folded up his bedroll, before the children were awake, only to bring it down again the next night.

Vincent noticed Beth was sure. She couldn't look at Vincent. She was afraid to ask Pat what he thought about as he lay on the sofa. She tried not to think, as she lay upstairs, aware of Pat's wakefulness, a sort of arrhythmic blip under the deep pattern of the children's sleep. She read Jane Austen. She popped her Trazodone. She tried not to let her mind climb out of bed, glide down the stairs, and walk down the street to stand yearning in front of the red house.

Returning Sam had been a decorous procedure; only George had wept.

They'd met with the social worker and then had a brief hearing in chambers with a family court judge. The judge had asked each of them, including Sam, who sat rigid in his chair, whether this was a decision made of free will. Beth spoke first. "With a great deal of sadness," she said. "But yes, freely."

"And Mr. Cappadora?"

There was a long interval of murderous silence, and then Pat said, "Yes."

He did not look at Beth, but she'd reached out and put her hand on his arm, touching the starched cotton of his long-sleeved shirt. The arm was still as marble; not even a nerve answered her touch. Asked about his willingness, George could only nod mutely. The judge then asked to speak to Samuel Karras Cappadora alone, and emerged, fifteen minutes later, slightly red about the eyes, his palms turned up. There would be, he explained, no formal custody decree granted at this time. The review of Cecilia's condition was pending; it was necessary to follow Sam in his return transition for a period of time not to exceed, say, three months.

"I think our goal should be to restore this boy's life to as much normalcy as possible as quickly as possible," the judge told George, Beth, and Pat. "I confess that I am troubled by this, by all your suffering, and touched by all your evident concern and love for this boy. I wish all of you luck and peace."

Sam, he said, would be permitted weekly visits, unsupervised, with his natural parents, the duration of those visits to be determined by George in concordance with the Cappadoras. "I hope that he will have some interaction with his birth siblings," the judge added. "For their emotional well-being as well as his own."

Kerry reacted to the news of Sam's imminent departure with frank grief, running up to her room and sobbing into her whale puppet until the plush was soggy. "We just found him," she told Beth. "Why doesn't he like us?" Miserable as the question was, Beth was relieved. Vincent greeted the departure with his trademark frost; but Beth knew that he would talk it over with Tom.

No one, except Beth, really understood what had happened. Even Candy, who struggled to retain a shred of professional detachment, could not hide her disgust. To Beth's gratitude, Rosie and Angelo were only sad, not outraged; but she was sure she would never spend another holiday in Monica's house or in Tree's. Her brothers, sideswiped by what they considered an impulsive Beth-move, tried to counsel a wait-and-see plan. Laurie was struck speechless, and Ellen had asked, "How can you, Beth? I don't mean, how could you? I mean, how can you bring yourself to do it?"

Fortunately, nobody had the energy to alert the media, and Sam was reinstated at George's house for a full week before they got wind of it. Then, there were ponderous quotes from psychologists about the quest for identity during adolescence and the nature of memory in the constitution of family. There were stories about how rarely the "reunions" of children adopted at birth with the parents who'd given birth to them gave rise to actual extended-family bonds. There were stray quotes from neighbors—Beth almost had to laugh at them—about how Sam had seemed quiet and content enough; they reminded her of the comments neighbors made after quiet, helpful men got up one day and shotgunned whole families.

But really, how could anyone grasp it? They had not seen Sam's face at the cedar chest. They had not seen his eyes.

It was the image that Beth kept in her mind throughout the formalities of the return. It sustained her. She could not describe it to anyone; it was like trying to describe "yellow" to a child sightless from birth. The feel of the sun? The velvet of a daffodil? Beth could only cling to the certainty that she had known, when Sam looked up at her after the inspection of his baby clothes, that she and Pat had guardianship only over Sam's physical body. She had felt the way Cecilia, in the sad safe room of her riddled mind, could never feel, and probably had never felt—like a kidnapper holding a child against his will.

And was he happy now? On their few desultory visits—one outing to Great America, once to dinner at Rosie's—both she and Pat had felt keenly Sam's nearly pitiful willingness to indulge them.

On the way home from dropping him off the last time, Pat had told her suddenly. "It's like he's trying to pay us back by being glad to see us. He's grateful to us for setting him free."

There had been nothing else to say. Years ago, during their one stab at marriage counseling, the cheerful MSW had suggested that they simply try to act as if they were happy. "It has a way of becoming habitual, just as a pattern of conflict does," he'd said. Beth understood that. She'd done it for the latter half of the nine years at least. And then after Pat's illness, she'd become a method actor, a loving wife or be damned. But only during the brief sojourn of Ben's return had there been the beginnings of a renewed, real tenderness between them. A few times, before the weekend of the Fourth of July when they had lain together, after lovemaking, and Beth had actually believed they were going to be whole again, in spite of themselves. By the time she knew for sure that was what she wanted, Beth reflected now, it was probably already too late.

Even now, she sometimes caught herself hoping that the simple habit of a lifetime of Pat-and-Beth would span the gulf. But Pat had given up after Sam left. And so emotion leaked steadily out of the air between them, until there was no shape or structure that didn't have to do with Vincent's habits or Kerry's schedules. Pat's rage on the morning after Vincent stole the car had been the most emotion he had showed toward Beth in weeks. Even anger had felt almost . . . heartening, in the sterility of their lives.

Pat's focus was now given over entirely to Vincent's rehabilitation. He drove his son to every counseling appointment with Tom, waiting for him outside; he visited the youth officer with Vincent; he closed Vincent's door behind them at night when he went in to say goodnight. Even when Beth offered to spell him, to take Vincent to see Tom on nights when she knew the session would make Pat late for opening at Wedding, Pat had refused. "I owe him, Beth," he told her. "I owe him, and even if I didn't owe him, he's the only son I have."

The day he said that, Beth sent for the catalogues, applications for the master's program in Fine Arts at the University of Wisconsin. She'd filled them out, sending her fee, not entirely certain what she was trying to accomplish. Did this mean she actually meant to leave Pat? Move away? Or was she simply trying to see if there would be a twig of pride for her to cling to if he demanded she go? And what if she did go back to school? Would she aim at teaching? Opening a studio of her own, back in Madison?

She'd left some papers lying on a coffee table, several days after they came, and caught Pat's glance on them.

"I thought," she said, stopping him in one of his headlong dashes in the door from some Vincent thing to grab his jacket for work, "I might consider taking some time, maybe a semester, so we can think things over. . . ."

And she was surprised how much it cut her when Pat said, "Whatever. Do whatever you want, Bethie."

So he would not try to stop her. Why had she thought he would?

Stubbornness, the Kerry family curse, had driven her on, then, to say more, make the point harder. "I thought I could maybe rent a little place. . . . Kerry and Vincent could go to school at Edgewood, maybe, if we can afford it. . . ."

He'd come full stop then, his look as if he were taking her by both shoulders, squaring her to face him.

"My children," he said, as slowly as if he were talking to a woman whose first language was not English, "are going noplace, Bethie. My children's home is here."

"Paddy," she began, "Kerry's still so little . . ."

And he seemed to relent, if only slightly. "Maybe . . . it's possible that Kerry would be okay. But Beth, she has friends here, and Scouts, and sports. She has Blythe, who's like her sister, and Georgia, who's like her—" He didn't, bless him, say "like her mother." "She might be okay, and it's something we can talk about after you make up your mind. But Vincent is not going to leave this house with you. Not ever. He is not going to leave this house until he goes to college, if, I pray to God, I can figure out how to get him out of high school in one piece, and get him to believe he can do anything except screw up his life." Beth loved him then, loved him desperately, his deep, utter Pat Cappadora goodness. It was, after all, a kindness, in a sense, that she might leave. If she had ever been worthy of him, she wasn't now.

And what, after all, Beth thought that night as she listened to Pat's drawer rummaging downstairs, was a marriage really except a collection of wishes that, after years of association, took on the coloration of facts? She wondered whether she and Pat, except in the early years of their college passion— which, she reasoned, could have ignited between any two healthy young people—had ever been more than a kind of brother and sister, raised to the assumption of safety in one another. She would settle even for safety now.

Beth woke one night, shaking, from a dream of Vincent. Vincent . . . injured. Aged about five, in the hospital, a broken wrist. She'd dreamed of bursting through swinging doors—not one, or two, but an endless series—to follow the trail of wails to Vincent.

She could have her son, Beth thought, sitting up. Her lost-on-purpose son. Not the one lost by accident. If she had the guts, if she had the time, if she could find the ropes. If miracles could really happen.

If miracles could really happen.

If she didn't leave him. If she took him with her ... but now could she do that? If she stayed ... but how could she do that?

And from Vincent's point of view, would it make any difference?

Beth remembered how, in college, she'd toyed with the idea of a career in special education (Laurie called it Beth's Annie Sullivan phase). Beth had read that all children experienced to some degree the phenomenon of erased recollection. It was one of the most difficult crossroads between parents and children: adults could remember the enraptured tenderness of the early bond; children, whose job was to fracture that bond, couldn't. At six, Vincent had looked at her with flinty eyes and explained that he hated her. Beth was aghast. Where behind those eyes was her princeling, who only a year before would quiet from fear in no other arms but hers, not Rosie's, not Pat's? Where was that child, back then?

Where was he now?

Oh, Vincent, Vincent-turned-Reese, another changeling child in a house that already, impossibly, contained America's best-known changeling child. What did Vincent remember? Anything, at all, of mother love unscored by family casualties? And not remembering was the same as not knowing. If Vincent thought of her in those terms, it was probably a gauzy recollection of the amusement and affection she'd felt for Ben just before he was lost. She had, yes, given Ben more of that. Ben was easier. She'd liked him better. But love? Amusement and affection no more comprised the sum of love than sex on your honeymoon compared with going through labor and delivery— pleasure compared with the world-without-end amen. Beth was struck with a sudden, vivid picture of herself, coming up the walk at night after an all-day shift at the afternoon daily in Madison where she'd worked when the boys were babies, seeing Ben dancing in his diaper on the window seat, and Vincent scooting through Jill's legs to jump on his mother. She remembered thinking, more than once, Imagine! I made them. All this beautiful, intelligent flesh I made. Actual, comical humans. And how she would think, then, aching with her abundance, I would die for them. For each of them, equally painfully, and eagerly.

If Vincent could look through her lens ... but that was it. That picture was hers, not his. There was no way to graft it onto his heart.

Suddenly panicky, Beth thought, I'll go downstairs and wake Pat and tell him: It had gotten colossally out of hand, this notion of separating; it was just a pose. Together, they would forge a relationship with Sam, and help Vincent and Kerry do that, too. It could happen. She would go down there, and get Pat to slide over on the couch, so she could crunch in next to him, as she had in his hospital bed. She pulled back the quilt and swung her bare feet to the floor.

And then she pictured Pat's mouth, as it had looked when he told her, "Vincent is not going to leave this house with you." She pulled up her quilt and lay flat, her hands laced on her chest.

Candy dropped by one night—girlish in jeans and a paint-spattered shirt. She kissed Pat in passing as he left for work, and plopped down on the porch.

"Give me vodka," she told Beth. "I have spent all day painting my disgusting single-girl flat, in preparation for my disgusting single girl's life, and I feel old as dirt."

They sat on the porch, and Beth wondered if she only imagined Candy shooting glances down toward the corner around which Sam lived. Both of them tipped their feet up on the railing and listened to the crickets.

"How's my man Reese?" Candy asked, midway through her second drink. "Does he brag to his friends about doing time? Even though it was only two days?"

"On the contrary," said Beth. "I really think he's ashamed of it."

"That's good," Candy said. "And life on probation?"

Relieved to be able to say anything, Beth told her, "It seems better." She sketched in Vincent's evident interest, or at least his show of interest, in the basketball camp for inner-city fifth graders he'd been assigned to help coach twice each week.

"He been driving up any oak trees lately?" Candy asked.

"Vincent will probably be drawing Social Security the next time he gets behind a wheel, if Pat has his way," Beth said. "His wings are basically clipped. I mean, he goes to community service, he goes to Wedding to help out, he goes to see Tom—"

"What does Tom say?"

"I . . . I haven't talked to him. I . . . usually don't."

"And has Reese seen Sam? Again?"

"No."

They rocked a little longer, and Beth added, "The one thing that seems to have made the biggest impression on him is taking away the boom box."

"What?" Candy sat up.

"That was my idea. Since he was a little kid, Vincent just . . . he gets lost in music. It's way beyond a teenager thing. I stripped it all," Beth said. "Tapes. CDs. I kept them; but I donated his boom box. I gave it to Saint Vincent De Paul. I told him it was a privilege. He had to know we mean business, and after all, it's the thing he loves the most. . . ."

She didn't notice, in the gathering dusk, how Candy's face had changed, so when Candy brought the chair she'd been balancing on two legs down with a crack and leveled a finger at Beth's face, Beth almost flinched.

"What he loves most," Candy said, "is right here in front of me. That's what he loves most, Beth."

Rage splashed in Beth's throat; she almost couldn't speak.

"I'm so sick of hearing it," she said finally. "I hear it even in my sleep! I'm so sick of hearing how this boy is only a delinquent because his mother didn't love him. . . . Candy, forgive me, it's not so simple. Vincent never . . . even before any of this ever happened, Vincent was convinced I loved Ben better."

"Did you?"

"Jesus God! Did I? How do I know? Candy, do you love your heart better than your brain? Your arm better than your leg? But then this happened, all of it, and Ben at the center, so there was no way I could ever convince Vincent . . ."

"Even if you tried."

"Which I didn't, yes, mea culpa, mea maxima culpa. But anyhow, shouldn't he have known? Shouldn't a normal kid have known? Did I have to tell him every day?"

"Did he have to tell *you* every day? I mean, shouldn't you know, too?"

"What's that supposed to mean? Are you taking up Freudian analysis now, Candy?"

"Beth, I've seen this kid when he looks at you. He wants you to forgive him so bad...."

"Forgive him? *Forgive* him?"

"For all the shit he's pulled. Or for something, some dumb thing you don't even know about. Why don't you talk to Tom? Why don't you? I have."

"And he said?"

"He said Reese is what they call a symptom bearer. He lives out everybody's else's pain with the stuff he does. And now, with Sam gone, how do you think he feels?"

"I have no idea," Beth said wearily, and then, "You know what? I think Pat and I are separating."

Candy tossed the remains of her drink out into the bushes and slammed down the glass. "Good Christ, Beth, why?" Beth shrugged. "Isn't enough enough?"

"Candy, he wants it."

"Did he say that?"

"He didn't have to. I can tell."

"No. No. I refuse to believe that. Pat thinks the sun comes up—"

"Not anymore. Not for a long time, I guess."

"Bethie, you have to do something about this. You guys can't take another loss. Come on."

"Candy, people get divorced all the time. Most people who ... lost a child get divorced. Look it up." Beth struggled to restore a lightness to her tone. "Even you got divorced."

"You can't sit here and compare Chris and me with ... You were meant for each other, Bethie. You and Pat."

"Another thing I'm sick of hearing. You know? I feel like I was born with

Pat's last name. Damn it. Maybe I can have a life, you know? Maybe what I need is what you have—real work, and a little place, by myself. Pat doesn't care."

"Did you ask him?"

"Yes, as a matter of fact, I did. And he said, 'Do what you want.'"

"That's just pride." Candy got up and sat on the railing. "He's just played out. You don't make these decisions after a summer like the one you had. And what about Reese? And Kerry?"

"He's going to fight to keep them here. He doesn't want me to take them back to Madison."

"To Madison?"

"Well, Candy, what's left for me here? Annual follow-ups of the many permutations and combinations of the Cappadora saga in the *Tribune* magazine? Even more nasties from his sisters? My father looking at me like I shot his favorite dog? No. Shit. I'm not doing it." Beth got up and sat down on the cement stoop. "Candy, I don't know how to even think of leaving Reese or Kerry. And I know that if I move, I'll hardly ever . . . I'll lose all my contact with Sam."

"But you're played out, too, aren't you, girlfriend?" Candy kneeled next to Beth's chair. "Oh, Bethie, Bethie." Candy rocked her then, and Beth felt her tears come like the letdown of milk when she'd nursed the babies, unstoppable, purging. "Okay now, okay. Listen. I just want you to do one thing for me. One thing. Will you?" Beth nodded, and Candy said, "Don't bolt the door behind you is all. Close it partway if you have to, but don't lock it. Give him one more chance to talk. You and Pat haven't lived apart for your entire adult lives. If you go, don't forget to listen to how that really feels. Don't talk yourself into anything, Bethie. You're fully capable of talking yourself into anything, remember? Just . . . wait and see."

Beth nodded.

"When are you leaving?" Candy asked.

"I don't know . . . maybe soon," Beth murmured. "If I go at all. School starts in January. And I'd be taking classes at the university."

"Oh, my God, my God," Candy said. "Pat's going to miss you like he's lost an arm." She stood up and gathered up her mammoth bag. "And Bethie, he's not the only one. I will, too."

"You sure you don't want another drink?" asked Beth, suddenly loath for Candy to leave.

"No, I don't want to have to give myself a field sobriety test. Even though I'm now out of the fertility sweepstakes for good."

Beth said, wondering if she was going too far, "I kind of hate that, Candy. I wanted you to have your baby."

"Yeah, yeah . . . I did, too," Candy said. "I wanted it, for real. I'm sorry for Chris, too, though he'll do a lot better with the next twenty-five-year-old to come down the pike. And maybe, now that I don't have to live on slave wages, I think sometimes there's this little girl living on a mountain in Chile somewhere who wants a crazy mama who carries a gun. So maybe . . ."

"I think that would be wonderful. You'd be a wonderful mother," Beth said.

"So would you, Beth," Candy said softly, and walked down the steps.

Reese

Chapter 35

It was after eleven when Reese thought he heard the clang of a basketball on the driveway. He stopped; he'd been writing, or trying to write, something in the stupid journal Tom insisted he mess with every night.

Yeah. Definitely. It was crazy hot for September. With the air on, and the house sealed like a pie under plastic wrap, he wouldn't have heard it if he'd had even a little music on. Which he would normally have had. Even so, he wasn't sure, until he raised the window and put his head out, that he wasn't imagining it.

But no. Somebody was down there.

Reese couldn't see; his dad had told him to replace the bulbs in the floods on the garage a month ago, and of course he hadn't. The night was moonless, murky, the only light from the street lamp a block away. The ball hit again, twice, sharply. Reese had to flip the bedside lamp off to be able to tell who it was.

It was Sam.

"What the hell are you doing?" he hissed. Mom and Dad's window was next to his, and though he knew they were long gone to dreamland, and that

Mom, especially, wouldn't be back until dawn, he didn't want to start anything.

"Nothing," said Sam.

"Does your dad know where you are?" asked Reese.

"Yeah," Sam replied.

"I'll just bet," said Reese, leaning out on his elbows.

"You want to play some?"

"Uh, roundhead, it's nearly midnight, in case you haven't noticed."

"Past your bedtime?"

"What I mean is, you waste, I'm in enough fucking trouble without getting Mrs. Pellicano or Mr. Becker to call me in for disturbing the peace, too."

"We could play quiet," Sam said. "Unless you're . . . like, too tired. Or too afraid."

"Fear is not in my vocabulary," Reese told him. "As you know, I could take you blindfolded. I took you every day last summer and sometimes twice on Sundays. As I recall, you had to move out to save what little lousy reputation you had left."

"I don't remember it that way," Sam said, and Reese could hear his grin. "Anyhow, that's pretty easy to say when you're up on the second floor."

"Start praying, wimp."

"I'm on my knees," Sam said.

Reese thought of putting on a shirt, but it was so damn hot anyway. He just jumped down the stairs by threes—what the hell was the kid doing hanging around their driveway at midnight? He was sure as hell George didn't know anything about this. George was probably already calling the fucking FBI or the networks or both. Jesus Christ.

He ran out the door, and Sam was standing there, sunburned, in cutoffs and Reese's White Sox jersey.

"That's my shirt," Reese said automatically.

"Awww, really?" Sam pretended to sound apologetic. "I thought it was a paint rag."

"Where'd you get it?"

"I . . . took it when I left. I'm sorry. You can have it."

"I don't need it," Reese said in a hurry, then thinking, What a complete asshole I am. "Have it. Or, have it if you beat me. So, that is, you might as well give it up now. Unless it smells." He couldn't take his eyes off the kid. It had been, like, weeks since he'd seen him at the jail. His dad and mom had taken Sam out twice, that he knew of, but Reese had been busy both times. And now, having spent two days in jail and many wonderful days and nights in the comfortable confines of his room except for the few moments they allowed him out in manacles to eat dinner did not make for easy surveillance of anything except Mr. Becker watering his hostas.

"Are you sure your dad knows where you are?" he asked again, checking the ball.

"You keep putting it off," Sam said. "I think you're scared."

"Make It—Take It, then," Reese said. "To eleven."

He had played with Sam enough to know his moves, so by rights they shouldn't have fooled him. He knew that the kid hardly ever looked at you, and that was one of his tricks. Sam had these slanty eyes, Dad's eyes, and he would narrow them down to slits and fasten his gaze over your right shoulder, as if there were some giant bedbug behind you, all the while dribbling in figure eights low between his legs. You almost had to be drawn off. And he talked the whole time—"Man, you are sorry, you're so sorry, which way you want me to take you? to the right? to the left?"—but it wasn't as if his patter was directed at you, even meant to rattle you; it was just like a motor running. He made you feel like you weren't there. And the goddamn thing was, it worked.

Sam looped right around Reese and went in for the lay-up. And then walked back with his arms out, punching the air, crowing, "What's up? What's up? You asleep? You asleep?" And Reese couldn't help laughing.

But then, when he finally got the ball, he swore to God Sam had grown three inches in the last month; the kid was all over him, clapping his hands, ignoring Reese's attempts to fake him out. Reese finally drove in to the left, but Sam knocked the shot down.

"That's goaltending," Reese said sharply, though he knew it wasn't; the ball was nowhere near the descending arc. Of course, you had to object, just for form.

"If you gotta cheat, you gotta cheat—I don't care, take it over," Sam said.

"Go ahead, little boy," Reese said then. "I'm going to go easy on you. Seeing it's late and all."

By the time the score stood seven–five, Reese ahead, both of them were gasping in the humid darkness. You could feel your lungs flap like wet gloves. "You got air inside?" Sam asked Reese.

"Full blast," said Reese. "You giving up?"

"Who's giving up?" Sam darted right and whirled, with this beautiful skyhook, which went nowhere but the bottom of the net.

"What the hell? How did you learn that?" Reese asked him. "That was your left hand."

"I'm a man of many talents," Sam laughed, checking the ball to Reese and going into his crouch.

"Call it," Reese said; then, "Keep the shirt. I pissed on it in June anyhow, that's why it was in the drawer."

"You have to stop pissing in your drawers," Sam said, and Reese reached under the ball, knocking it up so it just glanced off Sam's chin.

"You got to say 'beat,' though," Sam egged him on. "You're beat, right?"

"I let you," Reese told him, "and you know it. But let's call it a night. Come back tomorrow for a rematch."

That was when Sam put his hands up and pushed the wet hair up over his forehead, so it stuck straight up, like mowed grass. And took a deep breath. He didn't move. Reese stopped, heaving and sweating, flatfooted in the driveway.

"I ... The thing is," Sam said then, "I'm not going back."

"What do you mean?"

Sam jerked his head over his right shoulder, and there, at the end of the driveway in the dark, where Reese had not even noticed it, was a huge, battered suitcase.

"Sam," he said slowly, "man, what are you doing?"

"My dad knows," Sam answered, hurriedly. "I mean, we talked about it a lot last week, for a long time, and he said I have to do what I have to do, and he even knows why I came over here so late at night...."

"Which is why?"

Sam looked up at the darkened bedroom windows. "I didn't want to have this whole big number," he said. "You know. With your ... with Beth and Pat. And, like, what if the press found out?" That killed Reese, the way he said "the press," like he was forty years old or something. "They probably already think I'm out of my mind for going home—I mean back—I mean to George ..."

"So he let you come out this late?"

"We walked down here before. A little while ago. I saw your light."

"Okay," Reese said, and added, almost swallowing his tongue over the words, "but, is this, like, permanent?"

Sam looked down at his feet, his mouth clamped shut, and then looked up at Reese—still, Reese thought, an inch shorter maybe—his eyes widening in the dark, as if they had no color, as if they were dark little mirrors in which Reese was sure, if he could get close enough, he could see his own pale face. "I don't know," he said. "I don't know. Maybe. If I can ... I hope—"

Reese made a motion, stopping him, and Sam stopped, turned, and went down to the end of the driveway to get his suitcase. After a beat, Reese followed. He didn't want to push him, but he had to move, to do something; he'd go crazy if he didn't.

"Loser carries," Reese said. "Fairsies fairsie." The thing weighed a ton. "What, do you collect anvils?"

Reese rounded his shoulders, strained, hefted the handle into his right hand; and then Sam reached out and closed his own hand over Reese's. Reese jerked; he felt the touch up his whole arm, as if the kid had pressure-pointed him.

"No problem. I can do it," he said.

But Sam didn't loosen his grip.

You felt like you were diving in a quarry, it was so dark. Reese had to strain to see Sam's expression in the faint cast from that corner light, the corner around which you would walk, cross one side street, and then spot the ▢d house, the only one on that block that wasn't blue or gray or brown. ▢ ld picture it now clearer than he could the sweat-shaped brim of ▢ feel of the wild goose pillow on Tom's couch. The red ▢ ▢ house, now not Sam's. Maybe. He could ask again, b▢ make any difference.

It was like everything. You just had to wait until morning and then count and see who was left. You had to keep walking until you figured out what was the right place, keep on searching until somebody found you. Reese looked up at the light, then back at the patch of darker dark that contained his brother. He could only feel him, the sweat on his palm—the kid calluses, the strength in those oversized fingers. Reese put the suitcase down; he was shivering. It was one of those times he thought he understood the way his dad felt when his heart brought down the hammer. We should just go in, is all. But fuck, thought Reese, I have to. I have to sometime. I have to now.

"I was the one," he said. "I was the one who let go of your hand."

Sam shifted his feet. Reese could hear him sigh.

"Well ..." Sam said.

They picked up the suitcase then, even weight, like it was a mattress, and carried it between them onto the porch.

"We're locked out?" Sam asked.

"They don't make a lock that can resist the charms of Reese Cappadora," Reese said, pulling his jimmy out of his back pocket. "I get in this way half the time." Laughing, then, they struggled into the hall. Beowulf stirred on his rug, got up stretching painfully, and clicked down the hall, chuffing his graying muzzle into Sam's palm.

"Old dog," said Sam. "Good old dog." Then he noticed the stack of Beth's bags, her suitcase and equipment. "Who's going on a trip?"

"My mom is maybe going to Wisconsin for ... a job," said Reese.

Maybe. Now maybe not. Suitcases could be packed. Suitcases could be unpacked. You just had to wait. "You want to put that in here? We can take it up later." They shoved Sam's bag into the living room next to the piano.

"I could eat," Sam said.

In the kitchen, the refrigerator's glow was the only light. Reese flipped a piece of cheese to Beowulf, who gobbled it noisily. Sam reached around him to dislodge a Coke from the pyramid of stacked cans on the bottom shelf, and leaped back when all of them rolled. In the silence, they hit the linoleum like M-80s.

"Jesus Christ," hissed Reese. "Wreck the joint." They scrambled after the ns, which kept rolling out, leisurely, smoothly, one after another. One a corner of the baseboard, spun, and popped open. Soda geysered; Beowulf yipped. "For God's sake," Reese whispered, grinning, "shut up!"

The cans seemed endless, like a film strip of logs rolling down a chute.

"This isn't your fault," Reese gasped. "This is Dad, the master engineer of the universe. This one winter, when they were working on the restaurant, and Dad was going to save all the leftover tiles ... so he spends all day getting them up in the rafters of the garage, and he stands there and shuts the garage door, and the rafters crack, and the whole goddamn ceiling. . . ."

Helplessly, Sam spit his Coke, which only made Reese more determined to make him laugh. "And so every fucking tile, every single tile goes crashing down, one by one, on the floor of the—"

But they both heard her step.

"Vincent!" Beth called from the top of the stairs, her voice sleep-slurred but laced with a tang of panic. "What's that noise? Are you in the house?"

Reese put his finger to his lips. "You don't want her up," he told Sam. "Not now. Trust me on this." Sam reached silently into the refrigerator for a flat box of cold pizza, and Reese held up his palm in warning. "Wait," he ordered. Sam stopped.

Beth called, "Vincent?"

"It's okay, Mom," he yelled. "I dropped something. Go back to bed. I'm here."

Reese turned to follow Sam to the kitchen table. From the upper floor came a whoosh of water, a settling sound. He could feel Beth's urgent presence recede, down the hall. They sat down at the table, and Sam delicately opened the pizza box, grimacing disgustedly at the slabs cemented to the lid. Reese went out to the kitchen for a butter knife, and stood for a moment, his ear pitched to the creak of the floorboards overhead, the soft sponge of the bed as she lay down, and then nothing but quiet, the tick and gust of the air conditioner going on, the sounds of a house, anyone's ordinary house, at rest.

"It's pretty ickining-say," Sam said of the pizza. "On the other hand, I'm pretty starving." He sat back after quickly polishing off two slices. "You think she's asleep?"

"Probably," Reese told him. "Hang on a minute more. And then, when you go up there, just sleep in my room. Just for tonight. So we don't have to get out all the sheets and stuff. The whole house will be up."

"Where will you sleep?"

"I don't know," Reese said. "Down here on the couch. With the Wulf. And I'm not even tired."

"It seems kind of crummy to come along and kick you out of your bed."

"No, really," Reese insisted. "I'll take first watch, okay?"

Sam smiled. "Okay."

"I'll walk the perimeter," said Reese, as Sam got up, rummaged in his suitcase, and extracted his toothbrush. Always the good kid.

"Look for suspicious activity," Sam whispered back.

"Right-o, sir, and have a good sleep. I won't rest until the encampment is secured," said Reese.

"Well done."

Reese sat down at the kitchen table, propping his chin on his hands. It was a lie about being wide awake; he was dogged. He felt as though he hadn't really slept in weeks. Overhead, the telltale complaint of his old bed sounded as Sam lay down. Reese looked out the big window, past his reflection, deep into the thick dark of the yard. Was it his imagination, or was there already a lightening out at the edge, where the lawn chairs were?

Out there at the perimeter?

He could just flop on the couch. It was unoccupied, for once. Not like the last few weeks. Dad was sleeping upstairs in their bed. Reese had no idea whether that meant he was trying to get her to stay or saying goodbye. But anyway, it meant that there was vacant real estate on the first floor, and Reese would wake up if anybody moved; he always did. He'd given his word, though. And it was only a few more hours, the tail end of one night. Night could only last so long.

Until the encampment is secured, Reese thought. Or until morning. Whichever comes first.